INCONSTANT MOON

" . . . builds with great intensity toward a mystery that must be solved. The answers lie in understanding adult responsibility and knowing things aren't always as they appear."

—Debbi Mack

New York Times bestselling author of
Identity Crisis and **Least Wanted**

"Laurel L. Russwurm captures the inconstant nature of the college experience in her book,

INCONSTANT MOON

bringing to life a host of characters that may have been lost in another work, but manage to maintain their own identity throughout the story. "

—Eric Swett
author of
Apocalypse Rising

INCONSTANT MOON

~ *a novel* ~

LAUREL L RUSSWURM

Paperback Edition

Canada

This book is a work of fiction.
Names, characters, places and incidents are either the
product of the author's imagination or are used fictitiously.
Any resemblance to actual events, locales, institutions, or
persons (corporate, living or dead), is entirely coincidental.

The author's serialization is available online at
<http://inconstantmoon.russwurm.org/blogs/>

LIBRARY AND ARCHIVES CANADA CATALOGUING IN
PUBLICATION

Russwurm, Laurel L., 1959 -

Inconstant Moon / Laurel L. Russwurm
ISBN 978-0-9877183-3-4
ISBN-10:0987718339

dedicated to an amazing woman
and very good friend
who just happens to be
the world's best sister-in-law

for
Nienke Hinton
with love

"O, swear not by the moon!

The inconstant moon,

that monthly changes in her circled orb,

lest that thy love prove

likewise variable."

-- Juliet,

William Shakespeare's

ROMEO & JULIET

INCONSTANT MOON

dramatis personæ

Fyfield House Residence
Liz -- 1st Year, Photography
Natasha -- 1st Year, Photography
Elsie -- 2nd Year Med School
Maggie -- 2nd Year, Computer Science
Amelia -- 1st Year, English Lit
Mouse -- 1st Year, English Lit
Boris -- 1st Year, Photography
Jake -- 1st Year, Photography
Ethan -- grad student, Photography, Teaching Assistant
Oscar -- 2nd Year, Computer Science
Jose -- 1st Year, English Lit
Eric -- 1st Year, English Lit

Married Student Residence
Quentin -- 1st Year, Photography
Tamara -- 1st Year Med School
Kate -- 2nd Year, Computer Science
Nick -- 3rd year Med School, Teaching Assistant

Off Campus
Adam -- 2nd Year, Computer Science
Barbie -- 1st Year Med School
Krystal -- 2nd Year, Computer Science

1 . . . thursday

Given a choice, he'd be anywhere but here.

Although quite close to the street, the thick stand of trees means the road noise is almost nonexistent. A paved path meanders through the woods, interspersed every so often with concrete stanchions bearing street lights. The worst of it is all the leaf mold.

Tree stink. Fresh air. Cold. Who needs it? At least there's this stump to sit on.

Because there isn't any choice.

Concealed in forest shadow, elbows on knees, he takes a deep drag on the cigarette he's just lit. But then he tenses as he hears the sound of a female giggle. Holds his breath.

Listens.

Relax.

Exhale. Watch the smoke rise up and dissipate among the trees.

False alarm. Too loud, gotta be a pack.

He needs a cull; packs are dangerous.

He draws deeply on the cigarette and quietly strokes himself as he watches the long limbed college girls sweep past his hidey hole, never once glancing his way. After all, why would they? The world is theirs for the taking. Look at that firm flesh, so casually parading past. Teasing glimpses of breast and buttock make him stiffer than ever. He knows that he'll never be allowed to touch; so he touches himself as he watches them.

On parade. Just for him.

Then that bunch is gone, and he's left alone again. A smile touches his lips and he drags deeply, watching wisps of smoke curl sensuously in the air above the cigarette.

Watching the smoke he luxuriates in the cherished memory of that time in the elevator, his day with the Ice Queen from the seventeenth floor. The unattainable goddess never registered his existence.

She didn't see him. They never did.

But as the car filled up, and everyone pressed more tightly in the confines of the corporate box she brushed her buttocks deliciously against him. Teasing his penis, the Ice Queen swayed with the elevator's motion.

And she smelled *so* good. He felt his blood rising, his breath grow ragged, and he knew it was impossible but he couldn't stop.

Was it her soap or perfume or her very own girl smell? Whatever it was, he tightened his grip on the briefcase and tried to hold his breath, to pull away, but there was nowhere to go.

She leaned back into him and stiffened as his hardness strained into her softness. An unexpected rush of pleasure-- he knew she could feel him.

She froze in place, tantalizing, connected. He couldn't breathe... blood was pounding in his ears. He closed his eyes as she began squirming, rubbing against him deliberately.

He couldn't believe it. Surely this was more than any man should have to bear.

He breathed in deeply, more of a shudder as he could feel he was about to...

He bit his tongue so he wouldn't cry out as the elevator stopped. Tasted the blood as she went, waving those buttocks saucily at him as she left the elevator with the others on the seventeenth floor.

As if nothing had happened.

He tried for nonchalance, angled the briefcase in front, hiding the painful erection from the other passengers. She'd done it on purpose. Was hurrying off to laugh about it with her friends. He was the last out on nineteen and it was all he could do to make it to the privacy of the bathroom stall to finish up.

But the memory of her... it was glorious.

He breathes heavily, warmed by the remembrance of actual contact. The corners of his mouth twitch as he admires the memory, and savours its... deliciousness.

Footsteps. He snaps out of his reverie into the here and now.

Listen.

Footfalls clattering. Good. Stupid girl shoes.

No giggling, no talking even. That means it's just one. A cull.

Perfect.

He smiles and rubs. Coming into view around the bend, she heads into the zone. A little plump, that's good. Wavy brown hair, pulled back severely, tendrils escaping around the heavy looking backpack. Straps pull her sweater taut and emphasize juicy squeezable breasts.

Perfect. A quick tug and the pantyhose leg is tight over his head, distorting his features. She won't be able to recognize him. Best of all, she'll be scared. This is gonna be so good.

He pulls open his coat, and he's ready, manhood thrusting forward like a sword, swelling with power as he steps out of the shadow and into the sunshine.

He feels like a god.

Startled by his sudden appearance out of the bushes, the girl starts to smile an automatic greeting but she realizes right away that something is wrong. She registers the stocking mask, the open coat... then she sees the out-thrust penis. His weapon of love.

He's breathing harder now. She bites her lip, and he takes a step closer. Is she going to cry out at the sight of his power? He takes another step... she's shaking now, bowing to his...

Startled by the snorting noise she makes-- that's so unfeminine-- peering through the distorting fabric-- he realizes she's not doubled over in fear, she's shaking with laughter. Snickering, spluttering, guffawing.

What the fuck? This is disconcerting. It is just not right. He feels his masculine power draining away.

Her laughter gets louder. She lifts up a hand and points brazenly at his suddenly faltering manhood, still laughing. Her other hand rubs tears of laughter from her eyes and she says, "Is that the best you can do?"

This is wrong, he thinks, wrong, wrong, wrong, as her laughter gets louder and louder. What is the world coming to?

He whirls around and sprints back into the safety of the trees, trying to stuff himself back inside his pants. He has to get away from that foul woman. Get away from her. Away from her laughter. Away. Just away.

He grabs the bicycle from its cover and runs back toward the path, past where she stands and laughs. He heads in the direction she's just come from to get away. Out of her reach.

He throws a leg over the bike and grunts at the unexpected stab of pain generated by the impact of his sensitive bits with the bike's cross bar. His back to that dreadful hyena, he rips off the stocking mask and stuffs it in his pocket.

Grimly gripping the handlebars he rides like the hounds of hell are after him.

When, really, it is just a little bit of laughter.

2 . . .

Music leaks out of the building as the group of photography students approaches the pub. Liz complains, "I don't know about this, guys, we've got a nine a.m. lecture and I am just not a party girl."

Boris says, "Aw c'mon, Liz, it'll be fine. You don't have to stay late, but you have to go out at least some of the time. You're supposed to get rounded."

Natasha gushes, "But Boris, Dahhlink, Liz IS rounded." Liz feels a blush rise to her cheeks as Jake and Boris laugh.

Natasha gathers her friend in a hug. "Just try it,

OK? It isn't like high school where you have to smoke up or drink yourself cross-eyed to be cool. You might hate it but maybe you'll have fun. It isn't a party, so there is no social commitment. You can stay ten minutes or two hours. It's up to you."

"It's hanging out," says Jake.

"Unwinding," adds Boris.

Natasha grins. "Socializing."

Liz nods. "Okay, okay."

They go in and the music is loud, although not as bad as Liz thought it would be. Boris and Natasha lead the way through the crowd to a group of tables at the back. From here Liz can see the dance floor but the speakers aren't right in her lap either, so maybe it won't be so bad. Looking around, she recognizes a few of the faces.

One of the catchier **Beatles** songs is blasting; and Natasha mimes dancing to Boris, who nods, then follows her onto the dance floor. As Liz and Jake settle, they watch Boris and Natasha dance a little awkwardly, but then the song ends and the juke box replaces the high energy dance number with the sultry notes of a slow tune. They keep on gamely, although Boris glares darkly at the jukebox, maybe hoping to frighten it into a song with a faster tempo.

Clearly Boris and Natasha have never slow danced together, and Liz knows all too well what that's like. Still, she can't help but smile as she sees what a hard time Boris has trying to figure out where to put his hands while Natasha manages to stay just far enough out of range to ensure they don't accidentally wind up in full body contact.

The pub's terrible acoustics mean that she only hears snatches of song lyrics over the hubbub. Something about dreams and desires. As if on cue, another couple she recognizes from Fyfield House dance through her view. In stark contrast to Boris and Natasha's awkward circling, Eric and Elsie are engaged in a sinuous mating dance. As this couple sways in perfect unison it is clear Eric has no trouble knowing where to put his hands. Moving easily together, their synchronous movements appear almost choreographed as they float across the room. It would be a kick to photograph them.

Liz finds herself swaying and tapping her toe to the beat of the music, drawn in so she almost doesn't register Jake asking her if she wants to dance.

Snap.

Liz looks over at him with trepidation; she so hates this. They never believe her when she says, "Sorry, I don't dance."

Jake is crestfallen. "But I'm a good dancer."

Liz smiles. "But I'm a terrible dancer."

"Oh." Jake sucks it up and shrugs pragmatically. "Okay. Want something to drink? I don't think there's table service here."

Liz nods. "Oh sure, just a ginger ale or something."

Liz digs for money but then realizes Jake's is already off to the bar. Liz pulls out a Toonie and sets it on the table for when he gets back. She does not want

Jake thinking this is a date. Jake may be a brilliant photographer but he's too young for her. Well. She's almost twenty three, and Jake is maybe eighteen.

Sitting back, Liz's eyes are drawn to a flash of auburn hair as Elsie spins into Eric's arms like something out of one of those old black and white musicals she used to watch with Mom. Elsie draws Eric in, running her hands over his face then pulling him into a long slow kiss. They seem so secure in their own world, and Liz realizes their dance isn't so much composed of skill as foreplay.

Maybe that's what dancing is for, Liz thinks. Like a human mating ritual. It's getting more erotic by the moment, and Liz is starting to feel just a little hot and bothered.

Suddenly feeling like a voyeur, Liz turns away, flushed. With a start she realizes it's not just the make out dance. It's that the dance made her think about Ethan. Because she's half hoping Ethan will magically arrive.

Wait a minute. Where did that thought come from? Ethan. Huh. *Ethan.*

Like that isn't the last thing she needs. It's a good thing he isn't here. Except a bit of reflection makes her realize he's the real reason she allowed herself to be talked into coming. That she had the idea Ethan spends most evenings here. With the other stoners. Serves her right to be wrong.

But what on earth is she thinking? Well. Apparently she isn't. Thinking, that is. Well, not with her brain, anyway.

Being back in school isn't like she thought it would be, that's for sure. In some ways it's a chance to be a kid again, without having to relive the hell that was high school. But everything happens so fast, who has time to think? Hmmm. But Ethan? She knew he made her smile, but, apparently that's not all he makes her feel.

At least he's older than Jake. Liz wonders what it would be like to feel the way Elsie and Eric do. Those two are so obviously in love. Wonders how dancing like that feels, wonders how dancing with Ethan like that would feel. Again her eyes are drawn back to the lovers swaying in total disregard of the rest of the world. The world that doesn't seem to exist for them.

An acrid mix of cold air and smoke gets up her nose, and Liz looks up as Miese leads several smokers in from the cold. The vivacious Dutch girl is another Fyfield house mate, who's been inevitably nicknamed "Mouse." Liz wonders momentarily if it bothers Miese that no one calls her by her real name. But Mouse is perpetually cheerful, the kind that takes everything in stride.

Liz doesn't know any of the other smokers settling in at the adjacent table until she spots Ethan bringing up the rear. Liz feels an involuntary tingle at the sight of the guy she's been entertaining impure thoughts about. She looks away, afraid he'll see her telltale blush. Where's Jake? Or Natasha? She needs distraction.

Liz has no idea why she has a crush on Ethan. It makes no sense.

But then, maybe it is because he is so different. Relaxed. Liz herself is anything but. Ethan is a house mate, and he's a fine photographer, just not in Jake's league. But then, who is?

Ethan is Professor Mol's teaching assistant, so at least he's a bit older than most of them. Liz doesn't really know him, just something about the guy makes her mouth go dry. She'd like to run her fingers through his wild and curly mop of hair.

She glances furtively over but he looks up just as she does and catches her eye. Ethan winks right at her, inspiring another tingle. E embarrassed, she turns away, but it occurs to her that part of what makes the wink so great is the sexy dimple it brings out in his cheek.

Doesn't really matter anyway. Liz has been too tall for most guys since the second grade, and now she's too old, too. But that's good, right? She doesn't need complications. She's not here for romance, she's here for a degree.

But then, Liz is a little surprised to realize that Ethan is sitting over there juggling. Juggling. How cool is that?

Liz pinches herself under the table. She's got to stop this, it's getting ridiculous. Any minute now she's going to haul Ethan onto the dance floor. Which would be nuts because she really can't dance. It would be fun to be able to do a make out dance except that she has no rhythm. None at all. Maybe she just wants to make out.

Jake sets her innocuous glass of ginger ale glass in front of her and Liz grins in relief, sliding him the coin.

Sipping her drink, Liz glances nonchalantly over to see Ethan has finished juggling and is now listening to one of the computer geeks. What's so striking is that that Adam guy is about as far from being a druggie as you get. Even dressed casually his neck cries out for a power tie. Yet somehow Ethan puts him at ease. Relaxed.

Boris and Natasha come back to the table, and Liz rubs her eyes, realizing now she can leave without it looking like she's ditching Jake. As she slips on her jacket, Natasha asks, "Heading home?"

Liz nods.

"You want us to come?" asks Natasha.

Liz shakes her head. "No, that's alright. It's just a little loud for me. See you later."

"Wait a minute," says Jake. "Why don't we all blow this pop stand? There's this guy I want you all to meet, and since it's so mild, tonight would be perfect.   There might not be another chance for a while."

"Who is this guy Jake?" asks Boris.

But Jake is already heading for the door. "It's a surprise."

Following, Natasha says, "I love surprises."

Boris and Liz trail after, Liz happy they're using the rear exit because it saves her walking past Ethan. As she pulls the door shut behind her, Liz glances back and sees Ethan is still talking with Adam; as oblivious to her departure as he is to the solitary figures of Eric and Elsie dancing slowly through the pools of coloured light.

Just as well.

Liz follows her friends into the night, part of her wishing Ethan was coming, part of her relieved he's not.

3 . . . friday

Maggie and Amelia sip coffee at the big table in the Fyfield House common room when a bleary e eyed Liz comes down. She wasn't kidding when she said she wasn't a partier.

Maggie's make-up bag is open with pots of this and tubes of that scattered everywhere. Amelia reads from a very thick paperback. Maggie looks up from applying mascara to give Liz a big smile. "Look what the cat dragged in. Where were you 'til all hours last night Miss Lizzie?"

Liz pauses long enough to say, "Star gazing," flash a smile and continue on to the kitchen. She gets out a cup then starts a fruitless search of the fridge for milk.

There is milk.

Liz knows there is milk.

She knows because she bought a litre yesterday and hasn't even opened it. But where is it? It is not here. It's gone.

She feels herself tensing, then takes a deep breath and opens the cupboard where the disgusting powder cream substitute lives. Funny how *that* never runs out.

She sighs and pours herself some coffee.

Liz can't stomach black coffee at all, and she sure needs coffee this morning. The gritty powdered cream she dislikes is better than nothing. Sighing, she adds it to her cup then takes the disgusting concoction back to join the others.

As always, Amelia's nose is in her book. Focusing on the title, Liz sits down and says with a smile, "Don Quicks-Oat? Sounds like a breakfast cereal."

Maggie looks at Liz with a creased brow, then realizes Amelia is reading **Don Quixote** and Liz is talking about Amelia's book. Amelia looks up, then she gets it too. Amelia and Maggie share a look and begin to smirk... then splutter... then howl.

Liz watches them. Irritated.

"What?" she says. Amelia and Maggie just laugh harder.

"What!?" Liz says again in frustration.

Amelia is laughing, hugging herself trying to draw breath. Maggie brushes the tears of laughter away and says "Don Quicks-Oat," then doubles over again.

Liz purses her lips, folds her arms and sits back, watching. Any trace of her normally sunny disposition is gone.

She waits.

Finally they start calming down, getting under control.

Maggie grins at Liz and says, "Lizzie, you have just provided the laugh of the day." Catching a glimpse of her raccoon eyes in the makeup mirror, Maggie says, "Shit, I'm gonna have to start over."

Liz narrows her eyes. "Wanna let me in on the joke, Mary Margaret?" Venomous.

Maggie scowls. "There's no call to get mean."

Liz can't believe it. The urge to slap Maggie is strong.

"Slow down," says Amelia, realizing Liz is not a happy camper. "It's funny. Truly. The name is Spanish. The book is Spanish. You pronounce it 'Don Key-Ho-Tay'."

Liz rolls her eyes, getting it. "You mean the crazy old man and Sancho Panza? **Man of La Mancha**."

Nodding, Amelia says "That's the one, yeah. I know, I know, you've just never seen it written down. Part of what made it so funny is I remember the first time I saw it written. You're not the first one to sound it out English style."

"Okay," says Liz, "but tell me this. You're an English major. Why study **Don Quixote** if it's Spanish?"

"It's thought to be the first novel, and we're studying the novel form. Before this there were only epic poems and theatre."

"Oh."

"The musical is great, but the novel is the story Cervantes tells in the jail during the play." Waving the thick book she grins. "There's an awful lot more of it for one thing. The musical is about Cervantes being arrested for writing his seditious book **Don Quixote** during the Spanish Inquisition."

Maggie pipes up in perfect mimicry of the **Monty Python** faux Spanish accent, "No one expects the Spanish Inquisition!" and the three girls crack up. Together this time.

When they're quite done, Liz stirs her coffee and takes a sip. "My mom took me to see that show on Broadway when I was in high school. It was so great."

"That sounds awesome. Wanna trade moms?" asks Maggie. "Mine would never do anything like that."

Smiling, Liz thinks maybe Maggie isn't so bad.

"It was just us girls. It was fun taking the train to New York and then staying in a hotel. My Dad wouldn't go to a musical to save his life, so he stayed home with the boys. And it was great, but I was bawling my eyes out by the end, though."

"Wow," Amelia smiles, "I'd love to see it done live."

"The music was beautiful but it rocked visually, too. The set was amazing, I mean, it was a dungeon and all but it was like... um... grotty, but artistic. And the lighting was amazing."

"Broadway." Amelia says almost reverently. "That is so cool. The closest I've come is the Peter O'Toole movie."

Maggie asks, "Peter O'Toole?"

"He's an old movie star my Mom likes," says Liz. "He played Orlando's dad in that movie **Troy**."

Maggie nods, "Okay, yeah."

Amelia says, "He was good as Quixote but you could tell his singing was dubbed. You know, the play is as fictional as the novel, but I think the musical was a way to make points about the importance of free speech."

Maggie asks, "Isn't free speech always important?"

Amelia says, "I think so, yeah, but more when it's in danger of being taken away. The original play was a TV broadcast during the McCarthy witch hunt in the 1950's. Showing how nasty the Spanish Inquisition was, could imply the McCarthy 'UN-American' crap was as bad."

"Kinda like that Wikileaks business now," says Liz.

"Oh yeah, lots of similarities, out of touch government, erosion of civil liberties, like that. The irony is that there's no evidence Cervantes was ever jailed."

"It's still a good story," adds Maggie.

"Absolutely." Liz smiles, mostly restored to good humour, until she looks at her coffee and grimaces. "You know, I swear I bought a litre of milk yesterday and now there isn't any."

"Oh, that's right," Maggie nods, "Mouse got a care package from her mom with weird sugar cube things called Annie's blocks."

"Anise? I've seen that in the produce section but don't know what it's for."

Maggie says, "Yeah, that one. Annie's blocks are licorice sugar cubes you dissolve in warm milk."

Liz says, "Well, I like licorice. But putting it in milk?"

"I can't stand the stuff, and that's what it smelt like. But you know Mouse. Everybody had to try it and that was pretty much it for your milk."

Liz rolls her eyes, thinking about a year of powdered cream. Maybe she'll get used to it.

"Guess you don't like ouzo either," says Amelia.

Maggie shudders. "No way. Disgusting stuff."

Liz grimaces as she finishes her coffee. "Now I know why people buy those over priced mini fridges for their rooms."

"If you decide to get one," says Amelia, "you might want to make sure to get one that comes with a lock."

Liz stares at her in surprise. "What, I can't even trust my own roomie?"

Amelia laughs. "Yeah, you can trust me. But we're neither of us very good about keeping the room locked. There wouldn't be any point in having a private fridge without a lock."

"Nobody swipes my knickers, just my food."

Amelia laughs. "Probably because you're the only one who goes shopping on a regular basis. You've gotta realize that most of us are used to having magically filled fridges."

"When you live alone you darned well learn there aren't any house elves filling your cupboards at night. It's annoying when stuff gets swiped, not to mention hell on my budget," says Liz.

"So," says Maggie, pretending nonchalance as she peers over the top of her glasses at Liz. "What's this star gazing deal? I haven't heard about any stars being in town since they shot that Justin Bieber video last month."

Amelia's eyes widen. "Justin Bieber, you've gotta be kidding right? That boy looks like he's twelve years old."

"Yeah, but what can I say, I like his music. So sue me."

"Wrong kind of stars," explains Liz, pleased to know something Maggie doesn't for once. "You know, ones in the sky. The Seven Sisters, Betelgeuse, Mars, the Big Dipper. Like that."

Maggie looks aghast. "Its one thing to lay out under the stars in summer but at this time of year? Baby it's cold outside."

"Maybe that's why God invented winter coats."

"Meow," says Maggie swiping her talons through the air.

"What was it like?" asks Amelia.

"Pretty cool actually." Liz raises her eyebrows in Maggie's direction, "although not in a temperature kind of way. Jake's friend built his own telescope."

Amelia says, "Mars is a planet, not a star, though."

"Wait a minute, Jake?" Maggie turns to Liz. "You mean that little guy could pass for Justin Bieber's younger brother? The one looks all of 14?"

"Yeah, Jake. He may look young but he's an amazing photographer. Ferociously smart too."

Maggie says, "You're not... I mean..." rarely at a loss, Maggie stumbles, and Liz suddenly understands the question.

"No, we're not dating if that's what you're getting at. We're friends. If its any of your business, it wasn't just me and Jake. Natasha and Boris were there, too."

"Mmmm. Boris is pretty hot," says Amelia.

"Way too many muscles for me." says Maggie. "But I'd walk softly there 'cause Boris and Natasha are joined at the hip."

"I took some pretty cool shots of Mars through that telescope. They actually came out better than I thought. Not as good as NASA shots, but still, how cool is getting to take my own picture of Mars? Jake's friend Larry thinks the visibility is better this time of year. You should see his telescope, it's huge. Almost as tall as I am. Larry told me the mirror alone cost hundreds of dollars."

Maggie says, "Sounds like a mirror for Barbie."

"Barbie? Like the doll?" asks Liz.

"No, like the pre-med student."

"Barbie? There can't possibly be a real live girl who actually goes by the name Barbie? Not in med school? No way."

"Way." Maggie nods. "In pre-med. Can you believe it? She's even blonde. Boobs out to here, perfect skin, teeth, big blue eyes. Kate saw her file. It's not a nick-name, it's her honest-to-god name. I ask you, what kind of parents would name their kid after a doll?"

"Luckily, not mine," says Liz, "Never saw the point in those dolls myself."

"Yeah, talk about weird shaped." Amelia nods, "I mean forget the physics of how wide her bra straps would have to be just to hold those babies up. Have you looked at those feet? The damage to those poor little doll feet is as bad as that Chinese foot binding thing. Barbie doll feet look like they are in major pain. Can you imaging having to walk on tiptoes forever?"

"What do you know about physics?" asks Liz.

Amelia nods. "I was a Physics major last year. Just I lost my way in the math, so I kinda flunked out. Only other choice was English."

"That's a big jump." says Maggie.

"Not really. The plan was always to be a science fiction writer," Amelia tells them. "You know, maybe Barbie's mom is one of those crazed Barbie doll collectors you hear about."

"But a blonde," Liz snorts, "named Barbie. I mean, what kind of place IS this. I'd have shopped around for another school if I'd known what kind of students came here."

Amelia says, "You can't hardly hold it against her, Maggie. Her parents named her, and if she's pre-med, she must be smart."

Liz shudders. "I dunno, if my folks saddled me with a name like Barbie I'd have legally changed that sucker by now."

"Yeah really. Me too. Or at the very least told everybody my name was something like 'Moonbeam' or 'Peaches.' You know, something with a bit more credibility."

Liz snickers. She especially likes 'Moonbeam.'

"There's a reasonable probability Barbie may not actually be pre-med smart," says Maggie. "Nick thinks Barbie is in med school to shop for an MD, not become one."

"You mean marry a doctor?" asks Liz. "For real?"

"God. I thought we stopped doing that generations ago," grumbles Amelia. "Don't you need good grades for pre-med?"

Maggie says, "Not as good as you need to get into the U of G Veterinary College but still..."

"You need better marks to be a vet than a people

doctor?"

"Absolutely. The smart ones become vets." says Maggie.

"Bet you wouldn't say that if Kate was here." says Amelia.

"Of course I wouldn't." Maggie rolls her eyes. "I want to live, don't I? Doesn't mean it isn't true though."

Amelia says, "You have to be plenty smart and dedicated either way. More people want to be vets. After all, if you're a vet, your patients are guinea pigs, bunny rabbits and puppy dogs. They don't talk back. I bet the malpractice premiums are lower too."

"I don't know about that. You should have seen all the blood the first time I tried to give our cat a bath," says Liz.

Amelia grins. "Well, cats..."

"I miss my cat."

Maggie says, "I wouldn't mind having a cat around, Lizzie."

Liz rounds on Maggie and says, "For the last time, my name is not 'Lizzie', Mary Margaret."

Maggie narrows her eyes. "Fine. Be that way. Liz it is."

Liz nods. "While we're clearing the air, what I do and where I go is my business, so I'd appreciate it if you would stop giving me the third degree all the time."

"Third degree? That's called 'making conversation'. Sometimes I get worried when people aren't in when they ought to be. Last night I was up way late and you still weren't back. Then I thought maybe you had a hot date. So shoot me, I was just asking. You don't have to get your knickers in a twist."

"I don't meddle in your love life, so I'd appreciate it if you didn't stick your nose in mine."

"I wasn't meddling, girl, I was just hoping."

Liz scoops up her cup, and stomps off to the kitchen, and Amelia shoots Maggie a look.

"What?" Maggie asks, defensive. "She's mad at me for worrying about her?"

Amelia shakes her head, glancing pointedly at the clock. "Don't you have a computer to fix, or a class or something?"

4 . . .

The leaves crunch satisfyingly under foot, filling the air with the tang of autumn. The rich golds and reds seem to glow as they strike a satisfying contrast with the deep forest greens. The scents of trees, leaves, and mossy forest floor mingle with the last lingering sweetness of wildflowers.

Liz breathes a little easier, walking through the quiet forest, kicking at a drift of leaves makes her smile, even as the tension slowly melts away.

Unslinging the oblong case from her shoulder, she unzips it, t hen slides out the tripod, setting it up efficiently in the small clearing alongside the creek. Liz has been doing this for years, which is why the necessity of getting a degree galls her. Dad gave her her first camera before she even started school. When the pictures came back everyone laughed at how her perspective was so different, but being under three feet tall gave her a different world view and it showed. It made her realize, too, that people see the world differently. It was empowering to photograph her world. Addictive, too.

It wasn't long before her photographs started showing signs of technical mastery. The yellow plastic kiddie camera with the cute little gorilla face didn't have any manual settings. She learned how to position herself just the right distance from the subject. She had to figure out light by trial and error. They gave her a real s single-lens reflex camera for her seventh birthday. The grown up camera was amazing, but it was awkward and heavy for her small hands. She emptied her bank account to buy a light but flexible tripod because she couldn't wait until her eighth birthday. From then on, her allowance always went on film and developing. She couldn't get enough.

The folks wouldn't allow her to set up a darkroom at home because they worried the chemicals would be too dangerous to have in the house with the boys. They said. Liz thinks the real reason is Mom wanted her to take dance lessons, be more of a girlie girl. But in high school she started a camera club and it didn't take much to get a darkroom up and running. Enlargers, developer trays, timers and other darkroom gear was cheap because so many people were going digital. For the first time in her life, the popular girls wanted to be friends -- because they wanted her to photograph them for the paper or school yearbook.

Laurel L Russwurm

Screwing the camera on top of the tripod she perches on a fallen log to survey the terrain. There's pine, a bit of maple, a stand of larches. Peripheral motion catches her eye and she gets a few snaps of a raccoon as it lumbers across the clearing before disappearing into the woods.   It is so nice to be out in the real world breathing real air.   Warmed by the sunlight, Liz peers through the zoom to see what else there is to see in the forest.   A flash of movement draws her eye to three playful young squirrels chasing about. Maybe litter mates. Or perhaps it's just a bit of adolescent flirting.   Whatever they're doing it's sure not territorial warfare.

Not for the first time she wonders if winter will surprise the critters. Instinct ensures they gather food for the time ahead, but surely instinct can't prepare them for the cold desolation of snow. She wonders about the natural world when she's out taking photographs, although she rarely engages in any follow up research. Sometimes just knowing the questions is enough.

The long lens and the low light of the forest interior make it impossible to get good sharp shots of the little guys from this far away, but she fires off a series of photographs in burst mode for some interesting motion shots. It's so easy to be cavalier about how many digital pictures she actually takes. It's never the taking that is the problem, it's the sorting and filing later that eats up hours on end. Or days. Doing everything on a computer instead of in a dark room is still a little weird to get used to. But she is learning.

INCONSTANT MOON

Rubbing her neck ruefully she idly wishes she had a boyfriend. It would almost be worth the annoyance to have someone around just to give her a neck massage when she needs one. Since she wants to relax, Liz tries to avoid thinking about Ethan. To not think about his dimple that comes and goes, or the single silver skull earring that peeks out at her from under the curly dark hair he usually restrains in a ponytail. Although her initial tension has dissipated, there's still a dull ache at the base of her neck, and thinking about that guy isn't helping. Maybe she should see if she can find a more comfortable perch. Hoisting her gear packs over her shoulders she stands and snaps the tripod legs together with practiced ease before tucking it, still extended, under her arm.

As Liz moves back into the forest proper she realizes that the forest is just a little too tidy. Although there are different kinds of trees and complimentary vegetation, the groomed wood chip paths are the big tip off. Probably the lawn mower guys come here to shovel wood chips. The forest floor is somehow too manicured, that's what's wrong. No decaying logs, no moss, mold, or fungus. Fallen logs are probably hauled away for free firewood. City people don't realize fallen trees are a natural part of forest renewal. It is more a park than a forest, then, but better than a parking lot. There is some wildlife. The new subdivisions going up probably means the school won't care about forest renewal as much as selling off this 'empty space' to pay for new buildings. The forest is a part of why she chose Christie, but Liz knows she's the minority.

Laurel L Russwurm

At the creek, Liz sits on the wooden bridge, dangling her legs over the side. Taking the camera off the tripod, she hangs it round her neck and slides the tripod back in its case. Who is she kidding? She doesn't need any more nature shots. The assignment is covered and then some. As always.

That's not what's brought her out here today. What she really needs is a break from people. It's hard getting a chance to think when you're living in a house full of strangers. Liz knows her folks would have a conniption if they understood she was living in a co-ed residence with boys on the lower level. It was weird at first, but not much different from living with brothers. The girl's floor is supposed to be off limits to guys but they all share the downstairs common room. And though she's a grown woman who makes her own decisions, Liz is well aware that her dad would not best be pleased.

She's seen Eric sneaking up to Elsie's room, nights; and Elsie sleeps down in his even more. Sleeps. Right. It may not be allowed but it's an open secret. Thing is, Liz doesn't want to know who's sleeping with who. Or who's smoking up. Or who snores. She quit Facebook back in high school because of that stuff, but it's even worse here. Sometimes she thinks half of the students are here for the soap opera, with education coming last.

Although she'd thought she was well out of it, she'd found out the hard way she wasn't going to get anywhere in the 'real world' without a degree. Proving herself over and over didn't make a difference.

Her boss thought the only reason she brought in

good pictures was luck. She'd never seen him even hold a camera, but he could judge her because she didn't have a degree, and he was the boss. Did he turn down her best shots because he was jealous? He killed her low angle time-lapse 'artsy-fartsy' Ferris Wheel shot then was furious when that same shot won the **Canadian Geographic** contest. That was the straw that sent her to Christie.

Here she is back at school with all these kids. If she was going back to school the only choice *was* Christie, so she could study with award winning photo-journalist Annie Mol. Liz grew up poring over a world framed by Mol's eyepiece, award winning photos published in **This Magazine** and **Maclean's**.

Making good pictures is what it has always been about for Liz. Focal lengths, f-stops, and developing your own. But now those heady chemical smells are gone-- Christie doesn't even have a darkroom. The closest you come is printer ink, which is not the same thing at all. Everything she'd known about cameras and chemicals and photographic paper has changed.

Although digital is still photography, it comes with a different set of problems. It requires new technical skills and competence with a computer to get it all in hand. So, okay, there is stuff she needs to learn. All the computer background she's missed. So she is motivated after all.

But it's too expensive to not live in residence. Even after moving home last year and banking near every cent she made, between tuition and digital equipment that will be obsolete by the time she graduates, funds are tight. The government has only just begun giving grants to needy students, and it's more on the order of a gesture than actual help. Maybe it'll get better. Her folks aren't poor exactly, but with Mom staying home with the younger sibs it means there isn't family cash to help out.

It's most frustrating nobody warned her that most scholarships aren't even open to mature students. She's already decided to apply for a student loan next year, but she might need to take a part time job like Amelia this year.

Even so, money is not the real problem. It's more an annoyance. Even if it takes years to pay off, she will be able to get work at the other end, and a degree will ensure she's paid what she's worth. On to the big time. **Maclean's** maybe? **Canadian Geographic**? Sky's the limit. She knows very well what it will mean to her quality of life. She might even be able to help the folks send the boys to college. The ones that want to, anyway.

Not Randy, he's a maker, he'll need to go into an apprenticeship. He'll end up the one making money.

No, Liz's real problem is living in the dorm. What the city kids jokingly call "the Res." It's not t he same as living with family, even one big by today's standards like hers. You can shut the door on brothers.

It's all the other students. Sharing bathrooms with strangers. Communal showers are not her idea of fun. Different showers for men and women isn't enough, it's the idea of group bathing. Always being too tall made her an easy target. She isn't comfortable being stared at.

It's different when it's your own family. It's a lot harder with roommates, particularly the one who sleeps in the same room you do. She says a little prayer for being blessed with Amelia as a room mate. Liz knows she wouldn't have lasted five minutes with Maggie. Maggie is a trial. Just thinking of Maggie makes Liz tense. Like most of her house mates, Maggie came to Christie straight from high school. Even though she's years younger than Liz, Maggie seems to have elected herself house mother, wanting to know where Liz is going, what she is doing.

Is it prurient interest, or is it what Maggie says, that she just needs to know whether to worry? Either way it's driving Liz around the bend.

Okay, maybe, it makes sense to have some idea where people are. But that's why they have sign in sheets. It's not Maggie's job, she's just another student. They aren't even in the same program for God's sake. Back home, Mom and Dad trusted her to come in when she said. They never gave her the third degree. Why does Maggie? It's none of her business. And although Maggie is the worst, the city slickers think their life experience is more cutting edge because they grew up with drug dealers on every corner. Although Liz knows things most of them never will, to them she's a hick. Inexperienced. Just because she grew up in a small town she lacks 'street cred'.

Liz attended a school so small that all the teachers knew her name, so for sure it was harder to get away with anything.

But the biggest problem for small town kids is no public transit. Going to the movies requires a ride from somebody's parents, no fun for a date. So everybody rushes to get a driver's license at the crack of their sixteenth birthday. Farm kids have the edge over townies because they get the chance to boot around on the back forty, sometimes years before they're sixteen, like her friend Gabe's brother. Liz and Gabe had been inseparable since the third grade.

Gabe's brother loved driving the four by four, and their Dad let him take it to the Hallowe'en dance before he'd graduated to the full license. Except he was just a little bit cocky, and so he wrapped the truck around a bridge abutment. Although Gabe was thrown clear, his brother was killed on impact. And you know how it is, even though Gabe lived, he wouldn't see her anymore after the accident. It's tough being a fourteen year-old paraplegic.

Liz knows she hasn't exactly been wrapped in cotton, but it seems to make it worse that she doesn't do drugs or drink. Sure that's how she was raised but what's wrong with that? Her parents don't drink or smoke. She's seen people drunk and been around people wasted. She knows what can happen. Meh.

Besides, she knows she's capable of being stupid all by herself. She doesn't need alcohol or drugs to help, she can manage it all on her own, thanks.

Many of her classmates assume she's naïve because she doesn't try to fry her brain cells. But she knows she's just smarter. Liz smiles to herself.

Maybe that is enough.

Don't let them -- don't let Maggie -- get to her.

5 . . .

Professor Cootes looks right at Kate when he says, "I seem to be boring your partner Ms. Stone."

Kate looks at Maggie, canted to the right, her head resting on her fist, eyes closed, s softly snoring. Kate gives her a shake and Maggie's eyes snap open. Kate glances down to read a text message on her cell phone.

> **Oscar**
> How about this one: "Women can discover everything except the obvious."

Maggie drifts off while Kate gives Oscar the evil eye and texts back.

> **Kate**
> Ooooooh. That one was catty, Oz. You could get in big trouble repeating stuff like that.

> **Oscar**
> Wilde was frequently catty. Um Maggie's snoring again.

Kate tries nudging Maggie, but it just changes the timbre of her snores. A sharp kick to the ankle yields a better result.

Maggie wakes enough to realize Kate kicked her, so she glowers.

Kate whispers, "You have to stop snoring."

Maggie's eyes narrow. "I don't snore!"

Kate nods. "Do so, I've got witnesses to prove it."

Maggie smacks herself in the head, "No way."

"Way." Kate says, "Even the prof cracked jokes about it. Good thing you have nice little l lady-like snores. If it'd been Elsie's honking he'd have fled screaming."

"But I don't snore."

Kate grins. "If you want I can get a show of hands."

Maggie holds up her hands in surrender. "No no no. Okay, shhhh, I believe you. So what's the assignment?"

Somehow Maggie lives through the rest of her sleep deprived morning. Compensating with double doubles from the cafeteria keeps her moving, but she is in a fog nonetheless.

Only as the school day is ending does she begin to feel conscious. A bit more wired than awake, but it will do.

Oscar comes in trailing Jake and Kate. He peers at Maggie, then bends over, cups her chin, gently tilting her head back and forth as he examines her face in the afternoon sun. "Hate to tell you this, wee girl, they're called 'the whites of your eyes' -- not 'the reds of your eyes' -- for a reason."

Maggie wrenches her chin away and sticks out her tongue. "Sez you. It's the new look, Oz. Get with the program."

Kate says, "Maybe we should reschedule?"

Oscar is firm. "Can't do it. If we pack it in, we make Linux look bad to all the noobs who might've switched."

"Oscar's right," agrees Maggie, "We can't. Every **Ubuntu** group in the world is having their release party today. That's the point. I was just too excited to sleep. No way do we reschedule."

"You were playing Farmville, weren't you?" teases Jake.

"Of course I was. But only because I couldn't sleep."

Kate rolls her eyes at Maggie. "How about this then, you nip home for a nap."

"No, no, no. It's my party, I gotta be there."

"Look at it this way, kiddo, if you sneak a nap you'll have the pleasure of being conscious for your release party."

"I'm awake now, I will be then. Don't worry. If I slap on some war paint I'll even look conscious. It'll be fine."

Kate asks "Gonna paint eyeballs on your eyelids like Captain Jack?"

"Ha ha." Maggie rolls her eyes

Oscar's flipping though the school paper with a frown. "Wasn't Krystal doing publicity? I thought she said she'd get something in the paper."

"Yeah, I thought she had it all set up."

"Nothing in here." Oscar lays down the paper.

"Are you sure she's even coming?" asks Kate. "She wasn't in Gates' class this morning."

Maggie shakes her head. "You're right, she wasn't. I don't know. She said she would."

"Cheer up, girl, it will be fine. You know, Adam was saying that Canada's got a higher proportion of Linux users than the States. How cool is that?"

Maggie grins at Kate, "Pretty cool. Look, save my spot and guard my coffee with your lives, 'cause I know I'm gonna need every drop today. Back in a flash."

Maggie heads for the washroom where she splashes water on her face. Yup, Oscar's right on the money. She could be the poster girl for a horror movie. Much more red in them thar eyes than white. Another splash.

Coffee coffee and more coffee is just what this girl needs to get through the rest of the day.

6 . . .

The double lecture hall in the **Arts Centre** is quiet but for the tapping of hundreds of laptop keys. Behind the lectern the English prof skims her notes to make sure that everything's covered. She glances up at her audience. Smiling at the sight of all her students typing furiously, she she shuts down the PowerPoint presentation.

"That's it for today. If anyone needs to see me about the assignment I'm back on regular office hours this week." As the professor packs up her materials, a general exodus is underway in the cheap seats, as notebooks are shut down, and personal effects are gathered up.

Mouse looks over at Eric, bent over his cellphone. "You take very good notes. Maybe I could borrow the ones from the days I missed last week when I was sick?"

She watches Eric peering at the tiny screen then thumbing in a quick message before nodding to her.

"Sure thing, Mouse. Monday and Tuesday?" She nods. "Email later, okay?"

"Excellent, yes, Eric, thank you. That will be a big help."

A text flashes on his phone screen and suddenly Eric is in a hurry, nodding as he pockets the phone and snaps his laptop closed and stuffs it into the case.

"Later," he grins, and is gone in a blur.

Mouse turns to Amelia, who seems to be having a job repacking her computer case. Everything that came out doesn't want to fit back in. Mouse asks, "Would you care to join us for a walk in the woods?" but Amelia shakes her head no.

"Sorry, Mouse, I've got to work."

"OK," Mouse smiles. "Maybe next time," and Mouse follows Jose up the steps. Amelia watches them go. Or rather, watches Jose go. Watches his nice tight buns ascending the stairs. Too bad. A walk in the woods would have been nice.

Especially with Jose.

Amelia sighs, hoists the case over her shoulder.

7 · · ·

Maggie heads toward the corner cafeteria table

where Oscar's laptop is open at the **Oscar Wilde Quotations** Page.

Oscar pronounces, " 'Education is a wonderful thing, provided you always remember that nothing worth knowing can ever be taught.' "

Jake laughs, then chokes on the pop he's drinking. Kate pounds him on the back until he can breathe normally again. Jake grins, then asks, "Got any more, Oz?"

Oscar laughs. "That's the spirit. You'll be pleased to know there are scads of them. Wilde was the undisputed king of wit."

"So tell me another," prompts Jake.

" 'The only way to get rid of a temptation is to yield to it. Resist it and your soul grows sick with longing for the things it has forbidden to itself.' " says Oscar.

"Mmmm," says Kate, "I like that, it's wonderfully wicked. Permission to do pretty much anything."

Oscar does a Groucho Marx eyebrow waggle as he says, "How about this, 'The book of life begins with a man and a woman in a garden; it ends with Revelations.'"

Maggie laughs. "I don't think Liz would like that one."

"Or this-- one of my very favourites: 'Women are meant to be loved, not understood.' "

"Boo! Hiss!" Kate tosses a French fry at Oscar, who deftly catches it in his mouth.

Maggie slides in beside Oscar, who laughs, and says,

" 'Nothing succeeds like excess.' "

Kate looks over at Maggie. "Krystal still hasn't showed. I thought she was really up for the club."

Maggie shrugs. "She is. I don't know what happened but I'm sure she'll be here as soon as she can. How's everything else?"

Jake says, "Liz is coming to take photos for the paper, and Amelia will write the article."

"How we doing for food?"

"We've laid in a few cases of pop and chips, cheezies and pretzels. I thought instead of charging for it, we just leave a glass jar for people to drop donations in. And maybe order pizza if that isn't enough."

"No beer?" asks Oscar.

"No license. The **Computer Centre** doesn't have a liquor license. If we'd set this up earlier we'd have had time to apply for our own, but we didn't. So, no license, no beer."

"Too bad, it would have been a good fund raiser."

"I doubt Gates would let us use the room if we had beer."

"Good point. Cootes would've gone for it, though."

"Of course Cootes would go for it. He left most of his brain cells in the sixties. I swear the old geezer still thinks he's a student. We'd all be so much better off if he retired."

Oscar looks over at Maggie. She still looks a bit rough. "You sure you're up to this Mag? Still time for a nap."

She sticks out her tongue again but this time Oscar

leers, "Don't tempt me girl."

Suddenly uncomfortable, Maggie gathers her things to cover her embarrassment. "I'm fine, lets just start. I'll sleep later."

They gather their things and head out, waving at Eric seated by the glass wall overlooking the oval.

Eric smiles and waves back at Maggie, then turns back to his laptop. A quick re-read of the draft email doesn't pass muster, so he deletes it. He doesn't want to sound whiny is all.

Beginning again, he types:

> Where are you? You said to meet you here. I thought we were going to get something to eat before the computer party. I could have eaten without you but now it's too late, they've shut down so only the vending machines are open. Joy. Rapture even.

He looks up and scans the room again, but it's emptying fast. With everything closed down nobody is coming in. He sighs. Elsie never wants to go out.

> If you weren't coming why did say you were? I could be working on the essay due tomorrow, or researching my thesis, but no, here I am. Waiting for you.

Not that he minds staying in with her. The sex is incredible.

But.

He doesn't know what her favourite colour is or

even if she likes jazz. Just sometimes he'd like to be able to talk with her, find out what makes her tick.

He smiles to himself. Well, besides *that*.

> O.K. look, how 'bout this. I'm heading over to Callaghan's. If you want me to bring you something let me know. I have my cell. Call. Tweet. Something.
> xo eric

This time Eric doesn't read it, he just hits **send** then shuts down the laptop. Pulling on his jacket, he zips up, feeling in his pocket for his car keys. Not there. Must be back at the Res.

He stuffs the laptop unceremoniously into the bag, shouldering it and heads back to Fyfield House. It's a long way to Callaghan's without wheels.

At the building Eric waves at the night porter and heads for the stairs. He's been sitting too long and energy is bursting out of his pores so he takes the stairs two at a time, running all the way up to the fifth.

A swipe of his card and he's in. Heading for his room, he thinks how quiet it is.

Not a soul in the common room. Everybody out and about doing something or other. As he should be... would be... will be when he finds his keys. He's left the room open as usual, and drops the computer case on the desk, then roots through the knee hole drawer, but his keys aren't there either. He frowns, where? Checks the floor by the desk. Bedside. Closet. Nothing.

Nobody would bother to steal his keys. His car is a beater.

Eric thinks. Last night after the pub with Elsie. He could hardly believe she came out with him. Damn the girl can dance. He smiles. Dancing together was so great. Gotta do that again. He probably left the keys in her room. God knows he couldn't see straight when he came back down after. Maybe she'll be there and they can go to Callaghan's and get a bite together. So he heads back through the common room and up the stairs to the girl's floor.

Strictly speaking, it's off limits. But as Romeo says, "with love's light wings did I o'erperch these walls, for stony limits cannot hold love out." Eric smiles to himself as he heads down the corridor toward Elsie's room. Who is he to argue with Shakespeare?

There's a crack of light under the door. Good.

Elsie must have come back, great. Maybe she's changing for him. He smiles, taps softly once and pushes open the door to the room he knows as well as his own.

Except it looks a bit different just now. The point of view is just wrong.

Well.

There's Elsie's unmistakable cascade of auburn hair, fanned out over the pillow in erotic waves of spun silk that contrast with the soft pale skin adorned with a delicate tracery of pale blue veins. Her face is flushed, her eyes closed as she undulates on the bed.

Her long legs are bent and spread and her red polished toes knead the bedding. That's his Elsie all right. The thing that's not right is the sweaty guy kneeling at the side of the bed, with his head buried between her legs.

They're going at it so hot and heavy they haven't even heard him. Elsie did a good job training him to move quietly to be able to slip in and out without disturbing the dorm mates. Right. Softly, on little cat feet.

Eric watches a moment, stunned, not really taking it in.

At first.

Not until the guy's hands begin to slide up her torso.

Shaken by the enormity of the betrayal, Eric chokes back a sob and withdraws, softly pulling the door closed. He leans against the wall and squeezes his eyes closed. Trying to breathe.

Well.

That's a picture that'll be hard to get out of his head.

Like ever.

Eric shudders and starts shuffling down the hall in a daze. It's hard work, pushing his way through the heavy air. As though walking under water.

He stops at the fire door to the stairwell and it hits him that Elsie was...

As the anger wells up he knows he can't even think about going back. Pushing open the door he thunders down five flights of stairs and bursts out into the chill of the evening.

Outdoors.

Fresh air.

Clean air. Not like the shit in his head.

He breathes in great gulps, suddenly feeling nauseous. Blowing air out his nose he decides to jog to Callaghan's. Only a couple kilometres.

What the hell else is there to do?

8...

Jake uses Blu-Tack to stick up the **'Ubuntu Party,'** arrowed signs that will direct people down to the basement computer lab. They're hoping for a decent turnout of non-nerds; it's reassuring that there are already a handful of early arrivals.

Technically speaking he himself is not a computer nerd. He takes photography. Right. Like that saves him from nerd-dom?

Not.

Jake knows he's a nerd to his toes and always will be. And maybe the jocks got the glory and the girls in high school, but more and more it's the nerds who are running the world. One of the things Jake likes best about being a university man is the discovery that there are girl nerds. He doesn't know why he never knew any girl nerds in high school, maybe they had better protective colouration then. Or maybe because he was too busy lusting after cheer leaders to notice them.

Well, he's sure noticing them now. He hears the rattle of the exterior doors and the security guard talking, then a handful of students start down, following

Jake's arrows. A cute girl waves at him. Wow. This is so great.

People are coming out for this and he is one of he organizers. Heck, in high school you didn't dare even think words like **Ubuntu**, let alone suggest people might wanna dump **Windows** for FLOSS.

All done, last arrow stuck, time to head to the lab. Maybe he'll be able to help the cute girl with her installation. Another clump of customers follows him down. As Jake enters the room he sees Maggie settling people around the tables so they can plug in at the central power outlets. From the slide show running behind Oscar's presentation at the back of the room, Jake can hear Oz giving a fairly standard talk about free/libre open source software, or FLOSS.

Adam is set up in the corner, answering questions, showing people how to set up hard drive partitions so they can try **Ubuntu**. A touch on his shoulder makes Jake's heart race, and when he turns he's not disappointed because it's Krystal with a big smile for him. "Hey there, Jake, sorry I missed the meeting."

"That's okay. The important thing is you're here now. We don't even officially start for ten minutes yet and look at the turnout. Excellent." Jake produces an orange **Ubuntu** lanyard with an 'organizer' badge out of his bag and passes it to Krystal. His is clipped to his belt.

Krystal says, "Wow, these are great," slipping it on over her head. "Guess I'll just wander around to see who needs help."

"Good idea," Jake agrees as he glances at his watch. "Liz isn't here yet, so I'll take some pictures, cover until she is."

"Gotcha," says Krystal as she heads into the room. Maggie smiles and waves at her before going to help a couple who look lost. Jake sets up his tripod as Oscar greets a group of students he recognizes from Fyfield House. Oscar grins and bows, doffing an imaginary hat to Mouse and Barbie, who naturally giggle, while Ethan, Quentin and Jose roll their eyes as if on cue.

"Great to see you. Thanks for coming out to the Christie Computer Club **Ubuntu** Release Party. There are power bars in the centre of each workstation, so find a place to settle and we'll get you loaded up in no time."

Quentin raises a hand tentatively and Oscar smiles at him. "How can I help?"

"My wife couldn't make it out tonight, and I wonder if I'll be able to hook her up with this stuff when she has the time?"

Oscar laughs. "Of course, **Ubuntu** is available free all year round. There's a variety of different kinds of **GNU/Linux** distros. You might be happier with **Fedora** or **Mint**. But you'll be able to download any flavour you like off the Internet whenever."

Barbie says, "I thought fedora was a hat."

Oscar answers that "**Fedora** is made by a company called Red Hat," and Barbie laughs.

"Okay," Ethan asks, "Just, what if I don't like it?"

"Ah," Oscar raises his eyebrows, "A virgin."

"Woo hoo," Mouse and Barbie hoot, and the normally self assured Ethan looks about ready to melt through the floor.

"We'll help you download and install if you're ready, but since you're not sure, you'd be better off running it from one of Maggie's **live** disks so you can try it out without having to install."

"That's cool." Ethan nods and people start helping themselves to the freshly burned **Ubuntu** DVDs stacked on the table. Jose drifts over and sets up in an empty spot and Barbie squeezes into the corner beside Adam, flashing him a big smile as she sets up.

Maggie sets out bowls of munchies on the side counter while Kate builds a soft drink pyramid at the end.

Krystal crosses over to Jose, and looks over his shoulder, asking, "How are you doing there?"

"I want to try this **Ubuntu**, and I'm up for the partition thing. But I could use some help, you know?"

"That's what I'm here for." Krystal sits beside him, covering the hand holding his mouse with her own.

Jose asks, "It's not going to mess up my **Facebook**, is it?"

"Not at all." Krystal types in the password and connects the Wi-Fi. "Let's get started."

More students drift in and set up along the benches.

Adam is looking at Barbie's laptop screen with dismay. Her desktop is a mess of icons. "So what do you think?" Barbie asks.

"Ah, maybe the best thing would be to run off of a live disk for now, and see how that works for you. But you really should be better organized. How can you find anything? It looks as though all your documents are on the desktop."

Barbie looks up at him, tilting her head and frowning prettily. "Well yeah. What's wrong with that? I mean, that way I can find everything."

Adam frowns, "May I show you?" She nods and he slides over beside her. Reaching for her keyboard he creates a folder.

Adam says, "We will call this one assignments. Inside it we can make another for biology. We can make a folder for each of your courses so you can keep the work separate."

"You mean the way I keep my notes in binders?"

"Exactly."

Barbie's frown is replaced with a smile just for Adam. "Huh. I never really got the whole computer folder thing, but binders makes sense. It might be a good idea. Thanks Alan."

Liz and Amelia stand in the doorway, amazed at the turnout. The room is awash with students. Amelia holds a mic attached to a digital recorder clipped on her belt. Liz starts taking photographs before even stepping through the door.

"Wow," says Amelia, "looks like a hundred people in there. Let me see if anybody's done a head count. This is a good turnout for any club."

"I can't even see Maggie."

"There's Oz. I'll go talk to him first."

"Okay," Liz is just lifting her camera again when a touch on her shoulder startles her. She jumps with a little shriek, then glowers at Jake.

"Sorry. I just wanted to tell you I've that I've already taken some pictures. Won't do it again," raising two fingers, "Scouts' honour".

"You were a boy scout?" she asks, curious.

"Nawww," he grins, "You know they don't let in nerds." Liz laughs as he starts stowing his camera. "This is way more people than Maggie expected. And more are coming in all the time. Gotta go do my computer club job now."

Liz nods, edging around the room, photographing students helping students. Some faces are pensive, some squint in concentration, some are vacant with boredom. Others glance shyly at people they like, sparkle as they tell jokes, flutter in outrageous flirtation, discuss theories or argue with animation. Close shots of hands on mice, fingers tapping on keyboards.

Liz's camera captures them all, making sure to grab quick shots of faces for a photo essay she's been playing around with. Funny, she seems to be taking more photos of Ethan than just about anybody. Stop it girl. Do you really want to go there?

Ethan catches her eye and winks again. She can feel the flush starting at the roots of her hair. Down, girl. She turns away but she feels him watching. She tries to ignore him and concentrate on taking pictures. For the first time in her life, that isn't easy.

The crowd ebbs and flows throughout the evening, and Maggie is pleased with the level of interest. As it gets late, although she is well into her second wind people start drifting away.

Around about midnight the last of the release party guests straggle through the front doors of the **Computer Centre** and fan out in various directions. Barbie emerges into the cool night air flanked by Jose and Adam. Jose's glance lingers on Barbie, but it's late, and he's tired. He's not worried about Adam as competition. The guy is like Dilbert come to life.

"That's it for me." Jose says. "Later." and Barbie waves as he sets off along the path that will take him to the Fyfield House residence.

"I'm parked in C Lot," Barbie tells Adam, "How about you? Do you live on campus or off?"

"Oh, I live at home." confesses Adam, wishing for the first time that he didn't.

But Barbie giggles, "Me too. I thought I was the only one."

They walk companionably toward the parking lot, Adam lugging a laptop on each shoulder. They get to her car first. A shiny new looking compact car. She pushes the button to unlock it, and opens the door, turning to Adam and giving him a peck on the cheek.

"Thanks for all the help Alan, I really appreciate it."

Adam flushes and looks away, bashful under her intense blue eyed gaze. "It's no problem Barbie, I'll have it finished and back to you Monday, good as new. Better."

"That'd be great. I've got a family thing this weekend so I won't hardly even miss it. Just call me when it's ready and we'll get together. You're an angel, Alan." and she ducks into the driver's seat. Barbie flashes Adam a smile, then the lights, and away she goes.

Dazzled, Adam watches her drive away, head spinning as he makes his way to the back to his own car. Funny, he never cared what a hunk of junk it was before. He smiles to himself; he doesn't even mind she got his name wrong. Barbie kissed him! He's in such a good mood he pats his beater fondly on the roof.

His car is so old there isn't a remote -- you actually have to put a key in the lock. He opens the door and tucks Barbie's computer carefully behind the seat. He slides his computer in beside hers.

He can't help but grin as he slams the door. Barbie wants his help. She even gave him her phone number.

And her computer. Adam is simply amazed that a girl like that would even talk to him. He doesn't even mind that she calls him Alan. How can he possibly correct her? He's in a daze as he buckles the seat belt, then turns the key in the ignition. Before disengaging the emergency brake he touches his cheek in awe.

"She kissed me," he marvels. "Me."

As Adam drives out of the lot his lights illuminate Krystal and Jake emerging from the Computer Centre. He taps the horn and they wave as he goes past.

9 . . .

Maggie is curled up in bed, speaking softly into the cell phone.

"Oh I'm sorry babe... I can imagine... it's good you

saved the kittens... just a minute, Stu."

Dropping the phone on the bed, Maggie brushes her eyes with a tissue, then blows her nose before picking up the phone again.

"No, I haven't said anything to Kate or Oz. Krystal asked me not to say anything. And I understand why, really, but that doesn't make it any easier. I mean, Oz was ticked because she never got the release party plugged in the school paper, but since I'm sworn to secrecy I can't even stick up for her without saying anything."

10 . . .

Elsie sits at her computer, organizing her notes. Glancing at her watch, she rolls away from her desk, wondering where Eric is. He gives a mean massage and she could use one, but has to settle for neck stretches and rotations.

Surprising, really, he hasn't called or anything. Just as well, she has to get this done, and he's been becoming a bit of a pest lately. Pah. Men are supposed to be the ones who want sex without ties.

Except Eric. He wants commitment.

But she simply can't afford it. Sex is all she has time for. Some fun to ease the stress. Med school is the only priority. She simply does not have time to spend in relationships and emotional negotiations.

Which is not to say she doesn't want a nice uncomplicated roll in the hay every so often. Maybe a little more. Twice daily is good. She smiles at the memory of Chuck this afternoon. Talented, that one.

Distracting, even, so she checks email to see if Eric... oh shit. She was supposed to meet him for dinner, but, well, Chuck was a temptation she couldn't pass up.

Dinner date interruptis, so now there's petulant email from Eric. So much for a massage.

She'd thought a dalliance with Eric would be just the thing, but maybe it's been a mistake.

He has such wonderful skin though. Smiling she thinks about him, then shakes her head to realign her focus.

Work. This has to be done for tomorrow. Maybe she should think of cutting him loose. Not yet though. She's not done enjoying him just yet. There's something about the boy, addictive almost. Stop thinking about him. Get the work done. He probably just wants to punish her for standing him up.

But he won't be able to stay away. Rolling back to the desk she stubs her her toe on something hard and irregular.

Twisting around and under Elsie sees what it is. Eric's keys.

Hmmm.

11 . . .

Mouse drops anise blocks into two mugs of milk before putting them in the microwave, bopping to music only she hears through her ear buds while it counts down. When it beeps she takes the steaming mugs out and stirs them vigorously, shuddering in happy pleasure as she inhales the rich licorice scent of home.

Tucking her well thumbed copy of **Don Quixote** under her arm, she pops the spoon in the sink then carefully picks up the mugs and navigates the stairs to the common room.

Mouse sets one mug on the table in front of Amelia curled up on the sofa. Looking up from her own **Don Quixote**, Amelia smiles her thanks, not asking whose milk it is. Mouse settles at the other end and begins reading. Producing a pencil from behind her ear she makes margin notes now and again.

Mouse is just taking her own first sip of anise milk when she hears a thud from the stair door followed by giggling. Amelia and Mouse exchange glances. "I thought everybody was in already." whispers Amelia.

"Seems not," says Mouse, setting her mug back down, she stands and tightens her fuzzy robe then starts for the door. Amelia lays her book face down on the sofa to preserve her place and follows, curious.

The door creeps open as they approach and Amelia gasps-- there's a body on the floor. But then more giggling.

As they arrive at the door the "body" is revealed as an extremely inebriated Eric. The giggling comes in equal parts from Natasha and Liz.

"What happened to him?" hisses Amelia.

"Isn't it obvious? This is one plastered puppy," says Natasha, which encourages another round of giggling from Liz.

"Boris and I found him at Callaghan's passed out in the back booth. The waitress made us bring him home."

"Where is Boris?" asks Mouse.

"Putting away the car. When we got here Liz was on her way in so we drafted her to help," says Natasha.

Liz giggles. "He was conscious then. I guess the elevator rocked him to sleep. It was all we could do to get him out."

"He can't stay out here in the hall, he'll get in trouble. How about everybody grab corner?"

Natasha and Liz struggle to get Eric's dead weight elevated enough so they can get a grip under his arms, while Mouse and Amelia each hoist a foot. They stumble through the door and manhandle Eric onto the sofa.

"Funny," says Liz, "He didn't look that heavy."

"Thanks for your help, guys, but that's it for me," says Natasha. "G'night all."

Liz yawns, catching the scent of licorice she notes the two mugs of steaming milk on the coffee table and in a blink decides to let it go. "I'm calling it a night too. Sweet dreams," and she follows Natasha up.

Amelia and Mouse exchange glances.

"Well." Amelia says, "We could move to the chairs."

Just then, Eric begins to snore. It's a substantial sound, and Mouse shakes her head.

"Since the Incredible Hulk seems to have appropriated the room I think I will call it a night too."

Amelia nods. "Like we have a choice." She snaps off the reading lamp, and they pick up their mugs and start up the stairs. Amelia glances back at the sleeper. "I've got an extra blanket I can bring down for him."

Mouse smiles at her. "You've a good heart Ami. G'night." They separate at the top, heading to their rooms.

Amelia shares one of the big corner doubles with Liz, so she gives a quiet tap before entering. As she sets the mug on her desk she sees Liz is nearly asleep. Amelia pulls a fleece blanket down from her closet.

"I'm gonna run this down to sleeping beauty," she whispers.

Liz mumbles something unintelligible and rolls over, so Amelia turns the desk light off and slips out with the blanket. Boris is just coming in as she comes down the stairs.

Boris asks, "He's out again?"

Amelia grins. "Yup, and that was as far as we could get him." Taking an end of the blanket, Boris helps her drape it over the sleeper. Eric takes a deep shuddering breath and snores profoundly.

Boris and Amelia both cover their mouths in an effort to keep their laughter from waking the dead, and Boris whispers, "I hope I get treated so nicely when I show up in that condition."

"You?" whispers Amelia, "You're far too cool to end up like this, Bo. Goodnight."

Boris grins and gives her a courtly bow before he heads under the stairs on the way to his room. Amelia heads back up and is about to go into her own room when she realizes **Don Quixote** is still downstairs. And she's not finished the chapter. Damn.

So much for a quiet night to catch up on her reading. Back down the stairs. She looks at Eric sleeping so peacefully. Where would the book be? She had been sitting at the door end, meaning the book is probably somewhere under his neck. What are the odds on getting it out without waking him or wrecking the book?

Giving up is not an option if she's to finish the chapter and start the essay tomorrow. Gently peeling the blanket down she's rewarded with a glimpse of her book tucked in behind the small of his back. She tries to wriggle it out but no go. Sliding her hand under doesn't work, so she tries to roll him. A blast of stale beery breath in her face does not thrill her. Yuk.

Around the back of the sofa to try and get a hold of the book she reaches down and snags the corner, and is jiggling it to pull it out when Eric rolls off the sofa onto the floor.

Now Amelia's book is free, but she feels guilty for pitching the guy on the floor. Still, there's no way she is getting him back on the sofa by herself. Too bad Boris is gone, he probably bench presses more than Eric weighs. He could pick Eric up easy. No way she can. She takes a cushion and wrestles it under his head. He snuggles in and looks so sweet.

Too bad he reeks of stale beer. Reaching over she pulls the blanket across him again before heading back up the stairs for the night.

Pulling the door closed she sets the book on her table, drapes her robe over the chair and angles it to block the bedside lamplight. She switches it on. Not a twitch from Liz. Good.

She can finish her reading here. Curling in with Cervantes, she finds herself thinking about Eric. She's never seen him drunk. He always seemed to have it together. Most of the other guys get shitfaced, not him. At least not 'til now. Guess everybody takes a turn. Wonder what did it.

Elsie, probably.

Poor schmuck.

12 . . . the weekend

The good thing about Saturday morning shifts is there aren't many customers before noon.

But it's still hard when you were up too late the night before. Amelia unpacks a box of books, checking the contents against the shipping manifest. Lifting out a handful of physics texts she carries them out front to shelve.

When the bell tinkles she looks over to see that it's Adam. "I need a spindle of writable CDs this morning" he says.

"They're over here. Sure you want CDs? You know they're more expensive than DVDs because of the levy, right?"

"Yes, I do know, but I need them for an old laptop that only takes CDs."

"Too bad," commiserates Amelia. "Anything else?"

He thinks. "Let me look around a bit. There might be."

"OK," she says, "I'm just putting out some new books. Just give a holler when you're ready."

Adam looks through the rack of greeting cards, wondering what card you would get for the most beautiful girl in the world. These cards are all too foolish. Some have sexual implications that make him a little uncomfortable. Maybe a card isn't quite right anyway.

He's skips the iPad display. Even if they weren't beyond his price range the Apple toy doesn't fill any real need he knows of. But when Adam sees the **Ubuntu** mug he knows it is just perfect.

Not the big clunky travel mug, the delicate porcelain mug. It will remind her of him every time she sees it. Drinks from it. Every time her lips touch... wait a minute.

Calm down.

Surely it would be obvious to anyone how smitten he is with Barbie. Glancing around guiltily, Adam is relieved to see that Amelia is still in the back room.

Breathe deeply, from the belly, get a strong ki flow.

Adam feels himself coming back under control. Once in balance, he carries the mug back to the register just as Amelia emerges with more text books.

Amelia asks, "All set?" and Adam nods agreement, smiling. She sets the pile of texts on the counter to ring his purchases through.

Adam feels a little sorry for this drab, ordinary girl.

She seems pleasant enough but she's so... colourless. Poor thing, not blessed with golden hair like beautiful Barbie.

It's too bad all girls can't sparkle like his Barbie.

13 . . .

Boris, Natasha, Liz and Jake are walking along the creek, enjoying the great outdoors on the Christie campus grounds. Although there are still leaves on the trees, there are more are on the ground, now.

Jake says, "I can't believe how warm it is still."

"So where is this surprise?" asks Boris.

Natasha lightly punches his shoulder, "Stop buggin' her, Bo. We'll see it when we get there."

Liz knows there is no way any of them will capture any wildlife in their photographs today. Jake isn't bad but Boris and Natasha are simply too loud. City slickers. Every critter for miles is holed up somewhere else, hiding until these large noisy intruders go away.

Still, Liz can't help but grin. She's actually having fun here.

She can't wait to show them. Her friends. People she has stuff in common with.

Now that was something worth coming to Christie for. Imagine, people as interested in photography as she is. Heck, Jake is way ahead of her. For such a young guy he knows so much. And he's on top of all the digital stuff, too.

Boris and Natasha run ahead, throwing leaves at each other. Liz starts snapping shots of the leaf fight. Hah.

At first Liz doesn't notice Jake backing up behind her, taking pictures of her taking pictures. But when she does she whirls around to catch him dead on, camera obscuring much of his face but none of his intensity.

Natasha runs on ahead again, leaving Boris far behind. As she crests the hill she stops, and Liz knows she's seen it. Snapping on her lens cap, she tells Jake, "Come on!"

Liz turns and runs up the slope after Natasha, her long legs easily outdistancing Jake and passing Boris. Jake jogs over to Boris then drops into a walk beside him.

"Aren't you curious?" Jake asks, since Boris hasn't increased his walking speed at all.

"I expect whatever it is will still be there when we arrive."

Jake nods, and they continue up the sloping path. As they reach the top, they can see the hill follows the creek down the hill to a little valley. Beside the meandering creek at the bottom they see Natasha under a huge old oak tree, pushing an enormous tire swing suspended on a thick chain from one of the massive branches. A humongous tire.

The tire twists as it swings and they see Liz spreadeagled inside, arms and legs outstretched to hold on to the inner lip.

Boris grins and snaps off some shots as they start down the hill. "Good surprise. Think it's a tractor tire?"

"Monster truck maybe." And Jake realizes that even Boris will probably fit in that thing.

Cool.

14 . . .

Eyes closed, focusing on the spirit of breathing, Adam begins exhaling through his nose.

Slowly he opens his eyes and gazes at the far away spot.

Extending his arm he stretches and points toward the spot until the exhalation begins to wane. He allows his eyes to close and relaxes his arm, allowing it to fall to his side.

Adam inhales deeply, beginning ki breathing as he focuses internally now.

Until he feels a touch on his shoulder. Without altering his breathing, Adam reaches up and grasps the wrist of the hand that's touching him. Turning evasively while breaking free of the shoulder grip, he puts his attacker on the mat.

His brother angrily protests, "Hey!"

Adam stops and blinks, releasing the wrist. "What are you doing here?"

His brother shakes his head and says, "We've got to stop meeting like this. Could you maybe try to remember that I live here too?"

"But you snuck up on me." Adam is annoyed to hear the whine in his own voice. The problem is that his brother always makes him feel like a little kid.

There has never been any doubt that Adam was the smart one. But his brother has always had the far more valuable gift of sociability. Sometimes Adam has to quell a touch of jealousy for this older sibling who glides so effortlessly through life, as suave and charming as any Hugh Grant character.

Adam extends a hand and helps his brother up.

"I wish you wouldn't keep doing that. I just want to work out. That's why I put in the weight room."

"Sorry."

"You wanna spot me?"

Adam nods, "Alright."

Adam loves his brother. He just doesn't like to be startled.

15 . . . monday

Eric watches Elsie sitting in the window of the coffee shop, sipping her cappuccino. The sun angling through the plate glass lights her auburn mane afire like an erotic halo. He sighs heavily as he emerges from the bathroom, walking over to slip into the seat across from her.

This was 'their place.' The only place outside bed they ever frequented together with any regularity.

God, she is so gorgeous. Alabaster skin, sea green eyes. He smiles at her until he remembers, and then he looks away. He tells himself to stop it. Be a grown up here.

She smiles and says, "Hey, Eric." Like nothing's changed. He looks at the table. She's gotten him his usual dark roast with a sprinkle of chocolate, biscotti arranged on the side dish.

He can't stop the sigh. "Missed you at Callaghan's Friday." He looks at the coffee as he picks it up.

Not looking at her.

Blows on it, sips, sets it down. Stirs.

She looks at him closely. His skin looks grey this morning. Particularly in this glorious sunlight. Amazing sun for October. She can smell the alcohol wafting off him. Watching him not looking at her, she takes in the uncharacteristic stubble, the red rimmed eyes looking here, there, not knowing where to rest.

He licks his lips. Such lovely lips he has too, she thinks. Eric is possibly one of the best lovers she's ever had. "I got held up." she says, watching him, seeing his jaw clench. Not a good sign.

He's still not meeting her eye.

Eric is looking at her reflection. Stirring his coffee, looking out the window. Anything but to look in those eyes. She's so achingly beautiful. Maybe it was just a bad dream.

Stirring.

That's all she's going to say.

Maybe it was all in his imagination. Yeah right. He's got a great imagination but he's not a masochist.

Inconstant Moon

Wake up and smell the coffee.

She's acting like it's an everyday thing.

He stops, freezes, as an awesome and monstrous thought enters his mind. Eric's fingers go slack as the thought sucks all the air out of his heart. He lets go the spoon, it clatters to the tabletop, flinging a few drops of coffee on his shirt. Like he cares.

Monstrous.

Maybe it **is** an everyday thing.

She's bent over the table, digging for something in her bag. The waves of glorious hair fan out around that perfect neck. She purses those lips as she finds what she's looking for. Withdrawing her hand, clasping it tightly she reaches across the table then opens it. An offering of his keys cupped in the palm of her hand. He just stares at them with dead eyes.

"You forgot these the other day," she says.

As though nothing has happened. Her voice sounds exactly the same. As if everything is the same.

But it isn't.

Yesterday he loved her and thought she loved him.

Today he knows better.

He raises his eyes and meets hers. She drops the keys on the table, and withdraws her hand.

She knows. He knows. And she's still the most beautiful girl he's ever seen. She's probably the most beautiful girl he will ever see. And she's got such a brilliant mind. God she is smart. He thinks that was maybe more important than anything.

But.

She looks at him and sees him seeing her. Really seeing her for the first time, not the pedestal woman he had made of her, but the real woman.

She can see the lust in his eyes, mingling with the hurt and pain. The disgust. But the lust is still there.

And it's making her feel... she feels so... it's an arousal so strong she can't believe it. She bites her lip as the flush spreads across her face. She wants to knock all the bloody coffee stuff off the table and fuck him silly right here on this table in the window in front of god and everybody. She's never wanted anything this badly in her life.

He picks up his keys and hooks them over his little finger, just like always, and it hits her that he's leaving. Then he pulls out his wallet and throws some bills on the table. He's leaving her. He walks out.

Elsie grabs her bag and follows him out into the sun.

"Eric," she calls. "Wait." He stops. Frozen. Still tense.

She runs after him, comes around in front of him. Standing inches away. She stares in his eyes a moment, then reaches up and pulls his face to hers. And the kiss is the most amazing thing she's ever felt, the most sexually charged kiss she's ever had, she can't breathe, she needs him-- needs him-- right now. She doesn't want it to end.

But he wrenches free and walks away.

"It didn't mean anything." she calls after him. She can't believe it as she watches him walking away. From her.

Bastard.

16 . . .

The sun is shining, the trees are flaunting their glorious autumn plumage, but Maggie and Krystal walk in the woods oblivious to the beauty all around them.

Maggie asks, "So what did the doctor say, Krys?"

They keep walking, Krystal doesn't say anything for a bit.

Just thinking, they scuff their way through the fallen leaves. As they approach the bench beside the wooden bridge that spans the creek, Krystal says, "Let's sit a while, O.K?"

Maggie nods and they sit. Krystal clears her throat, but doesn't look at Maggie, stares into the creek instead.

"Nothing's changed. It's not growing as fast as they thought. But it is growing."

"Can't they zap it with radiation or something?" Maggie asks hopefully.

Krystal sighs sadly. "Maybe there will be a breakthrough down the road. But there's nothing to be done now."

Maggie doesn't say anything. She's not sure what to say. She's still not sure that she understands.

"Look I'm sorry I told you, Maggie. I didn't mean to. It just kind of slipped out."

"What can I do to help, Krystal?"

"Just keep being my friend, Maggie. It's great to have some support, you know? But there isn't really anything else anyone can do at this point."

"Oh god, Krystal, I'm sorry... "

Maggie's tears are flowing and Krystal reaches over and pulls her into a hug. Patting her awkwardly on the back, Krystal says, "Don't cry, Maggie. Please don't cry."

17 . . .

Ensconced in his basement domain, Adam works hard; clearly, in his element.

Computers in all states of being, some live and Internet ready, others gaping with all their chips exposed, are set up along the wall to wall work bench.

Motherboards, cables and capacitors are tidily stored in boxes and bins.

But the only computer he has eyes for today is Barbie's. He spent the weekend getting it done. Such chaos; files scattered all over the laptop.

It was close, getting it all done for today, but that's what he promised. Now every thing is backed up and the defrag is finally done. Adam can't wait to give it to her. To Barbie.

18 . . .

The circle of friends reclines on the grass in their special clearing off the beaten track. Soaking up rays beside the creek running through the woodlot, Barbie languorously passes the joint to Jose, stretched out beside her. He takes a satisfying drag and smiles.

"Nice of Mister Sunshine to drop in for a visit, eh?"

He passes it on to Tamara, who takes just a light pull before handing it off to Quentin. Q takes a couple of tokes and passes it on to Mouse.

Tamara sits up, feeling just a bit spinny, taking in a deep breath in an attempt to clear her head before the dissection lab she has this afternoon. She smiles down at Quentin, who flashes his own pearly whites in a wolfish grin.

"You're not leaving," he asks.

"Yeah, babe, I can't afford to miss the lab." She leans over and gives him a kiss before she struggles to her feet. She looks down at Barbie laying there. The girl is totally wasted. "You coming Barb?"

"I don't think it'd be such a good idea Tam. I think they'd notice." And she starts in giggling.

"Yeah, you're probably right. Later." Tamara waves to the group and hurries off to the Bio building. The air feels good, the sun is soft and warm but she's got a bit of a head. That's it for me, she thinks, not for the first time. Can't afford to toke up at lunch any more. No way no how.

Tamara has wanted to be a doctor since she was small. Since her brother got the doctor kit she wanted for Christmas.

But she'll have a real doctor kit soon. She's worked too hard and too long to get here. Slaving night and day to get the math, but she did it. And now Tamara realizes that she has to get her head into the program or she's gonna end up booted out. That is not in the plan. Stick to the program. Get it done.

Yes.

19 . . .

Adam walks through the Oval carrying Barbie's laptop. It is indeed crowded with students sitting, eating, walking, talking and enjoying the beautiful weather.

Adam stops, and starts slowly scanning the sea of humanity. She said she would be here. As his eyes travel from group to group, always looking for the brightest blondes, he simply can not see Barbie anywhere.

It is a poser. She said she would meet him here. But it is so crowded. Her cellphone must be switched off. He has already used the cafeteria pay phone to leave messages on her voice mail, so she must know he is trying to find her.

He starts to walk along the path, careful not to trip over students or gear spread out along the way. Adam carefully checks every blonde girl, but there is no sign.

He is getting some funny looks when he makes the circuit fruitlessly a second time.

But now at least he is sure she is not here. He knows Barbie is pre-med, but he has no idea of her schedule. They have no overlapping classes. He doubts the registrar will give out her information.

He knows she does not live on campus so there is no point checking the residences. Wait a minute. He has her computer. He came where she told him to come.

He's searched diligently, and she is just not here.

But she will need the laptop for just about everything. He smiles as he pictures her making pencil notes in a lecture hall where everyone else is using a laptop or a tablet.

Barbie will want her computer back. She will come looking for him. Having a woman like Barbie searching him out, asking people if they know where he is, would be good.

Act natural, don't deviate from his normal activities. Stay in character. Go to the library.

Let her find him. Adam smiles. It is just what his brother would do.

20 . . .

Tamara pushes open the door of the Med School wing of Christie General. The facility was originally built in a sleepy rural backwater in the 19th Century. Deliberately removed from urban centres of industry and disease, quiet and fresh air was more responsible for the high rate of patient survival than many of the dubious medical practices of the day.

Sixty years later the institutional quiet was breached forever with an influx of Great War casualties no other facility had the beds to accept. The survivors of mustard gas, battlefield surgery and shell shock desperately needed housing and treatment. No longer just a quiet place where the railroad petered into a train yard, the town expanded to accommodate an ever increasing flow of visitors, sprawling down the valley to meet the river.

With an end to the war, several military surgeons followed their former patients to Christie, bringing with them surgical innovations developed in wretched battlefield conditions, triggering the transformation from sanatorium to teaching hospital. It wasn't long before Christie University grew up around the bustling hospital.

Tamara undresses in the locker room, slipping into scrubs and stuffing her clothes in the locker. She notes the quiet, but brushes her unease aside as she hurries to the Lab. It's later than she thought. Damn.

Opening the door she's surprised to find the lab empty.

Nobody here.

Nothing to cut.

WTF? Maybe she got the day wrong? Must have been rescheduled. Wish somebody had told her, given her a call, something. She could have stayed in the sun with her baby. Maybe she can still catch him.

She goes back into the hall when the men's locker room door slams open and startles her. She whirls to look but it's only Nick, backing out with a wheelie bin.

"Gee, Nick, you scared me. What happened to the dissection?"

Nick looks at her. He thinks she's intelligent enough, but he knows if she doesn't get it together soon she's gonna be history. Her big brown eyes look so open, so serious.

Probably because her pupils are so widely dilated.

"The dissection went off as scheduled at one, Tamara."

"At one. I thought... it's after one?"

Nick nods toward the wall clock, "It's after three."

She stares at him, aghast. "Oh no."

Nick starts wheeling the sharps cart away, but he feels sorry for the girl standing there, conflicted. Maybe she'll pull it up if he gives her a word. She looks pretty devastated. So he stops.

"Look, I know you're really smart, Tamara. But if you don't focus you are just not going to make it. There are too many people who want your spot. If you're looking for an easy ride you're in the wrong program, you want to transfer to something else 'cause there just isn't any slack for a pre-med. Maybe you want to consider something in the arts instead."

Her head is bowed and her shoulders are shaking. But when she speaks her words are steady, though her voice is thick with tears. "Can I make up the dissection with another class?"

"Come by the office after five. I'll see what I can do." Nick shrugs. "I think you might make a good doctor, Tamara, but maybe not. What you do on your own time is your business, but I can smell the pot from here. And that sure isn't the way."

Tamara says. "It won't happen again."

Pushing the bin toward the store room he hears her say softly, "Thanks Nick."

21 . . .

Quentin snores gently, Barbie and Jose are asleep too. Mouse gathers her things and jiggles Quentin's shoulder.

"I have to go to a class Quentin, but somebody should be awake. Too easy to rob sleeping people, yes?"

Bleary eyed, Quentin nods, rubbing his head, "I got it, Mousie." He struggles to sit up. "Man, that was good shit."

She grins enthusiastically and waves before jogging back toward the main path.

Quentin flips open his phone, and scrolls through the calendar. He's missed one class already, but he could probably slip into the art theory snooze without getting busted. School just makes him tired. But he wants Tamara to be happy.

So.

Much as he'd rather kick back in the sun, he knows he has to go, so Quentin reaches over and gives Jose a shake.

"Hey man, Mouse's gone, and I've gotta go too." Stretching, himself awake. "You guys probably don't wanna sleep out here, you know."

Staring up at the clouds, Jose says, "Yeah. I know."

Quentin grins, "Later, dude," and is gone.

Jose stretches and yawns hugely before rooting around in his backpack and pulling out a water bottle.

He unscrews it and takes a swig, then sets it down beside him, crosses his arms and rests them on his knees and watches the water running along the creek bed. Jose does more stretching, then some yawning and now he's awake. He wants something sweet. And Goldilocks is laying there waiting for him.

He sure likes the girl. What's not to like? Does she like him though? She seems to, flirting all the time. Not a bad time to find out. Another sip of water, and he lays back again on the grass. Rolls on his side, watching her sleep. Pretty girl all right. WASP. White Anglo Saxon Protestant. Doesn't act it though, smoking up with Catholic boys like him and Q. Hell, he's the Latin lover type, right? The corner of his mouth turns up as he thinks about that one.

Watching the girl sleep is pretty intimate. Her breath is on him. Better wake her up. He reaches out a finger and runs it along her jaw. She smiles, mumbles something. He leans closer, to hear. Right. He touches her shoulder.

"Hey Barbie, it's getting late, we gotta go."

"Mmmm, just a few more minutes."

He smiles, this time running a finger along her lips. Her eyes open, she looks right at him, "Mmmm, Jose, hey."

He sees an invitation in those blue blue eyes, and he leans in, kisses her gently. Oh wow, she's kissing back.

He can't believe his luck. She pulls him close, really going to town. He hugs her back, enjoys the way she's so aggressive, the way her curves feel against him, kinda nice. Really, really nice.

Barbie's legs circle him, pulling him in.

He's almost light headed from the kissing when her hands grab his and push them under her sweater...

Oh my. He can't believe this is actually happening, maybe he's still asleep and this is the mother of all wet dreams, oh much better than he could have imagined. This is the real deal here in his arms, this is Malibu Barbie rubbing all over him and it is sure happening. He's rising manfully to the occasion and ...

Then all of a sudden it isn't. Barbie sits up and tugs her sweater down, suddenly modest. Or maybe just awake. Dammit.

"Oh my god Jose, what are you doing?"

"Me?" Jose shrugs, lowering his eyes "I was just trying to wake you up. You're the one jumping me, girl." he smiles his soft smile at her. "Not that I mind or anything."

She sits up and looks at him. His big brown eyes look away, suddenly embarrassed. Cast downward, those gorgeous thick eyelashes veiling those bedroom eyes. "Oh my god," she thinks, "he's blushing." She doesn't have trouble buying his story because, Jesus, she's wet. She smiles; he is yummy. And she has thought about Jose, dreamt about him too.

More than once.

And man she's ready for him. More than ready. He's a better kisser than she'd expected but. Sexy as the boy is, he is just not a hustler. Jose is hot, alright. But he's not going to set the world on fire. He's not going anywhere extraordinary, and he won't be hot when he gets a pot belly, starts balding. He'll teach elementary school in some nowhere town, married with kids. Be a good dad, join the Lions, PTA, with a wife, couple of kids in soccer, the works. Great life for some girl.

Just not this girl. Seeing her cousin get hitched this weekend 'cause the silly twit got herself knocked up was like a warning from God. That's not happening to her. Bright lights, big city, glamour and glitz, that's the ticket.

"It's okay, Jose. Sorry, I didn't mean to, um, bother you."

She glances down at his straining jeans then quickly looks away, her breathing shallow. So easy to scratch the itch, but she knows damn well Jose would expect her to be *his* woman. Which would mean she'd have to chuck her plans. No, no. no.

He nods. Looking over at her with those big dark eyes. Licks his lips, her turn to blush. He's not being subtle at all as he looks longingly at her. She better watch it or she'll be the one making babies. Uh uh. No way. No how. Not this girl.

"I gotta go." She grabs her stuff and takes off without a backward glance.

Jose lays back and sighs. It was too good to be true.

22 . . .

Natasha, stands with hands planted on her hips, "I think it's just about perfect."

Boris chuckles. "You can't be serious."

But she is serious, staring up at the black metal statue. The horseman is mightily gripping the reigns of the rearing horse delicately balanced on its two rear legs. The statue's tail touches the concrete base making the third leg of the tripod, but it still looks precarious.

"She wants us to find a new way of looking at the world, a different point of view. This will be different."

"Well," Boris says, "Just how in hell do you think you're going to get up there?"

Natasha tilts her head and looks up at Boris, wearing a mischievous smile.

Boris holds both hands up in front of him, defensively. "Whoa there girl, You think I am going to help you get up on that ancient statue? I don't think so. I like it here at Christie and I don't really want to have to transfer out."

"Aw Boris, don't be such a poop. I only need a boost."

"Oh yeah? What happens if you wreck the thing, eh?"

"How am I gonna wreck it? It's made of metal for gods sake, and it's bolted to a concrete pedestal."

"Look, it's balanced OK now, but the horse is only standing on two feet. You go up there you might unbalance the whole thing. So let me ask you, is it worth the risk?"

Natasha looks into Bo's eyes. A big smile spreads from ear to ear, and she nods vigorously. "Oh yeah."

Boris claps himself on the head. "You're certifiable. Jeeze, Nat. If you get caught they might throw you out."

"Come on, Bo. I won't hurt anything... and nobody will catch me. It'll be fine."

"You're missing a really big point though."

"And that would be?"

"You take your shots from up there it would be evidence. Not a good idea. The pictures you hand in will bust you."

"Gee, that's an interesting point, Bo. I never would have thought of that." Natasha carefully winds the small camera bag around her wrist then scrambles up the side of the plinth, hoisting herself onto the pedestal.

"Wait, Nat, wait, you're not still gonna do it!"

"Sure I am." Natasha wraps one arm around the horse's near hind leg and reaches her other hand to Boris. "Now are you gonna help me or not?"

Boris looks at her outstretched right hand and her expectant face. Damn. "Okay okay." Boris waves away her hand, planting both of his on the top of the pedestal so he can vault up to join her.

Balancing precariously on top of the damned thing, he draws himself up to his full height and looks around.

From this vantage point Boris does in fact have a better view of the oval, pretty empty now in spite of the fabulous weather. Students are back in class or off campus this late in the day. Nobody is looking over this way. Seems safe enough.

"I just need you to give me a little boost up Bo."

Natasha extends her arms upward over her head,

her fully extended fingers just brush the bottom of the saddle. She won't make it without him. Unless she jumps, which would be incredibly dangerous. Boris sighs and takes one more stealthy glance around before reaching down and gently picking her up by the waist and raising her above his head. Natasha grasps the horse's metal mane, gets a good grip then throws her leg over the statue's withers, squeezing in between horse and general. Boris drapes his arm over the horse's rump while scanning the Oval, miserably hoping that they won't be caught and kicked out.

Natasha's camera is out, she aims here and there, checking the framing on the screen back against her view of the wider world. She looks around until she is satisfied that she is really seeing. Only then does she begin taking photographs. Getting the view from here, the buildings, plantings, scattered students hurrying along the paths.

"Are you almost finished?" Boris hisses urgently.

Making sure she's got a couple of incriminating shots of Boris, Natasha slides the little camera back in its bag. "All done."

She slips out of the general's grip and starts lowering herself down the side of the horse until Bo's hands encircle her waist. He carefully lowers her half way down so she can make a gentle jump to the grass below, then shakes his head, still surprised he's been dumb enough to go along with this crazy girl. His head is spinning, his heart racing as he glances around, certain that a contingent of campus cops will be coming for him any minute. But the coast is clear, so he jumps down, landing rather less gracefully. Rolling onto his back on the grass, weak as a kitten, he stares up at the impossibly blue sky, giddy with relief.

Natasha again offers him a hand, and this time he takes it, and she helps him up.

"Okay" she says brightly, "I've got mine, what's yours?"

Boris laughs, happy no one is slapping handcuffs on his wrists. Oh, it's good to be a free man. "I have no idea."

23 · · ·

Cameras slung around their necks, Liz follows Jake up the back stairs of the Art Centre. At the top Jake pushes open the door leading into a dimly lit corridor.

"So what's up here anyway?" Liz asks.

Jake smiles, touching a finger to his lips, then crooking it to indicate she should follow. Exasperated, she follows him anyway. Midway down the hall he stops and pushes a door inward, then walks into the dark.

"What is this brilliant idea anyway, Jake?"

He pops his head out, holding a finger to his lips, this time actually "shushing" her before disappearing inside. Liz doesn't know what to do, but follows him into the dark anyway.

Liz feels a little guarded. It's dark and there's a kind of weird ambiance. And what sounds kind of like... maybe water falling? She just feels more confused. But

Jake is already making his way through the darkness. So Liz trails after. It's a long, room, or maybe a hallway? Hulking shapes huddle along the walls. Some kind of containers. Barrels maybe? It's weird. Jake was so excited, he wouldn't steer her wrong. Would he?

Of course that's what everybody always thinks in the slasher movies. Reaching down to her fanny pack she makes sure she has her cellphone. Just in case. And she has the tripod if she needs some kind of a weapon. And she's a lot bigger than... Wait a minute, this is Jake here. What is she thinking?

Ahead the dim light from the camera's screen back illuminates the shadow that is Jake. Light stabs through the darkness and the sound volume swells. Liz realizes Jake is very cautiously opening yet another door. Suddenly she can clearly hear the rumble of a crowd, and puts it all together in a rush of relief. Vaguely Liz recalls Amelia saying something about the drama department hosting a play. The Stratford Touring Company, that was it.

It's easier going now that there's some illumination. Liz moves up to stand beside Jake. They look out at a lighting catwalk strung between large theatrical lights suspended from a latticework of metal struts mounted on the ceiling. Compared to the storeroom it's bright, but it's really just the spill, with the lion's share of illumination pouring down onto the stage.

Jake moves silently onto the catwalk to set up. There's no one else up here, so Liz assumes the lights have all been preset. Probably being run from a control board somewhere, maybe backstage. She watches Jake. He's clearly aiming straight down at the audience, sure to get some great shots of the tops of heads. Bald spots, dandruff, who knows what he'll capture, but whatever it is it'll sure be different. She smiles as she realizes he has come up with an interesting new perspective.

Liz fires up her own camera, adjusts her settings, feeling a little foolish for being worried.

About Jake.

She feels like an idiot.

Instead of stepping out onto the catwalk herself, Liz crouches and takes a series of photographs capturing Jake at work. Retrieving her cellphone from the fanny pack she turns it off. It wouldn't do to disrupt the show being put on below. Liz feels a bit of a stomach flutter as she steps out on the catwalk, moving away from Jake, toward the stage.

Jake brought her along so she can't very well poach his idea. She needs her own spin, make her own distinct images. It is warm here. A little hard to breathe.

Overheated by powerful lights and body heat from the audience below. No wonder. One of the big Shakespeare plays probably. Was there dancing in Macbeth? Doesn't matter, she feels supercharged as she applies herself to her task, photographing the mammoth lights that are so close she could almost touch them as they cast their magical glow on the stage below.

Liz feels a chill, but she's too busy, so she pushes it aside. She wants to get some good shots. She focuses on the stage, filled with masked revellers in flashing colours twirling to some kind of medieval music.

Following the colour and motion from this angle is interesting. A little dizzying. When she's got enough pictures, Liz shuts down her camera and stows it in her pouch.

Why is her heart racing like this? So hot. Turning back the way she came she doesn't see Jake at all. He must have finished. Maybe he's gone.

Now the work is done Liz realizes that she's having a bit of a problem. She tries to take a step in the darkness but... she can't make her foot rise. Now that she's looking through her own eyes and not the camera, she realizes the edges of her vision are ragged.

The dizziness is making her feel nauseous, along with a kind of falling sensation, pulling her to the side, drawing her to the audience. Down there. Now that she's not taking pictures, she realizes the physical discomfort she feels isn't excitement, it's fear. She does not want to be this high up. No. Her hand snakes out and grabs the catwalk railing.

This is silly. She walked out here, she should be able to go back again too. Looking down at her feet she can see the people below. Reflected light from the stage reveals them clearly through gaps in the metal mesh floor. Liz can feel the little holes in the floor through her shoes, she's mesmerized by the sight.

Heart pounding furiously Liz realizes she can't stay here.

She can't move either. Where is Jake? She can't lift her foot. Not the other one either. Lifting it off the floor is too scary. The nearly invisible floor. Not an option. Maybe she can slide it. Her death grip on the railing helps pull her forward a step. Progress. Slide the hand, slide the feet.

The heat is intense, Liz feels sweat running down her back. Got to get out of here. Dizzy.

The pounding in her chest is bad, now there's a pounding in her head, the rushing of the ocean, the blue of the water... white froth... Liz slumps to her knees, held upright by her mechanical grip on the rail.

As consciousness wanes, her fingers relax and she sprawls on the catwalk.

In the store room Jake is scrolling through the thumbnails of the images he's photographed. Looking good. He packs up his camera and wonders what's taking Liz so long. He goes back inside and takes a peek through the doorway. She's not there. Where did she go? He heads back out through the store room and into the hall. She must have left. That's annoying.

Not like Liz to just take off without a word though. Maybe she just thought it was stupid and didn't want to say anything.

He shakes his head in frustration, but he should be used to being ditched by girls by now. He starts down the stairs, feeling an increasing sense of annoyance. Just he didn't think Liz was like that. She's been a good friend until now. One of the very few here who don't treat him like a little kid.

As he reaches the exit door, it hits him.

When he was here this afternoon helping the crew set up the lights, he was all over the lighting grid. There is no other way out of there. The only way Liz could have left would have been to go right past him. And she didn't. So Liz must still be up there. But where was she? He turns and starts back up again.

24 . . .

Adam is tucked away in a study carrel in the back of the library, totally caught up in creating his software architecture plan. Crunching numbers, verifying, testing, he's totally oblivious to the world around him. Which is why he hasn't noticed it's getting dark. Or Barbie, when she finally makes an appearance.

Standing in the doorway, Barbie scans the room, trying to spot the computer guy who has her laptop. The library is cavernous, much bigger than she thought it'd be.

If she had actually looked for Alan in the oval she'd have it now. She could be home already. But it was so warm and snugglely in the sun, too much fun laying in the grass smoking up with her friends to go hunting up her laptop. Of course if she'd got her laptop from Alan things wouldn't have got out of hand with Jose. That's gonna be so awkward.

It's one thing to lust after him in her head and mess around with that great body in her fantasies, but she knows she's damn well given Jose ideas now. Hell, she's given herself ideas. That was too close, she needs to get laid.

And soon.

Inconstant Moon

But goddamn she is not gonna end up like Tam,
stuck with some loser. Or her dimwit cousin. God, who
is stupid enough to get knocked up these days? Even if
you don't want an abortion, there's always adoption.
You don't have to marry the guy and wreck your whole
life. She will just have to steer clear of Jose. Don't think
about it now. Just find the guy with her computer.

She walks through the main area, there are a few
guys who might be him, but she's not really sure what
Alan looks like actually. Ordinary looking. With a tie.
But it'd probably be a different tie today, so that might
not help very much.

Barbie cruises around the perimeter. Some of the
possibles catch her checking them out and look up
hopefully, but she ignores them.

He had brown hair. Or was it black? Not blond
anyway. Maybe dark, uh dirty blond. Um. No glasses.
Kinda like Dilbert, actually. Duh. For sure he isn't any
of the guys working at the common tables in the centre
of the room. She walks along peeking in the carrels,
looking for her computer case. That she'll recognize.

And finally, Barbie sees it. She comes up behind the
guy, taps his shoulder. Skinny, not muscular like Jose.
She's pleased to see she was right, he's got brown hair.
He turns around and smiles when he sees it's her. Yup.
He is wearing a tie too, with some kind of... what is that
spaceships?... yeah, spaceships on it.

"Hey, where were you? Couldn't find you at lunch."
Barbie bestows one of her brightest smiles. "It was so
crowded and I looked but you weren't anywhere. I think
the whole school was out in the sun."

"I am sorry, Barbie, I did try. We probably missed one another because it was crowded and we were both moving."

"Probably. Then I had a class. Sorry I missed you."

Adam smiles happily, "Oh that's fine. Have you got a moment now? We can go over it."

Barbie frowns prettily, "I wish I could but I promised my Dad I'd have dinner with him. My folks are divorced and I don't get to see him very much."

"That's alright." He pulls her computer case out from under the carrel desk and hands it to her. "Let me just tell you, I've installed the new **Ubuntu** distro, and upgraded all your open source software, **Libre Office**, **Gimp**, and **Firefox**. I set up a directory structure I think you'll like but if you have any problems give me a call and I'll get you fixed up, okay."

"Oh wow, you did all that? That's amazing." she gushes. Adam smiles, feeling terribly pleased with himself.

"Hey, you know," she says glancing down at the computer bag, "There's one more thing you could help me with, that is if you've got the time?"

"Yes, I have some time tonight. How can I help?"

"It's these," she says. Fishing a couple of CDs out of her purse she hands them to Adam.

Adam looks at the cases, **Black Eyed Peas' The E.N.D.** and **Coldplay**'s **Viva La Vida**. "What is the problem? Do they skip in your player?" he asks.

"No, they're fine. My friend loaned them to me but I always have so much trouble making copies, I thought maybe you could put them on my MP3 player. Or even just show me how to do it?"

Adam's face isn't happy any more. "You can't do that."

Frowning. "I know, that's why I'm asking for your help, because when I try to do it something always goes wrong. **The Peas** aren't supposed to sound like **The Chipmunks**, you know?"

"No, that's not what I meant at all, Barbie. I meant that it's illegal to make copies of CDs."

She shakes her head, frustrated. "I don't think so. Everybody does it, and that's why she gave these to me so that I could copy them. She knows I'm gonna, she said it was okay."

"That doesn't matter. She can't give you permission, she doesn't have the right to ... "

"Of course she does, they're her CDs. I was with her when she bought them."

"She may have bought them, but that doesn't mean you can copy them. That's against the law. You could get in trouble. She could get in trouble. If I copy them for you I could get in trouble."

Barbie stands up, frustrated "That's the stupidest thing I ever heard. She owns them, Alan, and she gave me permission."

Adam purses his lips and frowns. "Please let me explain. She owns the compact disks, right?"

Barbie's eyes narrow and she looks at the guy. She knows he likes her. Why is he giving her a hard time? It doesn't track. She'll give him one more chance. So she says tentatively, "Right."

"But that's not the same as owning what's on the CDs."

Barbie just stares at him, confused, like he's some kind of little green man getting out of one of the spaceships on his tie. She tosses her hair in frustration. "They aren't blank CDs. If they were blank CDs they wouldn't have cost as much."

"Yes she bought them," he waves the CD, "But she didn't buy the right to copy them."

"Of course she did. She owns them. Who else would have the right to copy them?" she asks, amused.

"Whoever made the CD."

Barbie crosses her arms, and looks at him, no longer confused or amused. "You're telling me the only one who can copy **The E.N.D.**" Barbie snatches the CDs from his hand and waves them in front of his nose, "is the **Black Eyed Peas**? That's ridiculous. How am I supposed to ask big stars for permission?"

Adam says, "Of course not, that is not what ... "

But Barbie can't hear him. She won't listen. "I mean just 'cause I can follow **will.i.am** on **Twitter** doesn't mean he has time to talk to all the Peabodies. I mean, he's brilliant but he's busy writing music. They don't print their phone number on the CD." she says, petulantly now. "Even if they did, am I gonna call up **will.i.am** or **Fergie** and ask if I can copy Tamara's CD? They'd be on the phone all the time, not making music anymore."

"It is unlikely that the band would be allowed to

give permission anyway. It would be the record label or ... "

"Wait a minute. I may be a blonde but I am not dumb enough to think that **will.i.am** can't give me permission to copy his own freaking CD. That's just nuts. Why are you giving me such a hard time? Are you mad I missed you at lunch? I said I was sorry."

"I am not trying to give you a hard time, but my brother is an Intellectual Property lawyer. Could I just show you?"

She looks at his outstretched hand and hesitates a moment. Just she really doesn't have any more time right now. Not after having had to chase all over looking for the guy. So she stuffs the CDs back in her purse. "Look, just forget it." She grabs the laptop case, mutters, "Thanks," then turns on her heel and stalks away.

Adam sits there, stunned. Watching her walk away.

Barbie is annoyed. No, not annoyed, angry.

She's really, really, angry.

How could he be so stupid? She liked him. She even kissed him once. Why couldn't he just enjoy it? Why does he always have to be so anal? Barbie was happy he fixed up her computer.

All he wanted was to help her. He doesn't want her to get in trouble. Why doesn't she understand? Now life is truly miserable.

It was better when she didn't know he existed.

When she had no idea he was alive, he could quietly admire her and hope she might talk to him some day.

Now that she knows who he is, he's made her hate him. Adam buries his face in his hands.

He didn't even have a chance to give her the mug.

25 . . .

Liz is dreaming and a woman is talking... speaking oddly, but somehow familiar... such pretty words.

> How camest thou hither, tell me, and
> wherefore?
> The orchard walls are high and hard to climb,
> and the place death, considering who thou art,
> if any of my kinsmen find thee here.

Then a man is saying,

> With love's light wings did I o'er-perch
> these walls
> for stony limits cannot hold love out.

And Liz thinks **Romeo.**

She smiles and opens her eyes and realizes her face is pressed against the metal grill work floor of the catwalk. Slam the eyes shut. Oh God.

Bad.

Very bad.

Her whole body is tense with fear. How the heck does she get out of this? Not opening her eyes. No how, no way.

Better not to look. Where did this come from? It's terrifying. Get the breathing under control. Try to

breathe deeply. Listen to the words in the play.
Breathe. In. Out. In. Out. Listen to the words.
Concentrate on Romeo's words.

Romeo
I have night's cloak to hide me from their sight,
and but thou love me, let them find me here.
My life were better ended by their hate,
than death prorogued wanting of thy love.

Liz knows it's the balcony scene, but she doesn't
much care. She has to concentrate, get control.
Breathe in, breathe out.

Juliet
By whose direction found'st thou this place?

Romeo
By love, who first did prompt me to inquire
He lent me counsel and I lent him eyes.

Liz remembers doing this scene in high school so
long ago. She always liked the music of the words but
had trouble with the reading. Eyes tight shut, Liz
reaches up feeling for the rail.

Waving her hand around... nothing... not a good
thing to do. Heart beating too fast again. Strained like it
will burst.

Breathe. Breathe. Concentrate on Juliet's words ...

Juliet
Dost thou love me?
I know thou wilt say 'Ay,'
And I will take thy word.
Yet if thou swear'st Thou mayst prove false;
At lover's perjuries they say Jove laughs.

Okay, the only way out is to crawl. But which way.
Think. Open eyes just now. She can see the stage just
there.

Juliet

O gentle Romeo, If thou dost love,
                  pronounce it faithfully:
Or if thou think'st I am too quickly won,
I'll frown and be perverse an say thee nay,

Back is the other way... breathe... listen...
breathe...

In truth fair Montague I am too fond.
And therefore thou mayst think
                my 'havior light
But trust me, gentleman I'll prove more true
than those that have more cunning
                to be strange.

... listen... breathe... concentrate... crawl...

I should have been more strange,
                I must confess...
But that thou overheard'st, ere I was ware,
          my true love's passion:
      therefore pardon me,
And not impute this yielding to light love,
Which the dark night hath so discovered.

... listen... concentrate... crawl...

Liz freezes as her head bumps something solid...
she pulls back and opens her eyes. Looking up she
sees Jake.

Romeo

Lady, by yonder blessed moon I swear that tips

with silver all these fruit-tree tops--"

Jake reaches out a hand but Liz shakes her head violently and waves him away, convulsively gripping the edges of the catwalk floor. A little hurt, not understanding, Jake steps back.

Liz closes her eyes and breathes, listening again.

Juliet
O, swear not by the moon!
The inconstant moon
that monthly changes in her circled orb,
Lest that thy love prove likewise variable.

Jake is confused but he does what she wants, backing out of the doorway. Liz's gingerly begins crawling again. Suddenly Liz feels cool tiles not mesh. Solid. Through the doorway then she collapses in a heap.

Romeo
What shall I swear by?

Jake steps around the really weird girl on the floor and carefully pushes the door closed soundlessly. With the theatre closed off it's safe to talk aloud.

"What's wrong Liz? Should I get a doctor?"

Liz looks pretty shaky but she's sitting up.

"Are you all right?"

"No. Yes. Sorry, Jake." She nods, breathing deeply. "I... I think I just discovered I'm scared of heights."

"Oh." Jake is trying to process this. "I guess this wasn't such a hot idea then."

"It was an awesome idea." Liz smiles shakily. "Maybe not for me, but I got some pictures anyway. But I'm done now. Boy am I done."

Liz gets shakily to her feet. "Lets just go, okay?"

They go back out and down the stairs. At the bottom Liz stops and rests against the bench just inside the rear doors. She flops down into the seat. "I've gotta rest a minute. You can go on, I know I've been a real pain, but I'm okay now."

"It's fine. I'll wait. I'm sorry Liz, I didn't know."

Liz smiles ruefully, "That's okay, I didn't know either."

Jake looks at her. "I don't get it. How can you not know something like that?"

"I guess because I've never been in that kind of situation before. Flimsy railings you can't hardly see and ... " she shudders. "Huh, maybe that's why I never liked carnival rides. That floor up there, it's made of holes. You can see all the people underneath. It's almost invisible." Liz closes her eyes. "Not doing that again real soon."

Jake points to Ethan and Oscar walking past outside. "Look, there's Oz. I'll just--"

"No!" snaps Liz. "Don't tell Ethan, or anybody! Look, just don't say anything to anybody."

Jake frowns at her. "Why not? If you get dizzy again."

"Now that I'm on solid ground I'm not dizzy. Just a little shaky. It's just a delayed reaction. Really."

"They can help me get you back to the residence."

"You don't have to, I'll get myself back. I'm all right now."

"Like I'm gonna leave you." Jake throws up his hands in frustration. "Why you don't want any help, it's not a big deal."

"People around here already think I'm enough of a freak, okay? I just don't need the aggro."

"You're just talking trash now, Liz. You're cool, nobody thinks you're a freak."

"That's nice of you to say."

Jake is examining her face, "It's Ethan, isn't it?"

Liz snaps, "I don't know what you're talking about."

"You weren't worried about Oz, you were worried about what Ethan thinks." Jake grins, examining her now flushed complexion. "You like him, don't you."

"Time to be getting back Jake."

"You do!"

"Just stop it."

"What's the big deal?"

"I don't have time for guys. I have stuff I need to do with my life."

"Don't worry." Jake grins. "I won't tell him."

Liz stands up and pushes open the door. "Good."

"But maybe I can find out if he likes you too."

Liz is mortified. "No! Don't even think that."

"I'll bet he does."

"Look Jake, just give it a rest. Besides, what makes you think he'd be interested in a giraffe anyway?" Liz pushes through the door. Jake works hard to match her deliberately fast pace.

"You aren't that much taller than Ethan-- probably only a few inches. What does that matter?"

"I'm taller than everybody except maybe Kobe Bryant. Trust me, it matters. Just give it a rest, Jake."

Jake stops in his tracks, watching Liz keep right on going. At least he's no longer worried she's going to pass out, but he is worried that she might not want to be his friend now he's tumbled to her secret.

That is so weird, Liz doesn't know she's cool. Or pretty. Maybe that's why she's his friend, she doesn't know any better. Come to think of it, Ethan doesn't know he's cool either. Hmmmm. Maybe he can fix them up. Nobody cares about how tall anybody is. Krystal is taller than he is. And that's not gonna stop *him*.

26 . . .

Hair wound in a towel atop her head, swaddled in her fluffy purple robe and green bunny slippers, Amelia carries her bathroom bag back to the corner room she shares with Liz.

Too bad Liz couldn't come along tonight. Some assignment she had to work on with Jake.

Amelia is so glad she could get the night off to see the play. It was exquisite. She smiles to herself as favourite scenes play out in her mind. That actress was an excellent Juliet. And the sword fight was incredible.

There's just something about Shakespeare.

Amelia is startled when Elsie's door opens abruptly just as she passes. She's about to say, 'hey' when she realizes it isn't Elsie -- or Eric either -- everyone on the floor is accustomed to his occasional illicit presence. But this... this is some total stranger guy. Good looking, in a biker kind of way, but a total stranger.

He grins broadly at Amelia, eyeing her up and down, then he winks and says, "Nice threads."

Amelia flushes violently at the ignominious reminder she's dressed for bed. The guy blows her a kiss then slips out the fire door. She waits a beat and then checks to make sure that the heavy door really did latch behind him. Overcome with fury, she leans against the door, shaking, as the anger washes over her.

§

Liz looks up from her desk with a smile as the dorm room door swings open, but the smile dissolves at the sight of Amelia's face. Liz asks, "What's wrong?"

"I just about ran into some strange man in the hall."

"Well heck, we've gotta report this." Liz is reaching for her cell phone when she sees Amelia's head shake. "Why not?"

"He was coming out of Elsie's room."

"You're kidding!" says Liz. "She only just dumped Eric."

Amelia nods, "Guess she's a fast worker."

Hanging her bathroom bag on its hook, she shrugs off the purple robe, revealing an equally purple nightgown. Kicking off the clashing slippers, she drapes the robe on her desk chair and climbs into bed, switching on the reading lamp.

"Let's hope it's a one time thing." Liz suggests hopefully.

"You know it wasn't that bad with Eric slinking around because at least we know him, but I'm not so keen on running into total strangers when I'm wandering around in my jammies."

Liz nods, "Lets see how it goes."

"I just hope it doesn't turn into a parade," replies Amelia as she picks up her book. Thinking, it was a parade when Elsie was with Eric. It's only gonna get worse now she's not.

27 . . .

The LEDs on the alarm clock show 3:00 a.m.

Maggie is laying on her back in bed, staring at the ceiling with red rimmed eyes when she hears her cellphone vibrate on the night table. She grabs it and rolls onto her side to talk into it softly.

"Hey baby. No that's Okay, I was awake. How was it?"

She listens to his stories for a while. Then it's her turn.

"I'm just having a bit of a hard time sleeping."

She listens, then, "No way, I wasn't worried about you and the strippers." Maggie listens to him talk a bit, then she says, "Yeah, of course I trust you. I mean you're my guy and all but more important is you know

I'd kill you stone dead if you stepped out on me."

Stuart talks some more, and Maggie giggles. "But it's not gonna be forever. Even if I was there no way would I be going to a stag with you."

Maggie listens some more, then smiles sadly, "Yeah, I was thinking about her. You know me too well."

She listens again. Then, "No, she doesn't want anybody to know, but yeah, I told her I'd tell you. You know she's right. If people knew they'd treat her different." Maggie brushes her eyes.

"Hell, I know I do. I try not to... no, not even Katie. Just talk to me ... " Tears are running silently down Maggie's face. "Yeah, I wish you were here too, babe, 'cause I could sure use a hug."

28 . . . tuesday

Adam sits at the wheel of his car outside the record store. He drums his fingers on the dashboard, waiting impatiently for the store to open.

The problem is that it doesn't even look like there's anyone inside yet. He glances at his watch, then gets out of the car and goes up to the door. White painted letters tell him the hours of operation. The store doesn't even open until ten. That's ridiculous. And people wonder why there's a recession on.

He'll be late for class if he stays and waits.

Ruin his perfect record.

A surge of anger prompts Adam to punch the wall by the door in frustration. The impulse is instantly regretted as skin breaks and pain shoots up his arm.

Clutching skinned knuckles he stuffs his wounded hand into the protection of his armpit. Clenching his teeth he paces back and forth in front of the unhelpful storefront. Eventually the waves of pain subside.

With the pain level dropping to manageable, Adam returns to the car and opens the door with his right hand. He climbs in, being very careful not to injure himself further as he pulls the door closed. Examining his knuckles he notes the scrape will certainly leave bruises. But the skin is only broken in two places.

Adam shakes his head ruefully. What a stupid thing to do.

Reaching under the passenger seat Adam pulls out his first aid kit. A little rubbing alcohol, a couple of Band-Aids, and a few breathing exercises later, he's good as new.

At this point he decides to stay.

Going back for Web Design now will make him miss at least part of Computer Architecture after lunch since he'll have to come back. Better for his schedule if he stays. Some people cut classes all the time. Of course, those people don't have his grade point average. Still, missing half a lecture is hardly going to ruin his life. Maybe it's time he started taking control. Be the master of his own destiny. Adam smiles.

He pulls out his laptop, he could at least do some work from here. While it cycles through the start up Adam waves around his Wi-Fi finder. Not a whiff. He's surprised. Sure, Canada may have terrible connection speeds and some of the worst price gouging in the world, but it's not the UK so there is usually some open Wi-Fi to be had.

Except there does not seem to be any around here. This is the old part of town, and, well, really, this store still calls itself a record store. A thought. Maybe they sell records not CDs. He jumps out of the car and goes to peer in the window. He's relieved to see CDs in there. Still, it is old tech when you get down to it. Maybe they don't even know what Wi-Fi is.

It doesn't look like that bad a neighbourhood.

Just nothing looks very new, maybe that's it. Older businesses run by older people probably. He pulls into a parking spot right in front.

Driving around will turn up something. Settling the computer in the passenger seat he pulls the seat belt around to secure it, then places the Wi-Fi finder on the dashboard. Snapping on his own seat belt he starts the car and drives more downtown, keeping an eye on the finder.

The LED starts to pulse as he nears the library. Something to be said for coming to the library before it opens; good parking anyway.

Adam's watch shows it is only eight thirty. Well. He can at least get some work done anyway while he's waiting.

29 . . .

Maggie is sitting at the games table absently

stirring her tea, ostensibly reading the paper when Oscar comes in with a steaming mug of coffee.

"Morning, Miss Maggie."

"Hey Oz," she murmurs without looking up.

Oscar settles across from her, taking in the circles under her red rimmed eyes that aren't meeting his.

"Maggie? Have I done something to offend?" he asks.

Maggie looks up, surprised. "Offend? No of course not. Why would you think that?"

"I don't know." Oscar sighs. "You've been distant, and now you're unhappy to see me, so I'd thought perhaps your Stuart had an objection to our friendship, or some such thing."

Her eyes are brimming with unshed tears, "Oh Oz, no, nothing like that. Actually, Stu suggested I talk to you."

Knowing he's on the wrong page, but it's not so bad as he feared, Oscar nods. "I'll do whatever I can do to help, Maggs."

Maggie blows her nose a then takes a fortifying breath. "I thought I could carry it myself but, I just can't. Someone I've been getting close to, am pretty close to, well, this friend is really sick."

"Sick? How, exactly."

"Very sick. Very very sick."

"Oh my god not Katie," blurts Oscar.

She shakes her head, "No, no. Not Katie, Oz, it's Krystal."

"What's wrong with Krystal?"

"She has a tumour."

"Oh, dear lord, I don't know what to say." He reaches over to squeeze her hand. "This is why you've been so moody?" she nods, not speaking, struggling to get under control.

"It's fine Maggie. Take your time."

Maggie says, "She was having headaches, and nausea too. But her family only moved here a couple of years ago so they don't have a family doctor. She had to go to a clinic for a referral, and it took a long time before they could get the tests scheduled, and, well, they took too long. The problem is a brain tumour, and it got too big."

"Too big?" asks Oscar, not quite getting it.

"Too big to take out. What they call inoperable,"

A gasp from behind grabs their attention. Maggie and Oscar turn to see Jake in the doorway, his face slack with shock.

"Oh, Maggie."

Oscar beckons Jake over. "You might as well join us lad. Come on and sit down."

Jake moves slowly across the room and pulls up a chair. He stares at Maggie, clearly stricken. "Maggie, that can't be right."

Maggie pushes the cup of tea she's been fiddling with over to Jake. "I'm afraid it is."

"But Maggie, you don't look, I mean, I'm so sorry."

Maggie doesn't really know the freshman very well, but his eyes are full of pity. Then she realizes he must only have heard the tail end of the conversation and thinks she's the one dying.

"It's not me, Jake. I'm healthy as a horse, it's a friend of mine who's sick, not me."

Oscar cocks an eyebrow. "That's what comes of listening at doors, misunderstanding and innuendo. Tsk, tsk."

Jake starts "I didn't ... "

Maggie turns to Oscar, "It's not his fault, Oz. Obviously this was not something we should have been discussing in the common room. It's my fault. I wasn't thinking."

Jake suddenly looks if anything even more upset.

"Oh, Kate! Oh how awful for poor Nick."

Maggie says, "Stop." She takes a breath. "Look, it's not my secret, but I see it'll drive you nuts if you don't know."

Jake says. "It's driving me nuts already."

"Here's the deal; I will tell you who my unlucky friend is. She doesn't want people to know, she wants to live her life the way she wants. She doesn't want pity. So you don't tell anyone, not your mother, your girlfriend or your priest. Okay?"

Oscar chips in, "It goes no farther, right?"

Both stare intently at Jake who says, "I won't say a word."

Maggie says, "Okay, then."

Jake leans in close to hear, Oscar scans the entrances and the upper balcony of the women's part of the Res above, making sure there are no other inadvertent listeners.

Maggie says, softly. "It's Krystal."

"Krystal." Jake is stricken. "No way. I mean, oh shit."

Maggie nods. "You can't tell anybody though."

"I wouldn't." Jake shakes his head. "I didn't... I mean, I thought she was a bit goth, I never thought she might be sick."

Oscar stands up, and puts on his sternest face, which surprises them both, since he's usually scattering blarney. He looks different, this burly serious man with smouldering grey eyes.

"So, this is a secret, right?" Oscar's eyes bore into Jake's, who nods fervently. "Just know that if this sad tale makes the rounds whoever spread it will answer to me."

Maggie appraises Oscar carefully as he crosses surprisingly muscular arms over his broad chest. This is a different Oscar, actually a pretty scary Oscar.

Jake nods, wide eyed. "Yes, Oscar." and he gets to his feet. "Uh, I've got a class." Jake can't leave fast enough.

Oscar sits back down. Maggie looks at him, biting her lip, beginning to giggle. Oscar relaxes and laughs along with her.

"Where," asks Maggie, "did you learn to do scary like that. That was amazing."

"Count yourself lucky, you've never had the pleasure of my sainted sister."

Maggie cracks up, a mixture of laughter and tears pour out of her in glorious release.

30 . . .

Ethan walks into the photography lab where Jake sits at a workbench, running a slide show on the large wall mounted flat screen.

It is a series of high contrast macro shots of really surprising things. Ethan's not sure what many of the images actually might be, but all are clean and sharp, yet with a pervasive aura of decay.

Not for the first time Ethan is overawed by young Jake's skill. Talent. genius. Whatever it is, Jake is good.

Ethan slips quietly into a chair by the door so as not to disturb Jake's series of photographs. Now it looks to be shots of some kind of fabric, nicotine yellow with a loose weave, maybe antique lace because it looks like it's crumbling to dust. Then there are images of some kind of fungal growth on what might be tree bark with an almost luminescent undertone to the lighting.

But the images that speak to Ethan are a series of metal connectors, ball bearings, and what he thinks might be the links of a bicycle chain. His favourite is a low angle shot of a rusted out bolt protruding from some kind of sheet metal.

What makes the image so interesting to Ethan is the refracted halo of light from above. Ethan's not sure if the light is the sun or a clever lighting effect.

The screen goes black and Ethan asks, "Are they

natural or have you been dipping into Photoshop?"

"Straight up, Ethan. I'm a purist. I don't do Photoshop."

"That's cool. They're really good Jake." Jake looks a little uncomfortable under the praise, so Ethan continues, "You're probably wondering why I've called you here today."

Jake nods, "What's on the agenda?"

"Professor Mol wants a slide show that can run during the Christmas party. You know, kind of a year book effect."

"Taking portraits of everybody? Not my kind of thing."

"That's not what she's looking for, Jake, she specifically said she doesn't want formal portraits. She wants a vérité kind of look and she liked my idea of a mix of sources. You know, web cam shots, cell pics, black and white, out of focus, blurry stuff, whatever. She said we should be canvassing the whole student population for contributions of their favourite candid shots of their friends."

Jake smiles as he thinks about it. "Sounds like a monster amount of work. But you know, it might be fun, but we'll need heaps of storage. More hands too."

Ethan flips open his laptop and logs into the Christie Photography Student wiki. Logging in under his Teaching Assistant account he starts a new page called 'Candid Submissions,'and says,

"How about this, then. People can upload their candids here then we can go though and pull the cream and assemble it all into a mammoth slide show. That's gonna be the gruelling part."

"Well, yeah, but first you've gotta get everybody's attention. Paper the campus with flyers, maybe make a Facebook fan page?"

Jake asks, "So what do we wanna say in our flyer?"

"How about 'We Want Your Pictures.'"

"Too boring, Ethan. How about: 'Star Quality'"

"Okay." Ethan nods, "Better. You have any ideas about people we can dragoon into helping? How about Q?"

Jake rolls his eyes. "I know he's your friend and all, but Q doesn't seem to be straight very often. We'd be a lot better off with Boris."

"Okay, yeah. And Natasha."

Jake watches for Ethan's reaction as he adds, "And Liz too."

"Um." Noncommittal, Ethan looks away. "I don't think so."

"What do you mean, you don't think so?" Jake says, "She's got a good eye."

"Maybe she does. But maybe I'd be happier without her."

"I don't get it. What's your problem with Liz?"

"You're too young to understand."

Jake closes his laptop forcefully. "Don't give me that crap. Ethan, you're not my dad, you're only a few years older than me. Funny I'm not too young to work on your extracurriculars but suddenly I'm too young?

You know Liz is a friend of mine."

"Okay, okay, you're right. I'm sorry." Chastened, Ethan rubs his eyebrow, staring at the table, the floor, anywhere but at Jake.

"Look, it's, well ... " he shakes his head. "Even though it's an extra-curricular I'm expected to work it. I can't afford to blow this T.A. gig, Jake, I need the cash. But it's just that Liz... whenever she's around it's like I can't open my mouth. I look at her and it's game over. I like her, okay. I really like her. But if she's on this crew I'm not gonna get diddly done. She.. distracts me."

"That is just too weird." Jake asks, incredulous. "You don't want her on the team because you like her?"

Ethan nods sheepishly.

"Don't be a goof, it would be a great chance to get to know her better," Jake says. "Why don't you ask her out?"

"I just can't, man."

Ethan swivels in his chair.

"She's a nice girl. She doesn't even drink. More than that she's a star. What's her average, in the nineties? Probably almost as good as yours. And me? I'm faking it. What am I, some goofball drinks too much, smokes up and parties. I'm just barely making the grade. She's sure as shit too good for me, Jake."

31 . . .

Amelia heads for the kitchen to grab a quick cup of Ramen soup to get through the afternoon. She plugs in

the kettle and nips upstairs for the book she needs.
They say **Kindles** might be free soon, maybe that'll make
it easier to have the right books every time. Returning
to the kitchen she's shocked to see a strange man
pouring water out of her kettle -- until she realizes it's
Eric.

"Hope you left enough for me," she says.

He nods to the soup bowl and she sees that he filled
it before filling his mug.

"Thanks. You're better trained than most." she
smiles, and he nods. God he looks rough. "You coming
to class today?"

Eric shrugs as he fishes out the tea bag, and starts
ladling in sugar. "Probably not," he mutters.

She leans back on the counter and looks at him.
Unkempt. Stubble does not suit this guy. "Why not?"

"'Cause I really don't feel like it, that's why not."

She cocks her head, "So what, you're gonna wallow
in self pity for the rest of your life?"

He takes a sip of his tea. She can see it's too hot and
he's burnt his tongue, but he sticks to the tough guy act
and pretends it doesn't. "Maybe."

"I'd think about it. You wanna kiss off the
semester, fine, but if it was me I'd be down at the office
dropping out formally so I'd get at least some of my
money back."

Eric nods, continuing to look miserable.

"'Course, it was me I wouldn't give her the
satisfaction."

He pins her with a glower, "But it wasn't you, was it."

She glowers right back, "No it wasn't. But you don't have the market cornered on pain and suffering. This is the first time you've said two words to me and you wanna be a jerk? I may not be a goddess but I sure don't deserve any crap. You wanna dump on somebody, dump on her, not me."

Amelia turns on her heel and stomps out of the kitchen, soup and notebook forgotten in the grip of overwhelming anger.

Eric's jaw drops, then he calls, "Wait." But she doesn't hear him, she's too angry. Feeling like a jerk Eric goes after her, "Wait. I'm sorry." She keeps on going for the door and is just getting it open when he catches up with her and stops the door with his hand.

"You're right. Look. I didn't mean to be a jerk. I haven't been thinking, and, and, you haven't even touched your soup."

His contrition drains away her annoyance. "No. I haven't."

"Look," says Eric, "Why don't you eat and I'll get cleaned up and can come to the lecture with you."

She looks at him, appraisingly.

"I'm really not a jerk."

Amelia raises an eyebrow.

"Not usually." Eric makes a pitiful stab at a smile.

"Okay. Go get cleaned up. If you're good I'll let you come to class with me." Amelia shakes her head, smiling ruefully.

His smile touches his eyes for moment. "Deal."

32 · · ·

Adam ignores the lecture, probably for the first time in his life, as he texts his brother on his new cellphone.

> Can you get me tickets to the Black Eyed Peas concert?

The reply from his brother is tersely to the point.

> For tonight? You're kidding.

> Never more serious. Whatever it takes.

> Have you even heard BEP?

> Just get them for me.

There's no response. Adam follows up with a single word:

> Please.

Adam watches, anxious. Finally a message appears.

> I'll see what I can do kid. Just don't hold your breath.

33 · · ·

"I can't believe this weather," says Krystal, stopping

beside the wooded path that leads to Fyfield House.

Oscar says, "I agree, it's better than what we had for summer." He shakes the blanket, letting it billow out and settle on the grass under the huge weeping willow.

"Pity it won't last," says Maggie as she sits cross legged in the middle of the blanket, balancing her laptop in her lap. Oscar positions his bag in the corner of the blanket and drops down beside Maggie, laying back and using the computer as a pillow.

Krystal holds a finger to her lips and cautions Maggie, "Shhhh... mother nature might hear you." Then she lays down along the blanket's other edge, parallel to Oscar, but on her stomach, propped on her elbows as she opens her email account.

Oscar laughs and says "Climate change seems pretty real to me. Never know what we're going to get. Perhaps winter will give us a miss altogether this year."

"In your dreams, Oz," says Krystal. "Hey, didn't you go home this summer?"

Oscar says, "If you knew my family, you'd understand why not."

Maggie watches Krystal type. "I don't know how you can type like that. I tried that once and lost all circulation."

Krystal smiles. "I dunno... works for me." She scans the subject column, routinely marking obvious spam for destruction.

Maggie clears her throat. "Uh, Krys, there's something I have to tell you." Maggie says. Krystal rolls over on her side, looking up at her friend.

"That doesn't sound good, Maggie."

"Yeah, because I think you're going to be mad." Krystal watches Maggie, who is having a hard time making eye contact. "I'm sorry Krys, but I was really down and I kind of told Oz."

"You what?"

From his side of the blanket, Oscar looks over at Krystal, meeting her eyes firmly. "I dragged it out of her. I am sorry. And in future we will be quite careful not to let it go any further."

"Further? What further?" Krystal's eyes narrow. "Who else knows? What did you do, run an ad on **Craigslist**?"

"Worse. We discussed it in the common room."

Krystal shakes her head and sits up. "I don't believe you Maggie. First you haunt me until I tell you, and when I do you broadcast it to the world. It's my life, don't you get that?"

"I'm sorry. I thought we were alone but Jake came in and heard too. I'm so sorry."

"It wasn't intentional, I promise you that." adds Oscar.

"Jake? Jesus, you guys. So that's everybody? You didn't tell anybody else? I mean, Jose doesn't know, right?" Both Oscar and Maggie shake their heads solemnly, looking dejected. "Look, you guys need to understand. It's hard enough for me to be here, but if the whole world knows I won't be able to stick it out."

"I get it Krystal, and I can't tell you enough that I'm so sorry." Maggie tells her with feeling.

"Okay."

"Can I ask you something?"

"You can ask, I may not tell." Krystal replies wryly.

"Why are you here? I mean, I don't know that I'd go to school if it was me."

"Really? Where else would I be? I'm here for the same reason you are, I love computers. I like working with them, getting them to do what I want them to. I like learning to make them do stuff I don't even know I want them to do. It's fun."

"But, if I only had... "

"You think so? I might outlive you, girl. You could be hit by a bus tomorrow, Maggie. Why waste your time if this isn't what you want to do?"

Maggie nods, "I guess. I hadn't thought about it."

"Well, I have, and I decided I want to live like I mean it."

"I guess you have. I can't tell you how sorry I am, Krys."

"Yeah, I know you are. So now you can stop apologizing and move on, okay?" Krystal holds her eye, "I just want a normal life."

"I understand." Maggie nods.

Krystal smiles, "On the other hand if Hugh Jackman called to ask me to come loll in the sun on the French Riviera it'd be different." Krystal looks at her unhappy companions. "Okay, who knows a good funny story?"

Sniffling, Maggie asks, "Funny story?"

"What I want is to hang with friends and have fun."

Krystal turns to Oscar. "Come on Oz, got any more Oscar Wilde stories? I liked the one about the cowboy."

"That was good, wasn't it." Oscar grins, "You know, Maggie has her own wild story. Did she ever tell you about her flasher?"

Krystal's eyes widen, "Flasher? No way. Tell!"

Maggie rolls her eyes. "But it wasn't funny."

"Ah, but it was," says Oscar.

Krystal turns to Oscar, "Come on, then, Oz, spill it."

34 . . .

Liz is sitting at one of the library tables with several weighty volumes spread open around her when Jake pulls up a chair.

"I tried texting you but didn't get an answer. You use paper books, huh? Interesting."

"Lots of stuff isn't digitized. Besides, I get tired of staring at a screen all the time, Jake. But listen, I've gotta get this essay finished and I'm almost there. Just a little more, then I can write it up. And writing is not my thing. So," she turns to smile sweetly at him. "What do I have to do to make you go away?"

"Well," Jake begins, "if you're gonna be like that."

Just looking at Jake's Cheshire cat grin, Liz can tell she'll want to know.

Hmmm. "Alright. What do you want to tell me?"

"Ask me how I can be of assistance to you."

Liz studies him, sighs, then decides to play the

game.

"Okay, how are you going to help me, Jake?"

"I'm working on a project for Professor Mol, a kick-ass slide show that'll run on every available surface during the school Christmas party."

"Sounds cool. You want me to help?"

"Um, no, actually."

Exasperated. "So what are you bugging me about then?"

"That's not what you're supposed to say."

Liz laughs, quickly clapping her hands over her mouth to avoid being ejected on a noise complaint. People are looking, so she ducks down to whisper, "What am supposed to ask?"

"Ask me why the organizer doesn't want your help."

"What? I get along great with the Prof. She's my hero. There's no problem, at least not that I know. Oh God, is there something I should know? What have I screwed up? Or does she just hate me? Why doesn't she want me?"

"Not Professor Mol," Jake can't keep from grinning as he says, "Professor Mol's T.A. is the organizer."

Liz narrows her eyes, looking hard at Jake.

"I don't have a problem with Ethan." Jake looks at her with eyebrows raised, and she feels the blood rising to her face. "You gonna harass me about this for the rest of my life or what? Ohmigod you didn't say anything."

"No," Jake leans in, "What I'm trying to do is tell

you a secret."

Sceptical. "What?"

"Ethan doesn't want you to help because he thinks you're too much of a distraction."

Liz opens her mouth then shuts it. She stares at Jake, waiting for him to give up on this monstrous tease and tell her the real story. But he's just sitting there. Smug.

"On the level. I told him he should ask you and he... look, he's got it bad. Real bad. But he's not gonna do anything about it."

"Why is that? Oh, I get it, I'm too tall for him, right?"

"No." Jake shakes his head, "He didn't say anything like that. More like you're too good for him."

"What? That's crazy."

"I'm just telling you what he said. But if you wanna get together with him, you're the one's gonna have to ask him out."

Heart pounding, Liz snaps, "Maybe I will."

"I'll watch your stuff. He's in Mol's room right now."

"OK, I will." She gets up and starts away, but turns back and leans in close.

"You're not making this up, right?"

35 · · ·

Ethan is collating paperwork when Liz comes in.

"Hey Ethan."

His grin gives credence to Jake's story. "Uh, hi."

Okay, she thinks, I can do this. "They're screening **Un Chien Andalou** at the Art Centre tonight, so do you want to go with me?"

"Uh, what? They're screening what?"

"**Un Chien Andalou.** It's this really weird old movie, I've read about it but I've never had a chance to see it. It's a collaboration between the famous French film director Louis Bunuel and the artist Salvador Dalí. You know Dalí, the guy who painted all those droopy clocks? Anyway It's an old movie, from the nineteen thirties, but the best part is that Salvadore Dalí didn't just work on it he's actually in it too. Anyway, it's supposed to be way weird, I mean it's Dalí;, right, of course it will be weird, with interesting cinematography and special effects and anyway I'm going. Um. So you want to come with me?" Liz is mad at herself for babbling until she realizes that Ethan is smiling big and nodding. She smiles back.

"It starts at seven, but I want real good seats so maybe meet out front at six thirty?" Ethan nods happily.

"See you then."

And she's gone. Ethan takes a tentative breath, trying to determine if he's been dreaming or what. Pressing his palms over his chest he sits back, smiling even bigger. Nope, he wouldn't have been able to dream up **Un chien** and whatever. Ethan knows Jake's paw prints are all over this sucker but he doesn't care.

Liz wants to go out with him.

Whooee.

36 . . .

Barbie and Tamara are coming out of the lecture hall when Barbie stops abruptly. Tamara asks, "Something wrong?"

"Nah, just getting a text." Barbie flips open her cell phone, eyes widen as she scans the text message.

"Get outta town, I can't believe he got them!"

Tamara shakes her head. "He who? Got what?"

Barbie's busily texting back, "This guy has Black Eyed Peas tickets for tonight. My god they're only in town one night."

"Wow," gushes Tamara. "Jose, right?"

"God no, if it was Jose, I'd have to say no. He's all wrong for me, you gotta know that Tam."

Tamara nods, thinking of Quentin, "Yes, I think you're right about that."

Barbie starts singing into an air microphone, "I wanna I wanna rock right now."

Barbie dances around the hall, Tamara joins in chanting, "I wanna I wanna," and Barbie starts strutting, doing her Fergie impression. "I wanna I wanna rock right now I wanna I wanna see the Black Eyed Peas."

Tamara stops cold and asks, "But what about the test tomorrow, Barb? You're not going to be able to study at all."

"Oh come on Tam, there will be lots of tests but this

is a chance to see Black Eyed Peas. Imma Peabody!"

"I hope you know what you're doing, girl."

"Imma gonna see the Peas... Imma be fine. Look, Tam, I gotta go. Can I leave you my laptop? I've gotta go right now!"

"Sure," says Tamara, taking her friend's case. "Have fun."

"Thanks Tam you're an angel!"

Tamara watches Barbie go and wonders, not for the first time, how Barbie's going to manage it. But then she always seems to have everything come out her way. Barbie really is a golden girl. Tamara sighs, and heads for her own home. Stepping outside she shivers; much colder than before. Gotta make dinner.

Maybe something nice, she's got to talk to Q.

37 · ·

Boris and Natasha are singing along with **The Spam Song** on one of Natasha's **Monty Python** DVDs in the common room when Eric and Amelia come in.

Eric starts to laugh. "What on earth is that?"

Natasha clutches her heart in mock horror, "Don't tell me you haven't heard **The Spam Song**?"

Eric looks around "Spam? I can't believe someone made up a song about spam!"

"Yeah, it tastes pretty rude, too."

Eric looks surprised. "Tastes?"

"'Spam' the food."

"There's food called 'spam'? Get outta town."

Boris asks, "Am I detecting a woeful lack of cultural grounding? How about **Monty Python**, Eric, you heard of them?"

"Ummm." Eric tilts his head to the side and frowns, "Wasn't that a comedy team from the sixties or something?"

"How can you be an English major if you've never seen **Monty Python**?" cries Amelia.

Natasha shakes her head. "Scootch over Boris, make room."

Natasha pats the sofa beside her as Boris dutifully "scootches" and makes room on the end of the sofa. Picking up the remote Boris asks, "Should we go back to episode one for the noob, or just start this one over?"

Natasha tucks up beside Boris. "I think starting this one over will be okay. I mean, after all, he might, " she peers over the tops of her glasses studying Eric, "not like Python."

"Don't speak heresy girl. Everybody likes Python." Unsure what he's letting himself in for, Eric allows Amelia to steer him to the sofa and he ends up sandwiched between her and Natasha.

"No wait, I lie," continues Boris. "My brother hates Python." He grins, "But of course he's a dickhead."

Boris leans forward with the remote but stops short of pressing the button when he turns to Eric, "**Monty Python and the Holy Grail**. You HAVE to have heard of that one, man."

"Well, yeah, I've heard of it, but I never saw it. I'm

not big on religious movies. I'm, well, I'm an agnostic." Three blank faces stare back at him for a shocked moment but then they all start laughing.

Amelia reaches for the remote, but Boris isn't giving it up so easily. But he does take the hint and starts the disk.

They watch the whole thing, and they are all-- Eric included-- laughing their faces off at the "**Argument Sketch**" when Elsie slips in with a new man.

She sees the group on the sofa, and decides she doesn't want to get into anything with Eric just now, so she quickly leads her new friend up the stairs.

Eric is laughing so hard he's brushing the tears out of his eyes, but Amelia's peripheral vision tracks the movement. Angling her head she gets a glimpse of Elsie taking some guy upstairs.

Some one completely different. A total stranger guy. Amelia decides to keep her trap shut just now. Eric's finally almost acting like a normal person, he sure doesn't need to see that.

38 . . .

Ethan and Liz come out of the **Art Centre** discussing the film. Or rather Liz is discussing the film.

Ethan didn't like it. It was too weird, and he thought the ants coming out of the guy's hand was decidedly creepy. He wishes that it had been a nice romantic comedy. A Hugh Grantish kind of movie.

Because then there might have been a chance to at

least hold Liz's hand.

But Ethan is enjoying watching Liz crackle and pop with excitement. She's babbling so animatedly about Salvador Dalí and the movie, her eyes are alight as she explains all kinds of stuff that's way over his head.

She finally starts winding down as they approach the Fyfield House back door. Liz finally asks Ethan if he liked the film.

Ethan shrugs, and tells her "Not really."

Her face falls. "Oh. Why didn't you say anything?"

"Because I liked the being with you part," he says, reaching in his pocket for his key card.

Liz looks away, but she can feel herself blush, and Ethan looks at her a moment, breathless, before reaching over and giving her a soft kiss. He stays nose to nose with her and they gaze into one anther's eyes a moment. He brushes her lips with his own before Liz slides her arms around his neck and kisses him back.

Eventually they go in.

39 . . . wednesday

Tamara pours a second glass of orange juice. The married student cottage isn't very big, with only a nook instead of a real eat in kitchen, but that's okay, she thinks. Better than the residence coffins with people stealing your food.

Quentin may be great in the sack but he's not much for cleaning. Smaller means less mess.

Or maybe more concentrated mess.

As she whisks the egg mixture she cocks an ear, but she doesn't hear the shower.

It occurs to her that he might have gone back to sleep. And here she is making his breakfast. Setting the bowl on the galley counter she nips down the hall into the bedroom. Hearing his snores reignites her annoyance and she shakes him.

"C'mon Q. You've gotta get up, baby."

He mutters and tries to roll away but she grabs his shoulders. "It's morning. You want breakfast you gotta get up."

He opens his eyes and smiles up at her. She loves his smile, but she's gotta get going.

Quentin licks his lips seductively. "Hey gorgeous," he says, nearly melting her resolve. "C'mon for a little cuddle first," reaching for her waist.

Determination causes her to step back, just out of reach. "I can't hon, I've got a 9:30 lecture. I'm making French toast. If you want some you'd better get your butt outta bed."

Quentin gives her puppy dog eyes in a pouty face but Tamara just grins wickedly. Points her finger at him, "If you're still in bed when I go I'm feedin' your French Toast to the birds."

He stares in horror. "You wouldn't do that. Would you?"

She tosses her head and heads out the door. "Think what you like. Just remember, you were warned."

She slams the door and returns to the kitchen.

He lays there a minute looking at the closed door. Hmm. Maybe she's mad he was out so late last night.

She was sleeping when he came in. Least she acted like she was sleeping. If she's mad, maybe she really would dump his breakfast out for the birds.

It wouldn't even be a question if she knew he'd been up half the night talking to another woman. The frying pan wouldn't be making French toast, it would be embedded in his skull.

Tamara would never believe it was just talking, but it's true just the same. So. Better not push it. Not this morning, anyway.

Quentin stretches and hauls himself out of bed.

Into the shower, hoping she's not mad enough to do that cold water thing again. He soaps up, letting the hot water pound him, helping relax tense muscles. It feels good as the tension starts to drain. They're going to have to talk, maybe tonight. He tilts his head back and takes a gulp of water, swishing it around in his mouth, spitting. The head is a little tender but he'll live.

Quentin clambers out of the shower stall and rubs himself down, winding the towel around his waist he steps into shower shoes. He opens the window to let the steam dissipate then moves on to the kitchen, where he admires Tamara efficiently tending the food cooking in the frying pan. Heaven.

Quentin comes up behind her and slides his hands around her waist. "Smells real good baby" he breathes in her ear and he rubs up against her. She wiggles free and whirls around to face him.

"Stop it Q-- I'm cooking!"

He recoils as if slapped, unprepared for the fury. He sighs as he feels "mister morning" droop.

Tamara looks at his dejected face and softens her tone a shade, "I don't exactly feel like getting burnt over here, Q."

He holds up his hands in apology, "Sorry, Babe."

Looking somewhat sheepish he heads back to sit at the table. He downs the OJ in one, and pours himself another.

Tamara feels mean for a moment, but having to flip the French toast gets her over it. Another moment and she scoops the golden breakfast food and carries the plates to the table. The way his face lights up melts some of her anger.

As he drowns his breakfast with the syrup, he tells her, "Looks good, baby."

When he takes a bite, moaning in rapture, she can't help but laugh at her man-child. Tamara sips her juice, picking at her food.

She's never been big on sweets, but he loves this stuff. She can pick up a cheese croissant at the coffee shop on her way in to class. After yesterday she just can't afford to be late.

Having vacuumed his food Quentin looks longingly at hers, and she passes it over and drains her coffee as he dives in.

She gets up and hangs the cute little apron on the hook by the door. "Gotta go." Opening the closet she grabs her jacket and slips into it but when she turns around Quentin is standing right there looking terribly contrite.

"I'm sorry I was so late last night, Babe." He reaches for her but she steps backward into the closet. His face falls as he realizes that she's rebuffing him again.

Now it's her turn, "Now you just wait a minute. Don't even think about laying a load of guilt on me. I do not have time to mess around with you this morning no matter how much I might want to. I have a 9:30 lecture and it's after nine already."

He turns away, and stomps out of the room.

Now her anger rears its head, and she calls after him down the hall, "You wanna mess around with me Q maybe you oughta try coming home nights." Tamara grabs her purse and stalks out, slamming the door behind her.

She is mad. In the bedroom Quentin slumps in a chair.

He hates it when she's right.

40 . . .

Professor Gates projects a presentation on the large screen, "Obviously it's easier to adopt a static layout because there is less to take into account." Gates walks around the lab, glancing at the CSS code the students are working on.

"To fully exploit the capabilities of the user's browser and screen real estate your content should be readable no matter how the user accesses it." She scans

Krystal's code.

"That's much better Krys, you're on track now."

Krystal smiles. "It's scaling the images that gets me."

Gates nods, says "It gets easier." Raising her voice to address the rest of the class, "I'll schedule office hours Friday for any problems you need to discuss. That's the day, people."

As Gates heads out, Kate announces "Computer Club tonight at my place," but most of the class is already streaming out the door.

"I'll be there!" says Maggie from the doorway, and Oscar calls "Me too," as he follows her out.

Adam intercepts Kate enroute to the door and says, "Excuse me, Kate, I don't know where 'your place' is."

"Oh, that's OK, we live in the Married Student bungalows, ours is number 37. I hope you come check it out?"

"I'm kind of tired from last night, but I may just do that."

"What happened last night?"

"The Black Eyed Peas concert."

"Oh, wow, that's cool. I love The E.N.D. but I don't have The Beginning yet. Are they as wild in person as I think they are?"

"That Fergie was quite impressive, she'd sing and then do a full body flip while holding her microphone, and then sing another line, then another flip. And he never seemed out of breath."

"Maybe you can tell me more tonight. We're just

starting up, tonight's agenda is to establish what the club will want to do."

"It sounds good," he yawns and says, "I will really try." Kate's grin is echoed by a Adam's own. "See you then."

Kate is tucking her laptop into its case when Krystal asks her, "What's up with Adam?"

Kate continues tucking away bits of paraphernalia as she says, "I don't know, but I've never seen him like that before. He's always so serious."

"Yeah. I don't think I've even seen him smile before."

"He went to the BEP concert."

"Adam? The world must've slipped on its axis."

Kate's ready to go when she realizes Krystal hasn't started packing up, and is still working on her web page. "Aren't you coming?"

Krystal shakes her head. "I don't have another class 'til after lunch, but this room's empty, so I stay and get more done."

"I hear you. It's funny, but a lot of the time I'm glad Nick's course load is so heavy because it leaves me the time I need to get my own stuff done. You coming tonight?"

"Absolutely."

41 . . .

Back at Fyfield House, Natasha is curled up in the

rocking chair, strawberry blonde hair jutting out at all angles. Scrolling through the images on her camera to make preliminary selections, she looks up to see a bleary eyed Boris, wearing only shapeless gray track pants, stumble through the common room en route to the kitchen.

Natasha grins. It's not that she's admiring the rippling muscles of his torso, or his washboard abs. It's more a kinship of bad hair. Boris is the only human being she's met in her life who has worse morning hair than she does.

She reaches for the dregs of her coffee and takes a sip as Boris comes back with his own. She says, "That's what I like about you Bo, you're even less of a morning person than I am."

Boris sets his coffee on the table and sprawls out on the red sofa with an inarticulate grunt.

"I'd be careful if I were you. If you nod off you'll end up missing composition." He groans this time. "Again," she says.

Boris pulls himself into a sitting position and picks up his coffee, taking a tentative sip. He glances over at Natasha. "You're awfully chipper for such an ungodly hour."

Natasha laughs. "It's almost eleven. Practically afternoon. I've been up for ... " she studies her watch "... minutes."

Boris snorts a laugh, making the hot coffee slop back and forth in the mug held dangerously above his lap. In an effort to boost consciousness, or perhaps sentience, he takes a somewhat bigger sip before returning the mug to the safety of the table. Flopping back he says, "We're soul mates, Nat."

"Naw, just too stupid to go to bed at a decent hour."

"Good we were smart not to schedule morning classes."

"Except Friday. That 9 am elective is nasty."

"Think they rescheduled it on purpose?"

"It's too early for conspiracy theories, Bo."

"Where'd you go last night?"

"Couldn't sleep so I went over to Callaghan's. You should've come if you were up. Man, Q was wasted. I sat up half the night with him, and you know what? Poor sap wants to make movies."

Boris fights down the pang of annoyance that Natasha was out with Q last night. "Better tell him he's in the wrong program."

"He knows. He's really just trying to work up the nerve to tell his wife. She's a med student."

Boris drinks his coffee. Wife? First he heard Q was married. Good. Then, "What are you doing?"

"Looking for pictures for Ethan's slide show."

"Your eyes must be more open than mine." Setting the coffee mug down again, Boris leans back and closes his eyes. "You know, that was interesting. Liz and Ethan, I mean."

Natasha says, "Yeah, I never would have guessed."

"I think they're both a little bugged by the height thing."

"Of course they are. She's an Amazon princess and

he's Eric Idle's shorter brother."

"Aww, cut 'em some slack. They make a pretty cute couple."

"Mmmmm."

"Like us," says Boris.

His eyes are closed but hers are not as she glances over at him. Danger signal if she ever heard one. What to do what to do what to do. Let it lay. It will pass. Concentrate on the pictures.

Natasha rocks a little faster, pretending she hasn't heard as she tries to keep focusing on the camera screen.

Boris watches Natasha's consternation through his veiled lashes. Why does she look like a deer in the headlights? It's not such a crazy notion. She just needs to get used to the idea.

Not a spare ounce on her but he kind of likes that. He was surprised at how good she felt in his arms when thy were scrambling around on that bloody statue. He hasn't been able to get it out of his mind. He opens his eyes and sits up, picking up his cup, looking at her. Sticking up hair and all. Hell, he's never known anyone else with worse morning hair than he has.

"Hey Nat? Wanna try having a date?"

"Aw, Bo ... " Natasha flushes a little, and looks over at him, "Why ruin a perfectly good friendship?"

"It doesn't have to ruin anything."

"It's not a good idea, Boris, I'm sorry."

Boris sits rigid, trying to keep her from seeing how hurt he feels. But of course she does.

"Look, I've gotta go take a shower." She sets her camera down on the table. "Later, O.K?"

Boris suggests hopefully, "Maybe I could wash your back?"

Natasha looks at his puppy dog eyes and... flees.

Boris closes his eyes again. Why can't she see it? They are so alike. It would be perfect. He sighs in frustration. She's his best friend dammit. Isn't that what women want? Maybe he needs to try the cave man approach. Be firm.

Don't ask, just kiss the girl. Make Natasha understand what she means to him.

42 . . .

Ethan sits at the terminal in the cramped TA room organizing the first submissions that have come in by email. He can't believe the volume of response.

Jake only stuck up a few posters yesterday, they haven't even put a notice on the photo blog. At this rate maybe better not to. Suddenly hands are pressed over his eyes, momentarily disconcerting him until he breathes in the heady scent of soap and girl that tells him it's Liz.

"Guess who!"

He swivels the chair around to face her, grabbing hold of her hands he kisses each palm in turn. Liz shivers in delight, then bends down and takes his breath away with a kiss. Coming up for air, she reaches back without looking and pushes the door closed, then smiles and straddles his lap to make smooching easier. Eventually both have to stop to catch their breath.

"Wow," he says, noticing even through his euphoria that they are eye to eye even though she's perching in his lap.

What legs.

Liz smiles and says, "Natasha and I are heading over to the Antique Car Show down at the Waterfront this afternoon. So I thought you might like to get lunch."

"Yeah, that was good."

She giggles. "I meant food. You know, like at the caf. Or the coffee shop."

"Uh. If you want me to go out in public, it's gonna be a little while before I can walk."

Liz flushes. "Oh I'm sorry."

Ethan laughs and tells her, "Oh, don't be sorry." and pulls her in for an encore.

43 . . .

Barbie and Tamara are depositing the remains of their lunch trays in the cafeteria garbage and recycling bins when Jose joins them.

He says, "Hey guys. Anybody up for a little walk in the woods?"

Tamara shakes her head, "I can't afford the time today, Jose. We've got to prep for a big test."

Tamara watches Jose's face fall, noting how intently he is looking at Barbie. And Barbie is just as intently not looking at him. Uh oh. Suddenly she gets the dynamic, realizing her friends have crossed the line. Bad shit. Trying to save face for both she says, "Maybe we can get together on the weekend. Supposed to be nice."

"I guess," Jose is realizing that Barbie won't look at him.

"You can probably catch Q later. He's finished after comp. Whyn't you guys go out for a pub crawl tonight? I'm not going to have any time for him today."

"Maybe." Jose mutters miserably, beating a hasty retreat.

Tamara watches him go, before turning back to her friend. "Barbie girl, what did you do to that boy?"

"The other day it was so warm out, and well, we all kinda dozed off. When I woke up it was down to just us, and Jose kissed me, and I kind of let him. I was half asleep, and I was half dreaming, you know. So. Maybe I kissed him." She shakes her head. "Either way big mistake."

"Too bad," says Tamara, watching Jose. "Yum."

"Stop it Tam." Barbie giggles wickedly, "You're a married woman now." They gather up their things from the table.

"Marriage may have taken me out of circulation, but it didn't take out my eyes. Maybe you can turn off your feelings but I can't. Married ladies can look, just not touch."

Barbie giggles. "You're baaaaad!"

"So who did you go to the concert with?"

"That guy who fixed up my computer. Alan."

"I would never have pegged him for a Peabody."

"Me either, but he got great seats. In the A's even."

"So was it great?"

"Oh, Tam, I could have reached out and touched Taboo."

"You are so lucky. But we better hurry now."

"Don't worry so much, Nick's only a T.A."

They step through the doors, Tamara pulls her sweater tighter, but Barbie doesn't have one. "Brrr, suddenly it's winter."

Barbie and Tamara briskly cross the oval toward the Bio Building extension off the Medical Centre. Hurrying because of the cold.

Everyone is hurrying because it's so cold.

§

Natasha walks fast across the oval. Huddled into her coat, she doesn't notice Boris until he falls in step beside her.

"We have to talk, Natasha."

"Not now Boris, I'm gonna be late."

"Then we can both be late. Can you please just look at me? I thought at least we were friends."

Natasha looks up at Boris and he's surprised to see tears in her eyes. "We are friends. I've never had a friend as good as you Boris. I mean it. You are my best friend."

"Then I don't see what the problem is. Isn't that a good way to start a relationship?"

"Sometimes it is. Just not this time."

§

Well, almost everyone. Tamara sees two people not hurrying. Standing still. But it's too cold. What's going on? Looks like Boris and Natasha. But it can't be. They're tense, body language says they're arguing. But they never argue. There's a joke around the school Boris and Natasha are actually the same person.

If it is Boris and Natasha.

It's too far away to hear, and anyway too damn cold to stop and watch.

But suddenly there's that computer guy again, Alan, on an interception path with Barbie. Tamara thinks, "Another one."

"Barbie." He's smiling big. "I was wondering if you'd have time for a coffee later?"

Barbie shakes her head. "Sorry, Al, not today. Can't talk now, I'm late for class!"

Adam's smile falls away as he sees she's not going to stop. Barbie doesn't even break stride.

Tamara spares the guy a shrug, thinking seats in the A's don't mean so much after all. Not after the concert is over, anyway. Poor Alan has the same look of desolation Jose had a minute ago. Tamara wonders if Barbie realizes her power.

Adam just watches his dream girl walking away. She couldn't spare him a minute. Of course, it is cold, and she's not wearing a coat. And he's heard how heavy the pre-med course load is. She probably has a lot to catch up after going out with him last night. Besides she isn't even wearing a sweater. That's probably it, it's just cold. Adam feels unaccountably deflated anyway. He decides to go get something to eat at the cafeteria.

§

Across the oval, Boris towers over Natasha. Trying to be calm and rational. But it's really hard because she's being so damned stubborn.

"You haven't even given it a chance, Nat. Just think about it. That's all I want. Just for you to think about it."

Natasha clenches her fists, "I don't have to think about it, Bo. I know it wouldn't work. It just wouldn't."

"You can't know that. Not without giving it a chance. Natasha I... I love you. I love you so much."

"Oh Boris, don't," she looks so sad.

Her eyes are all puffy, her nose is redder than the hair sticking out from under her hat in endearing little spikes and tendrils. He can't help it, he leans down and gathers her in his arms, and she's trying to push him away but he kisses her with a passion he didn't know he had. Except Natasha is wriggling and pounding on his chest. Then she stops fighting and lets him kiss her.

And it's glorious.

§

Barbie is almost at the Bio door when she suddenly stops dead. Completely unprepared, Tamara plows into Barbie's back. In spite of the cold, the two med students watch rapt as Boris gathers Natasha up in his grand passionate gesture.

"What?" asks Tamara and swivels her head to see what's captured her friend's attention.

§

Boris comes up for air and looks down at Natasha. Expecting to see the flushed look of love in her eyes he's disconcerted to see... anger.

Fury.

Uh oh.

"What?" Boris asks as Natasha hauls off and slugs him with every ounce of strength she can muster. He reels in shock followed by a surprising wave of pain radiating outward from the bridge of his nose.

§

Barbie and Tamara aren't the only people in the oval to be arrested by the sight of the tiny woman... it has got to be Natasha... hauling off and pounding the big guy... not Boris! How could she hit Boris? He's such a sweetie and but she just slugged him in the head. And Boris... he just falls over. Holy shit!

Boris finds himself sitting on the ground. There's a burning pain in his left eye and he claps his hand overs it. His other eye watches uncomprehendingly as Natasha whirls and stalks away, not looking back. Not even once.

Boris realizes this might not have been such a good idea.

Suddenly there are people coming up to him. A couple of cute girls actually.

Mmm the stacked blonde one is Barbie, Jose's friend. She's touching his forehead as she kneels beside him.

"Are you OK, Boris?" Boris looks at Barbie stupidly.

The other one says, "Maybe you wanna come into the Bio Building and we'll get your head looked at?"

More people are arriving. Crowding around. Half the school must have seen it. Oh great. Just what he needs.

"No. No, it's okay. Really." He scrambles to his feet. "No, I don't need a doctor, just some ice. I've been hit before."

Experience tells Boris it's gonna be a heck of a black eye. Maybe even a double shiner. You don't grow up with brothers without getting pounded occasionally. Leave it to Natasha.

He looks down at the pretty pre-meds, and then realizes that there are all kinds of people heading in this direction. Already a dozen people, mostly women, making a growing crowd. What happened? Where did all these people come from? Boris realizes he's got to do something if he wants any kind of a life here.

Smiling as rakishly as he can manage he says, "After the swelling goes down I expect I'll be drowning my sorrows at the pub tonight. Any lovely ladies care to help soothe my soul, that's where I'll be."

Barbie laughs, and reaches up to pat him on the shoulder. "You'll be all right."

The crowd starts to disperse-- it's too cold-- and Boris takes advantage to hustle back to the residence, to be alone.

§

Adam feels unsettled. Not sick exactly. But there is

a clenching in his stomach. Seeing that tiny little girl hit that really big guy was weird. Especially when the big guy just fell down.

The part that... hurt... was watching Barbie run over to the big guy and then laugh and... and... flirt with him. Some stupid jock. Barbie couldn't spare a minute to talk to him, the one who makes her computer work like clockwork, the one who spent a fortune to take her to that concert of noise. But she can find time to bat her eyes at that... that... jock.

Adam shuts his eyes. His ears are still ringing from all the noise last night. Maybe the best thing for him today would be to go home. Everyone else cuts classes. Why shouldn't he? He's as good as they are.

Better.

Mental Health day, that's what Oscar would call it. Just go home. Maybe he'd be better off staying away from girls altogether.

They just are too different. He doesn't know how... how to be with them. Why can't girls just be like regular people? It's like they have different rules.

His brother got him tickets-- really good tickets apparently -- to the concert. Sitting right beside giant speakers is supposed to be a good thing? Not to him.

Lights flashing, strobing. Giant screens showing videos of politicians and then there were those weird dancers. Lights and special effects pounding in your eyes, people yelling and screaming all through it. And it was just noise.

You couldn't call it music, not really. Music is

Sergei Prokofiev or Wolfgang Amadeus Mozart. Not noise so loud your ears ring for hours afterwards.

He knows Barbie enjoyed it. She jumped up and down, a lot, and even sang along with the noise when he couldn't even tell what the words were. She smelled good. Especially after all the jumping around. He guesses it was supposed to be dancing. Was watching her jiggle like that worth it? He'll be paying it off for weeks, but it was worth it. Wasn't it?

Barbie got so sweaty so he could kind of see through her shirt. He really wanted to touch her. He looks around quickly, feeling guilty for the thought. Even though it's cold he's getting sweaty himself, just thinking about Barbie. He wanted to touch her so much last night after the concert but he didn't. Couldn't.

She smelled so good in the car. Her car is so much nicer than his, he's glad he let her drive. For the very first time he understands why guys spend so much money on cars. He would have been embarrassed for her to ride in his car.

Walking down the path toward the parking lot now, the more he thinks about it the better the idea of a mental health day sounds. His head is still pounding from last night. He just wanted to touch her. Maybe it wasn't worth it, really.

She didn't even kiss him goodnight.

44 . . .

Krystal is still struggling with her CSS files. She always thinks she gets it in class, but when she goes to do it nothing works the way she thinks it should. Her concentration is broken when a shadow blocks the morning light and she looks up to see Jake, the little photographer who doesn't look old enough for high school, much less university. Oh hell, he's the one Oz told.

"You looking for somebody?" she asks. "Oz maybe?"

But even though he looks a little insecure, he holds out a gift box. Uh oh. Last thing she needs is a puppy dog.

She asks, "What's that?"

Jake looks nervous. "It's nothing much."

Krystal purses her lips. "Look, I don't need a present."

He grins. "Uh, look, I just wanted to say, um, I'm sorry I overheard Maggie and all, and I realize that it's none of my business, but I wanted you to know that if you need anything I'll do whatever I can to help. That's all I wanted to say."

He drops the box on the desk and turns to leave but she stops him with "Wait a minute."

He turns back.

She asks, "Look, Jake... " He nods mutely, hopeful.

"It was an accident you know, and I appreciate the offer and all, but I'll be okay. Really. I just don't want it to get around."

He nods again, "Don't worry, I wouldn't tell anybody even if Oscar hadn't pretty much threatened to kill me if I did."

Krystal laughs. "Okay. But I still don't need a present."

"I think you do." Jake takes the box, and opens it. "It's a photo key chain. I've put some pictures on it already so it's not like I could return it even if I wanted to. It's just a little thing, but it's nice because you can always keep a few of your favourite pictures with you."

Now curious, she says, "What pictures?"

"Just some I took at the **Ubuntu** party."

"Can I see?" she asks, now very curious.

"Sure." He hands it to her and she sees a glowing digital image of herself. "I made it for you, you can have it."

"How do I see the other pictures?"

"There's a little wheel along the bottom, you just roll it."

Jake watches as Krystal scrolls through the images, Maggie, Oz, Kate, the crowd in the lab, one of her and Jose she lingers over. Jake can tell she's liking it.

She looks up at Jake. "Can I change the pictures?"

He nods. "There's a USB connector in the box. It's really easy. Will you be going to the computer club meeting tonight?"

"Yeah, probably." Krystal stands up.

"Me too." Jake smiles at her, secretly pleased that she's not much taller than he is. "I've got to get to class but I'll show you how tonight if you haven't already figured it out yourself, Okay?"

Krystal smiles back. "Deal. Thanks Jake." She leans

over and gives him a peck on the cheek.

Jake smiles and preens as he floats away to his next class. Maybe Krystal could like him, just a little. He'll have to think of an even cooler gift next time.

Make sure the next kiss doesn't land on the cheek though.

45 . . .

Liz paces back and forth at the bus stop.

It's cold out here but it should be warm enough inside the Waterfront Mall.

If the bus doesn't get here soon she'll have to wait half an hour or more for her cameras to warm up when she gets there. She glances at her watch. Again. Where is Natasha? Stamping her feet to keep warm she looks back down the path to the Res.

The Auto Show was all Natasha's idea. Lets go take pictures of these great antique cars, Natasha said. Just us girls, she said. Smell the leather, she said. Get up close and personal with real history, she said.

So where is she? Liz spots the bus lumbering up the main road. Natasha will just have to come later on her own, Liz isn't waiting out here any longer. It's too cold.

Global warming. Hah.

46 . . .

He looks down at his feet crunching the leaves. Stomping them. Follow the path through the woods.

Take the short cut for the scenic route. Beautiful day. But so cold. Just like Barbie. Time to take control of his destiny. He is a man after all. He can't allow her to control him anymore.

He has to stop thinking about her beautiful hair. Bright as gold. Or the swell of her breasts. Her scent. Her lips.

He can feel his blood rushing now. Just from the thought of her. That's wrong because he can feel himself getting excited. Wrong wrong wrong, he thinks. And it's starting to hurt. Walking. He has to get off the path. It could be embarrassing, messy. She acts as though she's a princess and he's a... tool that she can use. Take what she wants then cast him aside.

He was a perfect gentleman. She should appreciate him. Instead she treats him as though he is less than dirt. Will she ever think he's good enough? Will he ever be real to her?

He stumbles off the path into the woods, feeling the rage mount with his erection. He can't control the power. He looks around, he's off the path, no one can see him here. He opens his pants thinking maybe if he relieves himself...

His face is wet, oh God. He's crying over her. Stop it. It's as though she's cast a spell over him. He has to get her out of his head because she is messing up his mind.

He reaches down and starts rubbing himself. He can feel the heat rising but then he flashes on the contempt in her eyes and his erection deflates with his sobs.

She made him feel so wonderful at first.

Staring down at the expression of his manhood dangling limp between his legs, he can't believe she has done this to him. Why? It's crazy. Couldn't she see how good it would have been? He has got to put her out of his mind. He rubs his sleeve across his face, trying to mop up the tears that seem endless. How can he be so weak? How could he let her do this to him?

The crack of a twig behind him is as loud as a rifle shot.

Oh God no.

He freezes in horror. Maybe it's imagination?

No. There is someone coming. That's bad.

Even worse is the girl voice coming through the trees, getting closer, calling out, "Are you all right?"

The idea of a woman seeing him all... all hanging out, snot running down his face... eyes red... crying. Men don't cry. As quick as they began the tears stop now.

He doesn't dare speak. His heart batters his chest, he hopes she will go somewhere else.

He can not be found like this. No one can see him like this, especially a woman. Quietly he moves behind the tree, leaning against the trunk to quiet his breathing. When he reaches to put himself back in his pants the erection is unaccountably back, even more insistent than before.

Maybe she's gone. No. He hears her call out again, "Hello?" Why can't she just leave him alone?

She should just go away. But no. Too much to hope for. He hears the leaves crunch as she pushes closer to him.

He moves farther back, working his way around some bushes. And now the erection won't go down. It seems to have a life of its own, sticking out in front of him like a lance. He can't. It just won't fit into his pants like this... what is that damned woman doing... he can't hear her.

Crouching behind the bushes he discovers a handy tree stump, and he sinks onto it. The thicker brush screens him, making him feel a bit safer. Looking down he's amazed to see if anything he's even harder than before. No way a zipper will be able to contain this. But the damned woman is still blundering around out there. Maybe if he takes off his jacket and covers himself, he can pretend...

No. He's a grown man. He shouldn't have to pretend anything. He shouldn't have to hide. He left the path for privacy. He is minding his own business. He didn't ask for company. He is entitled to find his own peace in the forest. He picks up a stick.

Flashes of her through the shrubbery. "Is there someone here? Do you need help?" It's that red haired girl, the nasty little Natasha. The one he saw punch out her boyfriend. That Boris is a big guy but she knocked him down and he didn't even fight back, he just took it like a sap.

Damn woman's almost found him.

That can't happen. It can't it can't it can't. Oh god in heaven she's going to find him.

He watches her move around the tree and tentatively step back onto the path. He can see her clearly from behind. How much damage does she need to do in a day? He tightens his grip on the stick and stands up.

The woman is dangerous.

47 . . .

Boris comes out of the shower, wrapped in a towel, heading up the stairs to the girl's kitchen. He knows the upper level is off limits but nobody's here and it's an emergency. Maggie has that bag of frozen peas she uses as an icepack when her trick ankle swells. Nobody will have stolen that because even the local food thieves know those peas have been defrosted and refrozen so many times that eating them would mean a sure trip to the hospital side.

Not that any of the students ever seem to actually eat anything as nutritious as peas, he starts to smile at the thought but the pain stops him cold. He needs those peas.

He's wrapping Maggie's bag of peas in a tea towel when Elsie comes in.

"What happened to you?"

Boris jumps, then realizes Elsie is more interested in his busted face than in busting him. He starts to smile but the pain stops it dead. "I assumed the whole school would know by now."

Elsie smiles. "I'm not the whole school. Let me

see."

She corners him, reaches up and tilts his chin back so she can examine his eye in the light.

"I've had black eyes before. I'll live."

"You can't be too careful with your eyes Boris. A trauma can detach a retina. Hang on a minute." Elsie leaves him leaning on the cupboard while she roots through the drawer.

"Natasha hit me."

"Ah." She holds up a small bright LED flashlight.

Boris swallows, afraid of what she'll find.

"Don't look so worried. I'm just looking, it won't hurt. I may only be a student but I can probably tell you if you need to go in and see a real doctor. All right?"

Boris nods. "It hurts more than my last black eye."

"Here, what I want you to do is lean back and look up. Tilt your head back. Just like that. Keep staring up and I'm going to shine the light in your eyes. Try not to blink."

"Okay." Boris leans back and concentrates on keeping his eyes open and still, trying not to flinch when she shines the powerful little flash in his eyes. It seems to take forever but then suddenly she switches it off. It's over.

"So what do you think," he asks nervously as she tucks the flashlight back into the drawer full of odds and ends.

She smiles at him. "I can't see anything wrong. Use the ice, take Tylenol. If it hurts tomorrow, you should see a real doctor."

He nods. "Thanks, Elsie."

She turns away and it occurs to him for the first time that Elsie the maneater has just had him pinned in the corner wearing nothing but a towel. Suddenly he feels a little hurt.

"Is that it?" he asks, wrapping the peas in the towel, and gently laying it against his eye.

She turns back and says, "I can't write you a prescription, I'm only a student." Then she registers the look of rejection on his face, and a smile plays around the corners of her mouth. "Ah. You mean," she points to him, and says, "boy," to herself, "girl" then pointing at his "towel?"

He starts to blush, says, "Well, uh, yeah."

"In the first place, you're a patient. The most important thing in my life is becoming a doctor. Even wannabe doctors have to take care not to dally with patients. That's one. And two, I have an exam to study for."

Boris is happy that at least she didn't say he was ugly.

Still.

"That's not what I meant. I mean from a woman's point of view, what's wrong with me?"

The smile reaches her eyes. "Not a thing, Boris." She appraises his form seriously, then continues, "You're very nearly perfect. You've got a great body. Good muscle tone, definition. Perhaps your nose is a bit too perfect, a touch too straight. A little jog would make it nearly irresistible. Maybe next time get her to go for the nose and leave your eyes alone. When they're not bashed in you have beautiful eyes. A good face."

Boris looks a little bit happier to hear how great he is. "Really? You really think so?"

"I wouldn't lie to you. I like you, Boris, but you're a romantic. And much as I'd enjoy divesting you of that towel, I don't think it would do either of us any good. Do you?"

Sadly he says, "Oh, I don't know."

She winks at him. "But I'm only human after all, so maybe you'd better go put some clothes on just the same." She smiles down at the towel, licks her lips, then turns on her heel and heads out of the kitchen.

Boris finds himself smiling in spite of himself. Maybe he isn't a total loser. Maybe he will be fighting off the babes at the pub.

Good muscle tone she said. He flexes, making sure to keep a good grip on the frozen peas. Held gently against the sore eye. Ow.

Great body, eh?

48 . . .

Mouse and Amelia sit at the back of the lecture hall across the aisle from Jose and Eric. Mouse dutifully types notes, but Amelia finds herself spending all her time texting back and forth with Eric.

eric
do you think she misses me?

amelia
I don't know, why don't you ask her?

eric
does she seem different at all?

amelia
not to me... but I'm not really friends with her.
eric
Y not?

amelia
We're into different stuff

Eric looks across at Amelia. She's holding out on him. Hmm.

eric
the real reason?

amelia
she doesn't have friends.

eric
you think she's lonely?

amelia
i doubt it very much

Amelia glances at Eric. Let somebody else tell the poor schnook, She's not going to.

eric
you don't think she misses me?

amelia

she's pre-med. you know how heavy a course load that is.

eric

i miss her

amelia

i know you do, I'm sorry. you hear bout Boris and Natasha?

eric

no, what about b & n?

amelia

really? where were you at lunch?

eric

what about Boris and Natasha?

amelia

big fight

eric

about what?

amelia

don't know, nobody knows. one minute lovey dovey next minute Natasha decks him

eric

Natasha? U say five foot nothing Natasha decked 6 foot squared Boris? i don't believe it.

amelia
that's coz you're a 98 pound English geek

eric
hmmmph I'll have you know that I weigh at least 135

amelia
anyway, that's the story

eric
ur just making this up to make me feel better

amelia
it happened ask anybody

eric
anybody except me, eh?

amelia
didn't see it myself but seems everybody else did

eric
hmmm

amelia
what?

eric
was everybody texting about me and Elsie too?

amelia
not really

eric
what does 'not really' mean

amelia
nobody knew anything.

eric
Natasha really hit Boris?

amelia
knocked him down is what they say.

eric
what did people say about us?

amelia
one minute you and Elsie r joined at hip and the next ur not.

eric
what did he do when she hit him?

amelia
he fell down.

eric
figure of speech?

amelia
real deal

Eric looks at Amelia, who pantomimes crossing her heart.

Laurel L Russwurm

amelia
you know, most everybody will be out tonight

eric
and?

amelia
y don't we have a depression party

eric
a what?

eric
my girlfriend and i used to do that all the time in high school

eric
what u talking about A?

amelia
pretty much everybody's going out for computer club night.

eric
i know that. what i don't understand is "depression party"

amelia
popcorn & chocolate and depressing movies & depressing music. drink cheap wine 2 if u want

eric
movies like what?

158

amelia
maybe titanic?

eric
oh that's a great movie. excellent special effects and...

amelia
OK, that one's out then

eric
why? it's a great movie!

amelia
disqualified for fun parts. supposed to be depressing

eric
A? what IS the point?

amelia
idea of depression party is to wallow in your agony.

eric
ok... i know I have agony... i didn't know you have agony

amelia
i do... trust me on this

eric
great girl like you what could possibly be depressing in your life?

amelia
maybe i'll tell you sometime

eric
how bout Grave of the Fireflies.

amelia
nuclear aftermath? what i've heard, if i wasn't
depressed that'd give me depression, am i right?

eric
but why are you depressed?

amelia
why does anybody get depressed?

eric
ah. i didn't think you were going out with anybody.

amelia
that would about do it.

eric
what, guys aren't beating down your door?

amelia
lol... not hardly...

eric
i don't believe that

amelia
not the one i want beating down my door anyway

eric

oh... there's one you want. do tell, who's the lucky guy?

amelia

i'd have to kill you if i told you

eric

Not fair. you know the cause of my misery.

amelia

i hate to tell you this eric, but the entire world knows

eric

good point... come on A... i'll never tell.

amelia

so, i hear Fireflies is supposed to be really heavy.

eric

uh, yeah, it is. I've got Requiem for a Dream, too

amelia

get out. guess I'll bring La Jette to lighten it up

eric

what's that?

amelia

an old movie, but I think you'll like it.

eric

wait a minute A... this mean i'm your girlfriend?

amelia

lol... no stupid it means you're a friend... besides
my girlfriends don't hv 5 o'clock shadow ;D

eric

darn... thought if i was your girlfriend you'd have
to tell me who you have the hots for

amelia

c'mon why do you want to know?

eric

so i can make sure he treats my buddy tight

amelia

doesn't work that way unfortunately... *sigh*

eric

can't wait for the depression party kiddo

amelia

why is that?

eric

wallowing in agony is mighty appealing but i figure
i'll be able to pry your secret out of you

amelia

lol you fool

eric

you can tell me... really

amelia
maybe some day

eric
ve haff ways of making you talk

amelia
i'm not saying a word.

49 . . .

Liz is pacing in the the nearly empty cafeteria, cell phone pressed tightly to her ear. It rings and rings as she paces. Back and forth in front of the windows she peers out at the fall foliage without really seeing it. Why doesn't someone answer?

She waves at Jake coming in through the entrance, snapping the phone closed when he joins her.

"Anything?" she asks anxiously.

Shaking his head, Jake says, "Nobody's seen her."

"The car show was her idea."

"I agree it's not like her, but beating up Boris isn't either."

"Beating up Boris? What are you talking about?" Liz can see Jake's not kidding, but still. "You're saying Natasha beat up Boris?"

"Apparently she knocked him down in the oval, in full sight of pretty much the whole school. But that was at lunch and nobody's seen her since."

"I don't get it. I can't even imagine them having a disagreement, let alone a physical fight."

"Nobody heard what it was about, it was just the two of them. But everybody saw her deck him. Still, it's hard to know where she went after. Most people think she took the path to the parking lot, not the residence."

"That makes sense 'cause she was supposed to catch the bus with me. And nobody answers at the Res. But it doesn't explain why she didn't come to the show."

"Keeping a low profile? Maybe she went to the mall."

"Then why doesn't she answer her phone?"

"I don't know. Maybe she doesn't want to talk to anybody. Did you try texting her?"

"She's not answering texts either." Liz flips open her phone again, and redials. This time the phone at the Res is picked up. "Hi who's this?" Liz asks hopefully.

"Elsie. Is that you Liz?"

"Yeah, look, is Natasha there?"

"No, she's not. Do you want to talk to Boris?"

Liz can hear Boris, saying in the background, "I don't want to."

Liz rolls her eyes. Uh oh. Boris and Elsie alone in the Res, not answering the phone. That's bad. Uh oh.

Then Elsie says, "But it isn't Natasha."

Then Boris is on the line. "Yo."

Although she knows the answer, Liz has to ask, "Boris, is Natasha there?"

"No. I don't know where she is but she sure isn't here."

"Could you just check her room please?"

"You know what, I really don't care where she is."

"Bo, I'm worried." Liz flashes on Maggie saying "I was worried about you." There's a clunk as the receiver drops.

"Boris! Boris don't."

Elsie is on the line again. "Sorry. He bailed and went back to his room. Is there something I can do to help?"

"Could you just check Natasha's room, see if she's there? Nobody has seen her."

"I'm sure she's not, but I'll check." Elsie gently lays the phone down beside its receiver." Liz covers the mouthpiece and tells Jake, "Elsie's gone to look."

"That's good." Jake nods. "Boris didn't want to talk?"

"Nope." Liz resumes pacing. "Jerk."

"Jerk? Why is he a jerk?"

"He doesn't care about Natasha."

"Liz, some on. She punched him out in front of the whole school. He's probably mad at her."

"But she could be... "

"She humiliated him in front of the whole world. She hit him." Jake explains.

"Oh, come on he's a big guy. She couldn't hurt him."

"What do you mean? Of course she could hurt him." Jake shakes his head. "You think a person's size has anything to do with whether they feel pain?"

"I didn't say that."

"Even if Boris was impervious to physical pain, which I doubt, then there's the psychic pain of being humiliated in public. She knocked him down, Liz. Legally it's 'assault and battery'."

"Why are you making such a big deal out of it?"

"You don't think it's a big deal?"

"Well no, not really."

Jake shakes his head in disgust. "Would it be a big deal if Boris hit Natasha?"

"Well, sure."

"So why is this any different?"

"Because she's tiny. Because he's big. Because..."

"You're saying it's okay to hit someone bigger than you?"

"I never, I mean, well I didn't say that. Exactly. I guess I never really thought about it." she says.

Jake looks up at Liz. "You're bigger than I am. Does that make it okay for me to punch you?"

"No, of course not."

"So it's not all right for small guys to hit big girls, but it's okay for small girls to hit big guys."

"When you put it like that... Well... I don't know."

"I do know. Gender does not give anybody the right to hurt anybody. The only justification for violence is self defence."

"I guess you're right, Jake, it's just that, well you just don't think about stuff like that."

"Maybe you don't. But women aren't the only people who have violence done to them you know."

"Violence against women was condoned for a long time."

"And that was wrong. Just like violence against men is wrong. Or violence against children. There's always something, maybe skin colour, sexual orientation or simple geekiness that gets the shit kicked out of you. But it doesn't really matter whether the excuse is gender or religion. It's still just an excuse for people who want to kick the shit out of you. It's violence that's the problem."

Liz holds up a finger to indicate Elsie's back on the phone. "No sign, huh? If she shows, can you ask her to call me? I'm gonna look for her. Sure I'll let you know when I find her. Thanks, Elsie."

She hangs up and stows it again, this time pulling on her jacket. "Elsie says she's not there. She'll tell the house mother and the residence security guard to keep a look out."

"So now what?"

"I'm gonna find her," shaking her head, "I just don't understand what happened."

"Hang on a minute." She looks over and sees he's pulling a fleece sweater out of his bag. "I'll help." As they cross the lobby, Liz detours to the security desk, where a gaunt older man in a baggy security uniform is writing in a log book.

"Hey Vlad. I'm looking for my friend Natasha."

Jake is surprised to see the slightly sinister looking man, the one that reminds him of Underworld's Victor, take one look at Liz and undergo a transformation worthy of any good horror flick. Vlad's usually stern countenance is replaced by a smile of happy recognition. "Hello, Miss Liz," he rumbles in a deep thickly accented voice, "This is little red haired girl you work late at night with?"

"Yes. She's missed classes and no one has seen her."

"I'm sorry I have not seen her either. It is not long enough for official search but I can ask other guards to watch out for her." He unclips the Blackberry from his waist and sets it on the counter.

"Do you have a picture?" He gestures to her phone.

Liz beams. "Great idea!" She scrolls through the images then sends a face shot of Natasha to Vladimir's Blackberry. Then reaches over and gives him a peck on the cheek, and says, "Thanks so much, Vlad."

The guard looks like he's about to implode with pleasure, but he masters himself and holds up a finger, "Just remember this is very unofficial Miss Liz".

Liz nods. "I understand. We're gonna go check the paths." Vlad eyes Jake, clearly wondering how much help the boy will be, worried he will be no help at all if there is trouble.

"Maybe I should accompany you also." he mutters.

"No, I don't want you to get into trouble Vlad. Just spreading the word will help a lot."

"Hey look," says Jake, "There's Quentin. He was gonna come to the computer club meeting but I'll bet he'll help look for her." Jake and Liz wave at Vlad and hurry after Quentin who is just stepping though the main doors into the waning light. Following him out, Liz sees he's heading toward the married student residence complex. Liz yells, "Hey Q! Wait up," and Quentin, turns and waits for them to catch up with him.

Quentin tells Jake, "Sorry, can't make the meeting tonight."

"This is different," says Liz, "Have you seen Natasha, Q?"

"She's probably laying low." he smiles. "I know I would."

"But Nobody's seen her all afternoon. I'm worried about her. We were going to The Auto Show together, but she never showed. Jake and I are going to search for her. Can you help?"

"You think she's out here somewhere?"

"I don't know Q. She didn't go home, or make any classes, so I'm worried. Maybe she's off campus, but she might be out there. And you know how stubborn she is. She might think freezing her butt off is better than having to face Bo."

"I guess we could just walk the paths, see if she's running around out here." Quentin agrees. "Have you tried calling her?"

Liz nods miserably. "All afternoon. Ever since she stood me up. I've left messages, but her phone's off." Liz brushes at her eyes. "Oh Q, where is she?" Liz starts to sniffle.

Ethan joins the trio, smiling rapturously at Liz until he sees how upset she is. Opting for neutrality Ethan says, "Hey, guys, what's happening?" He's a little disconcerted no one answers him.

Quentin says, "Don't worry, when me and Tammy fight, first thing I do is turn off my phone. The last thing you wanna do in a fight is talk on the phone. Fighting has to be in person."

Ethan asks, "What's wrong?"

Liz says, "Natasha's missing." Then she bursts into tears.

Ethan tentatively steps toward her and pulls her into a hug. "It'll be okay, Liz." He awkwardly pats her back.

"She was here at lunch, so she's only been gone a couple of hours right? Let's just find her, then, okay?" Ethan asks, "Uh... would she have a camera with her?"

"Oh yeah. She always has the little Nikon 'cause it fits in her pocket." Liz wipes her eyes on her sleeve. "Coming to The Auto Show she'd have at least one of her digital SLRS." She rubs her eyes.

"So maybe she's just out there taking pictures."

"Maybe. But the light's almost gone. She should be back by now if she was on a shoot. It's just I've got a bad feeling."

Her face is all blotchy and wet, her nose is puffy, and Ethan's breath catches as he thinks how gorgeous she is. Not sure what his role is, he digs in his pocket and offers Liz a handful of paper napkins accumulated from fast food restaurants over the life of the pea coat.

Liz accepts the napkins gratefully, using the offering to mop her face. "OK, I'm OK. Lets go look. It is broad day light after all, I'm probably being silly."

As they start off across the oval, Ethan's arm comfortably around her waist, Liz looks brighter.

"Maybe we ought to split up. Cover more ground," Jake suggests. "Q and I can head for the Res, you guys take the path to the parking lot."

Ethan adds, "Good idea. And we'll cruise over to check the bus stop too. If she's not running around in the bush taking pictures, maybe she's just hiding out in the shelter."

50 . . .

Tamara slams the teapot down on the table. Startled, Barbie recoils, then asks, "What's wrong Tam?"

"I'm just so mad at Q. I hurried home last night and made dinner and he never showed. Didn't even call. He was in bed when I woke up, but I don't have a clue when he came in."

"That stinks."

"I feel so stupid." Tamara slides into her seat. "Everybody was right. We shouldn't have gotten married. Wait til after college my mom said. Be a doctor first and then be a wife."

Pouring tea for both, Barbie asks, "So why didn't you?"

"I couldn't stand the thought of losing him. Then he proposed. And like the song says, we're the now generation. I wanted him now, you know? I didn't see he's not very grown up. All he wants to do is play. Probably why he's so good at playing."

"But play is important. He still turns your crank, right?"

"That's half the problem. He can turn my crank whenever he wants. It's hard to have a serious conversation when you're makin' whoopee. Just thinking about him gets me hot. Still." Tamara shakes her head ruefully, smiling dreamily. "Even when I'm mad as hell. You just can't imagine how good the sex is, girl. I just wish he'd grow up."

Barbie giggles. Flashing on the clinch with Jose, she says, "Oh, I can imagine."

Tamara sighs. "I didn't know his idea of higher education was access to a better class of drugs. Pretty much all he wants to do, hang out with the gang and smoke up. I mean I like partying, just not twenty four seven. I have to work hard at it if I'm gonna be a doctor." Tamara takes a deep breath and says, "You know, I've been thinking about this a lot, and being a doctor is more important to me than being married. I know I'll be a good doctor. And I want it so bad I can taste it. But Q just hasn't been there for me."

"Is it that bad?" Barbie asks, surprised.

Tamara nods miserably. "I can't party all the time or I'll wash out. I have to focus on my studies. But how can I even concentrate if I'm spending half my life wondering where he is."

Barbie shakes her head, "Wow, Tam, I had no idea. What are you gonna do?"

"I've been hoping it'd pass, telling myself he'll settle down. Start participating in his coursework, get involved. But if anything it's getting worse." Tamara sips her tea, staring at the steam rising up out of the mug, "I just don't know, Barb. I didn't hardly get any sleep last night, trying to wait up for him. It was after three when I put out the light and he still wasn't back."

"You have to talk to him about it."

"I try to but every time we end up in bed having even better sex than the time before. I freaked on his head this morning and he still almost got me back in the sack. Just talking about it hours later I still feel equal parts lust and anger. How do you handle that?"

"Whoooo, sounds kind of tempting actually." giggles Barbie.

"You are not helping. But it sounds like you regret not giving Jose a tumble. Maybe you should, release a little tension."

"If there was any chance at all of a no strings roll in the hay with Jose I'd be there in a heartbeat. Maybe what I'm really afraid of is that once would never be enough and we end up game over. Married and dead." Barbie blushes and claps a hand over her mouth. "Oh Tam, I'm sorry I didn't mean..."

Tamara smiles sadly, "You did, and you'd be right. I gotta figure something out 'cause this married thing is gonna kill me."

Barbie suggests, "Maybe it would help to talk in public so he can't put the moves on you. Go to the pub or something."

"Maybe. He swore to me he'd be here for dinner tonight but he just blew it off. He knows I've got a lab and he'll miss me again."

"Maybe he missed on purpose 'cause he knows you're mad."

"If he doesn't bother to show up it only makes me madder. He knows that too."

"Yeah, but guys, don't they all do that? We all make choices, and it's hard to know what we'll regret later."

Tamara leans on her hand, dejected. "I regret too many things now, I can't afford to worry about later. What are you worried about regretting?"

"When I'm a little old lady sitting in my rocking chair in the old folks home, when I stare into the fireplace and think about my life, will I regret passing up a chance at Jose? Oh hell, I was doing so well keeping the fantasy Jose separate from the real one until, god, I was such a slut, I practically attacked him, and you know, it was so close, Tam. It was way better than my imagination. And part of me still wishes I did jump him."

Tamara says, "Sounds like regret right now."

"What I really better do is call Terrence."

Tamara snorts. "Barbie girl, you are the only woman I know whose vibrator has a name."

51 . . .

Jake and Quentin have the path to the Fyfield House Res to themselves.

Gesturing, Jake says, "Lets check this one too."

The side path Jake is pointing at isn't groomed with wood chips, it's just worn into the undergrowth by students creating their own shortcut. Jake has no idea where it goes although Quentin knows it leads to his circle's favourite clearing, surely littered with roaches. Still, they need to check it. His friends won't have been back since it got so cold.

"Liz is probably being a bit alarmist," Quentin tells Jake. "Nat's probably just out buying shoes or something."

Jake nods, not really believing it.

Natasha has never struck him as one of the girls who buys truckloads of shoes. She's willing to get dirty if it'll get her a good picture. She never seems to care what she wears or if it's a mess. He doesn't quite get the bond with Boris, either. Boris is the one he can see maxing the plastic buying new clothes to make himself feel better. Bo always makes him aware of how tattered his own off the rack wardrobe is. Boris generally looks like he just stepped out of GQ or something, but Natasha's favourite couturier is Goodwill.

"Natasha!" Jake calls. They stop and listen but hear nothing but the distant sounds of the creek.

"I hope you're right." They follow it to the clearing where they find lots of trampled grass, cigarette butts and roach ends. But no Natasha. No anybody.

Quentin peers into the bushes as he does a circuit of the clearing. "Natasha!" he calls, but gets no response.

Looking through the parking at the path going through the woods.

On the opposite branch of the path Ethan and Liz walk toward the parking lot. Periodically Liz calls out "Natasha!" but there's no sound beyond the rustling of leaves in the trees.

Liz says, "We have to find her. I have such a bad feeling."

"We'll find her." Ethan gives her hand a squeeze, then looks into the woods.

Most Christie students are off somewhere eating, or studying, or whatever, leaving the walkways nearly unused as night falls.

As it gets darker the sensors activate and the lights mounted on the poles lining the path wink on, one by one. They're losing light fast so it's getting harder to see.

Ethan says, "Let's just check the parking lot."

Liz nods and they hurry up to where the footpath widens into the lot that's used by day students with cars. Unless something's scheduled in the Arts Centre, its pretty empty nights, so now only a handful of cars are flung across a space large enough to accommodate a few hundred.

Although the bus shelter looks empty, Liz crosses the lot to check while Ethan starts peering in car windows.

Approaching the residence, Jake rubs his hands together vigorously, then stuffs them in his pockets. "I'll just be a minute."

Quentin nods. "Go on up, Jake, I'll keep looking around down here."

"Why don't you come up with me. Warm up."

Quentin laughs. "Then it'll just be harder to come back out. I'll keep moving thanks. Bring flashlights, that'll help."

Jake nods and keys his way in the side door.

Walking around the back of the building Quentin peers through the trees. Although the forest is thinner here it is almost dark. No sign of anyone, certainly no one taking pictures. He doesn't want to scare Jake, but he is starting to get worried. Maybe it's just because Liz is so worked up.

But.

Turning it over in his mind, Quentin knows hiding out is terribly out of character for Natasha. Or shoe shopping for that matter. The Natasha Quentin knows would have gone to the shoot and taken a bunch of fantastic photos of antique cars. When she came back she'd either apologize to Bo or knock him down again.

Rounding the building he comes to the residence parking lot. A quick scan of the cars tells him they all have Christie parking stickers. He doesn't think Natasha has a car, but he looks in car windows just the same. Maybe she's catching a nap or something.

Nothing. Looking back at the building, he notes a line of dumpsters backed up against the lower wall. The higher floors all have windows, but most of the lights are out. Students seem to resist going into their tiny cells until they have to to sleep.

Quentin looks at the dumpsters, but isn't sure he really wants to even think about them, let alone look.

Back home in Ottawa his brother is a cop, and he's heard too many grisly dumpster stories.

Please don't be in a dumpster, Natasha.

Upstairs Jake lets himself into the residence, passing through the common room where Elsie is curled in a chair eating a cream cheese bagel. Elsie smiles at him. She always smiles at him. That's part of what scares him. Jake knows other guys think she's hot, and he'd probably think so too if she wasn't so frightening. She'd make a great Lady MacBeth or a wild haired Boudica leading a charge on the Romans. But in real life she's a bit much.

"Have you seen Natasha?" he asks heading to the kitchen.

Elsie watches Jake, clearly amused at the reaction she always provokes in the boy. "I'd expect her to lay low a while."

Opening the junk drawer Jake roots around until he finds a couple of pencil flashlights. Then he decides they really need a big one, too. Coming back through the common room he asks Elsie, "You haven't seen her, have you?"

Elsie laughs. "No, just the results of her handiwork." Jake looks confused, until she adds, "I had to ice Bo's eyes and put him to bed."

Elsie makes eye contact with Jake, who'd momentarily forgotten how uncomfortable this woman makes him. But when she smiles and runs her tongue suggestively through the cream cheese Jake mutters, "Oh" and turns and escapes to his room.

Watching Jake flee makes Elsie smile. God that little one is too easy. Maybe she should take him to bed. Been a while since she's had a virgin. Then she chastises herself. Stop it. She's already made a mess in her nest, better not compound it.

Safe in his room Jake slips into his coat, wondering if he should wake Boris. Better not, probably wouldn't be a good thing to have him there when they find Natasha. She'll probably be mad.

He reaches into the night table drawer for the lantern flashlight his mom gave him. He pockets spare batteries fresh from the charger, since it eats batteries ridiculously fast, but it's bright.

Locking the room Jake wishes Q had come up just to get him get past Elsie. Bracing himself for the gauntlet, he's relieved Elsie's not in the common room this time, and he hurries to the stairwell. Jake hopes Liz is over-reacting, but he's afraid she's not.

52 . . .

The computer club members spread out in Kate and Nick's married student bungalow. Although the same size and floor plan as Tamara's, Kate has merged the intended dining area with the living room to make one larger living space. Sofas anchor either end with two folding tables down the middle.

Oscar and Maggie sit on junk shop easy chairs flanking the Jelly Belly bowl; Krystal and Adam sit along the side on two of Kate's vintage vinyl and chrome tube chairs.

Kate sets a bowl of ChedACorn beside Krystal before curling up on the window sofa. "I thought Jake was coming."

Krystal nods, "Me too. He was gonna try and bring along some other photography students."

Oscar very formally announces, "The Christie Computer Club Is Now In Session. Hear ye hear ye hear..." When they start pelting him with jellybeans and ChedACorn Oscar shuts up.

"Who died and made you president?" asks Maggie.

"No one," answers Oscar as he picks jellybeans out of his lap and pops them into his mouth. "I assumed possession of the biggest mouth and the largest ego made me a shoo-in." Lifting a ChedACorn from his shoulder he sends it after the jellybeans.

"Well," suggests Kate, "Far as I'm concerned if you've got an agenda you can have the job. I have no idea how to run a club." Gesturing toward the snack food array,'"Parties yes, clubs no. Whose idea was this anyway?"

Kate looks at Maggie who says, "Uh. Yeah, that'd be me."

"What is on the agenda today, Maggie?" Adam asks.

"That's the problem," says Maggie. "I don't have one. This meeting is to figure out what we want the club to be for."

Adams says, "Why not evaluate and compare software?"

"That's a great idea. Give us a focus right off." Oscar nods. "A ratings website. We could post software and hardware reviews."

"Not bad," says Maggie, "Call it **Computer Science Department**. It should be easy enough to do it for our coursework web pages."

Krystal says, "It would be fun to have something besides celebrity gossip to tweet about. I could plug the website."

Maggie says, "I signed up to Twitter for Stu, but we hardly ever use it; we're more likely to just text each other."

Oscar shakes his head. "I can't believe you lot call yourselves computer geeks."

"Wait just a minute, there. Oz, microblogging is more social network than a geek haven." says Kate.

"I prefer the term 'nerd'." Maggie grins.

"Depends on who you hang out with, doesn't it now."

"There are plenty of geeks and nerds on Twitter," says Krystal. "You guys just gave it up without giving it a chance."

"I connect to Twitter through Identi.ca" says Oscar. "All the better to be anonymous."

Krystal's eyes widen. "Are you in Anonymous, Oz?"

Oscar smiles, "If I told you, I'd have to kill you."

"Twitter is simply too frivolous." says Adam. "If I want to connect with programmers I'll go though IRC."

Krystal frowns. "What's that?"

"Internet relay channel. Live chatting without that 'following' business, so everyone can see the conversation.

Maggie laughs. "It's what Sheldon Cooper would use instead of Twitter".

Krystal asks, "Who?"

Oscar says "To live chat with Moss and Roy no doubt."

Krystal frowns. "Now what are you guys talking about?"

"Geek sitcoms."

Krystal shakes her head. "There are Geek sitcoms?"

Maggie says, "Oh yeah. I've only seen bits of I.T. Crowd on YouTube but I told my folks I want the boxed set for Christmas. Oz and I have a running argument about which is better, Big Bang Theory or I.T. Crowd. My favourite I.T. Crowd clip is where the cops break down the door and gun down the girl."

Krystal says, "Uh huh. Sounds real funny. Not."

"No really, you have to see it. I didn't explain it very well," Maggie says. "It's a take off on those theatre piracy ads."

Adam says, "I am sick of being lumped in with criminals. All computer people are not pirates. I wish pirates would stop downloading and making me look bad. It is illegal after all."

Kate says, "But all downloading isn't illegal, and an awful lot doesn't even infringe copyright. They're trying to make it sound as though all downloading is illegal."

Oscar adds, "You should look at the laws they're pushing before you judge. The worst of them require no conviction nor evidence. You don't even have to download anything to get barred from the interwebs. Accusations can evict you, and not just you, but everyone at your address, innocent family, flatmates."

Adam says, "That doesn't sound right. Are you certain?"

Kate says, "I thought it was to stop copyright infringement."

Oscar says, "That's what they want you to think, Kate. But in this brave new world you're guilty until proven innocent."

Adam says, "But they have to do that to stop the pirates."

"You mean like at our terribly depraved Ubuntu release party with all of those torrents."

"That's not what I mean," says Adam.

Maggie says, "I hadn't thought of that, Oz. That means when they throttle torrents it means they target Ubuntu parties."

"Of course that's wrong, but that's not what I mean though. What I'm talking about is people who steal music and movies."

Oscar says, "Lets think about that a minute, Adam, shall we? How are people stealing music exactly?"

"People download it then share it with other people."

"Have you ever watched a movie on TV Adam?"

"Of course."

"Was that stealing?"

"No, but we pay for cable."

Kate reaches for the remote and switches on the TV. "You know what? I pay for cable too."

Adam says, "Of course you do. I didn't mean to imply you wouldn't. I mean..."

It's the new **House** episode. Adam trails off as he notes that Kate isn't really listening, she's intently watching the doctor wheel out a crash cart and shock the patient until she's stable.

When the show breaks into a commercial, Kate mutes it, then turns to Adam. "How is watching my cable different than if we shared a download?"

Adam opens his mouth to answer, then closes it again, frowning. Then, "I will have to think about that, Kate."

53 · · ·

The darkness of the night is emphasized by the flashing lights of the police car angled across the parking lot behind Fyfield House. Jake's stomach drops as the worst case scenario catches his throat and he hurries over.

But wait. This isn't it. This is something else. Quentin spread eagled against the car in the time honoured tradition of TV cop shows. Why is the cop frisking Q like they do on TV? This is bad too. Just a different bad.

As Jake approaches he realizes it isn't a real police car, it's campus security. "Hey, what's the problem?"

The burly guard dismisses Jake with, "Move along

son."

Jake moves in closer, ignoring Q's warning head shake. "You're making a mistake here." says Jake firmly. Facing up to this beefy guard is nothing compared to dealing with Elsie.

Planting his hands on his hips to maximize his chest inflation, the guard glares down at Jake, irritated at the skinny kid's challenge. "I caught this guy lurking around down here, but that isn't any of your concern kid. So just move along."

Jake crosses his arms. "Q wasn't "lurking", he was waiting for me. Now just let him go."

"Just piss off kid."

Righteously indignant, Jake says, "Didn't you hear what I said? You have no call to harass him."

"Oooh, are you a lawyer, boy?"

Quentin is shaking his head more emphatically, trying to get Jake to stand down, eyes wide, trying to will Jake into silence.

"I live in Fyfield House, he lives in the cottages. We're both Christie students, boy , so that means we pay your salary. Now are you gonna let him go or do I call a real cop?"

Quentin is aghast, now worried that young Jake's heroics are gonna get them both killed.

Quentin says, "It's OK, Jake, really," when the guard rounds on him with raised fist.

"You. SHUT UP," shouts the guard as Elsie comes out of the building and barges into the tableau lit by strobing cruiser lights.

Elsie says, "Just get into the car, I'll tell you where to go."

"What the hell are you talking about girl?" The guard is not about to take any more crap from these snotty rich kids.

Elsie shifts the large cloth bag she has over her shoulder so she can whip out her cell phone. She punches a single digit then says, "We're having a problem, can you come out to the lot?"

Elsie snaps the phone shut and tucks it in her coat, folding her arms and glowering up at him. "I'm sorry, I mistook you for someone with a brain."

"You aren't making it any better for yourself, bitch," bellows the guard, "I don't know what you smart ass kids think you are up to but I'm going to take you all in, and then we will get it straightened out."

The guard is startled by a very large hand clamping itself on his shoulder. "I don't think so," says the owner of the hand, who wears the same uniform but with a bit of gold braid on the shoulder boards. Val Thompson, the campus security chief, has a physique roughly equivalent to the Incredible Hulk's. "I think you're about done here, Connor."

"Uh, sir, but I was on my rounds and these people were behaving suspiciously." Val fixes him with a look; Connor pales and shuts up.

"This is what we're gonna do. You are going to give me the keys to this car and then you will go inside and cover the main desk until I get back. You will be polite. And deferential. Think you can handle that Connor?"

Connor swallows, "Uh, sir," carefully avoiding looking at anyone but Val, "I'm not sure what deferential means."

Val pins him with a laser glare. "Deferential means you kiss ass. Do you think you can handle that Connor?"

Wearing a poker face Connor executes a military precision salute. "Yes sir."

Val holds out his palm and Connor digs the car keys out of his pocket and hands them over before marching back to the building, head held high.

Disgusted, Val gets into the driver's seat. "Guys, if you'll get in back, please, Elsie will ride shotgun."

Quentin and Jake pile in although they have no idea what is happening. After belting up, Elsie twists around in her seat to tell them, "Liz found Natasha and she's hurt. When we get there you'll need to stay on the path to flag down the ambulance."

Elsie says, "Val, this is my roommate Jake, and his friend..."

"Quentin Bradbury. I live in the cottages."

Val nods, carefully backing out, doing a three point turn onto the footpath, then driving slowly. "Tomorrow I'm gonna want to talk to you about what was happening with Connor."

"He was acting like a Nazi thug." protests Jake.

Quentin nods, "No problem, I'd love to come by and give you a statement."

"Sorry. Our budget doesn't buy us the cream of the crop. I've had suspicions about him but suspicion isn't grounds for termination. That's why I'd like to talk to you both. Later."

"Elsie, what happened to Natasha?" asks Jake.

"Liz said she was attacked. She's probably been out there most of the day, and she's hurt, so it's really lucky Liz found her."

Quentin mutters, "Luck, my ass."

The campus security car arrives at the fork in the path. Val makes the tight turn and drives toward the parking lot.

"Please keep your eyes open for..."

"There!" yells Jake. As the car approaches they see Ethan standing at the side of the road, shivering in a T shirt. Val stops the car, and Elsie is first out, handing Ethan a large sweatshirt.

He starts "They're in here."

Elsie shakes her head. "Put it on, you're freezing, then you can take me." Ethan nods and pulls it over his head, while Jake climbs out and hands Elsie his brightest flash light, then gives one of the penlights to Ethan. Elsie flashes Jake a non-predatory smile and follows Ethan into the woods.

Quentin climbs out of the car and positions himself with Jake just off the path, and they watch Val take the campus car down the path to the parking lot. Sirens wail in the distance.

Elsie's light bounces along the path, variously skidding off trees and shrubs until it lands on Liz kneeling at the side of the path, cradling Natasha's head in her lap.

Elsie bites back an admonition; a lay person should never move a head injury. Blood encrusted in her hair clearly indicates Natasha has one. She has also been bundled in Ethan's voluminous pea coat. Elsie fleetingly hopes the rescuers haven't done more damage than good as she passes the big flash to Ethan and she opens her bag. Ethan fiddles with the flash light until it slides open, transforming into a lantern.

Elsie pulls out a gray felt blanket and kneels beside Natasha's supine figure. Ethan goes around and crouches beside Liz, one hand holding up the lantern for Elsie, the other arm slipping protectively around Liz's shoulder.

Elsie can see matted blood on Natasha's head, quite a lot of it, clotted into her hair. Reaching out to gently touch Natasha's neck, Elsie deftly takes her pulse. "Getting her warm was good, and her pulse is strong." she tells Liz matter-of-factly. "May I have the light please?"

Ethan hands it over silently, and Elsie lifts the corner of the coat and shines the light in.

Liz asks, "Is she going to be okay?"

Natasha's clothes are ripped and bloody, the beginning of heavy bruising forming on her thighs. Looks like blood and semen. Elsie lightly probes her arms and legs.

"Nothing seems broken."

"But there's so much blood."

"Scalp wounds bleed a lot. Doesn't have to be serious. I can't tell about the head injury, it could be bad or she might be fine. I'm just here for first aid. We are not even going to try to move her, we just keep her warm until the paramedics arrive. I'd say she's in damn good shape for someone who's been laying out here for hours."

She passes the light back to Ethan, and settles the heavy wool blanket over the unconscious girl. "I think they're here."

The thrum of the ambulance engine slows and stops out on the footpath. Doors open and close and lights strobe as Val leads the paramedics through the trees.

With practiced ease a portable gurney is set up, and Elsie gets up and steps out of the way. The paramedics squat on either side of Liz, expertly sliding a board under the unconscious Natasha smoothly transferring her to the gurney.

Ethan gets up, and Liz tries to as well, but she's shaky from squatting so long. Ethan encircles her with his arms and pulls her to her feet. Liz rotates one ankle and flexes her knee, to restore circulation, then the other. She leans back into Ethan, and they watch the gurney being carried out.

54 . . .

The **'Untrue'** lyrics are like a knife slicing pieces off his heart, Eric thinks as he listens to the song on the CD player in the common room. It might have been written expressly for Elsie. God, that Amelia can sure pick depressing songs. He thinks he might counter with

Queen's '**Somebody To Love**', but then he decides against it. That might be too cruel.

In the kitchen, the air heats up and the popcorn kernels begin to rattle, then explode one by one. Amelia tucks a bowl under the outlet to catch the popped corn shooting out. Eric tries not to let the '**Untrue**' lyrics get to him. The butter is exploding so he shuts off the microwave before it can beep.

Eric says, "So we listen to depressing music."

Amelia nods. "Yup. I pick, you pick. Having fun yet?"

Eric wonders, is it just this song, or will every break up song rip out his heart out now?

It's starting to get to him but Amelia's popcorn machine is going nuts. The popping is picking up and shooting popped corn kernels into the bowl with such force they are bouncing out, landing on the counter or the floor.

Eric and Amelia scramble to catch errant popcorn, with little luck. The comedy inherent in being pelted with flying popcorn removes some of the sting from lyrics that are just a touch too close to home. The laughter they're sharing isn't exactly something he expected from Amelia's description of a 'depression party'.

Finally the corn is all popped so Amelia pulls the plug. "That was an exercise in stupidity."

"I have to tell you, your popper's design kind of sucks." he says as he opens the broom closet and pulls out the whisk broom to sweep the mess from the floor.

"Only kind of? Try massive fail. This is the first time I've used it. But my mom didn't think I would actually go off to college again without one, so she bought me this hunk of junk new."

Eric asks, "Popcorn junkie?"

"Oh yeah, the worst."

"Me too." He dumps the dustpan contents in the trash. "Do we decide what movies the same way, you pick I pick?"

"Yeah, and the best part is we can whine about our love lives as much as we want."

Eric cocks an eyebrow, "You know all about mine, but I am at a disadvantage since I have no idea what your problem is."

Sighing, Amelia says, "Just the usual, unrequited love. He doesn't know I exist." She opens the cupboard and she gathers up a half dozen spice bottles-- popcorn toppings.

"This is for the popcorn?" he asks in surprise.

Amelia drizzles melted margarine over the popcorn. "We can do this one of two ways. Pick one flavor. Or if you're boring we could just sprinkle it with the salt. But the other way we can go is to dump a bit of each topping into these Chinese tea cups and then dip as desired. Kind of like popcorn dim sum."

Eric laughs. "Popcorn dim sum. I love it." As they pour toppings into the little cups, Eric says, "Tell you what-- next time we do scratch toppings."

"Oooh. A connoisseur!" Amelia laughs, "Looks like I've uncovered another popcorn junkie."

Eric stacks the desert bowls and carries them in to the common room. He sets them out in a semicircle on the coffee table by the sectional sofa.

As the song fades down he crosses to the equipment stack and opens the DVD player, popping in a disk while Amelia opens the wine. She carries it out and sets the bottle beside the wine glasses and the popcorn, then flops down on half of the sectional. Eric flips through his CDs, selecting one before returning the **Tim Louis** CD to its case so he can put on his own choice, one guaranteed to rip her heart out. Time to get depressing.

"What've you got?" she asks.

"An oldie but goodie."

Amelia begins to eat popcorn but it's not long before she's captivated by the lyrics of the song '**Loneliness**', and stops eating, her hand poised above the bowl, staring up into nothingness as she listens to the words.

"Oh, this is good." Amelia closes her eyes to feel the music.

Eric drops onto the adjacent sectional section.

"Told you." But when he looks over at Amelia he is suddenly uncomfortable. There are actual tears trickling out of Amelia's closed eyes. He wants to pat her shoulder or something. Watching Amelia's tears flow as the words about hopelessness and the darkness in your heart pour out of the speakers, Eric wishes he'd chosen something else.

Finally unable to stand it, Eric asks, "You Okay?"

Amelia sits up and shushes him and they sit in

silence as the song plays out.

As the last note fades he says, "I'm so sorry I should have picked something else, I didn't mean to."

"No, that was perfect." She brushes her eyes with her sleeve and says, "You did good. That's the point!"

"What? I didn't mean to make you cry."

"Shut up and hand me a tissue." Eric passes the box.

Amelia grabs a wad and blows her nose. He watches as she scrubs at her blotchy face and mops her eyes, then gives him an unexpected smile through her tears. "You surprised, me that's all, Eric. Guys aren't supposed to know about the really good depressing shit like this."

"But I thought that's what you wanted?"

"God, it was perfect. Whining about people we love, crying our eyes out, maybe interspersed with a bit of hysterical giggling-- THAT's what a depression party is for, it's cathartic. You're an English major, you know what cathartic means right?"

"Yes, I know what cathartic means."

Munching on popcorn Amelia asks, "Who's the singer?"

"Annie Lennox. She writes awesome lyrics. Hang on." Eric jumps up and gets his PDA out of the CD box, passes it to her so she can read the words of the song they just heard.

"You've got all your favourite the lyrics on this?"

"Not all, but a lot. There are tons of lyrics online."

"Huh. I didn't know that. I can't tell you how many times I've sat there stopping and starting a CD to get down all the words to a song I love. I mean look at this, they're brilliant."

"Yeah, powerful imagery. Sometimes I toy with the idea of writing song lyrics, 'cause lyrics are like the poetry of today."

"I never thought about it before but that makes sense. Poetry used to be huge but it sure doesn't come across as being cool nowadays."

"Guys can't admit we read or write poetry, but writing songs is acceptable. Only thing is, I'm not very musical."

"If you're good at picking songs with great lyrics, you might be good at writing them."

"Thanks, I think I'd like that. So what do you think, isn't it time? I think so."

"Time for the first movie?"

"No, time to tell me why you are depressed."

"But you've got a movie ready to go."

"And it'll stay ready. I'm not letting you off so easily. What's getting you down?"

"It's just the usual. Unrequited love shit."

"Maybe you could get it requited?"

"Don't be such a man."

"What do you mean?"

"Trying to solve my problems. That's a man thing."

Eric says, "What I can possibly say to that? I hate to have to tell you this, but I am. A man, I mean." His words just hang in the air for a minute.

Amelia nods. "Uh, I will admit that I have noticed

you are in fact a man. Thing is, what I'm really looking for is a friend." Amelia sees the frustration written on his face and tries again, "Look I'm not trying to drive you nuts, really. It's just, how do I explain a depression party? It's about sharing feelings. We're not trying to fix them, just to process the feelings and let them out."

Eric says, "Wallowing, you mean."

"Yes! Exactly. Except it sounds better when you call it catharsis. The thing is, it It helps make it easier to cope with all the crap. That's why blubbering is good, though you don't seem comfortable with that part."

Eric says, "That would be a man thing."

"I'm not trying to--"

"Yes you are, but it's fine. I have an older sister. And she never actually talked to me about anything. The only time I ever saw her cry was when I think she'd just been dumped."

"Oh, that's so sad."

Eric holds up a finger. "Just let me finish, Okay?" Amelia nods so he continues, "I heard her crying in her room. So, you have to understand, the rule was I wasn't supposed to go in without permission but she was crying, and so I went in to give her a hug. But she threw her radio at my head, but I ducked and it hit the wall and smashed into a million pieces, which was apparently my fault too. My allowance was docked for months to pay for the new one."

"But that's not fair."

"Yeah, well she told our folks that I broke it, and I didn't realize until years later that it really wasn't my fault. I mean, I made her mad, right?"

"How old were you?"

"First or second grade, I think. What's that, six or seven or something? Guess I still don't know how to deal with girls." Seeing Amelia start to open her mouth he self corrects. "Women. You know I don't do so well in the girlfriend department."

"Oh, Eric, no one's keeping score. It's just, well, you can't 'fix' feelings. You just have to live through them. And besides, your sister sounds like a bitch."

"You got that right." Eric grins. "So. What do I do to help?"

"Just listen, it works wonders." She looks over with brows raised and he shrugs and then nods. Amelia takes a deep breath, then says, "Okay. I'll tell you. The guy wouldn't know who I was if he tripped over me. But for some stupid reason, well, I just fell hard for him. I mean, he's not even really that bright, which is unusual for me. Usually I get all hung up on brilliant geeky guys who don't know I'm alive."

"But not this time?"

"No this time I'm just hung up on a drop dead gorgeous guy who doesn't know I'm alive."

"I can see where that might be a problem. So," he glances over at her, "I'm not allowed to ask why you don't ask him out?"

Amelia giggles. "Am I that bossy?"

Eric nods, "Understatement."

Amelia laughs. "It isn't gonna work that way. If we're gonna be friends I guess I can't give you a hard time for being a guy. Do-over. You can do or say whatever you want to do or say."

"Gee thanks."

"Da nada."

"So why don't you just ask the guy out?"

"He's carrying a torch for someone else, and it is huge, his torch, I mean. Me, well, I've got a crush. Unrequited, the oldest snub in the book. A couple of depression parties and I'll be over him. But he doesn't even see anyone except her. And I'm hung up on the guy knowing that. I mean how pathetic is that?"

"I'll grab the chocolate and we can watch a movie."

"Chocolate? You know about chocolate?"

"Oh yeah, you need chocolate at a depression party. Gotta keep those endorphins flowing."

55 · · ·

Jose sits across from Mouse at a table by the jukebox. "What I don't understand, I mean, she likes me, she came onto me. So it's not that I'm repulsive to her or anything."

Mouse laughs and reaches out to touch his cheek.

"Poor boy. Of course she likes you, Jose, you're beautiful. But you are only an English major. Maybe you will be a teacher, yes? A good life, but Barbie expects more than an ordinary life."

"That sucks, Mouse." Jose sips his beer pensively.

"Maybe, but I think that has always been how the

world works. Used to be the man would always pick, but now the woman gets to pick too."

"So who do you pick, Mouse?"

She laughs. "I'm too young, I just want to have fun. Later. Maybe. Perhaps I will be a famous writer like Erica Jong first yes?"

"Maybe I'll become a famous writer too. Win the Booker Prize, maybe even a Pulitzer."

"You must be American to get that one."

"Okay. The Nobel then."

Mouse laughs "That's the spirit. Maybe then she will regret. But Barbie wants to go places now. She doesn't want to wait, has never had to because her beauty opens doors. She wants her power to find a star or a millionaire."

"That lets me out." Jose thumps his empty glass down and nibbles on peanuts from the bowl.

"Just relax and try to have some fun, Jose."

"I guess." Jose nods at the bar. "Hey, isn't that Boris?"

Mouse says, "Boris has even worse trouble than you."

§

Boris sits at the bar, staring morosely into his glass of beer. He's depressed, not just because he's been rejected by the girl he loves, or even that he's been so publicly humiliated. What bothers him the most, the thing that has shaken his self image is that until now he had never realized that he was such a loser.

He always thought girls liked him. That at least he

was okay, they at least didn't think he was repulsive. But maybe all these years when girls smiled at him they were really laughing at him. And he was too stupid to realize. Big dumb jock.

A couple of girls at the end of the bar are pointing and whispering. He knows they're looking at his black eye. Eyes. Leave it to Natasha to give him *two*. Hadda catch him in the sweet spot at the bridge of his nose. Feeling his jaw clench, Boris tracks the whispering girls in his peripheral vision.

Classic A- type personality, Natasha. She can't just tell him to take a hike like any normal girl. No, she's gotta make a laughing stock of him. Give him a double shiner, decking him in front of the whole world. Which has of course put him smack-dab in the middle of the kind of story that makes the rounds so often that even the people who weren't there tell it as though they were.

The kind of story that will never die.

Ever.

They'll probably be telling it decades from now. But in the here and now his whole university career will be a living hell.

And for what, because he likes her?

Because he's just another poor sap who wants to be more than friends? God. Every other girl in the world bitches about guys not wanting commitment. Not Natasha. She'd as soon knock you down as look at you.

They could've at least stayed friends if it wasn't for that stupid spectacle, but now? Just thinking of the flashing light in her eyes just before she knocked him down makes him seethe.

Why couldn't she have given him a chance?

Bitch.

Downing the rest of the beer he catches Billie the bartender's eye, points at his empty. She nods and pulls him a fresh draught. Watching her set it in front of him with a smile, he realizes morosely Billie probably knows the whole story too.

It's bad enough being humiliated by one woman but two in the same day? Hell, Elsie sleeps with everybody, but nooo, not him. Not Boris the loser. Even Elsie the easy is too good for him.

Bitch.

Drinking more beer he asks himself, not for the first time, how could he live this long and not have known he was a loser? Talk about living in denial.

Maybe denial is a loser survival trait. If you don't know you're a loser you don't jump out a window or slit your wrists. If you don't think you're a loser you can get out of bed in the morning and face the day. If you haven't realized you're a loser you can get on with your life, take your pictures, soak up some rays, pump a little iron, go out for a drink with your pal.

Except his pal Natasha decked him and in the process told him and everyone else what a loser he is.

What a fool, thinking you could be friends with a girl. Yeah.

The girls are giggling now, and he glowers over at them.

He can feel the giant "L" Natasha left imprinted in

the middle of his forehead.

One of the girls looks guiltily away, the other meets his eyes defiantly. She smiles, then suddenly blushes a deep crimson. Hmm, maybe she's... flirting? She holds his gaze. Nah. Probably just fucking with his head, a popular pastime. Make this a new civic holiday, call it "Screw With Boris Day."

He turns his attention to his beer and drinks more, watching bubbles float up without caring what causes them. Women. The cause of all the problems in the world. Maybe there is something in that Garden of Eden stuff Papa was always going on about.

He'd always just chalked it up to the fact that Mama left. Ran off with that Russian artist. Maybe Papa was right.

Boris knows he had been ready to fly in the face of family, not just any family, his family, to defend her. Even knowing they would never accept any girl who wasn't Croatian.

He would have faced them for her.

And of all the non-Croatian girls in the world to bring home, the absolute worst would be a Russian girl. It might even get him disowned. But he'd have done it for Natasha. Stood up for her. Because he loves her, damn it. And what does she do? She hits him. Disrespects him like that. Papa says women are the root of all...

Boris freezes as he feels a gentle touch on his arm. His peripheral vision tells him that there's only one girl left at the end of the bar.

Great, they aren't happy with tormenting him from afar. He turns to look at her. She looks nervous. Good. He gives her his best death metal glower.

What can she possibly want from him?

"Hi." she smiles. "I'm Sarah. Would it be okay if I joined you?" Boris continues glowering but she just smiles again, nervously, and slides onto the stool. "You're Boris, right?"

Boris just stares at her blackly. She glances away, then beckons the bartender over.

Sipping his beer, Boris waits for the punchline. He can see it now, she's gonna order a Black Russian.

Because all the ignoramuses here at Christie think it's a certainty that he's a Russian because of his name. These university assholes are mostly too stupid to even know there's a difference.

Billie the bartender comes over, "Help ya?"

The girl nods. "Tequila Sunrise please."

Billie pours a shot of tequila into a glass, douses it with O.J. and deftly splashes grenadine over the top, then sets it on a cocktail napkin in front of the girl.

"And another for him." the girl is rooting in her purse for some money, which she passes across the bar as the fresh draught arrives.

Boris watches as the grenadine sinks to the bottom of her glass, glancing from glass to girl. Trying to find the joke, the put down. This is some hot babe, slinky as all get out. She's a lot softer looking than Natasha, is, that's for sure. Boris is still wondering what the punch line is.

Laurel L Russwurm

The bartender slaps the change on the counter before moving off to the other end of the bar, and the girl just leaves the coins lay, sipping at her drink. She sure is pretty. Not a tom-boy like Natasha, this girl is wearing a dress, even. Gold chain around her neck, hanging down and disappearing in her cleavage.

She looks over the rim of the highball glass, smiling mysteriously. She licks her lips and suddenly Boris is having a hard time catching his breath. This is like a classic femme fatale pick up scene straight out of film noir. This can't possibly be happening. Not to him.

God this is making him horny.

A quick glance down the bar tells him that the friend has gone. Hmmm. Boris feels a light touch along his calf, and he glances down, startled. Sarah's allowed her ridiculous red shoes --Natasha would never be caught dead in such absurd footwear-- to slide off her feet, and the naked toes of one foot are curled around the stool's lower crossbar, the other languorously rubs the inside of his leg.

Boris smiles, the black Slavic mood abruptly gone. This girl is not only buying him drinks, she is coming on to him. If it's a joke, he's willing to take it like a man. He looks over at her face, she's watching him through veiled lashes, breathing shallowly.

Nervous, but not stopping. Mmmm.

Boris is feeling less like a loser and more like a lion as he slides the empty glass away, and picks up the glass of draught beer she bought him. He leans over to clink glasses with her. Sarah. She smiles, takes a sip, licks her lips. Boris smiles back.

"Maybe we'd be a little more comfortable in a booth? Quieter anyway." he suggests.

"I think the one at the back is empty." she replies. Then wiggles her toes. "Maybe you could get my shoes?"

Sliding off the stool, Boris drops into a squat and picks up the first shoe. The sharp edges and pointy bits on these things look painful. She extends her foot, pointing her toe, and he slides the shoe on. His smile widens. This is kinda sexy.

Boris picks up the second shoe and lifts it toward her foot but she snakes it around and down to run those toes across his groin. Oh boy.

Boris grabs the foot and slides the shoe over it, before awkwardly rising to his feet. He looks into the girl's eyes, and they are smouldering. Oh.

She reaches out and rests her hands on his shoulders then slides off the stool, brushing against him all the way down. Then she turns and starts down to the aisle to the back booth.

Watching her walk Boris understands the point of those damned shoes. Swaying hips. Boris' breath catches again.

Oh my.

Natasha never swayed quite like that. Boris tears his eyes away from the sultry undulation just long enough to grab their glasses off the bar so he can follow her.

Maybe girls do like him.

56 . . .

Amelia weeps openly as the fireflies rise above the funeral pyre. The odd snuffle undermines Eric's attempts to maintain an image of stoicism.

"That was depressing all right." Amelia blows her nose as the credits roll. "But it was the wrong kind of depressing."

"Wait a minute, wait just one minute-- what do you mean the wrong kind of depressing! You never said anything about there being different types of depressing."

"Uh no, but I figured any guy who could come up with that Loneliness song would understand we're talking love-lorn depression here. You know, star crossed lovers, like that. What my mom would call a tear jerker, and my dad would call mush."

"Sorry, next time put on a qualifier. I guess this means it's your turn?"

"Sure is, and I've got just the thing." Amelia says, as she puts **City of Angels** in the machine.

Eric says, "You still haven't told me who the guy is.

"Guy?" Amelia asks innocently. "What guy?"

"Your guy."

"Oh, he's not my guy. If he was my guy would I be here with you?" She laughs.

"Amelia?"

"What?"

"Why didn't anybody tell me Elsie was fucking every guy she clapped eyes on?"

"Well." Amelia clears her throat. He's watching her expectantly, so she can't dodge it outright. "Not every guy."

Holding up his hands, Eric says, "Stop. I don't want to know, really." He slumps back in his corner of the sofa. "Just now that it's too late everybody's happy to fill me in on the gory details."

"I haven't."

"Huh. No. You haven't. Why haven't you?"

"Would it help?"

"No."

"And you might get back together with her."

"No way. No how. Never."

"Really?"

He meets her eye. "Maybe. But why didn't anybody tell me then?"

"Would you have listened?"

"Probably not. But I feel seriously stupid now. But even so I miss her. I'll be laying in my room, all by myself and then suddenly I can smell her. Instant hard on." Eric claps his hand over his mouth. "Sorry, I mean..."

"Bodily functions happen to the best of us." Amelia grins. "But I know what you mean, and they say scent memory is the worst. Maybe wash your sheets, any clothes she wore, like that."

"That's a good idea. But it's so weird to be discussing this..."

Laurel L Russwurm

"With a girl?" Amelia laughs. "So tell me, what guy can you discuss this with?"

"Uh. I guess there isn't one. Jose would be closest, but really, we're just drinking buddies. I haven't really discussed her with him. I hooked up with Elsie in the first week and, well. I guess there wasn't time for anybody except school and Elsie. Once in a while I'd maybe have a beer with the guys after class. Mostly I haven't really been available to be friends with anyone." He smiles over at her. "Until now."

"Maybe that's part of why nobody told you. Acquaintances aren't usually willing to go out on a limb for you. It's a big risk telling anyone they're being stepped out on. Messengers do get shot you know."

"Yeah, I guess. And in a lot of ways I'm still hung up on her, and sometimes I think if she just looked at me the right way, well maybe I would go back to her.

"Really?"

"Well. Maybe. I can't get her out of my head."

"Just take it easy, that's all. Try to give it time."

"Are you attracted to me?"

"Um." Amelia purses her lips. "Maybe I shouldn't answer."

"Aw hell, Amelia, I'm not 'the guy' am I? I mean, I like you a lot, but I'm not remotely attracted to you.

"Oh that's a relief." Amelia bursts out laughing.

Eric frowns. "What?"

"I was worried you were eyeing me up for a rebound. I like you as a friend, and you're not bad looking, and you are the kind of guy I ought to be attracted to. But I'm just not. Sorry."

"So why wouldn't you just say that before?"

"Because I figured you've had your heart stomped pretty good, I didn't want to stomp it more. But I do like you and I'd be honoured to be your friend. Just not your squeeze."

Eric snorts. "Squeeze, who says squeeze?"

"If we're gonna hang around together you better know up front that after Asimov my favourite author is Dash Hammett. I love anything noir but Dash is the man. So sometimes words like 'squeeze' and 'gunsel' just pop right out in my conversation."

Eric looks at her and bursts out laughing.

"What's so funny about that?"

"That's great. You talk like a Bogart character and we aren't romantically attracted to each other. Great."

"Does that mean we can be friends?"

"Sure. But only on one condition. You have to tell me who the guy is."

Amelia glances around, making sure no one is lurking, listening. She puts in the DVD and comes back to sit beside Eric. Leaning close she whispers in his ear, "Jose."

"Jose? You're talking about Jose? You think Jose is a hunk?"

"Shhh!"

"But he's, he's, ordinary. He doesn't even have muscles or anything. Even I probably have a better body than he does."

"Most girls aren't into the muscle man thing. That's more a guy thing, to want to look like that, part of the whole alpha male deal. Not to say we don't want a guy to have a good body, but that's not the most important thing. But Jose's body is pretty good."

He looks at her in surprise. "Why on earth would you like Jose? I mean he's a nice guy and all, but he's... you're really smart and, how do I say this... He doesn't have two brain cells to rub together."

"It isn't his brains that get me hot."

"Uh. This is a weird thing to be discussing with a girl."

"Look, I have brothers so I doubt you could shock me."

"Well I have a sister and you sure as shit can shock me."

"Sorry."

"No, don't be. This is interesting. What do you see in Jose?"

"He may not be Einstein, but he's not as dim as you think, he just keeps stuff inside."

"You think so?" Eric asks thoughtfully.

"Yeah. There's a lot going on behind his eyes. You know, the strong silent type. He may be sacrificing more brain cells than he can afford smoking up, but he has a few. That's not the point."

"But what is the point then? I don't get it."

"Because you're a straight guy, Eric." She closes her eyes a moment. "I think he exudes pheromones. And of course it doesn't hurt he's got great buns. What can I say, there's something about the guy that makes me want to rip off his clothes. Maybe it's his bedroom eyes. They are just so deep. And he's got great eyelashes too, and yummy lips, you know. Kissable.

"Stop... no more. This is farther than I really wanna go here, okay? Jose is a friend, we eat lunch together and stuff. I really don't need this picture in my head."

"The only girl he even looks at is that Barbie bimbo."

"Well."

"Ahhh. I get it. You think she's hot too."

"Well, duh. I am a straight male."

"Uh huh. One that doesn't find me at all alluring."

"Uh... well Barbie's got..."

"Hooters. I get it Eric."

"Not that I'd want to go there."

"Because of Jose?"

"Yes. No. I don't know."

"The girl is drop dead gorgeous."

"Sure, and she'd be fine in a wet dream but I just can't see having a conversation with her."

Amelia smiles. "I kind of feel sorry for her."

"I thought girls were supposed to instinctively hate classic golden girls. You did call her a bimbo.."

"I admit I'd be happier if Jose wasn't hung up on her. But that's another urban myth. Beyond the odd loner like Elsie, women hang together. Sisterhood wasn't invented in the 60's. Historically women looked out for each other and built the community while the hunters wandered around hoping for something to kill."

"So why do you feel sorry for her?"

"It's that intelligence thing. I think she was bright once but hasn't actually had to use her brain in so long she's forgotten how. It's easier to let everyone do for you than to do it yourself."

"She seems to enjoy it."

"I'd expect it seems fun at first, like getting something for nothing. But for me it'd get old awfully fast. There's a rush you get from doing it yourself. First time I had a poem published in the paper I was eleven. It was cool, but it wouldn't have been as good if somebody else had helped me, or heaven forbid, written it for me."

57 · · ·

Nick comes in and grins at the sight of the computer club members glued to the television. He can't believe it. They aren't even watching streaming video, they're watching regular cable TV.

Some computer geeks.

He crosses over to sit with Kate.

The others keep watching the program, but Nick and Kate cuddle with their heads together, talking quietly.

"How was your night class?"

"Not too bad, most of the kids are coming along nicely. Only a couple in doubt at this point. One in serious doubt."

"Uh oh, what did she do this time?"

"They were supposed to be writing up their dissection notes because he's going to be marking them this weekend."

"Who's going to be marking them?"

"Shhh. Yes, it will be grunt work. You know how it goes."

"Yeah, I do. So tell me, what did she do?"

"She hadn't actually bothered to do a dissection."

"You're kidding. Why not?"

"Tamara missed it too, but she came in and made it up."

"After one of your famous chats?"

"Hey, I just gave her a bit of brotherly advice."

"Tamara's shaping up so it's just Barbie in the doo doo?"

Adam hears Barbie's name, realizing with an uncomfortable shock that Nick is talking about 'his' Barbie.

Although he continues to face the television set, Adam's real attention focuses on the quiet discussion on the sofa.

"You know, I did offer her some re-scheduling choices but she never showed," Nick continues. "That's it. So I didn't expect her to show up tonight. I mean, what's she going to write? She didn't do the procedure, game over. But she's making notes during the Q and A, sitting by Tamara. It's nuts to crib from Tamara because she's barely hanging on. I couldn't believe Barbie's... audacity."

"Not trying at all?"

"She doesn't think rules apply to her. There always has to be a special dispensation, just for her. She was trying to catch up, not by applying herself but by slapping together info she's picked up from the others. That's what she wants to hand in."

"That's crazy. How can she hand in notes on a procedure she hasn't done?"

"I don't know where her head is, but it's a class, so I'm not gonna talk to her until after, right? Anyway we're done the review and class breaks up so most of them are heading out. All except Barbie. Tamara looked like she was gonna wait too, but Barbie waved her out."

"I almost feel sorry for her."

"How can you say that?"

"It's not hard. You have to realize honey, it's because she's so pretty. People have probably been giving her things and doing for her her whole life. That's just how her world works. This is probably the first time anyone has expected her to actually do the work. I don't get why she just doesn't go to Hollywood or something."

"Probably because the serious competition there would be on her looks. Katie, you are so forgiving. Wait til you hear the rest before giving her a free pass babe. I'm gathering up my stuff and loading everything on the cart, when all of a sudden I can just tell she's coming up behind me."

"Like Freddie Kruger, right."

"Shhh... everyone's watching **House**."

"So what happened next?"

"You've seen her, she simpers, you know, in that gushy helpless voice that makes me want to smack her upside the head. She goes, 'Oh, hi Nick, what a great class, I learned so much. Can we talk?' so I told her, 'but you know I'm only a TA.' "

"Oh that's great, hon. What'd she say to that?"

"She asked me to help her write up her dissection notes."

"The girl has chutzpah."

Nick shakes his head. "I tried to explain that you have to actually do the dissection to be able to write it up but she doesn't listen, she's telling me about the troubles she has, organizing her schedule."

"You know she spends half her life in the woods smoking up with Jose and that crowd, right?" Kate says softly.

"Of course I know, I can smell it on her whenever I see her after she's cut class. But she can't submit dissection notes without having done the dissection. I mean what's she thinking? So I asked her if she's plans to con other doctors into doing her work for her after she gets her MD? I don't think so."

"Oh, sweetie. She threaten to go over your head again?"

"No, this time she burst into tears and ran out."

"Aw, poor thing. What did you do, follow and

apologize?"

"Hardly. I finished packing up. It's late, I'm done, I'm wheeling the cart up the aisle and the door opens."

"She came back after the big dramatic exit?"

"Hey, what else was she gonna do? I didn't follow her. She had to try some other kind of scam."

"Uh oh, I'm getting the idea here. What was the scam?"

"I've shut off most of the lights, so she's back lit, in a halo of light, so it's impossible to miss the shape on the girl."

"Oh, poor you, forced to admire perfectly formed nubile college girls."

"She gives it the old college try, 'Please Nick, you could help if you wanted to'. So I asked if she can't keep up now when it's beginner stuff, how she's gonna get by when things get difficult?"

"She lets the door swing closed and she comes in and I realize it isn't just fluffier hair. She's unbuttoned her blouse and it was, uh, painfully obvious that she'd taken off her bra."

"Sounds like it got your attention."

"Wait for it, I haven't got to the best part. She brushes up against me and tells me I look tired and we could help each other out. Only now she's talking in a breathy 'Marilyn' kind of voice."

"Not your type?"

"You know better than that, darlin'. Here's me trying to push the cart away and she's licking her lips and trying to do that slutty girl pout. It was actually kind of funny."

"Not as slinky as Thirteen?"

Nick nods at the actress on screen. "Not a prayer."

"No sale, huh?"

"You know better than that. So I tell her, 'Look that might have worked in high school, but it will not fly here. You need to think seriously about changing majors because the only way to get an MD is to earn it and the only way to earn it is to work for it.' Then she starts buttoning her cleavage back up and pfffft, 'Marilyn' has been replaced by the Snow Queen."

The end credit percussion signals the end of the House episode.

Nick glances up and sees that the computer club has dropped all pretence of watching TV in favour of his story.

"That really happened?" Jake asks.

"Sadly, yes."

Holding up his hands, "Look guys, I'd appreciate it if what I've said to Kate doesn't go any further. It's, er, privileged TA stuff. I didn't realize I was telling everyone."

"Don't worry about it, we'll never tell," smiles Krystal.

Oscar says, "Your soap opera was better than the one on **House**."

Adam's ordinarily well ordered mind reels chaotically. He needs to get somewhere quiet and think this through. Perhaps the pedestal he has Barbie on is not after all appropriate.

58 . . .

Cigarette smoke, perfume and alcohol waft off Boris as he stumbles through the common room on the way to bed but he's irritated by a nearly subliminal humming noise.

He thinks for a moment, blearily trying to recall which way he needs to go to find his bed. He shakes his head, but the annoying hum doesn't go away. Then he realizes some idiot hasn't switched the TV off.

Boris is stumbling over to the large screen TV when he bumps the corner of the blue sectional. A snore gets his attention, and he looks down to see Eric and Amelia curled up together, popcorn debris and chocolate wrappers scattered all around.

Boris is happy for Eric. About time he got over Elsie.

Grabbing the afghan from the red sofa, Boris brings it back to carefully drape over the sleepers. Then he switches the TV set off and creeps down the hall to his bedroom.

59 . . .

The transition to morning goes unnoticed by Val Thompson, Christie's Night Security Chief. He leans against the wall inside the waiting room doorway, radiating tension, unhappy to have a student attack on his watch.

Bad for business. Bad for the school. Having law enforcement wannabes like Connor as the rule rather than the exception doesn't help. More retired cops like Vlad would be best.

Quentin paces in the waiting room, Jake sits stiffly on one of the hard plastic chairs. Liz shelters under Ethan's arm with a kind of vacant look in her eyes.

Elsie pushes her way past Val and takes a position in the centre of the room so she can address the student contingent. "Natasha's still unconscious but all her vital signs are good. The doctor thinks she'll probably be fine. But they won't know for sure until she wakes up."

"There was so much blood," says Jake, "I was afraid that she might be, I thought she was... dead."

"Scalp wounds bleed. The doctor said the blow to her head wasn't so bad. They were worried about exposure, she was in the cold so long, but she's warmed up, so that's good."

Liz looks up at Elsie and asks, "Was it, was she...?

Elsie nods, "Yes, she was raped. But she's alive. It's looking pretty good for her. If she'd been out there all night before anybody even looked for her, it might be a lot different."

Liz nods miserably and Ethan hugs her more tightly.

"There is some brain swelling, so they're considering inducing a coma if she starts waking up too soon."

Ethan says, "That doesn't sound too good Else."

"It's precautionary, to prevent brain damage. Anyway, the cops are talking to the doc, but they want to talk to us all before we go home."

Quentin raises his hand, "Uh, can I go first? I haven't been able to get through to my wife, she's gonna be steamed."

Val nods. "I don't see why not."

The door opens and a couple of uniformed officers come in. Val asks if they'll speak to Quentin first. The officer nods and Quentin follows them out into the hall.

They all cram into a small office barely big enough to house a desk and three chairs. The younger officer says, "I'm P.C. McKay. Maybe you can tell me how you came to be involved in the search tonight Mr. Bradbury?"

Back in the waiting room Elsie puts some change in the drinks machine and pulls out a bottle of Gatorade.

Jake tells Val, "I've never been interviewed by cops."

"You'll be fine." Val says. "Just answer their questions."

Jake shrugs, "You know, what happened to Natasha was horrible, but in a sick way it's kind of exciting too."

"That's normal." smiles Val. "Look, can you and your friend come by security tomorrow? Today. I'd like to get your statements about Connor."

"That guy's a real creep."

"True. But I can't fire him for being a creep. That's why I need your statements about what happened tonight. The smart guys come to Christie for an education, so we're left with a pretty shallow gene pool for guards. Still, I'd rather be short handed than keep Connor. So your help would be appreciated."

"Oh sure. And I think Q will be happy to help too."

"Thanks." says Val.

Jake nods, and goes back to sit with Ethan and Liz. Val keeps his position by the door, and Elsie offers him a sip of her Gatorade.

Across the room, Ethan watches the way Elsie extends the bottle cautiously to the big man, almost like she's afraid she's gonna get bitten. Ethan wishes he had his camera since the combination of the gritty institutional room under fluorescents would make an excellent backdrop to the picture they cast, kind of a beauty and the beast motif, with the guard's bloated bodybuilder physique angled against Elsie's delicate beauty. Still, Ethan has a pretty good idea which one is the beast.

"Do you think they'll let us see Natasha?" Jake asks.

"Maybe tomorrow. I hope she'll be OK."

Ethan says "She'll be okay. She's got good friends."

"Oh God," Liz's eyes are wide, "Nobody told Boris."

"Nobody told anybody."

"But Boris, he'll be devastated."

Ethan and Jake exchange looks. It has occurred to both of them that Boris may very well be the prime suspect.

Over by the door, Val hands the bottle back to Elsie.

"So how've you been." she asks.

Val answers guardedly, "Good."

"Still married?"

"Very happily. Best thing that ever happened to me."

"Too bad."

"I'm happy, Else."

Elsie's eyes flash as she says, "You shouldn't be happy damn it. You should be a doctor." She stops abruptly, knowing she's spoken with more heat than intended, then glances over at the others, gratified to see that they're in their own world.

"It's over, Elsie. Just let it lay."

Under icy control Elsie says, "Whatever."

Val looks at her sharply, "Are you happy?"

"Yes, thank you, I'm ecstatic. Rapturous even."

Val smiles. "I worry about you sometimes still."

"Oh don't. You wouldn't believe how very many talented men there are in the world. I'm having the time of my life, dear."

"I'd be happy to hear you're happy, Else."

"I'm happy one of us will have our dream come true."

Val shakes his head, "It wasn't ever my dream, babe. I just went along because you wanted it so much."

"Is that what you tell yourself?"

"That's what's true. I know you never really listened to me, but I tried to tell you that for a long time."

The younger police officer sticks his head in to the

waiting room. "Who's next?" he asks. Jake stands up with alacrity, and the officer nods, so Jake follows him down the hall to a small office adjacent to the nurse's station.

The uniformed cop's deferential posture makes it clear the guy in plain clothes seated behind the desk is the top dog. Jake assumes he's a detective. The uniformed cop takes the seat by the wall and flips open the netbook perched on the corner of the desk.

The plainclothes cop stands, extends a hand to Jake and says, "I'm Detective Wolfrom, this is P.C. McKay. And you are?"

"Jake Ellis." Gingerly shaking Wolfrom's hand, Jake is relieved his hand is only a little crushed when the detective releases it. Wolfram gestures toward the chair and they sit.

Wolfrom asks "So, you were one of the searchers tonight, is that right?" The uniformed officer quietly transcribes the interview, typing everything into the small computer.

Jake says, "Yeah. Liz was worried because Natasha didn't show up at the car show."

"Lets try and keep it to what you know directly, okay? What you yourself saw, heard and did."

Jake nods. "You mean Liz asked me to help find Natasha?"

Wolfrom nods. "Right, knowledge you know yourself, not what you've heard, or inferred. How did that happen?"

"Okay, I guess it was around four thirty or so, and I

was looking to see if anybody wanted to come to the computer club meeting when I ran into Liz."

"And where was this?"

"In the library. Liz was looking for Natasha, and she was mad because Natasha didn't come to the car show. Which was weird because it was her idea, Natasha's I mean."

"That's the Antique Car Show at the Waterfront Mall?"

"That's right. Natasha never showed up. Liz said she couldn't get Natasha on her cell either. So Liz was mad at Natasha, but she didn't know about the fight."

Wolfrom frowns. "Fight?"

"Yeah, I didn't see it though so maybe."

Wolfrom shakes his head, "No, no, it's okay, it can provide the background. Tell me about the fight."

"Well, Boris and Natasha had a big fight at lunch, and she took a swing at him."

Wolfrom fixes Jake with a look. "Son, this isn't a game."

Jake frowns, then he gets it. "Oh, the names. It's their real names, Boris Horvat and Natasha Panov. they're both photography majors."

Mollified, Wolfrom nods. "Oh. Alright, then." Glancing down at his notebook, he asks, "How did you get involved the search?"

"When Liz got back she was looking for Natasha, so I helped ask around but nobody'd seen Natasha since the fight. That's when Liz got worried, so she rounded us up and got us out looking, and then, well, we found her."

Wolfrom nods. "What was the fight about?"

Jake shrugs. "They say Natasha knocked him down."

"How did you know where to look for her?"

"After the fight people said she took off into the woods. But there were conflicting stories as to which path she took."

"Where were you this afternoon?"

"A lecture after lunch, then I was taking pictures."

"Where?"

"Here in the hospital. The nursery. My prof recommended me." Jake frowns. "Wait a minute, you mean I'm a suspect?"

"Every male anywhere near this campus is a suspect."

60 . . .

Jake and Elsie stumble companionably into the residence. She's far too drained to give him a hard time, and he's much too tired to care.

"Goodnight Elsie. Thanks." says Jake, surprised at how much he really means it, as he heads down the hall.

Elsie nods and is crossing through the common room toward the interior stairs when she notices the sectional is occupied. She's started up the stairs when she realizes that it's Eric's unmistakable profile against the blue cushions. He's snoring a little, and some one's draped the afghan over him.

Hmm, she smiles, thinking, he's been waiting up for her. That's a rush. Tired or not, she decides she might like to enjoy a little Eric. He always liked her special way of waking him.

Drifting back down the stairs, loosening her blouse on the way she's a little surprised at just how excited she actually is. Maybe she misses Eric. But as she rounds the sofa she realizes that something's not right. Ah. The lump in his armpit isn't the dreadful pink afghan, it's that bitch Amelia. Guess she read that wrong. Elsie beats a retreat. Back to Plan A.

At least the batteries will be charged by now.

61 . . .

Detective Lewis notes the police cars blocking the university lot as she changes lanes for the hospital entrance. She finds a parking spot and hurries into the building. But when she sees her partner sitting outside a closed door, hunched over his iphone, his look of concentration tells her he's playing a video game.

"And you needed me urgently because...?"

Detective Wolfrom grins sheepishly. "Sorry. I figured it was better to lob some angry birds than lose it with a suspect. I didn't think you'd mind coming back on rotation a little early. Getting a jump on it." He stows the cell phone in its holster on his belt.

"Suspect?" Lewis asks. "What have we got?"

"Group of students arranged an unofficial search party for a missing classmate, Natasha Panov. The searchers found her in the woods behind the campus. Raped and badly beaten."

"Not rape, sexual assault. How's the vic doing?"

"Unconscious. The doc seems to think she'll live."

"And you have a suspect already?"

"Well. Kind of." Wolfrom shrugs, indicating the closed door behind him. "This guy was one of the searchers, but when I ask him anything, he just won't answer." Lewis shoots him a look. "Well, everybody's a suspect."

"Yes, but remember the doer is usually exactly who you expect. The boyfriend or the guy she wouldn't go out with. Or come across for. Real people don't screw around with complicated plots, Wolfie. They don't plan elaborate strategies and join search parties to throw the intrepid cops off the scent like in the movies. In real life people just act on impulse 'cause they're mad or frustrated. Being in the search party doesn't make the guy more likely."

"So why won't he answer even the simplest questions?"

Lewis shrugs. "Like every other fricken college kid he probably read that damn Boingboing article warning civilians never to talk to cops."

"Oh. I must've missed that one."

"You know, Wolfie, next time that Doctorow's in town lecturing at Christie I'll have a few choice words for the guy. What do you want from me?"

"I was kind of hoping you'd, I dunno, maybe bat your eyelashes at the guy or slap him around or something."

"Yeah right." Lewis laughs. "Seriously, though, do you have any reason for thinking he's the guy?"

"Well, no. I don't know anything about him because he won't talk." Wolfrom shakes his head.

"You have the guy's name?"

"Pretty much name rank and serial number. Ethan Sumner, teaching assistant, third year photography, lives in residence. Vic is a photography first year, lives in the same res."

"All right, let me take a run at him."

Wolfrom opens the door and reveals Ethan sitting stiffly in the patient chair across the desk in the small office. He looks up sullenly when the door opens.

"Hello Mr. Sumner, I'm detective Lewis. I understand you were with the search party. Is there any information you can help us out with tonight?"

"I've helped as much as I'm able."

"Detective Wolfrom tells me you're not answering questions."

Ethan nods. "That's correct."

"I don't understand that, Mr. Sumner." Detective Lewis asks, "Don't you want to help your friend? I mean, you went out searching to help find her, and you found her. Now that she's safe we want the guy who did it. I don't understand how not talking to us helps her."

Ethan says, "I have a right to remain silent."

"Ah. Well, that's true enough, but just so you know, real life in Canada is just a little different than what you see on American television. You do have the right to remain silent, but we have the right to hold it against you later in court. Still, you're not charged, so I don't see why you won't talk to us."

Ethan repeats, "I have a right to remain silent."

"Are you saying that we should be arresting you?" Detective Wolfrom speaks from behind Ethan, where he's leaning against the door jamb. "Was it you who attacked her, then?"

Ethan turns to glare at Wolfrom. "No, it wasn't me, but I still don't have to tell you anything."

Lewis says, "You do realize that as long as you stand mute, we can't eliminate you as a suspect."

"You people will do what you want either way. You can either arrest me or let me go."

Lewis shrugs. "You're not making it any easier, Mr. Sumner. I certainly hope that no one else gets raped because you chose not to share information with us."

Ethan just glares. "Am I free to leave?"

Lewis and Wolfrom exchange glances. They don't have anything on the guy beyond belligerence. "You have always been free to go. You aren't under arrest, we've only asked you questions as a witness. We may need to speak with you again."

"Will I get a lawyer then?"

Lewis shakes her head. "Mr. Sumner, you are free to consult with a lawyer at any time you like. However the only time the court appoints a lawyer is after your arrest if you are unable to hire your own."

"Fine. Maybe I'll talk to you then." Lewis notes a

little yellow button affixed to the backpack as he takes it off the back of the chair and slings it over his shoulder.

Wolfrom starts to open his mouth to explain that lawyers aren't allowed in interrogations, but Lewis just shakes her head, so he subsides and watches the student stomp out of the room.

As the door swings closed, Wolfrom says, "I wish they would stop getting legal advice from American cop shows."

"That's life, Wolfie."

"Wouldn't you think he'd be friends with the vic, he was out searching for her. You think he's the doer?"

Lewis shrugs. "No idea. But did you see the 'Free Byron' button on his backpack?"

"No." Wolfrom frowns. "What's that mean?"

"It means this Sumner kid supports the G20 protesters."

"Oh shit."

Lewis says, "Since all cops are assholes, talking to us is bad."

"But that was nothing to do with us. That was Toronto."

"Tell it to the Internet."

"Yeah." Wolfrom sighs. "And that crazy Boingboing."

"All I know is it makes the job that much more impossible. Let's just hope that they're not all like that, 'cause if they are we'll never catch this fuckin' perp."

62 . . .

Police have stretched crime scene tape around the wooded path, and crime scene technicians comb the immediate area where Natasha was found.

In the light of day, Val Thompson, the security chief, is gray with exhaustion as he walks Detective Lewis along the route Natasha most likely followed. Detective Lewis scans the path carefully, but it just looks like wood chips to her.

A uniformed officer calls, "I need a tech over here."

Lewis and Val leg it over to where the smug officer waits.

"What've you got?" asks Lewis.

"Looks like somebody's been laying in wait in here. Lots of cigarette butts, stomped down earth, screened by the shrubs.

"That's great," says Val. "You can get DNA off the butts?"

"Maybe. None of them look too fresh."

"Maybe this was where he scoped things out. Great work Harris."

Harris preens as Lewis leads Val back to the paved path, saying. "Just don't expect magic here, Val. CSI is only a TV show, and DNA only helps when there is a suspect to match."

"Yes, I am aware of that, Detective Lewis."

"Good, then. We may get something out of canvassing the neighbourhood."

Val asks, "What can we do to help you, Detective?"

"We're gonna have to interview students. Her friends, classmates. Anyone who might have information. Can you round up a room we can use for on site interviews?"

"Yeah. Sure." says Val, "That's a surprise. The other rape we had didn't get nearly this much law enforcement attention."

"You talking date rape,Val?"

"Yeah. It was at a frat party."

"This is different for two reasons. She holds up her index finger and says, "One, it looks premeditated. Laying in wait. Possibly a stranger, but maybe not. Either way, a predator."

"Uh oh. You're saying this isn't going to be the only one?"

"That's why we're coming down on it hard, Val. The level of violence is very disturbing." Lewis holds up a second finger. "He hit her hard enough to knock her out. Maybe she knows him, and he didn't want her to identify him, but the perp didn't just rape her, he used her as a punching bag, and when he was done he just walked away. Leaving her out in the elements without even an anonymous tip. Pretty cold."

"You're saying it's not just a crime of opportunity."

"We don't know much of anything yet, but it's a strong possibility. And, number three," adding a final finger Lewis says, "The worst is that the perp doesn't need a conscious victim."

Val blanches as he gets the implication. "That's

bad."

Lewis nods. "I have to get to the hospital. The victim's regained consciousness. Maybe she can tell us something so we can keep it from happening again."

"I'll get you that interview room."

63 . . .

With hair swaddled in bandages and her forehead approximating a rainbow that ends in violet rings around her eyes, Natasha knows she's looked better. Propped up in a hospital bed, she tries to listen to the cop asking her questions but it's hard staying focused.

Detective Lewis asks, "Did you see anyone? Or anything out of the ordinary?"

"It's fuzzy, but no, I didn't see anything. I was on my way to catch a bus, meet Liz, take some pictures. I heard crying."

Lewis frowns, "Crying?"

"In the bushes, well that's what I thought, anyway. I was gonna keep going, 'cause I'd just had a big fight with my best friend, but then I thought hey, maybe I can help, you know? Famous last words."

Natasha smiles ruefully and tries to shake her head but the quick movement triggers a wave of agony causing her to freeze mid wince. "Owww."

Natasha grips the bed rail tightly for a minute to allow the pain to subside. "Okay, I gotta try to remember that the only reason I don't feel like total crap is the heavy shit they're pumping into me." Her breathing is returning to normal. "Um. Where was I?"

Glancing at her notebook Lewis says, "You heard crying and were going to try to help."

"Okay, right. So I went off the path where I thought the crying was coming from but then I couldn't hear it anymore so I called and blundered in through the trees. Dumb, eh?"

"No", Lewis says, "Not dumb. You were trying to help someone. That's never dumb. Going so far of the path-- now that was dumb."

Natasha winces, "Don't make me laugh."

Lewis pulls a face, "Sorry. You were really lucky your friends went looking for you. If they hadn't found you when they did you would be in much worse shape."

"Yeah," agrees Natasha quietly. "The doctor said."

"That's all for now, here's my card, " Lewis sets it on the night table, "In case you remember anything else. You got a pretty good thump. When you're feeling better things might come back to you. So you'll give me a call if you remember anything, right?"

"Sure," Natasha smiles, dreamily watching Lewis leave. And then here comes Liz and Ethan. Natasha smiles wider, careful not to laugh because more than anything they look like the undead.

"You guys look like crap. Do I look that bad?"

"Oh Natasha, I'm so glad you're gonna be OK." smiles Liz through moist eyes,

"I heard you're the only reason I'm still kicking, girl, and I want to tell you I appre... app... bleh... you know."

Liz nods, and Ethan says, "Good drugs, eh Nat?"

"Oh yeah. But I think I'm gonna..." and her eyes slide closed. A small trilling snore escapes her lips.

Ethan gives Liz a hug, and tells her, "Okay, she's gonna live. I don't know about you but I need sleep or coffee. Or both."

64 . . .

Eric stands at the counter, waiting for the kettle to boil he pops opens the tin of Darjeeling and measures the leaves into the tea ball then drops it into the cup. But he almost drops the tin when he feels arms encircle him from behind.

Elsie.

Eric can feel his body betray him at the familiar feel of her pressing into him from behind, and she slips her hands inside the waistband of his track pants.

"Mmmm," she says. "You missed me."

"Elsie stop it." he says quietly. He turns around and is struck by how ethereal she looks. Probably worn out from fucking the other half of the guys on campus last night.

He smiles, "Involuntary reaction. Old habits die hard."

"They don't have to die hard, we can put them to use."

Of course she lets her robe fall tantalizingly open but even the provocative glimpse of that perfect body can't get the taste of betrayal out of his mouth.

He just shakes his head. "I don't think so."

The kettle starts to whistle, and he turns to shut it off, then pours the boiling water over the tea bell in his over sized mug. With the tea safely steeping he turns back and she's gone.

Eric sags back against the counter, weak with relief.

65 . . .

Adam is late arriving at school. The lot he normally parks in has been blocked by the police crime scene investigators. He and the other disgruntled students had to park in the overflow lot, necessitating an additional ten minute walk. Not an auspicious start to the day. He falls into step beside a guy he's seen in various lecture halls, the two of them trail the larger group of students hurrying to cover the ground between purgatory and the school.

"What happened?" he asks the guy.

"No idea. Just the cops were waving me away from the Lester Street lot."

"Yes, me too. Perhaps there was an accident. I hope no one was injured, but I would rather it was cleared up today."

"You and me both. I don't feature this much of a schlep twice daily."

"We might end up in very good shape." Adam says.

The guy laughs. "Buff. What a concept."

Inconstant Moon

As they enter the oval from the north, a red sports car speeds up the ring road. "Wow," Adam's companion says admiringly. "Porsche Boxter Spyder. That one might even be this year's model. I haven't seen one offline before. Sweet."

Adam says, "I didn't think you could park there."

"Oh, you can't, it's just a drop zone. Usually nobody uses it except for commencement ceremonies when they have celeb guest speakers. Limos. VIPs, that kind of thing."

"Ah. I'm Adam by the way. I believe we have some classes together."

The other guy extends a hand for a quick shake. "Dave. Yeah, I've seen you around too. How are you getting along?"

"Okay, I guess. Not quite what I was expecting, though."

Dave laughs. "Yeah, I know what you mean."

"How so?" asks Adam, curious.

"Well, it happened to me too. Quite the shock to suddenly not be the smartest guy in school, eh?"

"You know, that never occurred to me." Adam stops and suddenly everything is clear. That seems to answer everything. He looks at Dave gratefully. "You may well be correct ." Adam shakes his head and laughs. "I've been feeling as though I've lost my identity."

"Once you understand that, its not quite so bad."

Adam grins. "I suspect that if we'd gone to the same high school, I would have been the second smartest student."

"We'll never know. My first class is over in the Arts Centre this morning. Maybe I'll catch you at lunch, Adam."

"That would be good." Adam smiles.

Dave nods toward the Porsche, still idling in front of the Medical Centre. "If that thing's still there when you go by, give one of the tires a kick for me."

Adam laughs. "I certainly will, Dave."

The two students go their separate ways and Adam's curiosity about the hot car draws him toward it. Dave seemed seriously impressed. Even Adam knows that a Porsche is a very expensive machine. He's never paid much attention to cars, that's one of the things his brother knows about. Looking at the Spyder it he can kind of understand the appeal. It doesn't look like an ordinary car. Certainly nothing like his beater.

Maybe it's some specialist here to lecture the pre-meds. The med school gets lots of extra perks, probably paid for with the donations they get from doctors they graduate.

As Adam draws near his good mood evaporates when he realizes that the blonde woman in the passenger seat is Barbie.

Last night Adam had hoped what Nick said was all lies, but part of him didn't really believe it, even then. Why would Nick lie? It doesn't look like he did, now that Adam sees beautiful Barbie wound around the driver.

They're kissing and... the man's hand is inside Barbie's blouse and he's *touching* her. They are practically having coitus in public, like one of those terrible movies his brother hides in the back of the cabinet at home. Adam can hardly breathe. But he pauses long enough to kick the rear tire before hurrying past to the tech building.

She liked him.

At least he thought she liked him. She smiled at him, she even kissed him. How can she kiss this other man? How can she let another man touch her like that. Adam should be the only one who gets to touch her like that.

Not some rich creep with a hot car.

66 . . .

Oscar is running late for his first class when he spots Jake weaving down the hall. The freshman looks wrecked.

"Jake my man, we missed you at the meeting. The girls were wondering what happened because we thought you'd be joining us. Although you look as though you've had a busy night."

Jake shakes his head and waves Oscar away as he ducks into the mens room.

Curious, Oscar follows. Pushing the door open he sees Jake bent over the sink looking as though he's about to pass out.

"Are you sick? Should I bring you 'round to the medic?"

Jake shakes his head, then turns on the water and splashes some on his face, then uses the bottom of his sweatshirt as a towel.

Oscar watches with concern as Jake leans against the wall. "I should have stayed in bed. I'm sorry I missed the meeting, Oz. Something happened."

"That's okay." says Oscar, "Just, you look like hell and I'm not leaving you here by yourself. Lets take a bit of a wander to the caf and let me get a few of the major food groups into you."

"You can't do that, Oz. You'll miss your class."

"I've missed classes for worse reasons."

"The caf isn't even open."

"Ah, there you're wrong. The machines are open always.

"What about the food groups?"

"The vending machines are amply provisioned with salt, sugar, starch, fat and chocolate. Surely that's all the food groups represented."

67 . . .

Eric smiles at the detective. She's not bad for an older woman. "So," he asks, "Why did you decide to become a cop?"

Detective Lewis says, "I get to ask the questions."

"I'm gonna be a writer, one day I might write about cops."

"Well, when that time comes, you can ask me then. I wouldn't even charge you much."

Eric raises an eyebrow, "Charge? You'd charge a

writer?"

"It's called a consultation fee. But lets get on track here," she glances at her notebook, "Eric. This is a serious situation. What I really need to know about is your relationship with Natasha."

Eric shrugs. "Acquaintances at most. We live in the same place but don't usually spend much time together. She introduced me to Monty Python the other night if that helps."

"Was it just the two of you?"

"No, she was watching her DVDs with Boris when Amelia and I came in after the Branagh Hamlet at the Kingsway. So it was just the four of us sitting around the common room, you know?"

"So, you're saying you never dated Natasha?"

Eric shakes his head. "No. Nothing like that. Natasha was with Boris, and until recently I was seeing Elsie."

The low whistle from behind startles Eric, rudely reminding him of Detective Wolfrom leaning against the door back there. He'd forgotten Wolfrom. It occurs to him that that is probably the point. Eric swivels around to face him. "So you hang out back there to pounce on inconsistencies? Keep the bad guys from taking it on the lam? You're the bad cop, right?"

Wolfrom just looks at him. Lewis bites her tongue so the kid won't see her laugh. Problem is Wolfie looks like he might crack up at any moment. Lewis can't let the subject control the interview, she has to get back the lead.

"How long have Boris and Natasha been together?"

"Pretty much from day one, I think."

"And were they getting along well, would you say?"

"Wait a minute, you can't pin this on Boris. No way."

"We're not looking to 'pin it on' anyone. We're looking for facts." Lewis looks at him. "Can you vouch for Boris? Can you say you were with him every minute of the afternoon?"

"Well, no, but that isn't fair."

"How about you. Can anyone vouch for your own whereabouts yesterday afternoon

"I was in a lecture for part of it."

Wolfrom asks, "And would anyone testify to that?"

"Am I a suspect?"

"Certainly, until cleared, yes, you are. Maybe we can start with why you broke up with your girlfriend."

68 . . .

Oscar comes into the computer lab, settling at his usual machine between Maggie and Adam.

Maggie looks up, "Look at what the cat dragged in. And here I thought you'd tossed your alarm clock out the window again this morning."

Oscar shakes his head. He leans in and Maggie inclines closer to hear as he says, "I spent the last hour pouring coffee into young Jake. He had a disturbing tale to tell. It seems that Natasha was brutally attacked yesterday afternoon."

"Natasha? Oh no." Maggie covers her mouth.

"Seems she was only found because Liz led out the cavalry to search for her."

Maggie swivels around and psssts Kate and Krystal, who both roll closer for a mid-class confab.

"What's up?" asks Kate softly.

"One of the girls in my dorm was attacked yesterday."

Adam leans in to listen as well.

Kate frowns, "Who was it?"

Maggie says, "A frosh named Natasha."

"Not Bo's Natasha?" asks Kate.

Krystal gasps, "You mean the chick with the hay maker?"

"Same and same."

"Ohmigod, what happened?"

Oscar says grimly, "She was bashed in the head and raped."

"That would explain the police presence." says Adam.

Krystal swivels toward him. "Yeah cops were crawling all over the parking lot when I got off the bus, but they wouldn't give a straight answer why they were here. 'Procedure' was all they'd say."

"I was told 'routine'. There was crime scene tape across the near parking lot entrances this morning." Adam adds, " Those of us who drive in had to park in the overflow lot and hike back. There were security guards, and police officers throughout the woods."

"Oh that's so scary."

"I'll bet it was that Boris." says Krystal.

Kate shakes her head. "I don't think so. Nick works out with Bo, he's a really nice guy."

Maggie says, "Besides, Boris and Natasha are friends."

"Natasha wasn't very friendly when she clocked him yesterday." says Krystal.

Oscar shakes his head. "That was just friends having an argument. I hardly think rape would be the result."

Krystal asks, "Never heard of date rape? Or marital rape?"

Oscar looks thoughtful, "I stand corrected."

Maggie asks, "Is she okay?"

"I only know she's in hospital. Jake was so exhausted he hardly knew up from down. They were out searching whilst we watched House last night. That's why Jake missed the meeting."

"That's terrible." says Adam.

Kate asks, "So she was out there for hours?"

Oscar says, "Yes, Kate, she was hit on the head."

Kate says, "They would have had to warm her up and give her fluids if she was suffering from exposure."

"I'll bet it was Boris," says Krystal. "Any guy can become a wack job if he sucks up enough steroids."

"Boris power lifts but he doesn't use steroids." says Kate.

Krystal laughs. "Don't they all?"

Kate shakes her head. "No. They don't. Nick works with weights when he has the time and he doesn't use steroids. If he'd seen any sign in Bo I'm sure he'd have said something to me."

Maggie says, "That's terrible about Natasha."

"What does one do in a situation like this?" asks Adam.

"Do?" Maggie frowns at Adam. "You mean... like socially?"

Adam nods. "Yes. Would chocolate be appropriate?"

"Krystal snaps, "It's not like a date, Adam. That's twisted."

Adam looks uncomfortable, "I didn't really know her."

"Not 'didn't,'Adam, 'don't'. Natasha's not dead and gone, she's still here." snaps Krystal.

Adam blanches. "I didn't mean... I just thought we could let her know we supported her." mutters Adam.

"Yeah," Kate says, "we should do something like that. That's very thoughtful, Adam. Maybe flowers, or a plant maybe?"

"A couple of girls got raped in my high school," Maggie says.

Kate asks her, "Did they ever get the guy? Or guys?"

"Nope, never did."

Krystal says, "That's awful. What'd the girls do?"

"Both of them left school. I know one of them went

out west. All I know is I never saw either of them again."

"That's rough."

"You think Natasha will drop out?"

Genuinely perplexed, Adam asks, "I don't understand, why would they leave school?"

"They were probably afraid." says Krystal.

"Especially if the guy wasn't caught," adds Oscar.

Maggie nods. "That's about it. You don't know who to trust. And I gotta tell you, it sure didn't help male female relations at school."

"Weren't you and Stu high school sweethearts?"

Maggie smiles. "Yup."

"So how did you know you could trust him?"

"It helped that the first rape happened when we were on our first date. I knew it wasn't him, I could trust him. I wondered about other guys, though."

"That must have been hard on everyone."

Maggie nods. "It was. You know how when you first meet people you check them out? At our school every girl had to decide if she thought the guy was a rapist before even considering him as a boyfriend. The worst was nobody even knew for sure if it was somebody from school or not. Didn't make any difference, though. All the guys were suspect."

Adam says, "But that isn't fair."

"No it's not, but that's what happened, Adam."

"Like it was fair to the girls?" says Krystal. "Bad enough they were attacked but then having to drop out, too. They didn't do anything wrong. They were the victims and it screwed up their lives even worse."

"I don't know about you," says Maggie, "but this attack scares the hell out of me."

"Me too," agrees Krystal. "We won't be safe until they catch the guy."

Oscar says, "You do realize how naïve that is?"

"No, Oz, what do you mean?"

"There are always rapists and murderers and thieves, but we go through life not even thinking about them until something like this happens. People only think defensively when it's too bloody late. If we'd been on guard before it might not have happened."

Kate says, "Illogical or not, now is when I'm scared."

There's a loud bit of suggestive throat clearing from behind Adam and the group turns guiltily to face Professor Gates, who is looking fairly thunderous.

"Excuse me, Maggie, but would you mind sharing what's so interesting with the rest of the class?"

Maggie flushes, but rises to her feet. "Actually I do, but it's important that everyone knows so we can all take precautions."

Gates is floored by Maggie's unexpected response. "What?"

Maggie continues more loudly so everyone can hear. "Everyone should know that a frosh from my residence was attacked on campus yesterday."

There's a silence as Professor Gates looks stunned and the rest of the class takes in the disturbing information. Clearly even the Christie faculty has not yet been told of the incident.

"What happened?" Gates asks quietly.

"She was attacked and raped and left unconscious in the woods. If she hadn't been found she might have died."

Professor Gates looks stunned. But she knows she's lost the class for the day.

"Who was it, Maggie?" someone calls out.

"Natasha."

"No way!"

Someone else adds, "Goddamn I'll bet it was Boris."

Kate says, "Not Boris."

"Why not Boris?" mutters Krystal.

Kate replies, "Because Boris has been in my house."

The stunned silence gives way to muttering, both general and specific outpourings of outrage, fear and anger. Little discussions of safety precautions spring up throughout the class.

Oscar has been typing, and he interrupts the growing pandemonium to announce, "I'm just pulling together a quick and dirty web page. It isn't very pretty but to start I've popped on a few rape prevention links, and a few tips."

Gates interrupts. "Set it up as part of the ComSci wiki, Oz. Then anyone who logs in can add to it. Maybe Maggie might want to start a forum, for example."

"Include police contact information when we get it too," adds Kate.

Krystal says, "Read out a few of the main tips Oz."

"Be observant. Avoid walking alone. Keep to well

lighted areas. Avoid shortcuts through parks, vacant lots and the like."

"And don't turn your back on Boris." Krystal mutters. Kate shoots her a look.

Gates nods, "Be observant is probably most important. Try to use the buddy system."

"It's posted on the wiki so pass the word around. This is for everyone."

"Good job. Thanks Oz." says Gates. "I think that's it for today. Everyone please try to stay safe."

69 . . .

Jake comes into the common room and sniffs ostentatiously. He glares at Jose flaked out on the red sofa holding a burning roach in his hand.

Jose grins foolishly. "Hey there kid. How's it hanging?"

Jake comes in and sits in the arm chair, attempting to stare down Jose.

Doesn't work.

Jose says, "You look pretty rough, man. Want a hit?" pinching the stub in a roach clip he proffers it to Jake. Jake looks at the offering with dismay. Obviously subtlety has no hope of working.

"Jose, you can't smoke pot in here. We'll get in trouble."

Jose shakes his head. "Doesn't make sense man. If a man can't smoke up at home, where can he?"

"Nowhere. Smoking pot is against the law in

Canada. It's not legal anywhere, home or not. And think about it, if you get caught you could get kicked out of school. All it would take is for a porter or the don to wander in and you're cooked. We'd all get in trouble, too."

"Aw, sorry Jake." Jose puts the butt out in a portable ash tray, and snaps it shut. "I've just been having a crappy day, man, and I just wanted to get level, you know."

"What do you usually do?"

"I usually go smoke up in the woods but it's crawling with cops. And it's fucking cold out there." He laughs ruefully. "They warned me about Canadian winters but I didn't really get it."

In spite of himself Jake laughs. "I hate to tell you, but this isn't winter, it's fall. Winter is much colder."

"Are you shittin'me? That isn't winter out there?"

"Sorry. The way it works is that once we get used to this weather, that's when it gets really cold. But it really isn't so bad, you might even get to like snow."

"It gets worse? Oh man. I can't believe it. And I have to go outside to smoke? Isn't there anywhere warm to go?"

"Not really. It's even illegal to smoke cigarettes indoors in public spaces, and they're legal." Jake thinks a minute, then says, "If it's gonna be a problem for you maybe you ought to think about getting an off campus apartment."

"Maybe I should. Man, I wish I'd a known."

"Better take it outside there, Jose."

Jake and Jose look over and see Boris padding blearily through the common room on the way to the kitchen. Suddenly Jake looks a little queasy.

"Why is the campus crawling with cops?" asks Jose.

"Because Natasha got attacked yesterday. I was out searching for her half the night."

"Man, I'm sorry. I didn't know."

Suddenly towering over Jake, the only colour in his face made by black circles around his eyes, Boris asks, "What happened to Natasha?"

"Somebody attacked her in the woods."

"Is she OK?"

"She's in the hospital." Looking at the thunderous expression on Bo's face Jake isn't sure if it would be safer to tell him or not. He takes a deep breath and realizes there isn't a choice. He has to tell. "She was raped, Boris."

Boris sags, "Oh God. Did you see her? How was she?"

"She was unconscious. I came home to try and get some sleep but I couldn't, so I tried going to class, and I couldn't do that either. Liz and Ethan stayed at the hospital hoping to see her when she wakes up. They haven't come back yet."

Dropping to a sitting position on the floor Boris buries his face in his hands, shaking with heavy sobs.

Jake and Jose exchange awkward glances, wordlessly deciding the best course of action is withdrawal.

70 . . .

Adam is coming into the cafeteria just as Barbie and her annoying friend come out.

Isn't Barbie ever alone?

Adam wants so desperately to talk to her. All right all right, he's got to try anyway. Get under control. Deep breath.

"Hello, Barbie. How's your computer handling **Ubuntu**?"

"Oh, hi, uh, Alan, it's doing just great. You have a magic touch!" Barbie bestows a million dollar smile and then she's gone.

Instead of being dazzled, Adam feels as though he's taken a punch. Alan? She still doesn't even know his name? He's going to be paying his brother back for that god awful concert for years and she doesn't know his name.

Adam continues into the cafeteria. He grabs a tray, adds a pint of milk and the chicken entrée, slides it along the metal track. After paying he looks listlessly around for an empty seat when he notices someone is waving. At him? Oh, it's Dave. Adam smiles, and threads his way through the scattered tables and students to join his new friend over by the window.

§

Maggie, Kate and Krystal are sitting around their table in the sun. Krystal is looking a little off colour.

"Are you okay, Krys?" asks Maggie.

"I just need some lunch."

Kate looks a question at Maggie who almost imperceptibly waves her off. Suddenly Krystal flushes, and Maggie glances over to note it's a reaction to Quentin and Jose coming through the doors. "You still got a thing for that boy?"

"Yeah. I do."

"Why not go talk to him or something?"

"He's only interested in that Barbie doll. See he's looking all over the room, trying to catch a glimpse of the precious little bitch. But she's not here. Watch his face fall 'cause she's not here to lead him around by his prick."

Kate laughs. "You've got it bad, Krystal."

Krystal shakes her head, "Yeah, I know. Oh well, I'll have to make do. Admire from afar."

"He is good looking." Kate says, "Nice shoulders."

"Very," agrees Krystal. "Broad shoulders."

"Nice buns too," says Maggie.

Krystal says, "Mmmmmm."

"What's up with that?" asks Kate.

"What do you mean?" asks Krystal.

Kate says, "He's pretty sedentary. You never see him working out, or doing anything except being languid. What I want to know is why such a couch potato like Jose who smokes up and doesn't exercise has such a great butt while all I get is cellulite."

"Good genes," Maggie tells her.

"Real good jeans. All I want is one chance to chew

them off." Krystal smiles.

Maggie starts giggling, "God girl, watch yourself or you're gonna end up having an orgasm right here."

"Maybe then he'd notice me." says Krystal.

Kate throws up her hands. "Enough already. Anybody have anything interesting to talk about?"

"Uh, I had my interview with the cops." says Maggie.

"How'd that go? As bad as you thought?" asks Kate.

Maggie nods. "That Detective Lewis chewed me out for not reporting the flasher."

"It wouldn't be a flasher," says Krystal.

"Maybe they think the flasher graduated into rape." says Kate. "Deviant sexual offenders usually start small and then work up to the bigger shit."

Maggie shakes her head. "But the guy ran away when I laughed at him. Where would he get the balls to rape someone?"

"Don't need to be brave if you hit somebody over the head from behind." ventures Kate quietly.

"Oh god, I didn't think of that. Jesus maybe it was my fault."

"Look, it was probably Boris. It's always the boyfriend right?" Krystal shakes her head, "But even if it was your flasher, if you'd have gone to the cops with your flasher story what do you think they would they have done?"

"Maybe found the guy. Before he attacked Natasha."

Krystal shakes her head, "Naww, they'd have done the same thing we did, they'd have laughed."

Kate says, "Maggie, stop. Even if it was the flasher you didn't make the creep go out and do it. It isn't your fault, it's his. I am so sick of hearing excuses for bastards like that. Lots of people have crappy lives and don't go around attacking other people. He did. You didn't. End of story."

"They were interested when I told them about his bike."

"What?"

"It was a red Schwinn."

"What on earth is that?"

"A very expensive but very cool bike. Stu has one, which is why I recognized it. Maybe it'll lead to something."

"You guys do what you want, but far as I'm concerned, I'm watching my back when that Boris guy is around." Krystal says.

71 . . .

As Nick sits in the plastic chair across from Detective Lewis she asks, "What's your connection with Natasha Panov?"

Nick shakes his head. "We both go to Christie, but we don't really know each other. She's a friend of a friend."

"You reside in residence." Detective Wolfrom says from behind. Nick picks up the chair and turns it 45° so he can see both detectives. Lewis suppresses a smile at this simple method of defeating the interrogation ploy. Of course it wouldn't work in a real interrogation room, where the 'client' chair is generally bolted to the floor.

Nick nods. "Yes, I'm in a married student residence."

"You don't live in Fyfield House with Natasha Panov?"

"No, in one of the bungalows with my wife Kate."

"So, how's the home life, Mr. Stone?"

Nick bristles, but keeps his tone even. "I'm very happily married thank you. For the most part the only people I come in contact with are Christie personel and med students."

"Students like Barbie Janzen."

Nick looks at Lewis. "Along with my studies I am employed as a teaching assistant. Barbie Janzen is one of the first year students I've had occasion to supervise."

"There's been some suggestion that your relationship with Ms. Janzen may not be strictly platonic."

Lewis thinks she sees anger flash across the man's face, but it's gone so quickly she's not sure. "You must be kidding." Nick Stone clenches his jaw, but manages to keep it together when he answers. "Whoever told you that is way out in left field. In my opinion it's unlikely Ms. Janzen will complete the program."

"An untoward romantic entanglement, Nick?"

Nick shrugs. "More philosophical differences."

Lewis frowns. "Pardon me, Doc?"

"I'm not a doctor, detective, I'm a med student. Ms. Janzen's problem is a work ethic conflict. She thinks she can become a doctor without doing the work. In my books, that's a conflict."

"So, you're telling us there isn't any sexual harassment?"

Nick shrugs. "Not from me."

Wondering what that's supposed to mean, Detective Lewis studies Nick Stone. Most guys would be through the roof by this point, but this one is unnaturally calm. Is it because the guy is a sociopath or is he just good doctor material?

"How well do you know Ms. Panov?"

"I don't, actually. Pretty much the only reason I even know of Natasha is that I work out with her friend Boris. And I only know Boris because we hit the gym at the same time Tuesday nights."

"Would you know where Boris is?"

Nick frowns, startled. "Uh, no. You haven't talked to him?"

"There's been no sign of him. Although everyone seems to have watched his argument with Ms. Panov yesterday, no one appears to know where he is now."

72 . . .

Although cleaned up, Bo's dual black eyes make him look less than an upstanding citizen as he barrels through the hospital lobby. He heads for the information desk, where he gets directions to Natasha's room. He pays no attention to the receptionist picking up the phone as he heads toward the elevator.

Approaching Natasha's room, Boris slows down. What if she's still mad at him? Wait, he's supposed to be mad at her.

Never been very good at carrying a grudge though. He peeks around the door jamb to see if she's awake and Natasha's peal of laughter tells him she is. Boris is so relieved he smiles as he steps into the room but his face falls as he takes in her bandages and bruising.

"Oh Nat, I'm so sorry. I should have been there for you."

Natasha shakes her head. "What, after I did that to you? And then I laugh at you? I am such a bitch!"

"No you aren't."

"Yes I am," sniffling, Natasha looks perfectly miserable. "I'm sorry I hit you, god knows I've seen the error of my ways. Hitting is bad. Muy bad."

A little hopeful, Boris asks, "Does that mean there's a chance you'll go out with me?"

"No, it doesn't. Look, just pull that chair over here and sit so we can talk. It's important."

Boris does as she asks, and settles beside her. "Can I hold your hand at least?"

"Yes," she says, and he notices that her eyes are awfully moist. Up close he can also see quite a bit of bruising fanning out from her bandage.

"Look, I've been laying here in torment, not

knowing if you were ever gonna speak to me again. You're my best friend, Boris, I've never felt closer to anyone than I do to you. But I just don't have romantic feelings for you and I never will. I just can't."

"But the kiss? You let me kiss you."

"No. I stopped fighting you off because it wasn't doing any good. Anything good you got out of that kiss was all in your mind Bo. It was not good for me."

"You didn't like it even a little?"

"No. I thought you knew right from the start. I thought we were so great because you knew and you didn't care."

"Knew what?"

"That I'm a lesbian, Bo."

He gapes at her, not getting it.

"I like girls. You aren't my type, Bo, you're the competition."

Stunned, Boris lets go her hand. "Oh."

"You didn't know."

"Of course I didn't know. Do you think I'd have made a pass at you if I'd known? Why didn't you ever say anything? I thought we were friends. Jeeze Nat, I have to think about this."

"Here I thought you were such a cool guy and it turns out you weren't cool at all, you were just clueless." Natasha laughs, which turns into a prodigious yawn.

Boris shrugs. "Hey whaddayawant? I'm just a nice Croatian boy looking for love. Apparently in all the wrong places."

"Lots of guys think it's cool, they think they'll turn

me on so that they can have a threesome. Or 'reform' me which I very much doubt is possible. I am definitely hard wired." Natasha looks over at Boris, who sits there, still looking so stunned. "You taking any of this in, Bo?"

"Yeah. Oh man, I'm just realizing how shitty it's gotta be for you to get attacked like that."

"It's a weird one, Bo. See, I was knocked out first, so it doesn't seem real to me. Yet. I dunno. But even though it happened to my body, I wasn't around for it, so that's something. Of course, they've been keeping me so high I can't hardly feel anything, and I'm probably really messed up down there. But my head knows, and it is some pissed off, let me tell you. They did a rape kit, a pregnancy test and an AIDS test on me before I even came to."

"Oh god."

"I'm not knocked up, but there's good news and bad news."

"Okay, good. What's the bad news?"

"The bastard didn't have the decency to wear a rubber so I'll be doing a series of AIDS tests over the next couple of years."

"And the good news?"

"If they catch him they've got DNA to put him away."

"Great. I guess. Maybe I'm just selfish, because all I really care about is that you're alive. I'm so glad. I couldn't even imagine a world without you, Nat." He turns away, and she can tell he's sniffling.

"Come on Bo, can the mush. Talk about something

else."

"Like what? You're in a hospital bed. They aren't gonna let me smuggle in your Underworld DVDs."

"Why not? What else am I gonna do?" She yawns deeply again. "Except maybe sleep. Hey, you know, there is one good thing about this."

"What?" Boris can't imagine anything good from this.

"I'm out of the closet now. That's something. You know what, I was so scared about it but it feels great. But then maybe that's the drugs. You're still my friend, right Bo?"

"Don't be a stupid. Of course I am."

"And you know, now that I'm out, I can tell my best friend who I have the hots for."

"No. Uh uh. I don't want to think about that."

"Hmm. I guess if you like me, you can't possibly be a boob man. God, I love a good set."

"Oh. Nat, " In spite of himself Boris finds himself chuckling. "What you are doing to all my misconceptions!"

"This is so great. I feel so great to be able to talk to you about... guess who I have the hots for?" she yawns again, and Boris can see she's fading.

"I can't guess. Why don't you tell me, who do you have the hots for?"

"That's it, you're not gonna guess?"

"Lemme get used to the idea, okay? Besides, you know I don't have to guess, you'll tell me."

"Says who? Come on, just guess."

"Okay, how about Barbie?"

"No way, I need a woman with a brain. Come on Bo, you gotta have something to talk about afterwards."

"Maybe you do, but I don't."

"I never knew you were such a pig!"

"Oink. Okay then how about Elsie. That girl is so hot."

"Oh yeah she's great looking but she's got the personality of a Borg or something. Too tough. No, the one I like is Liz. She's such a sweetheart. I've got such a crush on that girl. Except I know she's so straight I cut myself just looking at her."

"You can tell?"

"Yeah, I can tell." Yawn. "I'm pretty sure anyway."

"This is a lot to get my head around Nat. Hell, I've been thinking of us as getting married for a long time now. Imagining what our kids would look like."

"Kids?" Natasha's jaw drops. "Get outta town, no way!"

"I think I still want to marry you."

"Look Bo, in the first place, you're way too young to get married. If I was straight, hell, I'd marry you in a heartbeat. But I'm not. And I'm never gonna be."

"But I don't want to grow old alone."

"I won't let you, you can come live with me when we're old. Although it's pretty unlikely, 'cause you set hearts a racing."

"That's BS Nat, and you know it."

"No, it's true Bo. I've been your biggest handicap

because they all think I've got you. So they stay away. What a selfish bitch I am, if I'd backed off a little, but I was afraid you'd stop being my friend if you hooked up with some chick."

"No way."

"You're my best friend Bo. That hasn't changed. We'll always be friends no matter where we are. Don't want to lose you."

"You know, when I was so mad at you yesterday it made me even madder that I couldn't talk it through with you."

"Are you going to be able to get over it?"

"Well," Boris smiles a little, "Maybe."

Natasha studies him, mouth twitching just a tad. "What aren't you telling me Bo?"

"I guess I can tell you, it won't hurt your feelings."

"Yes Bo. But tell me quick because the pain meds are about to put me out here." Natasha gestures with her wrist, showing him the attached I.V.

"I was really mad, so I just went back to the Res and Elsie fixed me up."

"I guess she could at that." Natasha smiles drowsily.

"No, you goof, with ice." Natasha raises her eyebrows questioningly. "Okay, I wasn't happy because Elsie just wouldn't play doctor with me even when I practically begged her."

"Oh poor Bo."

"I was seriously ragged so I had to go out and get pissed."

"I know how that goes. Did it help?"

"Funny thing, the beer didn't help much at all, really. But I have to tell you, the getting laid part really helped a lot."

"That's good, you tell me all the details." Natasha smiles and yawns. "Hard to believe you could get laid with a double shiner like that, but that's good Bo, tell me."

"It was," Boris smiles, remembering, "It was like something out of a movie. Out of one of Amelia's film noir movies."

Natasha smiles. "Sounds great, and I wanna hear everything but... when I'm 'wake... You'll have to... to... tell me all 'bout it..." And she's asleep.

Oddly, while watching Natasha sleep, Boris feels an overwhelming feeling of love for his friend, but without the slightest trace of lust. Any physical attraction he thought he had is gone. He leans down and gives her a light kiss on the forehead.

Looking down at her battered face he whispers, "I'm so glad you're gonna be okay, Nat."

73 · · ·

The detectives have been interviewing students living in residence with Natasha. Or in classes with her. Or both.

"Think that bike lead will go anywhere?" Wolfrom asks.

"I hope so. There were bunch of off trail bike tracks, but the tech said they were probably pretty old.

They took casts, and they'll need to check tread patterns before they'll give an opinion."

"Old tracks, old butts, all we can do is keep talking to people. What about the boyfriend?"

"Even if it's always the boyfriend, wouldn't he have to be a real bonehead to do something like that after she knocked him down in front of the whole school."

"What, perps aren't boneheads?"

"I know, I know. You're right. We gotta talk to him."

"I'm willing to take some of these accounts with a grain of salt. To hear the stories the whole school was there to see it. Probably half of them are telling what they heard, or what their friends who were there texted them. It comes to court, Wolfie, we're gonna have to be damn sure that only actual witnesses make it to the stand."

"Why would they say they were there if they weren't?"

"It was the social event of the season. Being there confers instant status. Didn't you ever want to be a Big Man on Campus?"

"Naw. I spent my life working on being invisible. Much safer that way."

Lewis laughs. "The lab says the Rape Kit produced viable DNA. So when we get the guy we'll be able to make it stick."

"Okay bring in the next customer."

Wolfrom goes to the door, opens it and surveys the group of male students seated in the waiting area. He beckons to Adam, who enters the small room nervously. Adam seems to relax as Wolfrom asks him all the easy questions, name, classes, course load, and everything is fine. Until it changes when Lewis asks, "How well do you know Natasha Panov?"

"I don't know her, really. I mean, I know her to see because I know several people who live in her residence. I've got classes with Maggie and Oscar and we are in a computer club together."

Adam looks at the detective, busy making notes. "I don't think I've ever really spoken to her. I see her taking pictures with that weight lifter, Boris."

Lewis nods, and Adam sees that the other detective is writing down everything he says.

"I know Jake as well. He's a photography student but he is also in the computer club."

"So what were you doing yesterday afternoon?"

"I... but... afternoon? I thought you would want to know about last night?"

"Just answer the question please Adam." she says.

"I was, I uh, I cut classes, and I went to the mall."

"Why would you do that?"

"Uh, I don't know, I just didn't feel like going."

"Hmmm." says Lewis, She flips back a few pages in her notebook, reading tiny cramped notes. then she looks up at him.

"But you don't cut classes, do you, Adam."

"Uh, how?" looking at the notebook in horror, "Has someone been talking about me?"

"That's confidential information, Adam." she shakes her head, studying him seriously.

"You can tell me, Adam, why did you really cut class yesterday afternoon?"

"Uh, I just did. It had nothing to do with that girl. I just went to the mall. Walked around a while. That's all. Then I got something to eat and came back to campus for the computer club meeting at Kate's house last night."

Leaning across the table toward Adam, Lewis says softly "I mean you had a perfect record up to yesterday. You never cut classes, Adam." Lewis frowns at him "Why did you pick yesterday to cut?"

"I just... I just did, that's all." He reaches into his interior jacket pocket and pulls out a wallet, and opens the billfold, rifling through receipts. He tosses one on the table in front of Lewis.

"There. You see, I was at Pad Thai Palace. That proves I was at the mall."

"Maybe. If the clerk remembers you."

From behind Adam, Wolfrom asks quietly. "Did you see Boris kiss Natasha at lunch? Or how about when she hit him, Adam. Which part got you all excited?"

Swivelling around Adam says, "Yes. No. I mean I saw her hit him but no it didn't... I mean I don't care about that girl. I don't know her. She's not even attractive. She's short. She's got red hair. Why would I? I could never get excited about someone like that." Face flushed with fury, Adam stands up and glares at Wolfrom. "Just leave me alone!"

Lewis says quietly, "Adam, sit down. You do not have an alibi. Even if the clerk remembers you, it does not cover you, do you understand that?"

Adam looks down at her, frowning. She gestures for him to sit back down, and he does. "Look, we need to know where people were to eliminate them. Did you see anyone you know at the mall?"

Adam shakes his head "no."

Wolfrom asks, "Did you buy anything else?"

"No," Adam says in a small voice.

"Why did you cut classes, Adam?"

He sighs deeply, staring intently at the plastic wood grain tabletop, "I was upset about a girl... a different girl. A beautiful one." Following the pattern of the plastic wood grain with his eyes. Mesmerizing. "I just had to go away. I was in the Sony store in the mall almost the whole time. I didn't buy anything."

"So they might remember you."

Adam shakes his head sadly. "People don't."

Lewis and Wolfrom exchange glances.

"Can I go?"

Lewis nods, "Yes, we're done here, for now, Adam."

Adam gets up and pushes his way out the door before they can change their minds.

Wolfrom shakes his head in admiration. "That was good, that notebook thing. How did you know?"

"You saw the guy's tie. Any tighter he couldn't breathe. Guys like that don't cut class just 'because'. There's always a reason."

"So there's a girl. Maybe our girl stumbled across his path when he was messed up over his girl."

"Could be. Just he seemed genuinely surprised we were looking at the afternoon, He thought he needed a night time alibi. That makes me doubt right there."

"Except you know he's smart. These kids are like rocket scientists, you know? Would it be so hard to play us?"

"Asshole." She shakes her head, "Get the next one in."

74 . . .

Jose slumps into the plastic interview chair, lacing his fingers together on top of his head, knees spread, legs crossed at the ankles, he gives Lewis a big shit eating grin.

She finds herself smiling back.

"So, Jose. Or is it Joe?"

"I'll answer to either. I'm easy, just not cheap." Jose grins, as if it wasn't a joke older than he is.

Keeping it neutral, Lewis asks, "What do you prefer?"

"My name is Jose, but you can call me whatever you want, whenever you wanna call me."

Wolfrom rolls his eyes from his position leaning against the door. He crosses his arms because he's feeling an impulse. A strong impulse. To slap the guy. He can't remember the last time he wanted to hit a citizen this bad. This kid is downright disrespectful.

You can smell the cannabis seeping out of his pores and polluting the air.

"Alright, Jose. How well do you know Natasha?"

"Okay, I guess. Not real well." Jose takes his hands down and rests them on the table.

Jose says, "We're both in Fyfield House but I'm an English major, she's in Photography. There isn't much crossover. I mean we say 'hey' but Boris and Natasha are the real deal, you know, like this." He crosses his fingers. "They mostly stuck to themselves. Never see one without the other, you know."

"So where were you yesterday afternoon then, Jose."

"I wasn't feeling very good. My stomach was a little off, tell you the truth, I think it was the crap lunch from the caf, you know, fish surprise. I felt pretty raunchy so I went back to the Res to take it easy."

"Did you see anyone there?"

"Naw. Seemed like everybody else was in class, so I just went to my room."

"Do you have a room mate?"

Grinning suggestively, Jose says, "I sleep alone, Officer."

Wolfrom wants to hit the little creep even more for hitting on Lewis. She's a nice looking lady, but she's old enough to be the little shit's mother, ferchrissake. That's bad enough. What's worse is that Lewis is eating it up.

Smiling back, Lewis says, "All I'm interested in is

what you were doing yesterday, Jose."

Jose shrugs, "Well, since I was feeling like sh... uh, bad, I tried sleeping but I wasn't tired or anything, so I ended up going online most of the afternoon, catching up my Facebook. I hadn't been on in a while 'cause of school stuff, you know, so I was online most of the afternoon."

"Jose, we might have to come back to you if things don't check out, but I think you're all right for now."

"Okay, cool. That's it then?"

Lewis nods and watches him gather himself and shoot her a smile on the way out. Wolfrom closes the door on him and turns back to the partner.

"I can't believe what I just saw!"

Lewis frowns at him, "What?"

"You were practically drooling, I couldn't believe it."

"Oh hey, get off it, he's a hunk, that's all. He was flirting, and his pheromones were definitely speaking to me, I'll tell you that. But he's a kid, Wolfie. Oozing sex maybe, but just a kid."

"The guy reeked of pot, doesn't that tell you something?"

"Yeah, it probably means he was scared to death so he smokes a joint to get the nerve to come talk to the scary cops."

"I dunno, he didn't look nervous."

"Isn't that the idea? Just give it a rest Wolfie. If you're worried don't be. I'm a big girl. I can look without touching. But even if I was into cradle robbing, which I am not, it damn sure wouldn't be with any subject under investigation."

"Good. Had me worried."

75 · · ·

Sitting side by side going through the images that have been submitted for the Christmas slide show, glancing over, Ethan is a little surprised at how fast Liz is whizzing through the images.

"Uh, Liz. Aren't you picking any?"

"No. They're all mostly crap."

"But we know that going in. There's probably only gonna be a couple of photographs. We're not looking for photographs, here, we're picking snapshots, babe, not art."

Liz frowns. "How do you mean?"

"This is more like a yearbook kind of thing, you know, candids of the student body, dances, pubs, fooling around, like that. Most of the pictures are going to be taken by people who can barely turn on a camera. Doesn't matter. We'll run 'em fast to some snappy music from Jamendo and it'll be a slide show."

"Oh." Liz mouses to the recycle bin and chooses 'select all' to restore hundreds of deleted images.

Ethan is aghast. "You've been deleting stuff?"

"Yeah, I thought, I mean they're just digital copies."

"Doesn't mean that everyone who submitted doesn't get a credit. Some people will want their pictures back. Mol suggested we put everything online forever. I don't know if that'll fly, but we don't toss anything no matter how bad."

"Then how do we make selections?"

"Put all the good stuff--" he notes her grimace and grins before continuing, "okay, the better stuff, in a first cut folder."

Liz covers her face with her hands. "Sorry sorry sorry."

"Look, it's okay, this is a bad time." Ethan swivels over and reaches out, enfolding Liz in his arms. "Maybe it'd be an idea to go back to the Res and get some sleep."

She looks up and says, "I can't. I close my eyes and I see Natasha laying there all covered in blood like she was. I can't get it out of my mind."

"Then why don't we head over to the hospital and see how she's doing?" asks Ethan.

76...

"You live in Fyfield House with Natasha Panov?

Though she's paying more attention to her notebook than to him, Oscar smiles at the woman detective.

"Yes, although the ladies sleep on the floor above, the lads sleep downstairs."

Now she looks up to ask, "Is that a problem?"

Oscar laughs nervously. He doesn't dare tell her the joke that's popped into his head, not to the filth. For a man who's never at a loss for something to say, he is now. What's she written in that book of hers already? It would make anyone nervous. The not knowing. God.

"No. It's fine. Most everyone contrives to be out most of the time." She writes it down, but doesn't say anything, pensively reading over what's already written. What if they find him out?

He doesn't know if he could stay here if it came out. Damn. Oscar feels the discomfort level increase exponentially. Understanding it is just an interrogation technique doesn't help, and suddenly the oppressive silence is more than he can bear.

Oscar says, "We go out when we can, to the pub, computer lab, library or the caf. Sometimes Callaghan's or a film for a change. Mostly people only stay in when they're short of funds."

"What's your relationship with Natasha Panov?" asks the male detective standing behind him. Oscar fancies he can feel the man's glare of the on the back of his neck. Disconcerting. Oscar has to twist around to address him.

"There isn't one, then, is there, other than that we're both in Fyfield. To be perfectly honest, this is the first I've heard her surname. Don't really know her, you see."

"She's not your girlfriend?" Detective Wolfrom asks.

"No, no, nothing like that. She's always with that weight lifter. They're both in the photography program, aren't they."

Wolfrom says, "You'd like to get to know her a little

better though."

Oscar shrugs. "I rather doubt we've anything in common. Girl didn't even come to the Ubuntu party."

"Do you have a girlfriend?"

"Not that it's anyone's business, but my own, but no. No, I don't."

"Are you gay?"

"Certainly not, "Oscar says, "Just I'm rather more interested in getting a degree at the moment." Oscar meets the man's eye, starting to feel a bit more confident. "There's actually very little fraternization."

The woman detective snorts derisively; Oscar turns back to her as she says, "That's not what we've been hearing. It sounds as though there's a lot of fraternization."

Oscar is getting angry. This is absurd. He's not some stupid kid for them to push around, he is a bloody grown up. He served in the 31st Southern Brigade for godsake. Why is he letting these wankers make him feel like a child? Shite. Don't get angry. Stay calm, and answer their questions.

Taking a deep breath, Oscar decides it would be better get it over so life can get back to normal. Or as normal as it can get.

"Oh, there's a fair bit 'o that in the Res, but it's cross program fraternization I was meaning. There's not so much as you'd think between students in the photography and computers, considering photography has gone digital, you see."

"That's all very interesting, but that's not what

makes me curious." The woman detective narrows her eyes at him. "What makes me curious is why you would come here."

"Christie is a very good school."

"Still, it's a long way from Tipperary."

"Seeing the world is a fine part of getting an education."

The woman studies him carefully. Oscar can feel sweat trickling down the back of his neck. Damn. Damn and damn. "Still, you could have gone to university in Ireland for free. Christie is expensive for foreign nationals. It doesn't make sense."

Oscar can feel his jaw tightening. This one's done some homework. The question is, how much. Does she know? He stares back, examining her. Looks like it is still a question.

"There were some family issues. I'd rather not say."

She frowns. "That could mean any number of things."

Oscar asks, "Why can't you just leave me in peace?"

She answers quietly, "Because there has been a particularly brutal attack on one of your classmates."

Studying her he decides she probably doesn't know. Yet. But if he tries to lead her along the garden path, she'll see it. And then she'll find out anyway. He sighs heavily. Father Ted always said confession was good for the soul. Maybe.

"Can what I tell you be kept in confidence?"

The woman shrugs. "It depends. If it isn't material

to the investigation, we'll do our best to be discreet. But."

"Anything can happen in a paramilitary organization," Oscar nods. "I know the drill. Army Reserve in Limerick was where I got into computers."

From behind him, the man says, "Family issues?"

Oscar wonders if the chip on his shoulder is playing havoc with his judgement. He thought it was all over. An ocean away. Maybe it will never go away. Like they say, you can run but you can't hide. "Yes, family troubles." Oscar deflates back into the chair. "Do your best to keep it to yourselves then."

Breaking eye contact with a sigh, Oscar leans back and closes his eyes before continuing. "My family was what they call dysfunctional. Textbook. My Da was crazy jealous of my Ma." Oscar stops a moment, takes a deep breath and decides, fuck it.

They'll find it out anyway. Better from him, and be done with it. "One fine day me Da up and killed her... he murdered Ma, strangled her with his hands."

Oscar opens his eyes, and sits up straighter, as though relieved of a weight. "See the world, Ma used to say, and if you must know, that's what it was that brought me here. After that there was nothing there for me. My sainted sister visits the bastard every weekend but as far as I'm concerned he can rot in hell, thanks. To be honest, I don't want to talk about this shite, so I left. No one here knows any of it and that's how I want it to stay." Oscar glares at the cop defiantly. She looks stunned. He asks, "So is that it then?"

Lewis nods, says, "I'm sorry for your loss. We may

have more questions later, but you can go."

Oscar leaves with alacrity, pushing his way past the man, striding into the hall, pushing out the door into the fresh air. Heading down the path, he fumbles in his pockets for the cigarette case. The one he inherited from Ma. Right now he doesn't care who sees him smoking. Even Maggie.

He fookin' needs it.

77 · · ·

Lewis asks, "Any more?" as Wolfrom opens the door and peers out.

"Just one." Wolfrom beckons, and Quentin gets up then comes in, taking the empty seat across from Lewis. He looks at them expectantly.

"Hey, how's it going? Have you got a bead on the guy yet?"

Wolfrom and Lewis exchange glances, then Lewis says, "The investigation is ongoing. I'm sure you understand."

"Okay, sure. Can you tell me how Nat's doing?" he asks.

"Sorry, you'll have to get that information from the hospital." Answers Lewis curtly. "And you are?"

"Quentin Bradbury. Photography, I know Natasha."

"I don't remember your name from the residence."

"I'm in Res, just not at Fyfield." The cop looks confused, so Quentin explains, "My wife and I live in a cottage. I helped Jake and Liz find Nat, and I already spoke to officers at the hospital last night, no I guess it was this morning."

Lewis flips through paperwork. When she finds his original statement she nods and skims it. "You spoke with PC McKay?"

"Yeah. I was wondering do you have any leads?"

"We're looking . Any idea who might have done this?"

"No. It just blows my mind. I hope you get the prick."

"So what can you tell us about Natasha?" she asks.

"She's a great girl, anybody knows that girl likes her. She's feisty, and there's definitely a mouth on her, but she's real, you know? Not a damn mean bone in her body."

"No ex-boyfriend? Bad blood with room mates, like that?"

"She's just... here let me tell you what I mean. I've been having a tough year. Okay, I have to say it was really dumb to get married before college, you know. Well, I know now, anyway. Too many big adjustments all at once. So I've been screwing up. My marriage is on the rocks, my work has been for shit, I'm been drinking too much. But Natasha, she doesn't judge, you know? The gal finds me passed out the other night and she doesn't call security, she kicks me awake and drags me back to the Res and shoves me into the shower. When I come to she sat beside me holding my hand while I threw everything up. Then she sits up all night with me, just talking. Or letting me talk, really. And I don't know how she did it or anything. Maybe just by letting me talk, cause she never even told me what to do."

"I'm sorry. Mr. Bradbury, I'm not sure I'm following you."

"It's that Natasha just, you know, she helped me see how much I've been screwing up. Of course my wife's pissed I came in so late, and I ended up sleeping most of the day, but when Liz was getting people to look for Natasha last night, I was right there. I'm in even bigger shit with my wife because of it, but finding Nat was more important, you know? She's a friend. I'm just glad we found her."

"So you were home alone sleeping for most of yesterday?"

"Yeah, that's right."

"Anyone to verify that?"

"Verify? Well no. I mean, it's a married student residence. They're those tiny little cottages. It's just me and Tamara and she was in class. I guess she'll be able to verify that I left a mess."

Lewis and Wolfrom exchange glances and Quentin is starting to feel as though he's just pinned a bulls eye to his chest. Shit. He knows better than to talk to cops. Hell, his brother is a cop. He's heard the stories. James would be some pissed he knew baby brother was babbling like a fool. James always said never talk to cops. Especially if you're innocent. But he needs to help. Natasha's a friend.

"What about Boris?"

"Boris is a great guy." Taking in their sceptical faces, Quentin is now just as certain that they're fitting Bo up for this. Hell, he can't let that happen either. Bo is a friend, too.

"No way man, Jake told me about the fight, but it doesn't matter, no way Boris is good for it. He might be pissed at her but he's not gonna lift a hand against that girl. He treasures Natasha. I mean, I didn't see him yesterday, but I know Boris, and he is no creep. Those two are tight. They have a closeness, well, if my marriage was that solid it wouldn't be in trouble, okay?"

"That's all for now, Mr. Bradbury. Thanks for your help. We may have more questions later," Wolfrom ushers Quentin to the door.

After closing the door, Lewis says to Wolfrom, "What did you think of that?"

"Hey, I think that had the ring of truth, don't you?"

"What, all they have to do is fess up to their little misdemeanours and they're off the hook? We gotta look at this guy, Wolfie. His marriage is in the toilet and he's out all night with the vic? Crying on her shoulder, he says. We check it out. Nobody's in, but nobody's out yet either. Except the ones with iron clad alibis."

"You mean like a room full of people swearing you were in class with them? Yeah, that works for me, too. But isn't it time we turn the boyfriend? Funny, he's the only one we haven't seen yet."

"Yeah," says Lewis, "he 'treasures' her, so where is he? He's gotta know we wanna talk to him."

"Not at the Res, hasn't been in class."

"Think, Wolfie. He's in the same place whether he did it or not."

Wolfrom's grin spreads. "The hospital, right?"

Lewis nods. "That's where he ought to be, either way."

"We pick up the boyfriend and haul his ass downtown."

"Yeah, we need to get that one in the box."

78 . . .

30's jazz plays softly on the radio while Amelia sits perched on the tall bar stool behind the cash register. Other than Billie Holiday's timeless music the store is quiet, and like any dedicated reader Amelia is entirely oblivious of her surroundings.

Until the cuckoo clock erupts in a cacophony of whistles and chirps. It's nine p.m. time to close up. The mood is broken. Amelia smiles as she slips a bookmark in the book before closing it and laying it on the counter. With a feline stretch she glances around the store to see who she'll have to hurry along so she can close up. But she doesn't see anyone. Nobody's here.

She starts the ancient register cashing out and it provides a rhythmic musical score as it spits out the tape. Amelia leaves it to do its thing as she slides off the stool and takes a quick walk around, checking the blind spots.

The place really is empty. Absolutely no one here; that's a first. Funny, it's a little disconcerting to realize she's the only person in the store. The only one. She's never been able to lock up without having to shoo out late browsers before. She goes to the front and slides the bolt into the floor.

Pulling the cash drawer, she drops the register tape in the bottom, then locks the drawer up in the fire safe in back. Good. Walking the aisles she doesn't notice anything gapingly amiss. Also good. What on earth was she thinking, reading something for enjoyment. That's one of the seven deadly sins for an English major. You're not supposed to have free time to read for enjoyment when you're an English major.

Christ, it must have been over an hour ago when she started reading. There were half dozen students scattered through the store then. She didn't notice any of them leave.

Please God don't let them have swiped half the merchandise. Not on her watch. That would be bad. Very bad indeed; she needs this job. Yes, the money's important but what other job lets you read on the job? She'll have to be careful, this can't happen again. Keep track of customers from here on in.

Nothing is wrong that she can see. Good. Sigh of relief. A bit of shelf straightening. Maybe she can hang onto this job at least 'til exams. She re-shelves a couple of misplaced books.

It's a little bit eerie to be the only one here. She's glad to be done. She tosses the paperback book in her backpack, and slips on her jacket. Yup. She needs this job. Student loan money doesn't stretch to luxuries like winter coats. It's not even winter yet, but she's felt half frozen for weeks.

Letting herself out the back door into the service hall she locks the deadbolt with the key and starts walking down the hall toward the back entrance.

Amelia wonders why the store was so quiet tonight.

Her heels echo on the tiles as she passes the huge trash compactor, happy the garbage here is just paper and dust. It positively reeks in the cafeteria's back hall.

Suddenly, it hits her. The store was quiet because of the attack. Shit. She hasn't seen a lone woman walking anywhere all day. Only her. Shit. Shit. Shit.

The exit door opens out into the faculty parking lot. The empty faculty lot. She opens the door and stops. Oh. Of course, all the faculty are long gone. Leaving an empty lot. And trees. Shadows. Amelia stares at the shadows. She does not want to step out there. Uh uh.

If this was a movie she'd be yelling 'Go back you idiot!'But it isn't a damn movie. No music warns her Jason hides through that doorway. If it was a movie the music could tell her if it was safe. Scary music, go back. Happy music, take the usual route.

Stay on the Road. Keep clear of the moors. Moors. Wait a minute. This is Ontario, there are no moors.

Oh, right. **American Werewolf in London**. She smiles to herself. Too many horror movies when she was a kid, Mom said. Maybe Mom was right?

Mom also told her to listen to her instincts. What are they saying? Hammering heart, clammy hands. Instinct says don't go out there.

Or is that imagination?

Who can tell?

Amelia withdraws her hand and allows the door to swing closed. She leans her head on the cool door, feeling stupid. What to do? Is this a panic attack or is it just being smart?

The place is deserted. The only way to know if there's a rapist out there is to go out there. Uh uh, no how, no way. She could live not knowing.

But that means spending the night here.

Here.

She looks around. It isn't as though there are any soft surfaces to sleep on. It's a book store. There is just no way she would be able to even fall asleep. In a bloody deserted building. If some psycho rapist wanted to get in it wouldn't be too hard. And it's not like there would be witnesses like there would in the Res. There may even be rats. Like Ben. Stop it now.

Get real. She can just imagine the scene if she stays. When the boss opens up in the morning and finds her flaked out in a corner it will surely be the end of the job. Not a good plan.

She has to decide. This is silly. She is a grown woman. She's got her cell phone. If there's anything out there she can always call for help, right? She can do this. Damn it.

Deep breath, push the door open. Step out. Walk confident. Don't look like a victim. Cross the parking lot. There's no one. Actually not so bad. No cars means no hiding places for bad guys. Bonus. Sometimes this imagination shit is more trouble than it's worth. She can always see twenty different outcomes for any scenario. Especially bad ones. Well, since she has at least as many demons as Stephen King. of course she'll be a best selling novelist.

That is, if she lives through the walk home tonight.

Okay, thinking about being scared is certainly not helping. Change tacks. Use the brain. Rational thought is good.

Try not to notice you're walking along the wood chip path.

Or that the lights are almost useless because the heavy foliage hasn't fallen from trees that have grown as tall or taller than the light standards. What does Christie have all those lawnmower guys for? Who cares how long the grass is, they need to get their asses out here pruning the frigging trees so that the light could get through. It doesn't feel safe in the dark.

Come on, no being a victim. Be rational. Think about the situation. Reality is much easier to take than any nightmare. Look it in the eye damn it. Who attacked Natasha?

People are saying that it had to be Boris. Up until the attack nobody had a word to say against Bo, a nice guy. But you can't tell from looking if someone has psychological scars or deviant tendencies. Could be Bo is a monster. She doesn't think so, but she doesn't know. You can't prove a negative. Bo sure seems like a what-you-see-is-what-you-get kind of guy. Why would Boris attack Natasha?

Amelia can't see it. Natasha popped him good, and

he took it. That had to hurt. If Bo was gonna hit back he would have done it then and there, in hot blood. Boris wouldn't have stalked her.

Amelia can't imagine Bo raping Natasha, either, but who really knows anybody else? It could as easily be any other guy in the Res. Now that's a creepy thought. Maybe a co-ed Res isn't such a cool idea after all. Surely nobody she knows could... The cops have to catch the guy, that's all there is to it.

It's more likely that Natasha was attacked by a serial rapist. A stranger. A predator. The kind of bastard who would lay in wait for unsuspecting victims, in the bushes, under cover of darkness.

Like now.

Except the rapist would have no earthly reason to be out right now. There's nobody out here.

All the students are in the library or the pub or the dorm. They sure aren't hanging around deserted parking lots or the paths at night.

Natasha was attacked in broad daylight. That's when a college rapist will be out on the hunt. A serial predator would pick a time and a place where there would be available prey.

That's it. She's gotta dump the psych minor. She knows too damn much about this motivation stuff. What an insane minor for someone with an imagination like hers. Stick to writing sci fi and forget about noir. She's got to change minors.

Maybe she could take shop class.

Do they have shop class in university? Maybe not

but something, anything that doesn't fill her head with information about sociopaths and serial rapists.

Jesus what is she doing out here alone?

Seriously, if the rapist was going to go hunting here, logically, the best selection on campus would be during the day when there is a pool of victims, lots of choices. There's a reason that's when Natasha was attacked.

No predator is gonna sit out here freezing his nuts off in the dead of night on the off chance some girl is gonna wander by. Stop being silly.

Amelia is just starting to breathe easily when it occurs to her: unless it is an organized predator.

One who selects his victims in advance. Does research. A predator like that might know there was one stupid and totally oblivious bimbo that closes the campus book store late at night. By herself. A girl with no social life and so never the slightest variation of routine.

Somehow nine p.m. didn't seem late before there was a rapist running around loose. Her pattern has been to lock up and walk the exact same route home, every night.

Walk with confidence. Yeah. Right.

79 · · ·

Lewis and Wolfrom take a peek in Natasha's room, but she's still out like a light. They make their way to the waiting room behind the elevators. Visiting hours are long over so there's only one occupant, and he's asleep, his bulk stretched out across a couple of miserable plastic waiting room chairs.

"How do we play it?" Wolfrom asks.

"Softly, Wolfie, always go in light first."

Lewis shakes Boris' shoulder, his eyes snap open.

She says, "That double shiner means you're Boris."

Boris asks, "What's wrong? Is Natasha okay, Doc?"

Lewis shakes her head. "We're police. Nothing has changed, but we'd like you to come down to the station with us, answer a few questions."

"Oh. sure. Anything I can do to help. Let me just go say goodbye..."

Lewis smiles and shakes her head. "We just came from there. She's asleep, and I think that's gotta be the best thing for her right now, don't you think?"

Boris nods, "Oh yeah, sure. Let's go do it then. I wanna be back when she wakes up."

Boris starts for the elevators and Wolfrom gives Lewis an appreciative salute as they follow him.

80 . . .

Jose is slouched across the table opposite Eric in the Christie library, an array of texts spread between them. They work companionably on their respective essays, sometimes reading, sometimes making notes, sometimes passing texts back and forth.

Quentin is in a corner study carrel, watching a movie under headphones. Every now and again he'll snort, laugh, or tap the desk, prompting chuckles or remarks from Jose or Eric.

Oscar and Krystal occupy carrels to the left of Quentin's. Oscar is curled around the partition more often than not, explaining things to Krystal, who is not really paying attention since she's focused instead on Jose over Oscar's shoulder. Oscar loses patience.

"You need to get your mind on this or moon over the lad, one or the other. Just now your sharp little brain is reduced to jelly and I am wasting my time because the carpet understands more of what I say than you do."

"I'm sorry Oz, it's just that..."

"I know what it's just. Ask him out? He'll say yes or he'll say no. Either way you'll know and you get on with your life."

She turns away, "It's not that simple, Oz. Besides, you're one to talk."

Suddenly a ringing cellphone disrupts the hush of normal ambient library sound. The librarian glares from the front desk as Eric dives for his laptop bag and mutes the phone. Jose is chuckling as Eric gets up and walks away from the table trying to find a good spot to have a private phone conversation.

"Hello. Yes, I'm in the library so of course texting would have been better. We were together almost two months and you don't know I'm in the library every Thursday? And that doesn't tell you anything?"

Eric paces, obviously uncomfortable as he listens. "No, you look. It's done. There isn't anything to talk about." Eric angrily snaps his phone closed and pockets it.

Returning to the table, in a foul mood now, Eric stares unseeing at the material spread out, then he gives his head a shake and starts packing up.

Jose shoots him a questioning look. "I didn't think you were done yet."

"Oh I'm done alright. My concentration is screwed. I'm going to grab a beer at the pub. Coming?"

"Sure." Jose stuffs his stuff into his bag. "You ever hear me turn down a beer? Never happen."

Eric grins. "Yeah." noticing the librarian is still glaring lasers at him across the room. "Lets get out of here before the dragon lady has us barred for life."

They pass by the main desk, Eric smiles winningly at the glowering librarian as they walk by. "Sorry Mrs. Jones, I didn't realize it was turned on."

The librarian nods, looking a little mollified. "Just make sure it's not next time, young man."

From across the room Krystal wistfully watches Jose's abrupt departure.

Once outside in the crisp night air Jose tells Eric, "I can't believe you man. What you wanna suck up to the old bat for?" Shaking his head, "Man I thought you had balls."

Eric stops and looks at Jose. Then he jumps up and down. And again.

Puzzled, Jose asks, "What are you doing man?"

"Just checking. They're still there."

Jose just stares at Eric. "What are you talking

about?"

"Don't tell me you didn't hear 'em clanking."

Jose breaks out laughing. "You're too much, man."

They start walking again and Eric tells him, "She's just doing her job. And I know how much I want to kill the asshole whose cellphone goes off in the library and screws up my concentration."

Jose laughs. "Yeah I know what you mean. Some people are just assholes, eh?"

"Hey, let's swing by the Book Store. It's around closing time so maybe Amelia will come get a beer with us."

Jose looks at him. "I didn't know you and Amelia were getting it on. Bit of a comedown after Elsie though, uh?"

"Naw, she'd be a step up if you ask me."

"That mousie little thing? After clouds of kinky red hair? I dunno, man, I could've gone to town with that redhead of yours."

"Elsie wasn't worth the aggro, tell the truth." They walk in silence for a bit before Eric just has to ask. "You mean you didn't?"

"What?" Jose looks over at Eric and immediately understands. "You're asking did I boff the red when you were with her? No way man." Jose shakes his head. "No way."

"Don't tell me she didn't come on to you."

"Uh, well, yeah, she did a couple of times."

"She did? And you really didn't?"

"Come on Eric, You're a friend. I wouldn't do that."

"Wow. I guess I just assumed everybody got a piece."

"Lets just say it wasn't easy to turn down, but you don't mess around with a friend's woman, that's all."

"Thanks, Jose."

"So what about this Amelia? How long has this been going on? She's not as hot as Elsie but then she's probably not banging the entire football team at lunch either."

"Let's not go there."

"Sorry."

"Okay. I just rather not talk about it, but I'm not ready to get mixed up with anyone. Amelia and I are just friends."

"Friends? With a girl? You gotta be kidding."

"Why not? I thought you were friends with Mouse."

"Talk about urban legends. You can't be friends with women." Jose shakes his head ruefully, "Mouse is a smoking buddy. She goes with the party but her real friend is the weed."

"Oh, hey, my mistake." They walk in silence for a bit, then Eric asks, "What about Barbie?"

Jose snaps, "Don't talk to me about that Barbie man."

"Oh. Okay, okay. I didn't know that went south on you." Eric says. "This is different with Amelia. This isn't dating, this is friendship. I mean I've had girlfriends before but I never had a girl for a friend before. And even though it's a little weird it's kind of interesting."

They walk in silence some more, then Eric continues, "Sometimes hearing what's going on in her head is kind of like making contact with an alien culture. Or being initiated into a secret society, you know?"

Jose shrugs. "No, I don't. I can't even imagine anything like it, but you're a weirdo anyway, so that's OK."

Weirdo. Eric laughs too. "You think it was Boris?"

Jose looks at him. "Now what are you talking about?"

"Some people are saying they think Boris raped Natasha."

Jose looks surprised. He turns the idea over but then shakes his head. "No way, man. Probably one of those stranger deals, you know. Bo doesn't have it in him."

Eric nods. "That's what I think too."

"He'll be okay. You should have seen the babe he hooked up with at the pub last night. Girl was some hot."

"Good for him."

Rounding the bend they come in sight of the Art Centre. Without saying a word, like a couple of little kids they erupt in a foot race that takes them across the Oval and up the steps to the Campus Book Store. Jose arrives first and dances a victory jig, waving his arms in the air like a victorious prizefighter. Eric chuckles and tries the door, only to find it locked. Pressing his face to the glass Eric cups his eyes with his hands to try to see inside.

"It's all closed up." says Jose. "It's just the night lights."

Eric nods. "Yeah, guess she's gone already. So on to the pub. I can hear a bottle of beer calling my name."

As they head back down the steps to the path, Jose asks, "Eric, what do you see yourself doing in ten years?"

"Me? I just want to be an English professor with leather elbow patches and lots of co-eds to oggle."

Jose laughs again. "Bullshit. Anybody dumb enough to be an English major secretly wants to be Hemingway."

"Not me, " laughs Eric. Then suddenly serious, "I want to be Steinbeck."

"But Hemingway got all the babes."

"Hemingway? He was gay, why did he need babes?"

"That's bullshit. No way Hemingway was gay. Hemingway ran with the bulls, man. He was macho."

"Hemingway only acted macho so nobody would know."

"You're making that up. You must mean Chandler."

"No way," Eric grins, "and you can't even mention Chandler in the same breath with Hemingway. That's sacrilege."

81 . . .

"Well," says Boris, staring morosely at the table bolted to the floor of the Interview Room, "It wasn't a big fight, exactly."

Lewis says, "Really." Unconvinced. "That's not the

consensus at the U."

Boris shrugs. "Well, it was really more like the mother of all misunderstandings."

Lewis studies him across the table, then says, "In my experience when people are knocked down it qualifies as a fight."

Boris looks up and meets her eye. "But it was my fault. She was right to hit me. I acted like an idiot, and I..." Boris sighs and breaks the eye contact, dropping his eyes. He spends a few moments staring at the fake wood grain imprinted on the plastic table as though it offered the meaning of life. Finally, he looks back at Lewis, and says quietly, "I deserved it. She tried to stop me with words, but I kissed her anyway. She was trying to, to push me away. And I... forced her."

Wolfrom says, "Sounds like more than a misunderstanding."

"Yes." Agrees Boris, before burying his face in his hands.

Wolfrom glances at Lewis, who nods then smashes her fist on the table to get the suspect's attention.

"You bastard, this isn't about you, it's about her. Stop your snivelling, it doesn't excuse what you've done! How could you do it? The girl isn't even half your size."

Boris's expression is pure misery. "Stupid me, I told myself that she wanted me to..."

Lewis shoves her chair back with such force it clatters into the wall, bounces off and falls over on the floor. "That is such bullshit. No woman on earth wants to be raped and used as a punching bag. You twisted bastards make me sick, you really do."

Shaking in fury Lewis stalks to the door and slams out of the room. Boris watches the door bang closed, mouth agape. Wolfrom sits quietly beside him, waiting.

Looking around Boris doesn't see any tissue box and he's not about to ask, so he mops his eyes with his sleeve. Boris looks at the other detective, sitting there impassive. Boris tells him, "I was going to say 'kiss her'. You know, like the crab says in that movie? I thought if I kissed her she'd fall madly in love with me. Dumb, eh? I'm not subtle, but, I never... I never... God that's sick."

Wolfrom sits back, folding his arms across his chest. "But somebody did. Your friend Natasha was punched and kicked and raped. Brutally. She was left in the woods, unconscious in the cold. Blunt force trauma, shock, exposure."

"Natasha is my closest friend. Wanting to be more than that doesn't make me a rapist."

"Alright, then help us out here. Tell us what happened. Who might have done it? We need to catch the guy who did it."

"Oh I'd like to catch the guy who did it, alright."

The student's tone sends a chill down Wolfrom's spine, and he studies Boris carefully. That had the ring of truth. But.

"You wanted to kiss her, she said no, but you forced yourself on her anyway. That's assault right there, Boris."

Boris nods. "Yes."

"So after all that, you expect us to believe you just

walked away?"

Boris shrugs. "That's what happened."

"After she made you look like an idiot to the whole school? That can't have been pleasant."

Ruefully, Boris nods. "No it wasn't. That's why I took off back to the residence. I didn't want to have to see anybody."

"So, you were alone the rest of the afternoon?"

"When I got back to the Res I jumped in the shower, but my eye hurt more than usual."

§

Quietly watching the interrogation through the one way glass, Detective Lewis thinks how convenient that shower was. Makes it damned near impossible to get any forensics off the guy. Nothing beats washing your hair in the shower for eradicating any microscopic evidence under the fingernails.

She is pleased to see that Wolfrom's doing such a good job.

Wolfrom asks, "This happens a lot?"

"It wasn't my first black eye-- I've got brothers. But it seemed to hurt more than I remembered. After the shower I was getting an ice pack when I ran into Elsie. She's a med student so she took a look at my eye."

Wolfrom raises his eyebrows. "Redhead? With the hair?"

Boris nods, "Yeah. She said my eye looked okay, and then I just holed up in my room. You know, updating my Facebook status. Unfriending Natasha."

INCONSTANT MOON

82 . . .

Natasha opens her eyes. She really is in the hospital. Damn, it wasn't a dream.

Her head is a little muzzy, tender.

Reaching up, she can feel bandages swaddling her head. Aches all over. Wiggle fingers, toes. All the bits work but everything is stiff and achy. She's sore, everything is sore, but no killing pain. Seems the drugs are pretty much worn off. The I.V. is out. Good, that means she must have enough fluids. Take it slow. It means she'll be able to get back to real life sooner. No time for laying around in bed. Things to do. Like find the bathroom.

She sits up slowly. Okay, not dizzy or anything, that's pretty good. Head a little sore. Gotta pee bad though. Very gingerly she turns sideways, slides her legs to the edge. Feet over. She can do this. She slides off the edge of the bed, feet on the floor.

Cold. A moment of dizzy, grip the bed rail. Hold on. Better. Cold feet, pee, no contest.

She pulls the thin top blanket off the bed and wraps it around her shoulders like a shawl and shuffles toward the doorway and sure enough the side door is a... closet. Next one is... yes. Natasha is acutely thankful for the metal bar positioned beside the toilet. As she lowers herself she is impressed with the accomplishment. You know you're at a low point when going to the potty by yourself gives you the same rush as climbing Everest. The thought triggers a giggle. Ouch. Hurts without drugs.

She's gonna have to check her face in the mirror when she's done. It will be bad.

Maybe better not to look.

No.

She has to know.

Finishing up, she flushes and toddles to the mirror. A mess of bruises down her face. A split lip. Teeth all present and accounted for. All in all not too bad. Considering.

She washes her hands, splashes water on her face. There's a shower stall, with a seat in here. A bath would be so good. Yes. She shuffles back to the door and peeks out. No lock on the bathroom door. Great, she thinks ruefully, that'd be handy if she were to fall and not be able to get up.

Just she wants privacy. She wants a lock, but she needs to wash. The shower head is on a hose clipped to the wall.

This is good. Get a nice gentle spray outta that. Draping the blanket over the towel rack, she lets the pathetic little hospital gown slip to the floor. The mirror above the sink shows a symphony of bruises running down her torso. Ga. Who could do something like this?

On purpose. Suddenly it feels personal.

The fragile balance she's been feeling slips and a surge of anger washes over her. God, what do women see in men? They are nothing but pigs. She grips the edge of the sink and closes her eyes, breathing deeply.

Breathe.

Bath. Think about sitting down in the soothing water. Only antibacterial hand soap liquid on the sink. But really, it's the water she wants, soothing water. Soap might hurt. Have to see. But water will help. Getting clean.

Oh yes.

Over to the bath, she sets the soap on a shelf, then unhooks the nozzle and suspends it to hang low to spray inside the tub enclosure while she gets the water to the right temperature. Brain is ticking. She takes it as a good sign she wasn't stupid enough to shock herself with cold water.

Now the water is warm so Natasha shuts it off and opens the door, stepping carefully into the bath. She pulls the tub enclosure door firmly closed. The last thing she wants is a flood and a bunch of people running in to help. Uh uh.

Natasha turns the water on and uses the the nozzle, gently spraying it all over. Feels nice. But with no lock, she can't get really relax. She feels too exposed.

She puts soap on her hands and lathers up, but rubbing it on her shoulders aches, so maybe not.

But.

She's been avoiding looking down.

Examining herself. She has always been comfortable in her own body. She just was. Until now. Now someone has done something unspeakable to her and she doesn't even know the extent of it.

Because she's afraid to even look. Breathe. Breathe

deeply, suck in the air. Think of something nice. Beach. Waves rolling in, the sun beating down, warming her. Yes. Okay. She can handle it.

No way is she letting that bastard win.

Taking a firm grip on the bar, just in case, she looks down. There are black and purple marks inside her thighs. The bruises and abrasions from the pummelling he gave her are nothing to seeing exactly where hands gripped the insides of her thighs as the bastard raped her.

Chills run down her spine as she stares in horror at the bruises in the shape of hand prints. Seeing where the fingers dug into her flesh makes it all too real and a wave of nausea overcomes Natasha and she vomits bile into the tub. Still she clings to the bar with all her strength.

Ignore the tears. They're tears of anger. Tears of strength. Grip the bar. Tight.

Falling down is not an option.

No fucking way is that asshole gonna get away with this. No fucking way. Open eyes. Turn the nozzle on the bile and spray until it's all gone. Soap. Lather up, rub it in. Damn but that stings.

Everything hurts. Let the water flow. Washing it all away along with the tears. She is alive.

He cold cocked her, she was out cold from the get go. She didn't fight.

Why did he punch the hell out of her? Wasn't raping her enough? She'd heard that rape was a crime of violence, and she can both see and feel how much anger has been unleashed on her. But still she can't make sense of it. It just hurts. Let the water flow. The warmth helps soothe the aches.

She's just starting to drift off when she hears a tentative knock on the door. A clutch of terror washes over her. Shut off the water, grip the nozzle. Some defensive weapon, eh? Rat bastard who did this. Made her scared of a knock on a door.

"Yes?" her voice is stronger than she thought it would be. Although muffled by the door, the voice is unmistakable.

"Natasha, It's Liz. I brought you some things. Do you need a hand in there?"

Uh oh. Sexual fantasy 101. Liz putting hands on her helpless body, helping dress her, Ohmigod, no. It can't happen. "I'm okay Liz. I'll be out in a minute."

"They said you were still sleeping but the IV was out. Want me to go get you some juice or something?"

"Yes please. That'd be awesome. Juice, food. Anything you can get, I'm starving here." She smiles as she hears Liz bounce away. Okay good, now get out and dressed before Liz comes back. She hopes Liz brought real clothes. If it's down to the hospital gown she'll just have to wear the blanket as a toga.

Natasha comes out and sure enough the bag on the bed has clothes, sweat pants. Soft and forgiving. Excellent choices. Oh hell, most of this was in a filthy heap on the floor under her bed. Why did Liz have to go and do her laundry? She'll never get over the silly crush at this rate.

Climbing back onto the bed she struggles into the fluffy sweats. She rests before wrestling her fuzzy socks on. Not hardly dizzy. How good does it get.

A gentle knock on the door. "Come in," Natasha calls, God, she thinks, I almost feel like a human again.

"Natasha, you're dressed. Shouldn't you be in bed?"

"Well I'm on the bed. I actually don't feel too bad, considering. This is so much better than that hospital gown. Girl, I'm gonna have to put you in my will for that."

Liz giggles. "Oh I'm so glad you're all right. You look a million times better." Liz hands Natasha a bottle of apple juice.

"Then I must have looked pretty bad."

Liz nods. "Ethan wanted to come, but I said no."

"Why? Oh, you mean because... I don't think it's him, it would be okay, you know. Ethan's a friend, he's a nice guy."

Liz smiles. "Yeah, I think so. You think he's nice?"

Natasha says, "Yeah, I do."

"They really had you doped to the eyeballs."

"I don't remember much, it was pretty surreal." Holding the juice bottle gingerly, Natasha takes a sip and the juice stings her split lip, but she needs the liquid. "But I'm close to clean and sober right now and... you know, I could swear all of these clothes were filthy, under my bed even." Natasha purses her lips. "What'd you have to go and do my laundry for? You didn't have to do that."

"You'd have done the same for me, I didn't want, I mean I wasn't trying to make you feel bad, but I felt a little guilty enough going in your room without permission and I didn't want to go through your drawers, too, that's so personal. So I just threw some of your stuff on the floor in with the load of laundry I was doing for myself anyway. No biggie."

"Don't be silly." Natasha sits back, relaxing a little. "Liz. You were doing a favour. I mean, really, getting clothes for somebody in the hospital isn't exactly the same as ransacking their drawers so you can read their diary." Thinking, ransack my drawers anytime.

"You have a diary? Oh the chances I missed."

"Yeah right. Even if I was insane enough to have a diary I sure wouldn't leave it laying around Fyfield House, at least not without heavy duty encryption, that's for sure. Did you bring chocolate?"

Liz pulls empties chocolate bars from her bag onto the bed. You should probably have some real food though."

Natasha asks, "Is the cafeteria still open? What time is it?"

"Only vending machines at this point. I can go out and get you a salad from Lick's if you want."

"Screw salad, I'm a carnivore. I want a Homeburger with extra Guk. French fries. Maybe two Homeburgers. I'm starving." Suddenly Natasha frowns, remembering, "Hey, where's Boris?"

"Oh, the cops were just taking him away when I got here."

Natasha sits up abruptly, scattering chocolate bars and clothes. "What?"

"The cops, they were putting him in a police car." seeing the look on Natasha's face Liz falters, "Why, shouldn't they have? Wasn't it him?"

Natasha shakes her head. "Shit no. They arrested Bo? No, it wasn't Bo. No way. Why would they think it was Bo? I told them I couldn't recognize who it was."

"Then they have to figure it out without your identification. I guess everybody told them about that big fight you had."

"But it wasn't Bo."

"How can you be so sure? I mean Nat, if you don't know who did it, how can you know who didn't do it?"

"For one thing, he was here today. There is no way he could have faced me if he's done it without me knowing. And even if Bo was capable of raping me, there is no way, there is just no way he could ever have beat on me like that."

Glancing at Natasha's bandaged head, she replies, "I thought that was just to knock you out so you couldn't recognize him,"

Natasha's pulls up the sweatshirt to show Liz the livid bruising on her stomach.

"Oh my god." breathes Liz.

"That is just the tip of the iceberg. I want you to get your camera and lights set up and take some good clear pictures. When they catch the bastard I want to make damn sure he goes to jail."

"Oh, uh, yeah, sure of course." Liz shivers. "But Natasha, if it wasn't Boris, who was it?"

"I don't know. Could have been almost anybody." Natasha slides off the bed. "Did you bring me shoes?"

"Oh yeah, they're right here." Liz pulls a pair of running shoes out from under the bed. Natasha steps into them without untying them, wiggling until her feet are inside.

"I should've brought your Crocs, that would have been the smart thing."

"It's okay, my feet are the only thing that don't hurt. Really, these are fine. You are an angel, girl." Natasha is pulling her fleece hoodie on as she walks gingerly toward the door. Liz says, "Hey, wait. Where are you going?"

"I have to go help Boris. The cops have got him, and he's not the guy."

"Wait, why not call? What's that cop's name, Lawrence?"

"Lewis. Okay, I guess that'd work. I just can't stand the idea of them picking on Bo."

Liz suppresses a smile as she flips open her phone.

How can Natasha be so worried about a guy like Boris getting picked on? Boris can take care of himself.

"Yes, could I speak to Detective Lewis please?"

Natasha leans on the closet door, breathing. Waiting, while Liz waits. How could they take in Boris! "No, I need to speak to her now." Liz rolls her eyes. "Yes, that's what we need to talk to her about. Natasha says he isn't the guy."

Natasha zips up the hoodie, and turns to leave the room.

"But she is sure." starting to sound angrier, "Look, I'm not four years old and I'm certainly not making this up. Look, Natasha needs to speak to the detective. No, not later. Now."

Glancing back at the door Liz sees Natasha is gone. She snaps the phone closed and hurries after her friend.

83 . . .

Amelia's heart pounds as she glances over her shoulder.

What was that noise?

Or that one. A footstep?

Oh, God. It sounded like somebody getting hit.

Why didn't she listen to her inner voice? What the heck is she doing walking around out here in the dark when there's a fucking rapist loose on campus?

Stupid stupid stupid.

There's a rustling in the trees beside her. She has no idea how to even guess what it is. Is it some kind of animal? Squirrels are sleeping now, right? What animals are awake at night? Skunks? Oh, wouldn't that be great. Owls. Mice too, oh and bats. Maybe a raccoon?

It could just as easily be a human predator. How do you tell? Characters in books and movies always know. How?

She's read about using keys as a weapon, so she

holds the ring in her palm, pushing the pointy ends of the keys between her knuckles. It's supposed to make a big impression if you have to punch somebody.

Well.

Gives her something to hold onto anyway.

Just walk faster. Take the right branch of the path and go to the pub instead. Much closer than the Res and there's bound to be somebody to walk home with from there. Someplace bright. She needs light and people and noise. Not quiet and dark like this.

Danger.

She should have thought all this through before blundering out into the night.

Stupid.

Why is it she can meticulously plan out every detail in an outline but her life is so totally haphazard? Start getting organized. Pay more attention to the real world, and less to fictional characters.

Just walk a little faster. Don't be such a wuss.

There's nothing out here. Nothing bad ever happens to her. She's too ordinary. Nothing here to interest a monster.

Just a boring middle class girl with boring middle class dreams and --

Crack.

What was that?

Shit. Her heart is pounding.

Where did that come from? What was that?

Walk a little faster.

Stop it. Nothing bad ever happens to her.

Nothing bad is likely to happen. Hell, it's hard to be a novelist with life experience this boring. Boring Amelia, follows the rules. Not at all interesting.

Never breaking a bone, getting knocked up, rolling the car, or getting caught shoplifting. Everybody else, never her. She doesn't do wild and crazy things. No. She's too boring. She's always tucked up somewhere with a book. Oh god.

Maybe that means it's her turn now.

No. Don't be an idiot. What are the odds? Well, let's think about this for a minute. Since all the intelligent women are taking sensible precautions, since they aren't running around in the dark all by themselves in the middle of the night. Well, those women have it made.

If the limp-dick-rat-bastard-rapist is out hunting, she is probably the easiest target going.

But what are the odds?

Probably better than she wants.

She's got her cell phone. What could happen?

Hmm. Quite a lot before help could possibly arrive.

That's the problem.

It can't be far to the pub now anyway.

Funny how close it always seemed in the daylight.

Stay calm, that's the ticket.

One time a nurse told her hospital medical staff aren't supposed run, even in an emergency, because it triggers the flight response and adrenaline floods through them and makes them all jittery. They need to keep calm to properly assess the nature of the medical emergency to treat it.

So the same thing should be true here, right? Running will just make her more scared.

Right?

Except the sound of feet pounding on the path behind her sends a cold spike of terror down her spine. Making her heart pound faster. Goddamn. Somebody is running toward her.

Fuck the path. She dives into the bushes and cowers behind a tree as the running feet come closer.

Screw this victim crap. Time to call Dudley Do-right. But Eric will have to do. She pulls out her cell phone and punches in his number. He's in the library tonight.

She holds her breath as the number dials while the pounding footsteps come closer. She squeezes her eyes closed and holds her breath as the sound of the feet get closer and then... run past. She is about to start breathing again when she realizes that there are a second pair of feet running past. Oh my god it IS the rapist and he's chasing somebody. Gotta help stop the bastard.

She steps out on the path and starts following the sound of running feet. Suddenly she hears the sound of a ringing cell phone. And Eric's voice is coming out of the phone still clutched in her hand, improbably saying, "I would've won if I didn't have to stop to answer the phone. Hello?"

And from the path ahead she hears Jose laughing. Jesus they scared her half to death and they were running a footrace? In the dark? In the middle of the night?

Men are nuts. Sheesh.

Amelia says into the phone, "Hey Eric is that you? I'm done work and I was gonna drop by the pub and grab a beer. You wanna come?"

84 . . .

Several empty beer glasses adorn the table in the booth Barbie and Tamara share along the back wall of the pub. Barbie looks clear as a button, but Tamara is swaying and unfocused. Slurring her words.

"That bastard, I have no idea when he even came in last night."

"Did you ask him?"

"I'm not gonna give him the satisfaction. He wants to know he can tell me."

Barbie bites back a chuckle, "You mean you're going to ask or you want him to tell you?"

"Yeah that's what I said."

85 . . .

The cab pulls up in front of the police station, and Liz pays the driver before going around to help Natasha get out.

Her friend looks smaller than usual and there is a gray cast to her skin Liz hadn't noticed at the hospital. But there's no stopping her, so she just helps, slamming the door and waving at the driver.

Liz follows Natasha through the doorway and to the front desk where she leans on the counter waiting for the officer to hang up the phone.

"No, he won't be back on until tomorrow. Yes, that's right. Thank you." He hangs up the phone and takes in the two girls. "Can I help you ladies?"

Natasha nods. "Yes, I'm here to see Detective Lewis."

He shakes his head, "I'm sorry ma'am, she's busy at the moment. Do you have an appointment?"

"No, no appointment, but I need to see her now." Natasha repeats quietly but firmly.

"Are you the lady who called earlier?" he asks, getting it.

"No," Liz tells him, "That was me. I was trying to keep her in the hospital."

"I need to see Detective Lewis."

Shaking his head in frustration, "I'm sorry ma'am, that's just not possible."

"Why can't you just tell her I'm here."

"I will, as soon as she comes out."

"And how long will that be?"

"I don't know. As long as it takes."

"And in the mean time she's questioning the one guy I know didn't attack me. How would you feel if that was you in there?" she frowns at him.

"What are you talking about, lady?"

"How would you like to spend an evening being interrogated about a rape you didn't do while a witness who could clear you was cooling their heels in the lobby? Wouldn't you rather..." suddenly all the colour just falls from Natasha's face and her eyes roll back as she collapses in a heap on the marble floor.

"Natasha!" Liz drops to the floor, cradling Natasha's head.

The officer comes out from behind the desk. Liz looks up. "Is there someplace she can lay down?"

"You said she was in the hospital?"

"Yes, she's the one who was attacked at Christie. Look, the floor is cold. Can we find a chair for her or something? She has to talk to Detective Lewis. If she can talk to Lewis, I can convince her to get back to the hospital." Liz looks earnestly at the young officer. "Please?"

"Here, let's get her off the floor." He helps Liz carry Natasha to an empty office, and settle her into a high backed swivel chair with arms.

The officer goes to find Lewis.

Natasha opens her eyes as the door closes behind him. "It worked, huh?"

Liz stares at her. "I can't believe you faked that."

"Not fake, I just stopped holding myself together and let go. Guess I'm in worse shape than I thought. Sitting is better anyway."

"Look, Nat, we have to get you back to the hospital."

Natasha sets her jaw, shaking her head. "Not until Boris is out of trouble."

"He's a big strong boy, and in case you haven't noticed, you're sick as a dog."

"I'm not sick, I'm hurt. And it wasn't Boris who hurt me, I'm telling you, and I won't be able to rest if I'm worried about Boris."

"But you can't know..."

"Yes, I can. We had a big fight, right. Who hit who? I hit *him* Liz, he didn't raise a finger, don't you get it? He would never hurt me on purpose. Never."

The door opens and Lewis comes into the room.

"You look as though you should still be in the hospital Ms. Panov."

"Natasha."

"I don't understand what you're doing here. You couldn't identify your attacker, so we're following leads. Let us do our job and you do yours by getting well."

"It wasn't Boris."

Lewis lightens up, "Look, I understand you want to help but you didn't see the man who attacked you, and we need to follow up all leads. That sad fact is that most attackers know their victims. They attack people they know. You were probably hit on the head so that you couldn't make an identification."

Natasha holds up her hand. "I know all that. Liz told me much the same thing but I know it wasn't Boris. I've been trying to figure out how I know it and I've just now figured it out."

Lewis crosses her arms, clearly sceptical. "Why do

you think it wasn't Mr. Horvat?"

"Because I know what he smells like. Look, you have to understand, Bo is my best friend. We're together all the time. I know what he smells like when he's just had a shower and I know what he smells like when he's had a few too many or he's stinking up the world after an all nighter. It was not Boris who attacked me, it was somebody who smells different. You have to let him go."

Lewis cocks her head, "What kind of smell?"

Natasha frowns. "I'm not sure. Just that it wasn't Bo. It was somebody else and you need to catch the guy. Look I don't want the asshole to get off, but I want it to be the real asshole in jail."

"It would help a lot if you could give some idea."

"I don't know, I'll think about it. Look, the nurse said they did a rape test when I was still out of it. Can't you check the DNA or something?"

Lewis nods, "Yes, Ms. Panov, we can and we will. Your Mr. Horvat is providing a sample right now, but it will be weeks before we have results."

"He's giving you a sample? Volunteering it, right?"

Lewis nods. "Why can't you just let him go then? I know it wasn't him. Why won't you believe me?"

"Victims are often unhelpful when they're in an abusive relationship."

Natasha looks at her.

"Oh. I get it." Sighs deeply. How does she do this? Fidgeting, staring intently at the floor, "I'm not in an abusive relationship. Boris is my best friend. It's the most important relationship I have but that's what it is, friendship. And I've never heard of an abusive friendship."

Lewis frowns, "That's not what everyone else thinks."

"I know. I, uh, kind of wanted it that way. But Boris and I are not involved romantically and never will be. Because I'm gay."

Lewis nods. "Ah."

Liz looks confused. "But, everybody saw you kiss Boris."

Afraid to even look at Liz, Natasha answers quietly, "Uh, no. Boris kissed me. Boris was trying it romantic. That's why I decked him, 'cause he kissed me and didn't let go."

"All the more reason he should be a suspect." says Lewis.

"You don't know him. He's big and he looks tough but he's the sweetest guy I've ever met. If it was Boris, I would know."

"I'll cut him loose for now, but he is still very much a suspect. You can be sure that if the DNA evidence says different--."

"It won't," Natasha says.

"Alright. Wait here." Lewis leaves to see about Boris.

"I'm sorry, Natasha. I didn't realize," Liz says Liz.

"Yeah, I know."

"We can still be friends, though, can't we?"

"Sure we can. Um. Have you ever known anybody gay before?"

"Well, not officially. I've got an uncle who might be, but he's not saying, it wouldn't go over well in a small town."

"Well, I was stupid enough to come out to my parents when I graduated from high school. My mom couldn't get me on a plane fast enough to the farthest away school she could think of. So. I just decided not to be anything. Celibate. It was like fate to meet Boris because we just clicked, you know?"

"Well," smiles Liz, "Of course it was fate. He's Boris and you're Natasha."

"Yeah, yeah, yeah. Boris thought it was funny."

"Uh, um, does this mean you're coming out of the closet?"

"Yeah. Everyone at school assumed Boris and I were a couple, and that gave me some protection, but if it hurts Boris it's gotta stop." Natasha rubs her eyes with her sleeve. "It's my fault he's in here. Even though it was kind of accidental I... guess I've kind of lead Boris on. I know that's no excuse but, oh I'm too tired and everything hurts. So tired." Natasha's head droops back on the chair. Asleep.

86 . . .

Oscar and Quentin walk Krystal to her car. "Look you guys don't have to do this."

"Don't be stupid. Until they catch the guy people

need to watch out for each other," says Oscar.

Quentin adds, "You don't want to end up like Natasha."

Krystal says, "But I don't want to be a bother," as they arrive at her car.

"One second," says Quentin as he peers through the rear window to make sure the back seat area is really empty. "Always check the back before unlocking the door."

Krystal nods then unlocks it. "Thanks, Q, I never would have thought of that. How's Tamara handling all this?"

"Damned if I know, she's not talking to me. Near as I can tell she's bunking with Barbie. At least she's not on her own."

"Oh Q, I'm sorry." she says.

"Don't worry, Krys. It might even be for the best."

Krystal slides in behind the wheel and starts the engine.

"Sorry I couldn't concentrate, Oz. I wasn't trying to totally wreck your evening."

Oscar grins. "No worries. The evening is just starting. We're heading out to the pub."

Krystal laughs. "Okay, you have fun then. Thanks guys."

"We'll do our best lass. Drive safe."

"Lets get a move on," suggests Quentin.

"Lead on McDuff, I'm bloody freezing." As she pulls out of the lot they jog back down the path.

87 . . .

Mouse, Maggie and Kate sit at the bar in the pub as Elsie intently tries to peel the label off her beer bottle. It isn't coming off easily, she has to scrape and fiddle with it. As fragments peel off she adds them to the pile of shreds on the bar.

Mouse says, "I think it sucks. Just because some creep is running around hurting women we're all supposed to cower behind closed doors waiting for big men to keep us safe?"

Elsie shakes her head. "This is the twenty first century for god's sake, not Victorian England."

"Works for me." Maggie sees how annoyed they are so she says, "All we need to do is buddy up until they get him."

Mouse turns to Maggie. "Kate said you met the rapist."

"Maybe, maybe not. It was a flasher. He jumped out of the woods in the rape zone."

"No!" Mouse laughs out loud. "What did you do?

"It was ridiculous. So I just laughed. At him. I guess he didn't know how to handle it and he just took off."

"That was brilliant, Maggie." says Mouse. "What made you think to do that?"

"No thinking, Mouse, it just happened."

Kate says, "It was brave."

"I hope this isn't the same guy 'cause I never reported it."

"This sounds like a timid man, not the same man I think."

"Maybe not, but Officer Wolfrom said it might be."

"I wouldn't worry about it," says Elsie. "Mouse is right. A flasher is minor. What happened to Natasha was not."

"They don't even know if it's some random guy or if Natasha was targeted specifically." says Maggie.

"Who would do something like that to Natasha on purpose? Surely she has no enemy that would do this thing." Mouse frowns. "It would have to be a serious enemy. I do not like to think this, but the rapist must still be out there."

It's quiet as they all stare at Mouse, wishing she hadn't said it out loud.

"I got the idea they think it might be Boris." Maggie says.

"Not a chance!" snaps Elsie.

"I don't think it's him either, but when it comes down to it, how do you know that about somebody?" asks Maggie.

"It isn't in his nature."

"You can't know that Elsie."

"Yes I can. I saw him that afternoon, Maggie. The guy was devastated."

"You think he's innocent because he was upset? How do you know he wasn't upset because he'd attacked Natasha?"

"I don't buy that." Elsie shakes her head. "He was too fragile."

"That's crap Else and you know it." Maggie says. "It could be anyone without a solid alibi. So maybe it is Boris. Or Eric. Or even Jake."

Elsie says, "Then don't leave out Oscar. Or Nick either for that matter."

Maggie nods slowly. "You're right we can't. How well does anyone know anyone? People see what they want to see. I mean look at Dexter."

Kate snorts. "Maggie, Dexter is a fictional character. Look, you guys can think what you want but I know it's not Nick."

"You know what they say," Elsie says, "The wife's always the last to know."

Kate glares at Elsie so Mouse leans in and says. "The police will investigate. Arguing will not solve anything."

Kate says, "It could be anybody. Except Nick."

Suddenly there's a strange man standing beside Elsie and they all startle, except Elsie.

Making eye contact with Elsie, he says, "Hey there, my name's Harry, and I was wondering if you'd maybe like to dance?"

Elsie smiles and slides off the stool. "Hi, Harry, I'm Elsie, and I would love to dance with you."

The others silently watch Elsie follow Harry to select songs from the jukebox before heading onto the tiny dance floor.

Mouse says, "How does she do that?"

"She must transmit some kind of subliminal 'come hither' signal," says Maggie.

Kate laughs. "That's it exactly. It's called pheromones."

Mouse says, "Maybe that's the guy."

"That'd be convenient."

"Well, yeah. Then it wouldn't have to be somebody we know."

"Don't say that, Maggie," insists Mouse. "I want to be able to sleep at night."

Elsie's chosen an Allison Crowe torch song from the jukebox. It's a very slow dance. Naturally. Elsie slides into Harry's arms and they begin to dance.

Sighing heavily, Maggie says, "If he is the guy, after Elsie's through with him he won't be bothering anyone tonight."

Elsie and Harry sway to the music, pressed as tightly together as is possible. Elsie's auburn mane undulates, drawing a veil across a good bit of the face to face contact.

Mouse frowns. "Rape isn't about sex, Maggie. It is about violent domination."

Maggie says, "Yeah I know. I was trying to make a joke."

Kate says, "Bad taste."

Harry and Elsie steam up the dance floor, clearly enjoying themselves as they bump and grind. And grind.

The side door to the pub opens and Jose walks in,

followed by Eric. On his way into the room Eric's attention is caught by the familiar torch song. He glances over at the dance floor and stops dead as his eyes light on Elsie. On the dance floor with some guy.

Coming in after, Amelia only just manages to not run into Eric. He just stands there, mesmerized, watching as Elsie running her hands down some guy's back and grabbing his butt. Elsie throws her head back and the guy nuzzles her neck, more groping than dancing.

Amelia grits her teeth at the sight of the Medusa screwing up some other poor schmuck. Eric certainly doesn't look like he's gotten over her. His rigid back tells her that Elsie is carving two notches for the price of one.

As Allison Crowe sings passionately about how she never loved a man, Amelia can't believe the wave of fury that washes over her while she watches that bitch Elsie giving all women a bad name.

Why do guys fall for women like that? Every time. Poor sap.

Elsie locks her eyes on Eric and smiles. She licks her lips and arches her back, doing some groping of her own, all the time keeping her eyes on Eric. Amelia is floored by the viciousness of it, just as Eric turns on his heel and stalks out.

Jose is ordering a drink at the bar before he realizes that he's lost Eric.

Jose sees Mouse, Maggie and Kate sitting on the other side of the bar when Maggie smiles and waves.

The three witches, Jose thinks, as Amelia joins him. "What happened to Eric?" he asks.

"She did," Amelia says, nodding gesturing back toward Elsie's display on the dance floor.

"Shit," mutters Jose.

"Look Jose, You've been his friend longer than me, is he gonna be all right?"

Jose says, "Probably not. I better go find him, take him to some nice bar far far away from the red menace."

"I didn't think she'd be here. She's never here."

"S'alright. You OK to get home?"

"Oh yeah, don't worry about me."

Jose takes a swig of his beer and starts to get out his wallet, but Amelia waves him away. "I'll get it, just go find him."

Jose smiles ruefully, "Thanks," then he heads out.

Amelia turns back to the bar and orders a fuzzy navel. One good thing, the guys didn't hear her order the sissy drink.

88 . . .

Liz kills the Tetris game she's been playing when she sees Detective Lewis leading Boris toward her. She stuffs the phone in her pocket.

Boris asks, "Where is she?"

Liz nods back at the office and says, "She's asleep. I just want to get her back to the hospital."

"Can I have a minute with her?" Liz nods, and Boris

heads into the office while Liz calls a cab.

Boris goes in and just stares at his sleeping friend a moment. A great lump is forming in his throat. He brushes at his eyes, but gets himself together. Crossing to where Natasha slumps awkwardly in the chair, he squats beside her.

From the doorway Lewis watches as the intensity of his gaze makes Natasha open her eyes. When Natasha sees Boris her relief is visible as she relaxes and gives him a wan smile.

"Oh Bo, you're OK."

"Of course I'm okay, but you're not, idiot. What the hell are you doing out of the hospital? You look like shit. Your skin is gray."

"I couldn't stand by and let 'em give you the third degree."

"It's okay, they didn't even use rubber hoses. I'm fine."

"But you were in trouble."

"The best thing you can do for me is for you to get better. Liz is calling a cab and we're gonna take you back and you are going to stay in the hospital until the doctors say you can go home if I have to get them to tie you to the bed, you hear?"

Natasha smiles wanly at Boris. "If you visit me every day."

Lewis thinks it's a touching scene.

Trouble is, she's seen too many instances of people hurting the ones they love.

89 . . .

Jose sees Eric disappear ahead of him on the forest path. It is cold. Pulling the zipper of his jacket all the way up to his neck still doesn't warm him up, so Jose jogs after, hoping the activity will help. But where did he go?

There he is.

"Hey Eric, wait up!" he calls into the night.

But Eric turns off the pavement and heads into the forest. "Jeeze," mutters Jose, "I don't need this shit."

Jose steps up his pace, catching up to where he thinks Eric might have gone off the path, but there is no obvious indication. Jose is no tracker, he is pure city boy.

"ERIC," he bellows. "Where the hell are you, you asshole?" Jose strains to hear, briskly rubbing his arms, then stamping his feet, trying to stay warm. Fat chance. It is goddamn cold out here. He peers into the adjoining forest. Can't see nothin' for the goddamn trees.

"Damn it Eric it's cold out here."

"Just leave me the fuck alone!"

Jose moves through the underbrush in the direction of the voice. "You got no call to sit out here and freeze to death over some no account bitch. You don't have to hang with me man, just come back to the Res. I'll even give you my forty pounder of Jack Daniels. You can drink all by your lonesome if you want."

"It's only half a bottle and you know it, you prick."

Jose steps into a small clearing. He's sure this is where the voice was coming from. But where is Eric?

"Come on out, you goof. Where the hell are you?"

"None of your fucking business. Just go away."

The voice is right there, but Jose can't see anything. He peers into the shadows. Then he looks up. Sure enough, Eric's legs dangle from a branch in an oak tree. "She ain't worth it man. Get your head outta your ass or you're gonna get your ass thrown outta school."

"Go 'way."

"Hey man it's cold. It's winter. C'mon down."

"You think this is winter you're in for a surprise."

"You'll be surprised when I pound you into dog food."

"I like it up here just fine. You go on without me."

"You stay there you're gonna get hypothermia. She's still back at the bar. Look, you want her to know she's fucked you up?"

"No way, Jose."

"Then get your ass down here."

"Okay, okay. I'm coming." Jose watches in horror as Eric just lets go and starts to topple off the branch.

"Wait, grab on!" yells Jose, startled, Eric grabs hold, and swings from the branch, feet dangling a few feet above the ground.

"Don't just fall out you shit, you break something I can't carry you back, just hang on, hang on." Eric dangles patiently while Jose positions himself just out of range, ready to do his best to assist the landing. "Okay, come on down."

Eric lets go and drops gracefully to the ground, allowing his legs to absorb the impact. Jose plants his hands on his hips. "You've done that before."

"No shit Sherlock. I'm a tree climbin' boy from way back. I like trees."

"I'm turning blue here man, and you're being an asshole."

"You play your cards right maybe I'll let you have some J.D. Maybe help you get warmed up."

Jose shakes his head in disgust and starts through the trees. Eric follows, biting his tongue, deciding he'd better not rag Jose about being a 'city boy' again.

90 . . .

Barbie smiles her thanks at Billie the bartender as she pays for two more bottles of beer, then carries to the back booth. Tamara looks fairly wretched.

"Why does he hafta be such a jerk, y'know? Just go to school, do whatcha gotta do. How hard is that? There's more to life than playing allatime."

§

Elsie and Harry are gone and Amelia sits in Elsie's seat between Maggie and Mouse. At the end of the bar Kate leans in and says, "No one was more surprised than I was when Elsie showed up with Mouse and Maggie. I think this is the first time I've seen her in here."

"Maybe she's having a hard time finding guys?" says Amelia.

Kate laughs. "Elsie? I doubt it. All she has to do is flip that hair and every male for miles around jumps to attention."

"I don't know, she's been pretty sexually active. I mean, if, uh, you know there's a Lotta concern about STDs out there." Maggie glances at Amelia, "Oh, hey, I'm sorry, I... "

"Sorry?" Amelia frowns. "What?"

Maggie says, "Poor guy. You know what they say, everyone your partner and all their partners..."

"You think..." Amelia frowns. "Wait a minute. I haven't slept with Eric. We're just friends."

Kate shrugs, "Well, Nick says Elsie's at the top of her class, so she's probably smart enough to use protection anyway."

The door swings open and Oscar and Quentin come in, Maggie waves and they drift over to join the girls at the bar, rubbing their hands together.

"Good evening ladies. How is everyone?"

"Just lovely, Oz." smiles Kate. "You guys look cold."

"We escorted Krystal to her car, farther than I realized. I do believe I'll be digging out my woollens."

"Still finding Canada a bit cold?"

"Yes," says Oscar, "but this year I am prepared."

Mouse leans in front of Oscar to ask Quentin, "Excuse me, Q, have you heard anything more about Natasha?"

"She'll survive, Mouse. She's busted up but there's no brain damage. They're keepin' her in the hospital another day for observation to make sure. She was beaten pretty badly."

Mouse sighs. "She'll get better then, that's good."

Oscar says, "I can't urge you ladies enough, stick together until they get the bastard. Don't go anywhere without a buddy."

There's a general wave of nodding through the company and Quentin says, "I just want a quick draught and then I need to head home hopefully in time to catch a word with my wife."

"Uh, Q... " Mouse stops him. "Tamara's here."

Quentin raises his eyebrows. "Where?"

Mouse nods. "In the booth at the back."

Quentin gets up and heads toward the back booth.

Maggie leans in, "What was that all about?"

Mouse sighs. "Paradise Lost, I think."

Barbie looks miserable sitting on the outer bench, Tamara sprawls at the back of the booth, slumped against the wall in the corner. The table is littered with empty glasses and beer bottles.

Tamara opens bleary eyes as Quentin slides in beside Barbie, and says, "Hey, doll."

Barbie rolls her eyes and looks away. Tamara sits up at the sound of his voice, and she focuses on Quentin. "Look what the cat dragged in."

He smiles at her. "Babe, I missed you."

"Missed me." Shaking her head, Tamara leans toward Barbie. "You hear that? Says he missed me." Turning back to Quentin, she glowers. "If you missed me... if you... if you gave a shit you woulda... would a...

aw shit... I am so mad at you."

Quentin turns to Barbie. "She's mad because?"

"You stood her up again, didn't even come home."

"I'm sorry, Tam, I was gonna see you last night. I tried calling but you never answered. It went straight to voicemail."

"You didn't leave a message, you din... din call back."

"No I didn't. Stuff happened, I was busy..." he shakes his head. "Look, I'm sorry. I was going to..."

"I'm sorry our marriage isn't 'portnat to you, goddammit." Tamara slides along the bench and out of the booth.

"It is important, I was on my way home when Jake asked me..."

"Always time for a bud, eh, Q. Just never any for me."

"... to help search for Natasha."

Tamara doesn't make the connection as she sways drunkenly beside the booth, but Barbie does. "That's the girl who was attacked."

"Yes. And when we found her we had to wait on cops and paramedics. And then we all went along to the hospital, and you know I couldn't even text you then, Tam."

Tamara blinks. "Oh."

"She'd been laying out there unconscious for hours. They think she was attacked in the afternoon."

Barbie shivers and says, "It got below freezing last

night."

Tamara softening. "The girl gonna be okay?"

"How right can anyone be after that? I don't know. But I was on my way home. Then everything happened so fast."

"So one time you had a good reason."

"Look, Tam, why don't we go home. Talk there."

Tamara makes eye contact with Quentin, or tries to. It's just that focusing is so damn difficult.

"Come on, we can work it out. We always have before."

Which is what he always says.

"No Q, we don't. Talk tomorrow. I'll call."

"I love you babe." Quentin turns on his heel.

Tamara watches him walk away through blurry eyes. Moving fast. Not looking back. Watches him open the door and go.

Barbie realizes that she's never really liked Q. Good riddance. When she's thinking clearly, even Tamara will probably realize she'll be better off without him. Calling her 'doll.' What a jerk.

"Are you all right?" Barbie asks, for the first time realizing that her swaying friend might not be. Tamara reaches for the booth back hoping for support but ends up nose down on the bench. From under the table she says, "I'm OK."

"Maybe we should just go." When there's no response Barbie gets up and goes around the table to check. "Tamara?"

"Yeah." Barbie helps Tamara sit. "God, I'm

wrecked."

"I think it's safe to say you've had too much to drink."

Tamara says. "Maybe we just need one for the road."

"I don't think so." Barbie reaches out a hand and Tamara takes it and Barbie pulls her friend to her feet.

Tamara says, "Maybe we could just sit, I feel a bit rocky."

Barbie shakes her head, sliding her arm around Tamara's shoulder. "Let's get you some fresh air, be good as new."

Barbie heads for the exit, half dragging Tamara.

Tamara suddenly swivels and pulls Barbie into a bear hug, says, "Jus a minute."

At a loss what to do, Barbie stands there, feeling exceedingly stupid as Tamara continues clutching at her, rocking, shaking. Oh god, she's crying. "Lets just go outside. It's only a few more feet." But Tamara just hugs her tighter. "Come on Tamara. Just walk."

Barbie tries to give her a push start and suddenly Tamara lets go and pulls back, her eyes roll around then focus on Barbie. Tamara's eyes clear as she smiles at her friend, but then she sways and leans forward, suddenly she's throwing up all over Barbie's matching skirt and shoes.

"Oh, gross!" shrieks Barbie. Leaping backward out of her shoes onto dry floor, leaving her pumps in the pool of vomit. "Oh Tamara, what a mess."

Disgusted to see Tamara doesn't have a drop on herself, Barbie snaps, "Just sit down and wait for me." As she bends to pick up her shoes, Barbie realizes this will be quite the trick since she doesn't want to actually touch the shoes since they are covered. Suppressing a shudder, Barbie sticks her hands inside them since that's the only clean part.

Wearing the filthy shoes like weird mittens, she hurries along the aisle on her way to the Ladies room.

Mouse watches Barbie's progress from the bar, not at first understanding why her friend is wearing her shoes on her hands. She can tell there is a problem, though, so Mouse asks, "Is everything okay?"

"No." snaps Barbie without stopping.

Mouse gets the picture when she looks back to see Tamara staring stupidly at the puddle by her feet.

Kate and Amelia follow Maggie over to find out what's happening. Mouse frantically signals Billie and the bartender hurries down the bar.

"Billie," Mouse asks, "Perhaps you have towels?"

Billie reaches under the counter, coming up with a wad of terry cloth hand towels she hands to Mouse.

"What's up?" asks Maggie while Mouse heads for Tamara.

Shaking her head at the state Tamara is in, Billie the bartender comes out from behind the bar and tells Maggie, "The other one's in the washroom. I'm going in back for the mop. Mind the store a minute?"

"Sure." Maggie steps behind the bar and can't resist texting Stu. Billie goes in back, Kate heads for the bathroom and Amelia helps Mouse with Tamara.

Reduced to blouse and underwear Barbie is bent over the sink trying to rinse out her skirt when Kate looks in.

"God. She really got you, huh?" Kate observes. "Anything I can do to help?"

Barbie says, "Hosing down my shoes would help."

Kate comes in, letting the door swing shut behind her. Seeing each vomit soaked shoe resting discarded in separate sinks, Kate carefully turns on the taps, not wanting to be splattered.

"Good thing it's all liquid," says Kate, watching the smelly mess swirl down the drain.

Barbie shakes her head, twisting the sodden skirt to ring it out. "If I'd known this was gonna happen I'd have sent her home with Q and he'd be cleaning up. Bastard."

Kate smiles, "Next time. Look, even if they come clean you can't go out in those clothes, you'll freeze. How about I get Nick to bring a change of clothes so you can get home?"

Although horrified at the idea, Barbie realizes she has no choice, so she agrees without enthusiasm. "Thanks."

91 . . . friday

Liz has dark circles under her eyes as she comes into the kitchen. The sink is full of unwashed dishes which she stacks neatly on the counter, then rinses her favourite mug under running water. A glimpse of the crud encrusted on the tea towel hanging on the stove makes her opt to let the mug air dry.

The coffee carafe gets the same treatment before Liz rummages in the cupboard looking for the tin. She pulls it down and squints at the contents. No way.

Liz squeezes her eyes closed, but when she opens them again nothing has changed. There's barely enough coffee for a weak pot. A small pot. Scooping the coffee into the filter she decides maybe there's enough for eight wimpy cups. So she'll make six okay cups. Liz adds a dash of salt, then slides the filter basket in and pours the water through. Waiting, she stretches like a cat, then begins doing a few warm-ups.

Touching her toes she is startled to see the shadow of a person stretching across the floor between her legs.

At the realization she's not alone Liz straightens up abruptly and whirls around to see Ethan leaned up against the door frame with a huge grin on his face.

"You don't have to stop on my account," he raises his eyebrows rakishly.

"Don't sneak up in me like that," she snaps.

His face falls. "Sorry. I didn't mean to scare you, I just wanted to walk you to class."

"You didn't scare me, you startled me is all." She turns to pour herself a cup of coffee, then opens the refrigerator. No milk. No half and half. Resigned, she gets the powdered stuff out, chisels off a chunk off and plops it in her cup. "You didn't used to walk me to class."

"You didn't used to be my girlfriend. I mean," he

pauses, watching Liz stir her coffee, not looking at him, "You are my girlfriend, aren't you?"

Liz sips her coffee, then turns to face him. "I don't know. I'm not sure I want a boyfriend. Lets just say we're dating, okay?"

"Uh, I'm not quite sure I see the difference. I always thought dating is what makes people girlfriends or boyfriends."

"Look, I'm sorry Ethan. It's been a little rough lately."

"Yeah, I know that Liz. I've been here too, remember."

"Yes you have, and you've been great."

"But." supplies Ethan quietly.

She nods. "But I don't know. I don't really think... " she looks at the bereft expression on his face and softens a little.

"Look. I don't know if I'm ready. I like you a lot," she looks down modestly, not quite able to meet his eyes, "No guy has ever made me feel like you do. But I don't know that I'm ready, or even if I want to be anybody's 'girlfriend.'There's implied ownership."

"I don't want to own anybody, Liz, I want to be with you."

"Then what's with this walking to class stuff? It's like you don't think I can take care of myself."

"You know what they said. Until they catch that guy nobody is supposed to be going anywhere on their own."

"Nobody isn't what they mean, or what you mean, either. It's just women. Put women in a cage instead of the predator and our menfolk protect us. Maybe we should wear burqahs too. I don't want to live in protective custody."

Ethan stops a moment, furrowed brow, thinking. "We live in the same residence, we're go to a lot of the same places. It makes sense for us to go together."

"But It doesn't. It might make sense for me to buddy up with Jake, or Natasha. But you're a T.A. so you're always in class way before and much later than me."

"Sometimes yeah, but not all the time."

"I'm an adult. I'm used to taking care of myself."

"Liz. forget the rapist a minute. It's not about him, it's about me and you. I want to spend time with you, even if only walking to class. But I guess you'd rather not be seen with me."

"It's not that at all." She steps closer and slides her arms around his neck. "I'm used to being on my own. My problem is the people everywhere. All the time. On campus, in class, out shooting, where I live, in the shower for god's sake. I need alone time, not a boyfriend to boss or a babysit me."

"Boyfriends don't have to be bossy." Liz can't help but melt into the moment as Ethan pulls her down into a lingering kiss. Coming up for air he adds, "I'd be honoured for the opportunity to join you in the shower anytime."

Liz can't help but giggle and the nuzzling resumes

on a much friendlier note, even beginning to get hot and heavy until ostentatious throat clearing from the doorway breaks the clinch. Liz looks embarrassed, turning self consciously to the counter stirring her cold coffee while Ethan treats Maggie to a goofy grin.

"Hey Maggie. We're going to be heading to class in a few minutes. You're welcome to join us."

"Thanks, but my classes don't start 'til eleven. I'll head over then with Mouse and Amelia." Pouring herself a tumbler of grapefruit juice Maggie can't resist adding, "Besides, looks like you've got the buddy system figured out."

92 . . .

Wolfrom hangs up the phone and grins at Lewis. "Looks like the bicycle lead paid off."

"We got something! It'll be great to get out of here. I'm just so damn tired of talking to college students. I don't know what's worse, the ones that wanna hang out with us or the ones that read Boingboing."

Lewis starts shutting down her laptop. "What've we got?"

"Turned up a good possibility at one of the white shoe law firms downtown." Wolfrom is packing up the stray bits of paper and file folders into a waiting banker's box.

"A lawyer? Please don't be talking about M & Ms."

"Well, yeah, Molony and Mulroney." Wolfrom frowns. "Terri, is there anything you want to tell me?"

"I should have known. Of course a designer bike is gonna belong to some lawyer. Real people can't afford to blow that kind of cash on a bicycle."

Lewis busies herself with wrapping cables and stowing the laptop in the case. She looks up to see Wolfrom staring at her, expectant. "I've got some history with the head honcho."

Wolfrom whistles. "One of the M's. How on earth did you manage that?"

Shaking her head. "It's a long story."

"Which M?"

"I doubt it matters, but it was Mulroney."

"When his wife went missing?"

"Yeah; I was on missing persons. Nobody knew she'd taken a powder. They thought it might be kidnap for ransom. The guy sends a minion in to report his wife missing."

"You're kidding!"

Shaking her head. "Nope. Apparently the minions even went shopping for gifts for his kids."

"Get out!"

"So I paid him a little visit."

"Shit. You kicked up a fuss?"

Stowing cables in the bag, Lewis says, "When a wife goes missing we've gotta look at the husband."

"But Terri you gotta go on tippie toes if it's an M!"

"I don't do politics very well, Wolfie. See, I don't much care if it's an M. Everybody's supposed to be equal under the law." Lewis zips the case closed, and glances around the broom closet sized office. "I think that's everything."

"So what happened? You bearded an M in the tower."

Shaking her head. "Yeah. That was me."

"And you got in his face?"

Shaking her head. "You might say that."

"And the wife saunters home a couple of days later with her tail between her legs."

"Yeah, that's my kinda luck alright." Lewis nods as she slings the laptop over her shoulder. "You know, Wolfie, it's not too late to put in for a new partner."

Wolfrom laughs. "You kidding? I'd miss all the fun."

Lewis grins and shakes her head. "Just tell me that we're not going to interview anybody named Molony."

"Source says the guy's not a lawyer, just a gofer, guy from the mail room or IT department, something like that."

"Praise the lord and pass the biscuits."

Wolfrom glances at her as they head out the door. "There's a lot I don't know about you, huh?"

Lewis laughs as she switches out the light.

93 · · ·

Mouse says, "This feels so stupid. People have been attacking people as long as there have been people." as she accompanies Maggie and Amelia on the path between Fyfield House and the central cluster of school buildings, which is now charmingly known as the 'rape zone.'"There was just as much need to be careful yesterday as today. This is not the first rape that has happened in Canada."

Amelia tells her, "Actually, there is no rape in Canada."

Maggie snorts dismissively. "What? Of course there is. What do you think happened to Natasha?"

"Under Canadian Law it's not called rape. It's called "sexual assault," Amelia explains. "And it covers the whole range of sex crimes."

"That's just semantics." says Maggie.

"It is important." Amelia says, "It's the legal definition."

"It's only important to English majors and lawyers, not to normal people." Maggie says, "It doesn't change the facts."

Amelia says, "Actually it does. That's why they try for precise language in framing laws. To cover every eventuality."

"People will still be confused. Besides, 'sexual assault' doesn't sound as bad as rape." says Maggie.

Mouse interrupts. "What does it matter what you call it if we have to give up our own freedom and cower in our beds?"

"Come on. It isn't that bad," says Maggie.

"I am already tired of travelling in a pack." says Mouse.

"All I care about is not ending up like Natasha."

"Maybe we could go and visit Natasha." suggests Mouse.

"That's a good idea," Amelia nods. "We could find out what really happened. Exactly. All I heard is she was found in the woods. Is that where she was attacked or what? Did she know him? Was he wearing a mask? If we know what actually happened we can all take better precautions."

"That sounds like writing a story." says Maggie flatly.

"Not at the moment. I'm not a journalist, Maggie. But I probably will write something eventually," agrees Amelia. "That's what I do. I'm a writer."

"That's sick. This is somebody you know."

"Yes, I do know Natasha, which is why I want to visit her to see with my own eyes that she's OK. If she wants to talk about it, fine. We're friends, I'm there for her. If I were to write it, it wouldn't be her story anymore. It won't be tomorrow, and it wouldn't be her life, it would be a story. Fiction."

"That sounds even worse. It just doesn't sound right."

"You're looking at it all wrong. Think about it like... you know when you guys talk about how an operating system is built around a kernel? Like that. Fiction is built around kernels of truth. Mixed up with imagination and reassembled as something completely different and new. Even fantasy and science fiction need to ring true or no one would read them."

"It still sounds creepy. Like you're being a vampire,

sucking out all her pain and suffering to use in a story."

Mouse silences their bickering by telling them, "Do you think Boris did it?"

Maggie says, "That's just silly. It must be somebody else."

"Why?" asks Mouse. "No one but you has seen the flasher but Boris is here all the time."

"And why not Boris?" adds Amelia.

Maggie is exasperated. "Boris is the last guy who'd harm Natasha. He loves her."

"I've done enough research to know women are usually hurt by their nearest and dearest. Cops always look at the husband or boyfriend. Boris has to be the prime suspect." Amelia sighs.

"It could be random, you know. It could have been any man hiding in the trees." says Mouse.

"Like my flasher."

Amelia says, "Yes, like your flasher. But it could be any guy. A teacher. A janitor. A security guy. But odds are it's another student, because predators almost always go after their own."

Maggie glares at her house mates. "But I don't want it to be somebody we know. Stop trying to scare me."

Amelia says, "It's smart to be aware. But being careful doesn't mean we have to run scared and hide. But being a little on edge can keep us from doing stupid things."

Mouse nods, "The world is wonderful but dangerous too."

Maggie says, "I just want to feel safe again.

94 . . .

Detectives Lewis and Wolfrom cross the expanse of concrete outside the ostentatious Molony and Mulroney office tower and enter the M&M lobby.

On the left are yogurt shops and boutiques while the right funnels visitors past the wide expanse of security desk before culminating at an impressive bank of elevators. As the detectives make their way to the security desk, Lewis pulls out her ID wallet to present to the guard. He nods after a cursory glance then looks expectantly up from scrutinizing the bank of security monitors spread out before him.

"Help you officer?" he asks.

"We're looking for the owner of the red Schwinn bicycle chained up outside there. If you can direct us to the owner, that'd be fine. If not just point us to the personnel department."

The guard looks a little shifty, glancing back at the monitors so as not to meet anyone's gaze. "Uh, well, I'm not really sure."

Wolfrom crosses his arms, not a sidekick anymore, but a stern representative of the law. Menacing even. "We need sure."

Bereft of his usual power to mess with those on the other side of the desk, the security guard knows he's out of his depth. And when he thinks about it, really, the little creep isn't worth running afoul of the law over.

"I don't know one bike from another, but I know

Neil comes in on a red bike. I can't swear it's that one."

Wolfrom asks, "Where will we find this Neil?"

"He's on twenty nine, in marketing."

"And that would be Neil who?" she presses.

The guard drops his gaze, sighing. This had been such a good gig. " Molony. Neil Molony."

Lewis tenses, then writes it in her book. She thanks him then they head for the elevators.

"Must be your lucky day," says Wolfrom, pushing the buttons. "Gonna get a shot at the other M."

95 . . .

The police on-site incident room is vacant when Ethan and Liz stop in. "They can't be done. What's happening?"

A quick look around reveals the police file boxes are gone. "I guess they talked to everybody already."

"They were ready to arrest Boris. How much can they have learned since then?"

"I don't know. Maybe the security people have an idea."

"Yeah, maybe. Lets check their office."

"Uh," Ethan looks uncomfortable, "I have to get to class."

"Yeah, I know. Go ahead. I just want to find out what's happening and then I'll head over too."

"OK. See you there." He starts for the door, but then turns back, gathers Liz in a big hug, gives her a kiss and a wink, then he's out the door and gone.

Liz smiles, touching her lips. Maybe this boyfriend thing will be okay. She heads down the hall toward security. Like most students, she's never been there but she knows where it is. The door is ajar so she walks in, noting a duty schedule on the board beside the desk.

Behind the desk the swivel chair is vacant. Keys hang from a rack, monitors span the desk. Liz peers over trying to get an idea of what areas are covered by cameras. It's hard to see from this side, so she slips around the desk and into the chair.

The monitors mostly cover the school's exterior entrances, parking lots, interior views of the lobby, cafeteria, corridors of this building. Liz glances at the closed door on the other side of the desk. It's marked Authorized Personnel Only. She pulls out her camera and rolls the chair toward the windows to get a better composition. Adjusting the camera settings for the daylight she takes some shots of the monitors.

Rolling back she slumps in the chair to shoot some low angle shots over the monitors with the daylight streaming brightly around them. Messing with the settings she brackets the exposures so she'll be able to choose from different versions. She's just getting into it when a flushing sound from behind the door brings her back. Snapping off the camera Liz hustles back to the civilian side before the running water stops and the door opens.

The security guy who helped find Natasha does a double take when he sees Liz leaning on the desk. Val says, "Hey there." Liz notes how gray and haggard he looks today.

"Hi, I just stopped in to see how the investigation is going. The cops seem to have gone."

He nods, "Liz, right?" She thinks he looked perfectly fit the other night but today he'd be a perfect candidate for one of those vampire movies Natasha likes.

"They've finished the preliminary student interviews. The neighbourhood canvas turned up a description of the flasher, so they're following up on both of those things."

Liz says, "That's good, I guess. You look terrible, you should be home in bed or something."

He laughs. "Not likely. Not til the campus is safe."

"Oh, well. You still look terrible."

"I'll catch up on my z's after things settle down a bit. How's your friend..." he glances down at a file spread open on the desk. "...Natasha?"

"Better than expected. She thinks they'll be letting her out of the hospital soon. So that's it for the cops on campus then?"

"Fingers crossed. They may re-interview people. I'm not sure if that'll be here or downtown though. We'll take it as it goes."

"Do you think it really is the flasher guy?"

Rubbing the beard stubble, Val shakes his head slowly. "I don't know. They haven't picked up the guy yet. I'd want more information before commenting. Better to err on the side of caution. But you might want to keep an eye on your boyfriend."

"What? What do you mean?"

"I shouldn't say this, but the cops are interested in him."

"Ethan? That's crazy."

Val shrugs. "He didn't give the cops an alibi. He wouldn't talk to them at all, actually."

"Oh." Liz frowns. "What is that supposed to mean? Are you saying you think Ethan is the rapist?"

"I'm just saying be careful."

96 . . .

Lewis and Wolfrom step out of the elevator and onto the gleaming golden hardwood floor. The word "Marketing" has been spelled out with a range of ornate hand carved wooden letters affixed to a stark white wall behind the wide reception desk.

Crafted from darker shades of wood, the massive desk almost looks as though it's growing into the space, dwarfing the tiny receptionist. She eyes them warily as they approach the desk. "Can I help you?"

Lewis raises an eyebrow and proffers her ID wallet. The receptionist accepts it, making a show of examining the badge before passing it back across the wide expanse of wood. Lewis tells her, "I see you've been expecting us. We're here to see Neil Molony. If you can just point us..."

The woman shakes her head, no, but Lewis smiles

and says, "That's alright. I'm sure I'll be able to find our way," and heads for the exceptionally dark wood panel door. The receptionist realizes there isn't any way out of it, so she comes out from behind the desk.

"I'll take you back." The receptionist snaps as she slips in front of Lewis, and hurries through the door ahead of them. Wolfrom and Lewis exchange glances as they follow along the elegantly appointed corridor. The doors inside the corridor are plain slab doors, differentiated by the objects affixed to their smooth surfaces rather than numbers.

Lewis notes a Kewpie doll, a tambourine, and a shimmery guitar-clutching frog interspersed with unlikely objects like gears and tire pumps framed and mounted on the walls between. Stopping just short of the end of the hall, the receptionist knocks on a door distinguished from all the rest by the representation of a hand tooled cowboy boot. As she pushes open the door to admit them, Lewis realizes that the cowboy boot is actually a real leather boot that's been sawn in half and somehow attached to the door. Glue maybe.

What a waste, she thinks as she gets a whiff of rich leather as she steps inside. Old fashioned venetian blinds cover the window, admitting bright stripes of sunlight into the room. The contrasting shadow seems all the darker because the sunlight is so bright. A drafting table leans against one wall, a desk and several file cabinets against the other with a long desk in between.

The young man seated there looks up from the video game he's playing. He's hard to see in the harsh strips of light, so Lewis moves to the window and adjust the blinds. The young man watches her warily. Wolfrom pulls the door behind him closed and extends a hand with a badge.

"Mr. Molony, I'm Detective Wolfrom, and this is Detective Lewis. We have a few questions for you." Molony nods, waving away the badge after a cursory glance, and Wolfrom perches on a corner of the desk. There are no other chairs in the room, so Lewis leans up against the cabinet beside the window.

"What can I do for you, officers?" asks Molony haughtily.

"You own a late model red Schwinn bicycle."

Molony nods, not sure where this is going. "It's more of a burgundy, but yes, It's a 2009 Classic Seven Deluxe." He looks at them and frowns. "It hasn't been stolen has it?"

"No," Wolfrom tells him, folding his arms across his chest, "But it was spotted on the Christie campus."

"At Christie?" Neil Molony goes very still. Then, "But that doesn't make any sense."

"It was seen there Mr. Molony. It's a very distinctive bicycle." Wolfrom watches him.

Neil splutters, "I never went there. That school is for losers. I went to UCLA. Even my bike wouldn't be caught dead at a dive like Christie."

Very softly, from behind, Lewis leans in and says into his ear, "It was used by a flasher, Neil." Molony has almost forgotten she's there, and nearly jumps out of his skin. Twisting around to face her, he insists "It wasn't me. Wasn't my bike. It had to be somebody else."

Wolfrom asks in a neutral tone, "When were you in college Mr. Molony?"

Molony swivels back to face him. "Uh, oh about five, no six years ago."

"And that prepared you for this job here, did it?"

"Uh, well, no, actually. I decided to help out here until I can find a suitable job in my field. This is really just a stop gap, just until I can put something better together."

"And your job here is?"

"I pull press clippings and keep the publicity files." Wolfrom nods, glancing around the spacious office. Although somewhat sterile, this office is far too grand for the job description. The guy is connected.

Again from behind Lewis asks, "What did you take?"

Without jumping this time, Molony swivels back to look at her. He's starting to feel more confident now. "I majored in film. That's where Spielberg and Lucas went too."

Wolfrom looks suitably impressed. "Wow, I'll bet that's hard work to find."

Neil haughtily explains "I'm an auteur, I don't work for some schmuck doesn't know from nothing. I intend to direct, which entails putting together a project and packaging. I'm not sure why you're here, though. I do have work to do, you know." Neil is trying for an imperious dismissal.

"Well," says Lewis as she comes around the desk, crossing her arms authoritatively. "What we want is for you to come downtown for a line-up."

Trying to hang onto imperious, "A line-up? That's ridiculous!" he says, now visibly nervous. Clenching her jaw, Lewis pins him with her flinty-eyed stare. Neil tries to keep it up, but cracks. "Uh, when do we do this?"

"Right now." Lewis hold Neil Molony's eye, then he swallows and nods and Lewis turns and makes for the door. Molony glances nervously back up at Wolfrom, standing by the desk, immobile, waiting. Molony looks away, then stuffs the game machine into a desk drawer and gets to his feet.

Wolfrom keeps his gaze neutral as he watches the creep come around the desk. Wolfrom feels the thrill. This is a wrong guy all right. Now to find out if it's the right wrong guy.

97 · · ·

The taxi arrives at the police station, and Maggie looks pale as she climbs out, so Oscar says, "It'll be fine." He holds the door to the building open, doffing an imaginary hat for Maggie. She tries a smile, then shrugs and squares her shoulders, marching through the door and heading for the front desk.

The duty sergeant looks up from his computer monitor expectantly. "Help you?"

Maggie clears her throat. "I'm uh, here for a line-up."

"And that would be with which officer?"

"Oh uh." Suddenly flustered. "Oh right, Detectives Lewis and, er, Wolf."

"That'd be Detective Wolfrom."

Maggie nods, "Yeah." The officer scrolls through pages of data, skimming until he finds what he's looking for. "Just have a seat over there and I'll get a PC to take you up."

"Okay." Maggie turns and follows Oscar over to the bank of plastic chairs by the window. "PC? Personal computer?"

Oscar smiles, "Police Constable."

Maggie nods. "Ah. Makes more sense than 'politically correct'."

98 . . .

Nick measures coffee beans into the hand grinder then sits beside Kate, hunched groggily over a bowl of porridge. Gripping the wooden grinder between his knees, Nick steadies it with his left hand and starts turning the crank.

As the mechanical chrish-chrish-chrish fills the air, the scent of the freshly ground beans wafts up from the grinder. Kate smiles over at Nick, breathing in the aroma. Nick shakes his head, "You know you don't have to get up this early, babe."

"Then I'd almost never get to see you."

"Who're you kidding? Your eyes aren't open yet. You're not seeing me now."

"I just need coffee."

"Almost done. What'd you decide about the meeting? Is it on for tonight?"

Kate sighs, "I don't know. Maybe."

"Did you hear they've caught the guy?"

"What do you mean caught him... caught who?"

"The cops brought the guy in this morning."

Kate says, "Yeah, but they brought Boris in too."

"Well, they let him go again too." Nick shrugs.

"After Natasha went down and made them let him out."

"Well, you know it wasn't Boris."

"No, I don't."

"Well sure you do."

"Honey, he's your friend. I don't really know him. It could very well be him no matter what Natasha thinks."

Nick shrugs. "Wait and see. I doubt it, though."

"Just 'cause you pump iron with the guy doesn't mean he couldn't be a rapist. I mean, come on."

Nick says, "I don't think... wasn't she badly beaten?"

"She was, but Boris is her boyfriend. You know how it goes, they naturally assumed it was him. She checked out of the hospital to get him released."

Nick shrugs. "This one's a little different. The campus flasher apparently. Some guy lurking in the woods, Val said."

"Maggie's flasher?"

"Probably. Val's taking the attack personally. He's annoyed nobody told him about the Christie flasher."

"You didn't tell him about Maggie?"

"It never came up. I mean, it was just a funny story. Who knew?"

"Don't worry babe, I won't rat you out."

"He's planning on going after the board of directors for a bigger budget so he can afford to hire guards with brains."

"It's about time. Sounds like he's got a handle on it, though."

99 . . .

Peering through the heavy glass at a uniformed officer flipping the pages on a clipboard, Maggie twists her hands together nervously .

"You're sure they won't be able to see me?"

"They won't be able to see you," Wolfrom assures her. "You're behind one way glass. They'll know somebody is here, but nobody can see who." Maggie nods.

Wolfrom doesn't tell her it will be different if it gets to court. He keys the mic. "Bring them in."

The officer opens the door and a half dozen men walk in and stand in front of the backdrop. Maggie thinks this is just like something on TV. Piece of cake.

The officer lines the men up, positioning each under a number stencilled on the wall behind them.

They all look roughly the same, white guys, under

six feet, brown hair, glasses, no facial hair. Gee, they all do look alike, what's that all about.

"Try not to look at them as a group." Wolfrom suggests, as though reading her mind. "Just look at them one at a time, focus on each one, individually."

Maggie nods and turns her attention to the first guy.

Wolfrom keys the mic again. "Number one step forward please."

As he does, Maggie looks at him. Tries to see a person. Okay, wide broad face. Looks a little like Boris maybe, only shorter. Not as built. The uniformed officer signals to the man to turn and he does. Maggie shakes her head. Not him.

Wolfrom speaks into the mic again. "Thank you. Number two step forward please."

Maggie looks at this guy.

Beyond the superficial average white guy looks these men all share, this one has sallow skin, lank hair hanging limply. The glasses reflect a wicked glint in the overhead light, making it difficult to see his eyes. Could it be this one? Or is it just because he doesn't look as clean cut as the first one.

"Turn please number two." As the man turns Maggie gets a good look at his profile. From this angle his nose is much more prominent. Pointy.

"Not him," she says softly.

Wolfrom nods, and tells the mic, "That's fine number two. Number three please. Step forward."

Maggie watches as number three looks around nervously.

Okay, this guy is acting guilty. The question is, is it the guy? He steps forward. Another clean cut one, a hint of beard along the jawline. One of those guys needs to shave three times a day. If it was me, I'd grow a beard, she thinks.

"Turn please."

Maggie purses her lips. Who the hell knows. He just looks like some guy. Like every other guy. So he's acting guilty. But she doesn't know him. She thinks. God. This is harder than she thought. Wolfrom is looking at her. She shrugs. "I don't know."

Wolfrom nods before keying the mic. "Thank you number three. Number four step forward please."

Oh god they all look the same. Like they were stamped out of the same mold. Wait. This one walks differently. There's something funny about him. Like he was assembled from parts. Wound tight. The way he walks. Tense. Lopsided. Does he look like the guy? Does anybody? Does she even remember after all this time?

"Turn please number four."

As number four turns he clenches his jaw, and Maggie can see that his jaw is out of alignment somehow. Is it because he's clenching it or is he clenching because it's out of alignment. There's something. Meh.

They need an artist or somebody who knows how to look. She doesn't know how to look at people. Or at least not how to see them. Or their parts, anyway.

What's wrong with this picture? This guy's glasses are a bit smaller than the others. His eyes are glittery. Is she imagining this? Is she trying to make it be one of these guys so it will be all over? Maybe.

"I don't know about this one either." she admits.

"Thank you number four. Number five step forward."

Gee, where do they get these creepy guys, she thinks as she takes in the half smirk on this one's face. Pointier chin. Glancing back at number four's chin for a comparison she thinks, gah, after that one anybody's chin would look pointy.

Okay okay. Look at him. Number five, Really look at him. But Maggie doesn't want to look at him.

He's making her feel uncomfortable. Look at him. Some wave in his hair. She doesn't remember his hair at all, it was under the pantyhose. No beard, not even stubble. Perfectly round glasses like Harry Potter. Looks a bit younger than the others. He's glancing around when Wolfrom says, "Turn please," and the guy startles. She sees the way he moves and she knows. It's him. Chills run down her back and she starts to shake.

"That's him. That's the one."

"Are you sure? Take your time."

"That's him that's him that's HIM." and Wolfrom draws back, while blood drains from Maggie's face and he thinks she's maybe gonna faint but then she bends down and grabs the waste paper basket.

Wolfrom looks away as she throws up. When she's done he passes her the box of tissues, then keys the mic.

"Thank you number five. Number six step forward please."

Maggie looks at him wanly. "But it's number five. I made the identification."

Wolfrom assures her, "Procedure."

100 . . .

Oscar's arms are protectively wound around Maggie's shaking form as they ride home in the back of a cab. He feels a little guilty because he's enjoying it so much as Maggie snuggles in closer.

It would be near perfect if the ruddy cabbie wasn't watching them in the mirror almost as much as he's watching the road. Oscar is going to say something, but then the taxi driver clears his throat, and says, "Don't worry, lady. You'll get through this. Look, I know this lawyer can probably help. I can give you his card, you want."

Oscar feels the difference in the timbre of Maggie's shaking, as she pulls her face away from his neck. Her eyes are red rimmed and her face is streaked with what used to be make up, but her lips are tightly clenched together to keep the giggles in.

"No, that won't be necessary, thanks." Oscar assures the cabbie as the cab pulls up in front of Fyfield House.

Oscar pays the guy and opens the cab door. Giggling, Maggie takes Oscar's hand for help getting out of the car. She slams the door and watches as the cab pulls away. Turning back to Oscar she says, "Look Oz,

I'm sorry I'm such a mess. I don't know why this is getting me so bad."

"It's fine Maggie. You just have too much imagination. Come on up, I'll buy you a drink."

101 . . .

painfully bright light. Covering her eyes with her hands she pulls the blanket over her head. Blanket?

It's a scratchy wool blanket. And it's heavy. Smells like flowers. Lavender maybe?

Where's the duvet? Peeking out from under the blanket again, and the light is like needles stabbing directly into her brain. A lot of frilly pink shit. She hates pink. She's not home, it's gotta be Barbie's dream house.

Meow, stop it girl. Barbie is a good friend, just cause you've got a hangover is no reason to dis the girl, not even in your own head. Not her fault her mom's so scary.

Stop it... stop it... you're being a bitch again. You drank that shit all by your lonesome. Barbie was a saint, bringing you home. Uh oh. Didn't you throw up on her?

God. And what day is it? What time? Can't risk missing any more classes.

Sit up. Whoa girl, way too fast, the world is too damned unfocused. Except for the pointy bits stabbing directly into her brain. Gotta do something about the light.

Tamara pushes the blanket off and lowers her feet

to the floor. Sure as hell seems a long way down. And it's moving. How much did she drink to be still having bed spins in full daylight?

Ohmigod. Move slow. Hold onto the bed til the world stops spinning. Oh boy. Gotta kill the damned sunlight or she'll never gonna get out of this world of pain.

Stumble to the window, pull the heavy drapes. Much better. Now it's muted. Cell phone... where is it?

Oh look. Her clothes are neatly folded on the delicate little café chair with the heart shaped back that sits so perkily in front of the vanity. Perched on top, like a cherry, is her cell phone.

Flipping it open she sees there's only one line of power. Of course the charger is at home. Oh who gives a shit It says it's Friday and only nine thirty.

That's something, anyway. No class til this afternoon. Thank god, time to get human. Might even be able to think by then.

Need the bathroom. Pull on the frilly pink -- what else -- kimono hanging from the back of the door.

Open the door a crack and peek out: the coast is clear. Tamara shuffles down to the bathroom.

Hanging the kimono on the hook, she kicks off panties and unsnaps her bra, dropping both on the floor and reaches behind the curtain to start the shower.

Running water reminds her she has to pee. As she settles on the toilet she thinks that's such a coarse way of putting it in such a delicate bathroom. The only word that could possibly be appropriate in this environment would be 'tinkle'. The mists starts to obscure the sparkly unicorn wallpaper. Thank God.

Tamara steps into the shower, standing under the nozzle and the waves of warmth stream over her head. She can feel the tension melting away. As the pounding in her head starts to ease off, she thinks maybe her life is starting to feel bearable.

Until the tapping sound. It takes a minute to realize that someone is tapping on the door. She shuts off the shower.

"Yes?" she says, wincing at the noise of her own voice.

"Tam, it's me." Barbie says through the door. "I'll be leaving for school in a half hour. You want a ride, be ready."

"Sure." Tamara says. Head or no head, she doesn't want to stay here with Godzilla mom. No way no how. "I'll be ready."

102 . . .

The doctor enters Natasha's room to find her asleep and snoring... no wait. The snoring is from behind the door where Boris sprawls in a chair. The doctor smiles, then pulls the privacy curtain around the hospital bed.

The squeak and rattle of the rollers makes Natasha stir. The doctor picks up the clipboard hung at the foot of the bed and flips through the pages of the chart.

Natasha's eyes snap open and the doctor hears the sudden intake of breath from her patient. Natasha relaxes as she realizes where she is. The doctor smiles at her. "Good to see you're getting some sleep Ms. Panov."

"It helps to have a bodyguard, Doc. Hey, where is... " the snore from behind the curtain answers her question and she smiles.

"Even bodyguards need their beauty sleep." Advancing with the stethoscope the doctor suggests "Let's see how we're doing here, shall we?"

103 . . .

Jake has only two cameras strung around his neck and a slim notepad under his arm when he comes along the hall and drops into step beside Krystal, who is juggling her laptop and book bag, along with a few loose manuals as she comes out of a nearly empty classroom.

"Hey Krystal, you look like you could use a hand."

She looks at him and smiles, "Oh hi, Jake. I've just got to learn to be a little better organized."

"I'll help," Jake holds out his hand, "Where're you off to?"

Passing him the loose manuals, Krystal says, "I've got a spare so I was heading to the cafeteria."

"But it's not open."

"They aren't serving food, but it's open. It'll be a great place to work on my laptop. I get a lot done when nobody's there. There's a ton of light from all the windows, lots more than the library, and if you can believe it, it's even quieter."

104 . . .

Draped in cameras, Liz makes her way toward Natasha's room. She's reaching for the door when it opens and Boris steps out. He looks beat but smiles when he sees it's Liz.

She asks, "Is everything OK?"

"Tired. The doc's giving her an examination."

"Mmm. I hate hospitals myself."

"I think they're probably gonna let her go. You could have waited and taken the pictures back at the Res."

Liz shakes her head while effortlessly performing a practiced shoulder roll to reposition the bags hanging there.

"Oh no, it's much better to do it here, Bo. The light will be better for one, but nothing beats an institutional setting for an insurance claim. I imagine it'll help just as much in criminal court."

"That sounds so cynical, Liz."

Liz laughs. "I am cynical. But think it through. By the time they catch the guy and bring him to court her cuts and bruises will probably be gone. Because Natasha was knocked out so she can't even tell a horrifying story on the stand. The pictures I take will probably go the farthest in convicting the guy."

Boris is looking at her. "How do you know all this stuff?"

"I was making a living off newspaper and insurance photos before I decided to go back to school."

"I didn't know that. I thought you were our age."

Liz laughs. "I'm only a couple years older. Close enough."

The door opens behind them and the doctor emerges. She looks at Liz and nods. "You'd better get in there fast if you want pictures because I'm releasing her."

Liz and Boris go in to find Natasha throwing some clothes in a bag. "Woo hoo! They're letting me out of here!"

"Wait. I have to take pictures first."

"We can do it later! The doc says I'm gonna be fine, other than being stiff and sore. Nothing's wrong medically except a lot of bruising. No concussion, nothing broken."

"That's great." nods Bo, "But let Liz take the pictures here. She's been holding out on us, she's already a professional. Insurance companies have paid her to take pictures."

"No way!" squeals Natasha. Why didn't you say something?"

"I'm just here to learn like everybody else." Liz stammers, suddenly uncomfortable, not wanting to stand out.

"Just let her take the pictures Nat. Liz knows what she's doing. Tell you what, I'll go round up some transport while you pose for her."

"All right already! Just go, Bo," urges Natasha as she

starts untying her robe. Boris looks like he'd like nothing better than to stay, but he turns and heads out.

105 . . .

Krystal's computer stuff is spread across the long back table of the cafeteria. Her laptop is disassembled, and various internal bits are sorted into plates and bowls.

A saucer holds the screws. She's shining a penlight into the DVD drive when Jake pops his head up from under the table.

"Ah ha!" he proffers a tiny screw. "Got it."

As Jake clambers out from under the table she says, "Oh Jake, that's great. You're a life saver. I was beginning to give up all hope."

Krystal positions the screw, then casts around for the tiny driver, which Jake lays in her hand.

"There you go, Doc." Looking around Jake notices students are beginning to flow into the cafeteria. "The lunch rush is starting. We're gonna be pressed for space in a few minutes, Krys."

"I'm going as fast as I can."

Oscar slides in beside her. "Want a hand?"

"Yeah, that'd be great. This is such a pain." She holds up a network card. "There's already an Ethernet card so I don't know what to do with this one."

Oscar starts sorting things out and putting it back together with far more assurance than Krystal had.

"Why did you decide to do this here and now?"

"It wasn't working right and I thought it just needed a good tweak. Except it's been a horror show."

"Way over my head." adds Jake.

"Yes, I imagine."

Krystal says, "Adam did a great web architecture presentation." Krystal tidies the surrounding area, tucking books and papers into her bag. "Too bad you guys missed it." Expecting an explanation.

Jake's looking at loose ends, so Oscar suggests, "Hey Jake," Oscar suggests, "Can I get you to grab me a cup of tea?"

"Oh yeah, sure." Oscar tosses him a Toonie and Jake heads down to the food dispensary.

Krystal says, "You're not gonna tell me where you were?"

"Maggie is tucked up in bed in the Res."

"You finally got her in the sack?" Krystal asks.

Oscar blushes. "No, nothing like that. She's just a bit shaken, since I took her down to identify her flasher."

"No! They got the guy? I don't believe it."

"She identified him, but she's having a hard time with it."

Krystal asks, "Why? If she IDed the creep she's a hero, Oz. We'll all be safe again."

"Really? As safe as Natasha was when she was attacked?"

Krystal tightly cinches the straps around her bag.

"Don't be a downer Oz. You know what I mean. Natasha's creep is caught."

"We don't really know that, love. A creep is caught. He may or may not be the right creep but he certainly will not be the only creep. Sadly there are many many creeps in the world." Krystal watches Oscar snap the case closed then she catches a glimpse of motion and her head turns. Sure enough, there's Jose. She turns her head away as Oz looks too. Jose trails Eric to the food counter, nodding to Jake in passing. Jake brings his tray of tea things back to rejoin his friends.

Oscar pushes the reassembled laptop back across the table to Krystal. "Good as new."

"Really?" she asks expectantly.

Oz laughs. "No, but all the bits are reattached anyway."

"Thanks, Oz. I would have got it together eventually."

"It's fine." Jake sets the tray down. They each take an anonymous white cafeteria mug, and Oscar paws through the pile of tea bags in the centre of the tray.

"Jake you're brilliant. How long have they had Earl Grey, Darjeeling and oh my god Oolong! The ladies have only ever given me that Orange Pekoe crap you Americans drink."

Jake holds up his hand, "Please Oz... Canadians."

"Sorry mate, didn't mean to offend."

Krystal drops a Darjeeling bag in her cup and pours hot water over it. "Could you pass me a creamer Jake?"

"I didn't bring any, they're terrible in tea."

Krystal frowns "What are those things then?"

Jake looks down. "These are milk."

"No, what do you call that thing? If it was cream you'd call it a 'creamer'. But it's milk."

Jake looks down at the tiny canister. "I don't know. A 'milker'?'

Oz snickers. "Isn't that what you'd call the great hairy beast who provides the milk?"

Jake laughs with Oz as Krystal reaches across to grab a couple of the milkers which she adds to her tea.

Across the room Jose is picking at a green salad while Eric eats a hamburger. "You know I used to think I was so incredibly lucky to have such an awesome girlfriend. Smart, gorgeous and built. And man oh man did she ever like sex. I mean how convenient can you get, just one floor up."

Jose nods sadly. "Yeah man, that's rough."

Eric pelts him with a French fry. "Don't be a jerk. It's a serious problem. I mean now, how do I get rid of her?"

"I don't get it man. I know she got around and all but what happened to all that undying love? How can you just turn it off?"

"Seeing her fucking some other guy was bad, but finding out he wasn't the only one. I guess it wasn't really love after all."

Jose nods. "Yeah. That might do it for me too."

"I just want to get one with my life. But now she's everywhere. I only used to see her when she'd text me to come to her room, coupla times she'd just show up in mine. She never wanted to go anywhere, do anything. But now I can't seem to get away from her. She's even coming out to the pub."

"Like they say man, careful what you wish for, 'cause you might just get it."

"She never wanted to go to the pub. Coursework and sex was all there was time for. If I was lucky I could get her to grab a bite if we managed to co-ordinate our dinner hour."

"That's a problem?" asks Jose. "Cheap date, man."

Eric shakes his head. "Thing is, once in a blue moon I could drag her out for breakfast, only if I caught after an all night lab. Maybe she was tired and her guard was down. Or something. No, wait, maybe she never had all night labs. Maybe that was all lies too. She was probably out fucking the football team those nights. No wonder she'd never go out in public with me."

"You dumped her, man. It's over now. Move on with your life. You like that Amelia, right. She's pretty smart for a girl."

"No, wait, Amelia and me, well, we're just friends. Not the same. She's more like a sister. Except I don't like my sister."

"Just, it sounds like you're not done with the redhead."

"I didn't think I would be, but I pretty much am. It's like she's not done with me, though. Everywhere I go, there she is. Yet she never spent much time with me outside the sack. Which is a sad commentary in itself."

"I dunno, bro, sounds like a perfect world to me. No talking just fucking."

"Not for me. I like talking. And I just never really saw it when we were together, but I guess my hormones were always running at full throttle. Really that's all she wanted."

"That wouldn't be a problem for me. The fact that she was messing with other guys, now, that'd be a problem."

"What do you think about her wanting to get back together? Do you think she's like, well, you know, stalking me?"

"What? 'Cause she went out to the pub?"

"Um, yeah. She never did before."

"Sorry to bust your bubble. she didn't have to before."

"I don't get it, what do you mean?"

Jose lays his fork down and looks at his friend. "She had her meat at home, and anything she wanted extra was on the side. You say you were humping like bunnies the whole time and it wasn't enough. That means she's got a big appetite, pal. So now that you're not there to provide service with a smile she's gotta cruise the meat markets 'cause she needs to find fresh every time."

"God you're a cynical bastard. I thought you Latins were supposed to be romantic."

"Stereotypes are for hacks, Eric. I don't see you gorging all day and hacking your enemies to bits every night either. Maybe you miss riding your Valkyrie."

Eric laughs. "You're such an asshole sometimes,

Jose."

Jose spears a tomato. "Aren't we all."

Jake watches Krystal, noting she's more attuned to Jose framed in the window across the room than to the people she's sitting here drinking tea with. Jake only half listens to the conversation, watching her in much the same way she watches Jose. It's better sitting beside her he could reach over and touch her cheek if he was brave enough. He can smell her hair from here.

Jake considers what would happen if he told Jose that Krystal was in love with him... hung up on him. That'd be the end of his friendship with Krys, one way or another. Either she'd end up as Jose's girlfriend and she'd never have time for him anymore, or maybe it wouldn't happen at all and she'll hate him for telling. Either way she'd probably kill him for telling.

Maybe she'll come around, he thinks, maybe she'll forget Jose. Jose's not very smart, he just looks like a Greek god. Jake sighs. Maybe in time she'll realize that even though he himself isn't a hunk like Jose, at least he's got a brain. And a heart. Maybe in time. Jake sips his tea, smiling as he watches her laugh at something Oscar said. Not that she has time. Why would God take someone so beautiful? So full of life. And then just take her out. It's just not fair.

Kate sees the gang along the back wall, noting Jake's eyes on Krystal, who is just as inevitably watching Jose across the room. She's so glad she doesn't have to do that dance any more, it leaves so much more time to actually get things done.

Oscar waves and she heads over. If Krystal is that hung up on the guy she should tell him.

Crossing the room Kate wonders if she should just tell Jose and get it over with. Put them all out of Krystal's misery. Or maybe she should tell Krystal to look at Jake. The problem there is that looking at Jake feels like cradle robbing.

"Hey guys!" Jake's reverie is broken by Kate's noisy entrance. "Who's up for a computer club meeting tonight?"

Jake says, "I didn't think you were gonna have any meetings til they caught the rapist."

"Didn't you hear?" interjects Krystal, "Oz told me they picked up Maggie's flasher."

"I heard there'd been an arrest." Kate doesn't mention that Nick had told her, unsure if it was supposed to be in confidence.

"That's good, now maybe we can get back to normal."

"So who's up for a club meeting tonight?" asks Kate.

Krystal says, "I can probably make it."

"Me too," chimes in Jake.

"Don't know about Maggie," Oscar says, "but I'll be along."

"That's great guys."

"Do you have a topic picked out yet?" Jake asks.

"There's a couple of new add-ons I thought we could try out. I'm thinking maybe be could brainstorm our own."

Oscar asks, "Brainstorm our own what?"

"Maybe we come up with an add-on for Firefox or a game or something. Create our own, do it all open source, and if we can get it together maybe we can get it bundled with the next **Ubuntu** distro."

Krystal grins. "Holy cow, what an awesome idea. I like it. Count me in."

"Thinking big, I like it too." smiles Jake, watching Krystal's eyes following Jose as he gathers up his tray. "Just I don't see I can be much help. I use software, I don't develop it."

Kate grins, "You could be a beta tester, Jake."

Oscar adds, "You take great pictures, maybe marketing?"

Krystal says, "It would be a hot addition to a CV. Put us head and shoulders above the rest of our graduating year."

Kate says, "Great, then, see you all there. There's Adam, I'm gonna see if he'll be able to come to the meeting."

Kate makes her way past Eric and Jose on their way out, and joins Adam and another buttoned down guy Jake doesn't know.

Kate perches on the third chair as she launches in to her pitch. One of the things Jake likes about Kate is that she's such a power house. Organizing, co-coordinating, never tiring of making them all do the things that are good for all of them.

When Jake turns back, Oscar has finished his tea and is clearing up, so Jake drains his mug and adds it to the tray. Glancing at Krystal he's shocked all the colour has drained out of her face. Damn Jose. She's so pallid, if there was something he could do.

"See you tonight then," Oscar says then carries off the tray.

"Where are you off to next Krystal?"

"I've got an elective, but all of a sudden i feel pretty beat, so I think I'm just gonna go home."

"I'll help you get your stuff out to your car then."

Krystal looks tired. "Thanks Jake, you're a real sweetie."

Jake smiles, "It's OK when I'm around to help, but you really gotta stop trying to drag around so much crap."

Krystal smiles back. "You think?

106 . . .

Oscar bends to tighten the laces of his running shoes, then does some stretching exercises. From a distance it rather looks like he might be dancing until he indulges in a little shadow boxing before stepping onto the cinder track. Making the circuit at a leisurely lope he's startled to be passed by Jose running at a much faster pace.

Biological imperative forces Oscar to increase his pace. He doesn't catch up exactly, but with effort he can keep the same distance between them. As he runs, Oscar marvels that Jose doesn't seem to even break into a sweat. Effortless.

"Damn," thinks Oscar, who feels himself dying here.

Wondering how Jose can keep it up. As his breathing becomes more laboured, and a corresponding longing for a cigarette grows, Oscar decides living through the run is much more important. After all, no matter what he does he'll never look like Superman. He allows his speed to drop back. In fact, the bench up ahead looks awfully inviting.

So Oscar starts to slow down and stops altogether.

He's overcome by a deep fit of coughing, and he grabs the back of the bench for support. Jose goes by, but slows, watching Oscar a moment, decides he's not gonna die and sketches a salute before resuming his speed. Oscar unties the sweatshirt from around his waist and mops his shaved head, then pulls it on, reaching into his pocket for the packet of cigarettes that isn't there. As his breathing returns to normal he watches Jose running with the grace of a natural athlete. Oscar knows he himself more resembles a lumbering bull. Taking up smoking was the stupidest thing he's ever done. His foot taps hyperactively. God, he wants a cigarette.

Even keeping it down to a handful a day, it's now three days without. Don't think about the filthy things. It's time to give it up, just have to allow his body to get used to the idea. Lacing his fingers behind his head he stretches. Jose passes again. Gliding. Now both of Oscars feet are tapping.

Jose. What a guy. All the women like him, but the guy doesn't even seem to try. At anything. He has perfect skin, golden, not pasty white. Not an acne scar or blemish on his face, straight teeth, long lean limbs. Thick bloody eyelashes. Soulful eyes. His movements are languorous, feline. Sensual. Right. He doesn't seem terribly bright, not stupid just not quick. It's not bloody fair.

And he's not even especially nice to women.

Well, at least he exercises, that's something, at least he has to work to keep up the body the women pant over. Still, it's the only time Oscar has seen Jose here. Not that he comes as often as he should, himself.

Okay, they pant over Boris's body too, but at least there's a reason. Boris has washboard abs from spending the other half of his life in the weight room, swimming, or on the track. When not taking pictures Bo is quite the jock. He even saw Bo running and taking pictures at the same time last week. Oscar smiles at the memory. Maybe video, you never know with the artsy guys. That Krystal though, she's just so single minded about Jose. Maybe Jose should be told. The girl is just so bloody hung up on the guy, and if Jose gave her a tumble it'd brighten her last days.

There he goes again. Doesn't the bastard sweat at all? Oscar reaches for his non-existent cigarettes again, then realizes what he's done. Oscar gets to his feet and yanks off the sweatshirt, tossing it back on the bench before he does a 'Rocky' bouncy thing and gets back on the track again.

Running is just so god damned boring. Maybe he should bring his MP3 player, so at least his brain wouldn't shrivel up. Some good music would help him dance round the track. Maybe not. Maybe a couple of podcasts. Maybe enough running will beat down the craving for a smoke... no. Don't think about it.

Run run as fast as you can. Run. Running on a track is just too bloody boring, you don't even get to see anything interesting, each circuit the same, at least until you start dying because you're in such rotten shape when the oxygen overdose kicks in and makes the sky look pink and the track look gray.

Too much time at the keyboard surely. It is high time to find some way of moving the physical body parts on a regular basis. There must be a better way to get exercise than this running around in circles. Alright, this track is an oval. Still. Maybe he could get some of the others interested in some football. Soccer.

Pound... pound... pound... the shadow prepares him for being overtaken by Jose again so at least this time he won't jump out of his skin when startled. It's merely humiliation now. Jesus, Jose. Not too bright but apparently that's what women want.

Oscar shakes his head a little. If he told Jose about Krystal, and it led to Jose paying attention to her, hell, it would make Krystal happy. Or maybe not. But then, mooning over Jose from afar isn't getting her anywhere either. On the other hand maybe it is. This way it's a perfect dream unmarred by personalities, sticky sex or reality's grunge. If Oscar were to tell Jose and he didn't handle it well, what's left of her life could be screwed. Only not in a good way.

So it's for the best then. Telling the man would not be a good thing. She actually said she wouldn't want

Jose out of pity. Much better to leave things as they lay. The problem with having women for friends is knowing all this shit.

107 . . .

Mouse lays in back in the recliner with a bowl of pretzels balanced on her stomach and a bottle of beer in easy reach. Several more bottles crowd the edge of a coffee table buried in pizza boxes. Quentin perches on the sofa playing with the remote, flicking through the cable universe, the sound murmuring on low.

"So your Tamara thinks you did not come home out of spite?"

Quentin nods desultorily. "Yeah, that's about it. She always thinks the worst of me. Nothing I do is right. I've been afraid to tell her how bad I'm doing. I shoulda gone somewhere with a documentary program."

"Why didn't you, Q?"

"I want our marriage to work. It seemed more important for her to be at a good med school. You can do film anywhere. Or so I thought. Anywhere but here."

"I do not understand why you do not make your own movies? It is supposed to be so cheap to do."

"Problem is, when I'm supposed to be shooting some stupid still photos I end up making video."

"That sounds pretty good then Q. Why not just keep that up, then?"

"Truth be told, I'm not doing well with my assignments. I'm flunking out, Mouse. The hell of it is that the classwork and assignments are the opposite of what I need to learn, I need film theory. I've already learned what I can by trial and error. You can do any art on your own but you end up re-inventing the wheel."

"I don't understand."

"You make the same mistakes everybody else made before while you figure out what the rules are. A good arts course teaches you what's gone before, what works, what doesn't."

"That makes sense."

"Yeah. But it seemed easier to not think about being miserable, blow off assignments, let classes slip, smoke up, have a good time. But it's not a good time anymore and I couldn'ta pissed off Tamara more if I'd tried."

"What are you going to do? Maybe they would let you do film as independent study?"

"That's what Natasha said too, so I've been looking into it. The problem with that is there's no film community here."

Mouse asks, "Is that so important?"

"I think so, yeah. Isn't it important in English Lit too?"

Mouse nods, "Yes, you're right, I didn't think. Discussing the work is very important."

"Other people learning the same shit, you know? The counsellor I talked to said if I managed to pass any courses, I could probably port credits to another school if I transfer."

"That would be really good then Q. That would solve everything. What does Tamara think?"

"I don't know, Mouse. I've tried texting, calling, email, but she doesn't answer and she doesn't come home. Maybe she's staying at Barb's, but I'm not sure. She won't talk to me at all."

"You need to talk to her Q. What is her schedule?"

"It's on the fridge." Quentin balances the remote on the arm of the sofa and goes into the kitchen. Mouse follows carrying several of the empty beer bottles which she stows in the empty case in the corner of the kitchen. Reading Tamara's schedule magnetized to the fridge door, Quentin says, "She's in a lab until five today. I could maybe catch her when she's done."

"You must talk to her, Q."

"Don't you have a class this afternoon, Mouse?"

"No this is my break day. We find a movie to watch and then it will be time for you to wait for her, yes?"

"Do you think she'll talk to me?"

"Certainly she will. But she must stop being angry first. Just now find something to watch. I'll make some Kool-Aid. Relax now, talk to Tamara at five."

"That's not a bad idea, Mouse. Let me hook up the hard drive, I think **Die Beauty** came in."

"That would be good. I want to see that one because it looks so delightfully creepy."

Mouse shakes the packet into the pitcher of water, stirring lime Kool-Aid vigorously.

Mouse hears the doorbell ring as she carries the jug into the living room, where she finds Jose and Quentin huddled over the computer.

"Hey Jose, can you move the pizza boxes please?"

Jose grabs the stack of boxes so Mouse can put the pitcher down on the empty spot. Jose standing there holding the boxes, not sure what he's supposed to do with them. She grins and takes them into the kitchen, stacking them on the over flowing Blue Box for recycling, then grabs three glasses to take back out.

Quentin has the drive hooked up to the television, and now he's in the recliner. Jose's on the sofa leaned over the coffee table rolling a joint from the baggie of pot now laying beside the jug.

Quentin says, "Jose'd rather watch **Harold and Kumar Go to White Castle** instead. It's supposed to be pretty funny."

Jose shrugs, "I'm in the mood for a comedy, Mouse."

"I'm easy," Mouse smiles, fully appreciative of the double entendre as she looks over Jose, thinking about the blog post she will write later about the folly of marriage before university. She knows none of her classmates will bother to read it since she posts exclusively in Hollands. Blogging is excellent grounding for her future as a world renowned journalist.

After pouring the Kool-Aid into glasses, Miese stretches out on the sofa. As she slides her feet into Jose's lap she thinks that some things are better left unblogged.

Quentin starts the movie as Jose lights up.

108 . . .

Maggie is curled up in bed staring up at the ceiling. On her night table, cellphone, MP3 player and ear buds are twisted together in a clump atop her dark laptop. The blinds are drawn, and Maggie's blanket is pulled up to her chin.

There's a soft knock at the door and Maggie ignores it, hoping whoever it is will go away. It's too early to be Oz. She doesn't want to see anybody.

She just wants to sleep. Another knock, louder. Maybe if she covers her head with the pillow, too, whoever it is will just go the hell away. But no, more knocking. And a whispered "Maggie?"

"Go away Amelia. I'm sleeping."

From the other side of the door she hears a brief suppressed snort, then "Five minutes, Maggie, then I've got to get to work."

"Then come in already, just so I can get rid of you."

Amelia comes into the darkened room lit only by the bits of sun squeezing in around the edges of the heavy blind. She perches on the corner of the foot of the bed. "Oscar said you're really upset about the flasher."

"Yes I'm upset. But I don't plan on telling you anything. You might write it in a story sometime, and I'd rather you didn't."

"If you don't want me to write about something I wouldn't write about it. I'm not a vampire Maggie. I'm a writer. But I thought I was your friend too. Look, I'll just go then."

Amelia gets up and Maggie says, "Look, I'm sorry I'm being such a bitch but that's part of why I'm in here. I am really bummed by this all."

Amelia turns back, settling back down again. "I'm not trying to make it worse, but I am trying to help. Did you get flashed or abused when you were a kid or something?"

Maggie props herself up on one elbow. "That's what you think? No. It's nothing like that. It's that I feel like such a shit, because if I'd gone to the cops before, Natasha might not have gotten attacked. How much shittier can it be? It's all my fault."

"Don't be such a drama queen. What would the cops have done? Maybe they would have written it down. Maybe. If they didn't laugh at you. They might even think it was a prank. You think they've got manpower for a college flasher? An elementary school, sure. But the world doesn't revolve around you. It will get screwed up all by itself."

"What, that's supposed to make me feel better? Being told I'm an egomaniac? Well fuck you and the horse you rode in on." Maggie rolls over and pulls the blanket right over her head.

Amelia shakes her head. "Glad we had this chat. Oughta do it more often, but I gotta go, really. Talk to Stu, Maggie. And stop beating yourself up."

Amelia pulls the door closed softly behind her.

109 . . .

Wolfrom sits on his side of the table across from the suspect in the cramped Interrogation Room.

Neil Molony looks past Wolfrom, rigidly watching Detective Lewis pace. Speaking conversationally, Lewis says, "We've known for some time that it was your bicycle, Neil. But now we have witnesses placing you there, too. You could try to lie and say you weren't there, but we both know that will just make you look bad on the stand when our witnesses refute you. Why not just tell us your side of the story and maybe we can get it all straightened out."

She sounds reasonable. Helpful.

Surly. "It isn't a story. I didn't do anything."

Lewis softens her tone. "You know what they say, Neil, confession is good for the soul." She lays her palms flat on the table and meets his eyes.

Neil Molony looks at her.

Her lips are parted, she's hardly breathing, expectant. This woman is really looking at him. He can't remember the last time a woman made him the centre of attention like this.

An appealing woman.

It's intoxicating. Softly, she says, "You'll feel a lot better after."

Dropping his eyes he decides the suit jacket she wears to conceal her feminine form just makes it more tantalizing. Maybe if he tells her, she'll...

"No. You won't," an imperious voice snaps from the doorway. Lewis whirls to see Colm Molony fill the doorway like a bad dream.

The lawyer levels a glare at the detective. "Do not say another word to these people, Neil."

Neil nods, mute. If anything he looks more scared.

"Detective Lewis, why was I not informed?"

"Neil waived the right to an attorney. He's an adult."

Molony shakes his head. "Neil wouldn't do that." He directs his attention to Neil. "Would you, son?"

"I just told them... " Molony holds up a warning finger and Neil claps his hand over his mouth."

"You tell them nothing boy. Not another word." Molony leads Neil to the door while Lewis folds her arms in frustration. She knows the little bastard was about to spill it all at her feet.

Lewis grips the table tightly, knowing if she gives into her impulse to kick something it won't end well. It's so damn infuriating that a powerful bastard like Molony has enough clout to twist the law to suit himself.

At the door Colm Molony stops, levels a finger at Lewis. "You're on notice, Detective. No one talks to my nephew without legal counsel."

110 . . .

"So," Nick rinses a plate before stacking it in the drying rack. "She's asked you to talk to him?"

Kate wipes the kitchen table, pausing to say, "Uh, no, not exactly."

Nick concentrates on washing the dishes, careful not to look at his darling wife, whose tendencies he knows all too well. "So. She's asked you not to say anything to him?"

"Um, no, not really."

"So. You're planning on meddling in their lives just for the fun of it?"

"It's not really meddling, it's just so obvious that something has to be done. Whenever he's anywhere around it's like her radar goes off. She loses all ability to concentrate on anything else. Maybe he'd want to go out with her if he knew."

"He'd probably ask her out if he wanted to go out with her. It's none of your business, hon."

"Mmmm." Kate says, "Sometimes people just need the teensiest bit of encouragement."

Kate carries the cloth to the sink, where she slides her arms under Nick's, encircling his waist with her arms as she wrings out the dish cloth in the soapy water.

"Don't interfere, woman. If Krystal likes Jose she should just ask the guy out. If she isn't ready or whatever, that's her call, babe. Not yours."

Kate drops the cloth but tightens the casual embrace into a hug, resting her head on his back, he can feel her breath between his shoulder blades.

"She likes him too much. She'd be devastated if he turned her down."

"Are you trying to distract me?"

Kate giggles into his back. "You ought to know by now I'm not that subtle, babe. If I was trying to distract you I'd do this."

Nick swallows, applying all of his considerable willpower to focus on the tasks at hand. "Does she even talk to him?" Concentrate on getting the dishes done. "Do they have anything in common at all? I mean from what you've told me she doesn't even know him, it's just lust."

Unable to continue in the face of Kate's ministrations, Nick throws the dish brush in the sink and turns to enfold her. As Kate reaches up for a kiss, she murmurs, "Lust is good."

111 . . .

Detectives Lewis and Wolfrom sit in an unmarked sedan in front of the M & M Tower. "You know they're gonna cry harassment," Wolfrom says in his most reasonable tone.

"What harassment? We're police officers. We're on city property. No harm no foul."

"Don't go all innocent on me Lewis. My shield may be new but I'm not stupid. Pull it on the bosses all you like, but I'm your partner, and we're both of us sitting here in this official car, tempting fate."

"Sorry Wolfie. It's just I'm so pissed off, you know? That little prick was gonna crack. I know it."

"Probably. Uncle M knew it too."

"Think we can tag Uncle M as an accessory?"

Wolfrom laughs aloud at the absurdity of the suggestion.

Lewis tenses, suddenly alert. "Look there, the staff is starting to let out for the day."

They both open their doors and get out in unison. A half dozen women are crossing the pavement when the detectives approach, flashing badges. "Excuse me, I'm Detective Lewis, this is Detective Wolfrom. We're looking for information. I wonder if any of you might be able to help our investigation."

"Is this about Neil?" asks one of the women.

Lewis nods. "If any of you have anything to say, you can tell us in confidence."

"Right, and get in trouble," a short brunette says.

Another woman asks the brunette, "Just how does keeping that little creep out of jail help me?"

The brunette says, "Good jobs don't grow on trees, Mare," as another shakes her head and hurries away.

Wolfrom produces a stack of business cards, passing them out. "Ladies, just take a card, and if you know anything give us a call. Or if you think someone else might want to speak to us, pass the card along. That's all. We don't want to get anyone in trouble."

"Yeah, right," says the brunette, "there's a recession on, didn't you know?" but she palms a card anyway.

Lewis purses her lips and puts on her most concerned face. "The young lady who was attacked is getting out of the hospital today, but it will be some time before she's really right again. If you can help us out at all we'll do our best to keep it confidential."

"What do you mean, attacked?"

"Neil put somebody in the hospital?"

"That's what we're trying to find out."

"Ohmigod, I just thought he was a dirty little pervert."

"We're just conducting a routine investigation," says Wolfrom, pinning Lewis with a sharp look.

"What happened to the woman?"

"If you know anything that may help, just give us a call."

Some of the women are accepting Wolfrom's cards when Lewis feels a hand brush hers from behind.

The detective's instinct is to grab the hand but she suppresses the impulse, forcing herself to stay relaxed. Lewis smiles as she feels a bit of paper slip into her waiting palm. She closes her fingers around it then drops it in her pocket as the women scatter at the approach of the pretentious little M & M security guard across the concrete. Lewis plants a hand on her hip and badges him with the other.

"Detective Lewis. Can I help you?"

"This is private property, detective. You have to leave."

Lewis cocks an eyebrow. "Really."

Wolfrom grins and shakes his head. "Since when did city sidewalks become private property?"

Looking smug the guard tells them, "This is not city sidewalk, Officer. City property ends at the curb. What technically should be sidewalk is actually the curb lane. The sidewalk you are standing on is M & M private property. Mr. Molony said you'll be able to see it on the city plan he's having faxed to your lieutenant as we speak. You're being advised to leave. If that's a problem, I'll just have your badge numbers?"

"Here you go, slugger," Lewis tells him as she thrusts her business card at him. "Knock yourself out. We're leaving."

112 . . .

Maggie is curled up on her bed, staring at the wall, when she hears movement out in the hall. She pulls the duvet over her head. The sounds are muffled under the covers but they continue, to Maggie's increasing irritation. She just wants to be alone.

Everybody is supposed to be in class now anyway damn it.

But Maggie hears the rumble of a deep male voice, followed by a woman's laugh, and decides enough is enough. What the hell is Elsie doing bringing men up here. That's got to stop. Righteous anger fuels Maggie as she flings off the duvet and grabs her robe. Knotting the sash she yanks open her bedroom door and stomps down the hall.

But Elsie's door is closed. Is she in there screwing some guy? No wait, the next door, Natasha's door, is ajar with light spilling out. Unbelievable, is some shit stealing Natasha's expensive camera gear? What kind of rat would rip off Natasha while she's in the hospital?

Without a second thought, Maggie's anger swells and propels her down the hall where she bangs open the door and bellows, "Just what the hell do you..."

Maggie stops when she sees it isn't a gang of thieves, it's house mates. Like a deer in the headlights, Liz is frozen in the act of loading laundry into a green garbage bag, while Boris looks up from where he's hunched on the floor trying to screw a bedside table together under Natasha's watchful gaze. Incredibly, he's holding the screwdriver wrong. Maggie didn't think that was possible. But when she looks at Natasha, she's struck by the dramatic clash of red hair and bruises.

"Oh god Nat, sorry, sorry, I didn't know you were coming home today!"

"Hey Maggs, what'd you think..." Natasha grins, "Oh I get it, you thought I was getting burgled."

"Uh, yeah but..."

"That's sweet, but don't do anything that stupid again okay? My toys cost a bomb but everything's insured. Not worth getting a friend hurt over." She waves her hand dismissively and suddenly Maggie dissolves in great gasping sobs and her tears start to fall.

Boris looks like he wants to bolt, so when Natasha tells him to "Shoo" and he's out the door in record time, while Liz stuffs the last of the laundry into the bag, then rises with alacrity, hefting the full sack, she says, "I'll just take this down, then."

Natasha nods. "Thanks Liz. I really owe you girl."

Natasha raises her arms to Maggie, who crosses the room and sits on the bed and Natasha gathers Maggie into a hug and Maggie sobs on her shoulder as Liz flashes a smile and beats a hasty retreat away from Maggie's messy meltdown.

Unsure why Maggie needs comforting, though clearly she does, Natasha awkwardly pats Maggie's hair and slowly the crying eases. Finally Maggie detaches herself, "I'm so sorry Nat." Her red rimmed eyes dart around the room and Natasha tells her, "On the dresser." Maggie grabs the box of tissues and mops her face, blowing her nose, then depositing the soggy things in the waste basket. Standing by the dresser again Maggie looks awkward.

"Okay, Maggie, you seem to have scared Bo off, but that's probably for the best since he lacks affinity for tools. Maybe you could put the rest of the night table together while we talk?"

Maggie nods and kneels beside the nightstand box. Fitting the bits together she busies herself with furniture assembly. Mercifully, building furniture frees her from having to look Natasha in the eye. Maggie says, "I'm sorry you got attacked."

"That makes two of us," agrees Natasha equably. She knows there's more, but she watches Maggie work, giving her time.

Maggie inverts the partially finished table, screwing on supports and attaching the back and she says, "It's all my fault."

Natasha frowns, "What's all your fault?"

"Your attack."

"No offence Mags, but that's nuts. You didn't attack

me."

"If I'd gone to the cops it wouldn't have happened."

"What, you could have stopped me from getting raped? You know who did it?"

"Kind of, well, not exactly. It's just that I never reported the flasher."

Natasha shakes her head, "I wasn't flashed, I was hit over the head and raped. Two very different things."

"But they've arrested the flasher. If I'd gone to the police it wouldn't have happened."

Natasha shakes her head. "Maybe it was the same guy, I don't know. But I bet the penalty for flashing is isn't very much."

"But, still."

"So even if you made a report and the cops went to the trouble to find him, he'd probably be back out there attacking somebody sooner or later. Harder to catch maybe."

"Hmmm, I never thought of that."

"And until they get the guy, we won't really know. I mean, it might be anybody."

"But if it was the flasher..."

"It really doesn't matter. Flasher or no, the only one to blame is the asshole who attacked me, Maggie, not you. Not your fault any way you slice it. You may have made an error in judgement but even that's not cut and dried. I made a error in judgement wandering around out there by myself."

"It's not your fault. You're the victim here."

"Yeah, and I hate like hell being a victim, but you know, I wouldn't have gone to the cops over a flasher. Comedians have made them the butt of jokes forever."

"But--"

"No, Maggie, butt." Natasha says, "That was a joke," but clearly Maggie isn't laughing. "Look, Maggie, you can't fix the world and all the bad stuff that happens isn't your fault."

Maggie finishes screwing in the last screw. "I still feel bad."

"Hell, girl, you think you feel bad? You can't possibly feel as bad as I feel."

"I have to admit I've never seen anybody with skin the colour of yours." Maggie turns the night table right side up. "Which is your favourite, the fuchsia or the green?"

Maggie says, "The fuchsia, definitely."

Maggie is trying not to smile as she tucks all the packaging into a plastic bag. "So, the night stand is finished. What do you want on it?"

"The ipad and iphone so I don't have to move more than necessary."

Maggie offers to attach the power bar to the night table's side. Natasha watches rapt, thinking, you just have to keep Maggie busy and every thing's fine. Would be nice to be so uncomplicated. When Maggie finishes drilling in the screws, the power bar is mounted and plugged into the wall in minutes.

"Wow that's so great Maggie, thanks."

Maggie drops her eyes. "It's the least I could do."

Natasha looks at her. "You're responsible for what you do, Maggie, not what anybody else does."

"Yeah and I'm responsible for what I don't do too."

Natasha pushes herself into a sitting position leaning forward on her knees. "Are you trying to drive me nuts?"

Maggie looks up, shakes her head.

"How do I get through to you?"

"I feel what I feel, Nat." Maggie sets up the night stand.

Natasha looks at her. "What if it's the wrong guy?"

"I don't know. Then I guess I wouldn't feel guilty."

Perching on the edge of the bed she plugs it in and switches it then settles the iphone onto the shelf below. "There you go, wired for the twenty first century." Natasha nods.

Maggie drops the screws in the pocket of her robe, and picks up the drill. "If you need anything, just ask. I'd like to help if I can."

Natasha narrows her eyes. "Do you play backgammon?"

113 · · ·

Oscar asks, "Are you going to announce it in class?" as he dumps jelly beans into a bowl.

"No way," says Kate, mixing a jug of Kool-Aid. "Those bone heads were too good for our 'little computer club meetings'? Screw them. Nine to fivers, go punch a clock. We'll start our own Research in Motion."

Oscar laughs. "Absolutely. Love the passion, lass. Sure you'll not dump Nick and run away with me?"

"Not a chance buck-o. You just want extra shares."

"Something like that. What's the school's cut?"

"Why should Christie get anything if we do it our own time? I don't want to cut them in at all if anything comes of this, so I think it's best that we do everything on our own computers, and not use school equipment for anything, not even Googling research, OK?"

"What are we thinking about here. Hardware? Software? Data base program?"

Kate frowns. "It's gotta be something doable on student resources. Maybe a program or a game? The simpler the coding the better. Later on we can come up with more elaborate ideas. Establish a track record we'll be able to write our own ticket."

"You're right, a track record would make investment financing possible. Sounds great, Kate, count me in."

Kate looks over at Oscar, deciding to confide. "There's something else I wanted to ask you, Oz. Nick said I shouldn't talk to Jose about Krystal, but what do you think?"

"Oh, well, I didn't know you knew she was sick. Did Krys tell you, or did Nick suss it out?"

Kate stares at Oscar. uncomprehending, "Sick?"

Oscar closes his eyes. "Christ. You didn't know."

"Know what, Oz? Krystal is sick?"

Oscar looks at her sadly and nods. "Krys is very sick, Kate."

"How sick?"

"An inoperable tumour."

"Oh." Kate slides into her chair. "Is there anything..." Looking at Oscar she sees that there isn't. "That will make tonight awkward."

"Oh Christ, I'm sorry. Just when you mentioned talking to Jose about Krystal I just assumed it was to tell him. I know that's crossed my mind more than once, but she says she doesn't want his pity. And I've got to respect that."

"Absolutely. Gee, no, I just thought I'd suggest he ask her out or something. I had no idea. That sure explains a lot about why Maggie's been so emotional."

"Maggie wormed it out of Krystal, and I wormed it out of her." Oscar helps Kate move the sofa. "So although sworn to secrecy here I am spilling my guts. God I need a fag."

Kate glances sharply at him and then she realizes he's talking about a cigarette. Kate stops rearranging furniture and pelts him with a pillow. "No Oz! You're doing so well."

"I don't feel like I'm doing well."

"You just need distraction. Talk to me Oz."

"A quickie would make a lovely distraction, we could just pop round to the bedroom, no one will be along for a bit."

Kate lobs a pillow at him and starts moving the

chairs along the wall. "Of course if that's what you really want, Nick might not be asleep yet. And he might appreciate a cuddle."

"Oooh, the cat's got claws!" and Oscar laughs and tosses both pillows back at her. Kate deftly grabs both out of the air and replaces them on the sofa.

114 . . .

Tamara opens the door to the dark apartment. The air reeks of stale smoke, and she shakes her head as she makes her way through the empty living room without putting on the light. Bastard couldn't hardly wait for her to be gone before polluting the air. It's one thing smoking up outside. God, now all of the clothes she's come to collect will reek. The married student residence is not a very big space after all. She's reaching for the bedroom door when she hears groaning, then she pushes it open.

She freezes in the doorway as she is hit with the pungent smell of sex. The venetian blinds are cracked open just enough to illuminate flashes of the beast with two backs writhing in her bed.

Bastard.

A wave of red passes in front of Tamara's eyes and her jaw clenches for one brief moment as she wishes she had a gun or a chainsaw or something.

Tamara whirls and stomps out, tears washing away the red of pure fury that's blurring her vision just the same. Over the past year she's come to realize Quentin is a loser but at least he was her loser. She never in a million years thought he'd be fucking someone else.

In her bed.

Can't go five minutes without gettin' some.

Prick.

Couldn't wait for her.

Cocksucker.

Wouldn't go to class.

Motherfucker.

Didn't pull his own weight.

Bastard.

That is it, this marriage is done. No more being screwed over. She fumbles with the bolt and pushes the door open, then stumbles into the clean cold fresh air.

No. No. No. Oh god, what a mess she's made of her life. At least she hasn't totally fucked up school.

She fucking loved that sumbitch.

How could he DO this to her.

Daddy will be happy anyway, she thinks, as she makes her way along the path. He never did care for Q. She pulls out her cellphone but has to rub her eyes because she can't see to dial. Screw it. She's not gonna go back to Barbie's again. She's going to the pub.

Fuck him. Um, no. Not him. She smiles through her tears. Fuck somebody. Anybody. Somebody new. Sauce for the goose. This goose is gonna find a new friend tonight. A stud who'll take her home and fuck her blind. Oh yes. And a lawyer who will help her fuck that bastard Q over tomorrow.

Find a new apartment without any garbage.

Inconstant Moon

The cool night air seeps into the front room, chilling Quentin. He shivers on the recliner and opens his eyes. His back is stiff as hell and his head aches something fierce. The god damned door is hanging open.

Scrubbing his face with his hands he gets up and slams the door that's letting the cold air turn this dive into a walk-in freezer before stumbling into the kitchen.

Quentin splashes water on his face. He stiffens as he hears a noise behind him. Suddenly sober, Quentin whirls. But its only Jose padding out of the bedroom wearing only socks and underwear.

"Everything okay Q? I heard the door slam."

Quentin raises his eyebrows. "Making yourself at home?"

Glad at least that Tamara isn't here to see Jose in all his glory.

Jose grins. "You were passed out and Mouse got a little bit frisky so we borrowed your room. Hope that's okay, bro."

Quentin thinks it's disgusting. Last thing he wants it to sleep on somebody else's wet spot. But what he says is, "It's cool."

Jose leans against the counter, stretching. "She's gone all nervous like she's afraid you'd come in. Got any more beer?"

Turning to the the fridge Quentin feels a pang of remorse as he comes face to face with Tamara's schedule. Fucking smoking up. Totally forgot, and so he missed her again.

Quentin grabs a couple bottles of beer, passing one to Jose. They pop caps in unison then clink bottles before they drink. "Good times and good friends." says Quentin.

Hearing the bitterness Jose asks, "Heard from Tamara?"

Quentin just shakes his head.

"Bummer."

115 . . .

When Nick comes into the pub he sees Ethan sitting alone at the bar, staring morosely at the bubbles rising in his glass of beer. Sliding onto the next stool Nick pats him on the shoulder. "Hey Ethan."

Without looking up Ethan nods. "Surprised to see you in here." Billie the bartender glances over, and Nick points at Ethan's glass and holds up two fingers.

"It happens. You solo tonight?"

"Yeah. Hope I'm not back to solo every night."

"You don't want to be?"

Ethan shakes his head as the bartender sets two new bottles on the bar and accepts a bill from Nick.

"Don't see you in here very often," she says, raising her eyebrows. "Where's that pretty wife of yours?"

"Home home throwing a computer club night. Much quieter over here let me tell you."

"Then send them along here next time, get the joint

jumping." Billie laughs, counting out the change onto the bar and heads off to serve a table of hockey shirted jocks.

"How are you holding up under the TA stint? Prof driving you insane yet?"

"No, she's pretty good, hasn't buried me in crap and she's actually pretty fair with the students."

"That's great to hear. They're not all like that."

"I thought you enjoyed TAing."

"Oh I do. But the first prof I worked for was a real asshole, let me tell you. Thank god he retired because if he hadn't I don't think I'd still be here. He was just too much, and the last straw for my buddy. 'Course, not everyone takes to it."

Ethan drains his original glass, then picks up the one Nick has bought him and raises his glass to clink. "Thanks."

"You're welcome. You sure looked like you needed another."

Ethan smiles ruefully. "Probably not. Good I don't have to drive, but the companionship is sure welcome."

"Ah, you've been here a while then. So what's her name?"

"Liz."

Nick thinks, then grins, "Not that incredibly cheerful Amazon?"

"That's the one."

Nick lets out a low wolf whistle. "You been out with her?"

"Yeah, and I thought it was going great but she got

mad at me for wanting to walk her to class. She's keeping me guessing, so I'm not sure if we're dating or if she dumped me."

Nick nods. "And you don't want to be dumped."

"Hell no. She says she doesn't know if she wants to be in a relationship. I'm afraid she's looking for excuses to dump me."

"That's tough."

"Yeah."

116 . . .

Elsie sits with her back to the wall, legs extended along the length of the bench in back booth. Half a strawberry daiquiri and a basket of fries sit on the table, but all her attention is focused on the beat up medical textbook she's poring over.

Every now and again Elsie makes a notation in the margins. She's pretty oblivious to what's going on around her, so she startles when Tamara plops on the bench opposite.

"Hey, Elsie. How's it hanging."

Elsie narrows her eyes. "I'm studying for a test tomorrow. You look like you should be sleeping. Shouldn't you be home?"

Tamara just stares back. "I just wanted to ask you... um, how do you attract guys? What's your secret?"

Elsie laughs. "No commitment. If I want a guy I let him know. Look, you aren't going to get anywhere looking like that."

Tamara looks defiant. "Like what?"

"Like a mess. Men are romantics, they all want a princess." Elsie closes her book and sets it on the table beside the French fries. "Come on."

Elsie gets up and heads for the washroom door. Tamara grudgingly gets up and follows.

Standing beside Elsie at the mirror Tamara appraises her red rimmed eyes and face streaked with make up. A mess.

"Okay, I see your point," concedes Tamara.

"You're a pretty girl, just not right now."

"No Elsie, I'm an idiot. What can I say." Tamara turns on her heel and leaves.

Elsie watches Tamara disappear through the rear exit door. Elsie shakes her head and goes back to her booth, picks up the book and is again transported into the wonderful world of medicine. Idly she pops a French fry into her mouth.

117 . . .

Oscar sits at Kate's desktop computer on the table pushed against the living room wall when Kate ushers in Liz and Jake. Half a dozen people Liz doesn't recognize are gathered around as Oscar's fingers dance across the keys.

Liz tells Kate, "Maggie said she wasn't coming tonight."

"Thanks for letting me know. I thought she might

pass," Kate nods. "Glad you came out. She is all right though?"

Liz nods. "Yeah, just tired."

Kate holds out a hand, "I'm stacking coats in the bedroom."

Liz passes her jacket and turns at the sound of Adam's raised voice, "You can't do that, Oscar. It's illegal!"

"Nick isn't home very much, but when he is, he needs his news hit, Oz." Kate turns to Oscar, wagging a finger. "So don't be doing anything that's gonna endanger my Internet connection."

"I'm only downloading **Sita Sings the Blues**."

"All right, then. Except already I've got it, so stop using my bandwidth."

Adam is aghast. "But it's piracy if you download movies."

Oscar says, "No it isn't."

"He's right, Adam." Kate nods. "It's Creative Commons."

"Not really. How could that work for a movie?"

"You know," Adam's friend Dave says, "I remember reading that George Lucas didn't get rich from Star Wars, he got rich from Star Wars merch."

"Yeah," says Jake, "I heard that too."

Liz adds, "I put photos on Flickr under a CC license."

"But why?" asks Adam.

"When I take pictures I want people to see the good ones. If I put them online then that happens. It's that simple."

"But how can you make a living if you give stuff away?"

"I get paid when I get hired to do work."

"If your pictures are free on Flickr, why would anyone hire you?"

"My Flickr pics are an online portfolio. They show prospective clients just how good a photographer I am. And that's what gives them reason to hire me."

"But why pay for what they can get for free."

"They only get free what I put out there. Stock photos often don't cut it. Newspapers and magazines cover events. Insurance companies need proof if the claimant is a fraud. Performers want original album art. You can't get custom photographs online for free."

"And what about music?"

"I don't know about music."

Oscar asks, "Do you buy music you didn't like?"

"Of course not, I only buy music I like."

"And how do you know what you like?"

"Actually, I..." Adam stops, thinking. "Point taken. I never really thought it through."

Kate stuffs her fingers in her mouth and emits a loud piercing whistle. Everybody stops dead and looks over at her. Looking pointedly at Oscar, Kate says, "I am sick to death of copyright. You guys wanna argue it to death, do it at lunch on your own time. Who's up for watching Sita? Show of hands." Kate looks and all hands have shot up.

"Okay, good." Kate passes bowls of snack food as

Oscar hooks the cables from the large screen TV to her laptop.

Dave tells Adam, "Not a bad idea, Sita's a lot of fun and it has been pretty tense around here lately."

"I could use a little relaxing." agrees Liz, a little surprised to hear the guys have found the last few days tense.

"At least they caught the guy." says Kate.

"Have they?" Liz asks. "They've caught somebody. But what's to say this is the right guy?"

"Gee thanks Liz. Just when I was starting to feel safer."

"Sorry, Kate, I'm not trying to freak you out, I'm just saying it'd be good to keep being careful."

"Of course it is the guy." insists Adam. "The police wouldn't have arrested him if it wasn't."

"They caught Boris yesterday," says Jake. "Wasn't him."

"Maybe they'll settle for anybody just so life could return to normal?" suggests Kate.

Liz says, "Kate's right. The cops have to be under even more pressure than the school is to get the rapist caught."

"But if they've got the wrong guy," says Jake, "Then it still isn't safe."

"That would suck," says Kate.

Oscar flicks off the lights so the dusky cartoon goddess shows up more clearly against the wall. "Okay, who wants to watch the movie?" asks Oscar.

Dave starts clapping like a wild man and in moments the rest follow suit. Everyone moves their chairs around so they can see the picture to its best advantage. Liz notes Jake's sour look.

"Something wrong?" she whispers.

"Krystal is supposed to be coming." says Jake quietly. Liz tactfully looks away with smile as the movie begins. Oscar douses the remaining light, leaving only a hint of light trickling under the kitchen door so the wall projection is revealed in stunning colour.

"Where's Ethan?" Jake whispers to Liz.

Liz doesn't want to explain she didn't invite Ethan, so she touches her finger to her lips in the universal admonition to silence.

118 . . .

"Wow. that was an awesome movie, Oz." Liz says as Oscar unlocks the door to Fyfield House.

"You know, I read about **Sita Sings the Blues** in **Tech Dirt**, says Jake, "But I had no idea it was funny."

Oscar sighs. "The animation is what gets me. So beautifully well done. Whenever I watch something like that I curse my parents for neglecting to bequeath me the slightest touch of artistic talent."

"Have you ever tried to draw or anything, Oz?"

Oscar nods. "Years of persistence and I've barely mastered stick figures. And XKCD has that covered."

"We all have stuff we're not good at."

"True." Oscar shrugs as he locks the door behind

them. "That's it for me then. Night kiddies."

"Me too," says Liz. I am pooched." She knows if she sits up with Jake he'll want the lowdown on Ethan, so she hoofs it to the staircase tossing them a wave over her shoulder.

"I'm just gonna zone out with the tube, then." Jake says, clearly not happy to be ditched, watching Oz head down the hall to his room. "Night guys."

When Liz opens the door to their room she sees Amelia's not back yet, but nothing is marked on the calendar. Amelia's next scheduled shift isn't until tomorrow night.

As Liz undresses she feels a little uneasy. Is the right guy in jail? Where is Amelia? Her roomie should be back, it's after eleven on a school night. Amelia shouldn't be running around out there alone, darn it.

Climbing into bed, Liz sets her alarm, then grabs the beat up paperback off the night stand, admitting to herself that she's every bit as bad as Maggie. She tries to read but it's hard to concentrate. The heroes are negotiating a tricky cave system, and Le Cagot is ragging on Nikolai. It's a fun bit and she loves the larger than life character of the gruff Basque poet.

What a romantic. She'd love to find a man like him. Or would she?

Ethan. Half of her wishes Ethan was here right now and half of her wishes he wasn't such a good kisser. The last thing she needs is to think about Ethan.

Setting the book down, she reaches for the fanny pack and pulls out her cell. About to phone, it occurs to her that maybe Amelia's out getting lucky or something. She has been spending a lot of time with Eric. Maybe she's getting over her crush on Jose. Better not to call. Instead Liz Tweets:

@ameliawrites Hey girl what's your ETA?

Liz smiles thinking how much her Mom would give her a hard time for using the word "girl." The older generations just get so hung up on non essentials. Still, it's worrying that there is no response. Thank God Mom doesn't tweet. It would be too creepy having Mom lurking. Still no response. Maybe she could go back down and watch TV with Jake. Just too tired.

Liz props the phone on the table, plugging it into the charger to keep it online, just in case. Picking up the the book again, Liz reads until she drops off to sleep.

119 . . .

Jake is sprawled on the sofa watching the TV on low, but the sound of the lock turning gets his attention. Glancing at the opening hall door he sees Amelia and Eric come in.

"I didn't say he was a crappy actor," Amelia says, "I just said his Hamlet wasn't as good as Gibson's."

"But Branagh is awesome." insists Eric.

"Yeah, he is, but my problem was the production. He didn't follow the text, Eric. At least Zeffirelli follows the text. Sure, he drops bits for pacing, but they do that in the theatre, what ever it takes to make it work."

"I thought it did work."

"Not for me." Amelia shrugs. "What can I say, I'm a purist. If you wanna mess with Shakespeare do a remix and call it something else. You know, like West Side Story. Just don't pretend it's Romeo and Juliet."

"But it was Hamlet."

Jake says, "Wanna keep it down? People are sleeping."

Amelia flushes with embarrassment. "Sorry." Her gaze lights on the TV screen. "Is that... oh, wow, Rear Window."

Eric says, "What?"

Jake points to the television. "The movie."

"Classic noir," Amelia says, "I love Cornell Woolrich almost as much as I love Dash Hammet. That is a great movie, maybe Hitchcock's best. If I wasn't so pooched I'd join you. Oh well, g'night, guys," as she heads upstairs.

Eric drops into the bean bag chair, glancing up to make sure Amelia is really gone before admitting, "You know, I thought 'film noir' meant 'black and white'."

"A lot of the movies are black and white, but it's a genre." Jake laughs. "Hard boiled detectives, femme fatales, gritty cynicism." Seeing Eric has no idea, Jake smiles big. "Rear Window is a Hitchcock classic. You'll like it. This one has serious suspense."

120 . . .

Amelia smiles at Liz snoring with a book collapsed on her chest. She pries the book from Liz's fingers, setting it on the night table next to the charging phone.

Draping her jacket on the back of her chair, Amelia changes into her neon green nightgown, slides into her fuzzy green slippers, pulls on her purple robe and grabs the bathroom bag before switching Liz's bed lamp off. She leaves on a night light that will allow her to get back to bed without disturbing Liz.

Pulling the room door closed, she turns down the dimly lit hall toward the bathroom. Amelia has decided to settle for a pirate bath, saving a real shower until morning. And she just has to get the fur off her teeth or she'll never be able to sleep. Rounding the corner she runs into a strange man: her blood curdling shriek would put many a Hitchcock heroine to shame, it's more than enough to trigger the man's shriek in response.

The hall light comes on full, throwing the tableau into sharp relief. Amelia stares at the man she's never seen before as doors open and resident female students step into the hall or peer through cracked doorways. The sound of pounding feet from downstairs announces the arrival of reinforcements.

Maggie glares at the man, wearing a woman's pink chenille robe stretched rather tautly across his weight lifter form. She plants her hands on her hips and says, "Think we need to call the cops on you pal?"

"Hey, lady, I'm visiting with Elsie. Just using the bathroom," he says.

"It's like this," Maggie tells him, "This is private property and you are not authorized to be here." Seeing Amelia is shaking, Maggie throws a protective arm around her shoulder just as Eric and Jake burst into the scene.

"Are you okay?" Eric asks, and Amelia nods.

Jake is overwhelmed at being surrounded by a universe of scantily clad young women, so he averts his eyes and drops into a crouch, busily gathering up all the things that Amelia's bag has spilled over the floor. Eric joins Maggie in glaring at the interloper; he has never seen the guy before, but he damned well recognizes that robe.

Maggie says to the guy, "Aren't you leaving?"

"Okay, okay, I just have to go get dressed, then I'm outta this nut house." He pushes past and around the corner.

Joining the confab Liz asks, "What on earth is going on?"

Amelia squeezes Maggie's hand and says, "Thanks," then tells Liz. "I was just going to brush my teeth and I ran into that guy. It... um... he startled me, that's all. But maybe I over reacted."

Maggie folds her arms. "This has to stop." Amelia nods.

Jake hands the bag back to Amelia, still feeling somewhat embarrassed, "Uh, everything is under control here, time to go Eric." Jake flees down the hall. Eric looks to Amelia, "So everything is okay then?"

"Yeah, fine. Under control anyway. Go."

Eric wants to give her a reassuring hug, but isn't sure that it's allowed, so he just says, "Okay," and follows Jake.

Amelia calls after him, "Thanks, Eric."

Eric waves and heads out. As he rounds the bend to catch up with Jake, Elsie's door swings open and the strange man steps out, still tucking in his shirt, clearly in a rush to be gone. Now wrapped in the chenille robe, Elsie leans against the door frame, narrowing her eyes as Eric passes, pointedly ignoring her.

The guy follows Eric, calling, "Hey guy, wait up."

Eric doesn't slow down but the guy hurries to catch up. "No, really, bro. How the hell do I get out of here?"

Eric sighs. "Follow me." Eric starts down the central stairs into the common area. Having just turned off the television, Jake watches Eric lead the stranger to the exit. Opening the door, the guy asks, "What's the big deal?"

"We're all on on edge here because one of our roommates was raped."

"Oh, Jesus, man, I had no idea. I'm really sorry."

Eric shakes his head as the guy heads out. "Not your fault. Elsie isn't exactly the soul of tact."

Back in the upstairs hall the roused students mill around, discussing the general discomfiture they have all been feeling. It's quickly agreed that Maggie can lead the delegation. So the company follows Maggie to Elsie's firmly closed door. It opens immediately on Maggie's knock, and Elsie surveys the crowd.

"Ah. Maggie. Can I help you with something?"

Amelia says, "We've decided that there aren't going to be any more nocturnal guests."

"That was you who screamed?" Elsie asks. "You

scared the poor guy half to death."

Maggie interrupts, "No more, Elsie. That's part of the deal when you live in residence."

"Nobody said anything when it was Eric." says Elsie.

"No, but we all know who he is. He's a house mate."

Amelia adds, "I never ran into him up here."

"That's bullshit, Amelia. What's your problem anyway? You were screwing around with Eric in the common room the other night."

Amelia is momentarily shocked at the accusation, but then grins at Elsie, "You're jealous."

Liz shakes her head. "It isn't going to happen again. Natasha was just beaten to a pulp and raped. I'm sure she wouldn't like running into strange men in the dark, and she shouldn't have to. Have some compassion."

Elsie glares up at Liz. "And your point?"

Faces inches apart, Liz doesn't flinch, she shakes her head. "You're living in residence. The community is on edge. There will be no more strangers on this floor. Period."

Folding her arms, defiant, "And what if I say no?"

"Then I get you bounced out of residence quick as I can."

"I've been here longer than you have."

"Doesn't change the fact that you're breaking residence rules. Who knows, maybe it could even get you expelled."

The colour drains from Elsie's face as she stares in horror at this woman who has never even made it to her radar before.

"What have I ever done to you?" Petulant in the face of Liz's implacable calm.

"Nothing, until tonight when your lack of consideration caused harm to my friend."

Glaring at Amelia, Elsie says, "She looks fine to me."

"This is not negotiable."

"I'll think about it." Elsie retreats to her room, slamming the door. There are snickers and whispers as everyone disperses.

Amelia tells Liz, "That was awesome."

"I just said what we were all thinking."

Amelia nods, "That's right. But you said it."

§

In the dark, Natasha is pressed up against the head board, clutching a pillow, heart pounding, eyes wide in terror. Fuck fuck fuck fuck fuck fuck fuck fuck fuck fuck fuck fuck fu--

She holds her breath as there is a knock on the door. Then she hears Maggie say, "Natasha? Can I come in?"

Breathing again in relief, Natasha says, "Just a minute."

She tries to get her breathing under control as she crosses to the door and unlocks it to let Maggie in.

§

Inside her room, Elsie leans against her door. They're all stupid and jealous. She doesn't have time to find an apartment before Christmas. It's gonna be more expensive too. Just because they can't get laid enough, they want to make her conform. Maybe she could cut back a little, but it isn't fair though. She isn't hurting anybody. And it isn't any of their god damned business.

If anybody is hurting anybody it's that loser Amelia. Seems fucking Eric isn't enough for her. Elsie is not giving up sex. No way, no matter what those jealous bitches want. It's her release. It's therapeutic. As necessary as breathing. The physicality and the endorphins make it possible for her to stay on an even keel. With her course load she needs the release, damn it. It's healthy.

Okay, she can understand Natasha probably doesn't... damn it anyway. The problem is, she knows Liz is right.

Until she finds an apartment, sex will have to happen elsewhere. It's so unfair. She hasn't done anything wrong. Given a chance, she'd stake the fucking rapist down on an ant hill for messing up her life.

But getting turfed is not an option.

121 . . . saturday

Wolfrom stares miserably out the passenger window of the unmarked car as Lewis navigates the cul de sacs of the suburbs. Wolfrom shakes his head, "How do people live like this. Everything looks the same."

Lewis laughs. "Not exactly. The plans are the same, and the streets may be cookie cutter, but if you look closer you'll see signs of individualism."

"I don't see it." he stops as Lewis slows the car then turns into a driveway. This bungalow does look different. The lawn is overgrown, the paint is peeling and a general air of decay rests over the lot.

"This one looks like a crack house or something."

Lewis nods. "Good guess. Maybe a year ago we busted this one. Didn't recognize the address at first." Lewis winks at Wolfrom, "Crack houses are cheap. They all look alike."

Wolfrom rolls his eyes. "So what are we doing here?"

Lewis shrugs. "It's gotta have something to do with junior perv 'cause it's the address that woman slipped me."

As they get out of the car they are assailed by the cacophony of power lawnmowers throughout the neighbourhood. Mowers all through the subdivision are mowing lawns far shorter than the long bedraggled grass that Lewis and Wolfrom have to cross on this lawn in order to to reach the front door.

Lewis knocks.

Immediately the door opens a couple of inches before the chain catches it.

"Yes?" It's a young woman's voice, but it's dark inside so they can't see her.

"Police." says Lewis, fanning her badge. "We'd like to ask you some questions, Miss Brooks."

There's no response so she adds, "Routine investigation. Can we come in?"

The voice says, "Can you pass me your badge

officer? Waving it around like that it's awfully hard to see."

Lewis shrugs and passes it through the crack where it disappears. Wolfrom reaches into his breast pocket when the voice tells him, "Not you. Even if your badge looks legitimate you won't be coming inside."

Wolfrom frowns. "What?"

Lewis's badge is extended through the crack. "I'll allow you in by yourself Detective Lewis."

Lewis nods as she pockets her badge. "You'll have to wait in the car Wolfie."

Disconcerted, Wolfrom says, "What did I...?"

The voice says, "Nothing you did. You're a man."

"But..."

Lewis shoots him a look. "Just go."

Wolfrom stomps back to the car. He watches the front door close then reopen without the chain. The woman glimpsed in the shadows might be pretty if she cleaned herself up. Dressed nicer. Wolfrom wonders if he'll ever understand women. This is ridiculous. This is... this is... it's discrimination is what it is. He watches Lewis disappear inside.

Not for the first time, Wolfrom regrets having quit smoking. He opens his phone to play some Tetris.

122 . . .

The speakers project Pablo Lentini Riv's masterful Bach classical guitar renditions while Adam and Dave work side by side at the workbench in Adam's basement. Bits of metal and wire are scattered everywhere. Dave carefully solders a cellphone sized motherboard while Adam wires yellow LEDs into the metal face of the robot they are building.

123 . . .

The young woman stirs her coffee, looking deep into the mug, as if she'll find her fortune there. It helps avoid eye contact with the cop sitting across the table.

Quietly taking a sip, Lewis waits, patiently. She's seen this before, knows not to push. "This is good, thanks."

"You're welcome." the young woman shrugs. "Sorry about your partner. It's just, just..."

Lewis nods. "That he's a man."

"Yes." Eve Brooks looks at Lewis gratefully. "I can't have any men here. It's just too dangerous in this rape culture. Safer." She looks at Lewis. "You're here about that pig, Neil, aren't you?"

This time it's Lewis who looks away. "We're conducting an investigation. If there's anything you can tell me, it will be appreciated."

"You won't do anything." Miss Brooks shakes her head. "Nobody ever does."

"Look, I can't help you unless you talk to me."

Brooks laughs mirthlessly. "Even if I tell you everything you won't be able to help. Not in this world. This culture."

Lewis says, "I'll do what I can. That's all I can promise."

Brooks shakes her head again. "People say it's stupid and I'm over reacting. It was in an elevator full of people. He... was rubbing against me..."

Lewis is startled as Eve Brooks abruptly pushes her chair back with such force it overturns. Even so the woman barely makes it to the sink in time to heaves up the contents of her stomach. Lewis rights the chair, then returns to her own, carefully looking away, trying to offer what little privacy she can. Eve Brooks finishes, then washes everything down the drain before rinsing her mouth out with the clean running tap water. She remains at the counter, leaning over the sink.

"Sorry."

"Don't be." says Lewis, looking at the witness, she sees white knuckles gripping the lip of the sink for support.

"I'd better stay here."

"Whatever you want."

"Um. Look, I tell you, and then you go. Okay?"

Detective Lewis nods. "Alright. Can I call you later?"

"If you want. Just you won't want. What happened. Well. We were packed in the elevator like sardines, and I didn't realize. I mean I didn't notice him at first, and I didn't realize what was happening. it was so crowded. People couldn't help it we were all so close together. I thought we were just pushed against each other. But then... then I could feel his breath on my neck, hear him grunting.

"And I knew. But... but I was trapped in the back. And I could feel him rubbing... rubbing his penis against me, and I started having a panic attack but I was trapped. The elevator kept going and he kept pushing into me and... and... there was no air."

She stops to throw up some more and Lewis feels a cold chill as she realizes the young woman is right. No prosecutor will ever bring charges over a "she says he says" in an elevator.

Even if they believe her, the bastard will walk because she didn't say anything to stop him at the time. But the signs are there; Lewis knows. Eve Brooks was already a rape victim before that pig Neil Molony dry raped her in an elevator full of people.

124 . . .

Tamara comes into the apartment, not sure what horror to expect, especially late on a Saturday night. Just the thought of another night at Barbie's is worse than dealing with Q. She needs resolution.

Unlocking the door, her nose twitches as she reaches for the light. It smells different. No pot anyway. What is that odour? Perfume?

As light floods the living room she is startled to see that everything is in order. Neat. No dead bottles or pizza boxes, or ashtrays. Well. Now that she sees this unnatural sight she can identify the smell-- the perfume is Febreze. Maybe he's trying to change...

Wait a minute. Why is she giving him credit for this. She knows Q.

No way. Q does not clean.

It was probably the cunt he was fucking who cleaned the place up for him.

Tamara's moment of happiness is killed by fury that Q fucked another woman in her bed. The man she married wouldn't have done that.

Bastard.

Tamara sets down the cheap empty suitcase she's brought in the doorway. She'd better go see if he's here before packing. Make sure he's not fucking anyone else right now. Although, Saturday night. Great night for partying. Even students who work at their courses are out partying tonight.

Taking a deep breath -- Febreze, shit -- Tamara goes down the little hall to the bedroom. The bimbo probably bought it. Q would never... She opens the door, the window is open a crack, the bed is made, hell, it looks... clean sheets. Smells fresh in here. Hiding the evidence no doubt.

She opens her side of the closet. Reaching in she freezes when she sees his side only holds empty hangers. Tamara's breath catches in her throat and she sinks down on the bed.

Shit. He's moved out.

Tamara bursts into tears.

Bastard.

125 . . . sunday

Elsie sits in a coffee shop, poring over the browser. There are only a few possible rooms for rent left, and so far nothing has been even close.

All of these rooms are places with families, for god's sakes. The last thing she wants is a basement apartment with a precocious five year old at home rifling through her things, or the one where the Italian Mama is gonna watch her like a hawk to ensure she doesn't seduce one of the sons. Or worse yet tries to fix her up with one.

Isn't it possible to live privately anymore? She shakes her head and dials the number of the next one.

126 . . .

Ethan and Liz walk along the waterfront, taking pictures of seagulls, boats and each other. It's a beautiful day, great for wandering. A day for getting to know each other.

They end up in his old neighbourhood, or what's left of it, and Ethan shows her around his hometown. He tells her about the street where he grew up. About the house where the local witch lived, the one that cast the spell on him that made him fall out of her apple tree and break his arm. But the witch's house is gone, replaced by a parking lot.

Most of what Ethan shows Liz are the new buildings standing in the places where his personal history was forged. He shows her where the library his Mom used to bring him used to be, before it was torn down to make room for a burger joint. Before she married the jerk. The elementary school Ethan attended has long since been supplanted by the Waterfront Mall.

Liz finds herself warmed by the intimacy of seeing the world through Ethan's eyes as he shares his memories. As the sun is going down, they are walking hand in hand through the park at the water's edge, heading back to catch the bus back to Christie, Liz just has to ask, "Why won't you talk to the cops, Ethan?"

He stares out across the water. He doesn't want to look at her, afraid what he'll see in her eyes.

"I don't like cops." he says, quietly.

"Well, where were you that afternoon?"

Ethan shrugs. "Recording Professor Mol's lecture for the graduating class."

"Well, why didn't you just tell them? That's a great alibi. It's fantastic. Don't you see, it proves you're innocent."

Ethan shrugs. "They can find out themselves."

Liz stops and flops down on a bench overlooking the water.

It takes Ethan a minute to realize she's stopped walking with him, and he turns around and goes back to sit beside her.

"What?"

"The cops are wasting time thinking you're a suspect."

"Fuck 'em if they can't take a joke."

Liz flushes with anger. "Do you want people to think it was you? The cops aren't going to find the real rapist if they think you're it. They might not even look. It's not a joke, Ethan."

"I know it's no joke, Liz, but I was in Toronto during the G20 and I will never forget that shit. Reading the articles and seeing interviews after, well, the official line did not match what I saw. So I don't trust cops any more. So I don't talk to them. Ever."

"But that was a different time and place."

"Long as cops aren't accountable, they do what they want."

"But it wasn't even these cops."

"Doesn't matter, babe. I guess the Toronto cops had their reasons for arresting people who didn't do anything. These cops might have their reasons too. I don't know. I'll bet the school is leaning on them really hard to catch the guy. They might not even care if its the right guy. Well, it's not going to be me. It comes down to it, I'm not going to be the fall guy if they don't catch the real rapist."

Liz is shocked. "You don't think they'd do that?"

"I don't know, but I'm not willing to risk my freedom to find out."

Liz reaches over and squeezes his hand. "That's okay, I wouldn't want you to."

127 . . .

Krystal vigorously dries her hair. Shaking it free in

front of the mirror, she admires the new gold highlights before switching on the CD.

As music blares she starts her exercise routine. Admiring her body as she works her way through the well worn moves she wonders again why Jose hasn't asked her out.

Surely Oscar will have told Jose her sad story by now. That guy can't keep his mouth shut to save his life.

Well. It's bound to happen, if not Oscar, its only a matter of time before Maggie or Jake spills it. All Krystal needs is one date with Jose. Sure as shit pity will get him into her bed, and once there her newly sculpted bod ought to pin him to the sheets for as long as she wants him. Oh yes.

Who says you can't always get what you want?

128 . . . monday

Lewis smiles sweetly as Neil Molony and his powerful uncle come in to the conference room.

It irks her that she was told to use this room room instead of one of the grubby interrogation rooms. Whatever happened to the law being blind? Lewis finds it offensive to have to give a connected perp special treatment. But the bosses deemed the regular interrogation rooms too low rent for a high stakes player like Uncle M. Which simply serves to make her want to get Uncle M in a choke hold and put him on the floor. She pushes the urge down. Maybe next time. If there is a next time.

Still, she can feel waves of darkness pouring from Colm Molony. He is one ticked off lawyer. Good. His discomfiture is a soothing balm to her soul.

Neil Molony's skin has that freshly scrubbed look. The effect is that all sign of his arrogance appears to have been washed away. He keeps his eyes downcast as he takes the seat Wolfrom offers across the table. As Lewis sits beside Wolfrom the senior Molony goes around to join his nephew, but instead of sitting, the older man stands behind the adjacent chair, setting his briefcase on the seat before resting his hands on the chair back. Anything but subdued.

Colm Molony may well resent being here but he knows that there was no choice. Which is why he's made this grudging appearance at the police station on this lovely autumn day.

Lewis abruptly pulls out the chair beside Wolfrom and sits, laying her handful of file folders on the table.

"I'm not quite certain why you insisted on seeing Neil today, Detective Lewis."

"It isn't a big secret, counsellor." Lewis says, without bothering to look up. She opens the folder on top of the stack and pulls out a lab report, which she slides across the table.

"The DNA report is in. We have a definite match."

Molony pulls out the chair and sits. He holds out his hand and Lewis passes him the report. He flips through it, pausing here and there. "I'll need a copy of this." Lewis nods.

Neil squirms in his seat. "But I didn't..." Colm holds

Laurel L Russwurm

up his a hand and the young man subsides.

"The report indicates that the evidence was acquired from cigarette butts."

Lewis nods. "Yes, that's right."

"Old cigarette butts," continues Molony.

"They had some wear but there's no telling how long they'd been there."

"That's my point, Detective. The cigarette butts were not fresh, they could have been left there at any time."

"Oh sure," Wolfrom volunteers. But we have Neil's statement denying he was ever there. This proves he was." Both Molonys turn their attention on the formerly silent partner.

"There's indication the butts were left over a substantial period of time. Time when young Neil spent hours concealed in those bushes. In that spot, watching the girls go by, getting the lay of the land. Premeditating, as it were."

Neil explodes out of his seat. "No. You've got it all wrong. I didn't do that..."

Colm says, "Neil," in a cautionary paternal tone of voice.

Neil waves him off. "No! I will not shut up because I'm the one they want to put in jail. Yes, I was there, but that was months ago. I didn't attack anyone."

"What were you doing there then?"

"I was just..." Neil blinks as the realization of what he's just admitted to hits home. "Just watching girls."

He looks hopefully at Wolfrom, who just stares back, not giving any encouragement.

Lewis says, "Back when it was still warm, you mean."

Colm Molony glares at Neil, who deliberately ignores his uncle. Neil turns almost gratefully to Lewis.

"I went biking there in the summer and I had a blow out and the bike went off the path. I sat on the stump to fix the tire there and I... I heard girls giggling."

"Neil, don't."

Ignoring his uncle, Neil says, "I looked up and I could see them going by on the path, but they couldn't see me. It was, it was, well just a good spot. You know, a nice place to watch the girls. A terrific place to watch girls, really, because I could watch them but they didn't see me. That's all. It was a long time ago."

Dubious, Lewis says, "I don't know Neil, there were a lot of cigarette butts there. You went there a lot."

Quiet, he lowers his eyes again. "Yes."

"You expect me to believe that you just stopped going?"

"That's what happened. One day I just decided it was too much trouble." He looks at Lewis, trying to decide if she's buying it.

"You know, too far from work, too far from home."

"So you just stopped?"

Surly as the attitude seeps back. "Yeah, I just stopped."

"Why would you do that Neil? Perfect spot to watch girls. Must have made you feel really powerful to be able to watch them without them knowing you were there."

"Something like that."

Lewis leans across to him, speaking in a softer tone, "In a situation like that, I expect that while you watched the girls, you had to find something to do with your hands..."

Colm Molony slams his fist on the table. "That is it Detective. We are done."

Molony stands up and turns to the young man, "Come along, Neil."

Neil looks up at his uncle and says, "No Uncle Colm. I am not done. I did find something to do with my hands. I jacked off and watched the girls go by, and it was just great." He closes his eyes and smiles. "Just fucking great."

Colm sits back down. "Neil, you have to stop talking now." he turns back to Lewis, "Detective we need five minutes alone."

"No!" Neil's voice cracks, "I have to tell them and I'm gonna. I have to tell them, don't you see? You won't listen to me. Nobody ever listens to me. I have to tell it now 'cause I do not want to go to jail. So shut the fuck up, Uncle Colm, and let me tell my goddamn story."

Colm Molony slumps back in his chair as though struck.

Feeling his power, Neil tells Lewis, "So yeah, that's what I was doing in those bushes. I went to watch. And it was incredible because I was invisible. I could look where I wanted and not get any grief. The stupid bitches didn't ever see me. But you know, after a while, well," he shakes his head ruefully, "watching just wasn't enough anymore."

The elder Molony watches incredulous as his nephew reveals a side he has never seen before, and it isn't pretty. How could this... this... creature possibly be related to him? It's simply inconceivable. This confession has to stop, there is no way this can be allowed to get out in this town.

God, the firm could be embarrassed. Possibly even ruined. He would be a pariah. Why in gods name did he give this fucking little prick a pity job? Family responsibility. Shit. What did his bloody family ever do for him? And how did he end up with a brother dumb enough to father... this... this... pervert.

"After a while it was as though. It wasn't as good being invisible. It was, I don't know, somehow it was beneath me. I'm as good as everybody else, right?"

"And I started thinking... I guess that's when I started thinking that maybe the best thing to do would be to... to show them. I wanted to show them so badly. You know these girls, blonde, gorgeous with legs up to there... they would be going past in their little groups, you know? You can't talk to them when they're in packs. Not those girls and I knew... I just knew I wouldn't be able to do anything. Uh, could I get some water?"

Wolfram pours a glass of water and hands it to Neil, who takes a sip, clearly relishing the attention, the suspense.

Neil nods, "Then... then one day there was a girl by herself, she wasn't walking very fast because she was carrying too much stuff, and I was... I really needed, you know, needed something, and I had been pounding the meat, but it wasn't as good anymore. It wasn't good enough any more. So I decided well... so then I came out of the bushes to show her and she... and she," all eyes are on him and his voice fades and he swallows before finishing, "She... she... just laughed." His jaw tightens, and he is overcome with emotion.

Colm can't believe it. The rotten kid's eyes are filling up.

Neil isn't just disgusting, he's pitiful. If you're gonna be a god damned pervert at least be a man about it.

Neil savagely rubs his eyes and his demeanour turns surly. He can feel his uncle's contempt. In a twisted way it gives him the strength to go on. He stares at his uncle with glittering eyes, as if willing his uncle to really see him. Prick.

Neil takes a breath and plunges on, "That nasty assed bitch just laughed and laughed. I couldn't believe it and, well, it was too much for any man. So I grabbed my bike and took off.

"That was the last time. I couldn't go back there. Don't you see? I'd give anything to be able to go back there, back the way it was before. Just to watch. But I can't. I just can't."

Neil is starting to whine, stung by the injustice of it all. Why did it have to happen to him? He's special, his mother always told him he was special. Well, until she dumped him with insufferable Uncle Colm.

"That bitch laughing at me, that was, that was the end. I don't even ride my damned bike up there any more. I just couldn't. I mean I can't. What if I saw her again? What if she laughed at me again. It's just... there is no way. There is no way... I didn't do anything to anyone. I just stopped going there, I haven't even been there in weeks. It wasn't me, raped that girl. I can't even go there. Just don't put me in fucking jail, okay?"

Neil buries his face in his hands and starts snivelling. Colm looks away. Incredible. This alien thing can't really be his own flesh and blood. A wienie wagger. Unbelievable. And what's worse, not even a good one. A wimp. A bloody wimpy wienie wagger. By god, if you're going to be a pervert, be a world class pervert. Like Bernardo, say. Make your name stand for something. Striking terror in the hearts of men is far better than inspiring contempt. Sniggers. What in God's name did he ever do to deserve this indignity?

Lewis and Wolfrom exchange glances. Without saying a word they are agreed. They've got this kid cold on exposing himself but there is no way this kid did the rape. First offence. And they just know Uncle M is gonna pull every string in reach to keep this one out of the media.

Lewis feels the revulsion building. In her mind's eye she can see Neil smirking as he assaults Eve Brooks in the elevator. She wants to slap the little bastard silly, knee him in the groin, stomp his pitiful little pecker into paste so that the bastard never gets the chance to hurt anybody ever again.

Except the little fucker is going to walk. Maybe

there is something to the 'rape culture' idea.

Goddamnitalltohell.

She feels Wolfie's look of concern and she takes a breath, gets hold of herself and pulls it back in, pushes it down. Lewis breathes, and her vision returns to normal.

Good old Wolfie. He's walking talking proof there are good men still. Easy to forget in the job. If nothing else, being police teaches you to choose your battles. Mostly.

Colm Molony clears his throat. "I have to say I had no idea." Incredulity gives way to self preservation soon enough though. "I think it is safe to say that my nephew is in need of professional help here. Perhaps..."

Lewis cuts him off. "We need to bring in the crown prosecutor to look at disposition. Mr. Molony."

Molony glares. "You can't just..?"

Lewis shakes her head. "No sir. There are protocols."

129 . . .

Liz is hurrying across the courtyard because she's not dressed warmly enough. It's so hard to tell what to wear when the weather is all over the map.

She pulls open the door to the computer building and steps gratefully into the warmth.

At least there isn't any snow. Yet.

Vlad looks up and smiles at her from behind the security desk. She grins and waves and Vlad waves back.

But as Liz crosses the lobby toward the stairwell, she realizes her favourite security guard isn't just returning her wave, he's waving her over. Her watch tells her she has time, so she changes course to see what he wants.

"Hey Vlad, how's it going?"

"Things are happening Miss Liz, that I thought you might wish to know."

Liz can see from Vlad's expression she is not going to like what he is about to tell her. Her smile falls away and she asks, "What?"

"It's the police, Miss Liz. They are back again."

Liz pales. "Oh no. Was there another attack?

"No. No, nothing like that. It is the young man they arrested. Apparently they got the wrong man."

"Oh. Not good. But better than another attack, anyway."

"Yes, you are right about that."

"Are they in the same room?"

Vlad nods.

"Thanks for letting me know. I'll tell Natasha."

"How is Miss Natasha doing?"

"A lot better. She's still pretty sore though."

"Tell her I said hello, please."

130 . . .

Wolfrom is scrolling through computer files while Lewis flips through the box of physical file folders. Wolfrom asks, "Were there any that stood out that we should bring back for follow up, or do we just start over?"

"Nothing jumps out at me. We're back to square one, Wolfie."

"Think how easy it'd be if we could get a court order to make them all give us samples."

Lewis laughs. "Never happen."

A knock on the door, Wolfrom opens it to admit Liz.

"Do you have new information for us?" asks Lewis.

Liz hovers in the doorway, "Uh, no. I thought you had the guy. I'm wondering what you're doing back here?"

Lewis says, "As it turns out, the guy isn't the guy."

"So you're back here because? You think it's a student?"

"Could be. Might be staff, guest lecturer, former student, stranger. The possibilities are endless."

"Oh shit. What do I tell Natasha?"

"That we haven't caught the guy. That if she remembers anything she should let us know. She was going to think about smells, if you could remind her."

"Oh, I will." Liz nods. "Um. So, now what are you guys doing?"

"Interviewing the rest of the student body to start."

131 . . .

When Tamara steps out of the shower she knows she's not alone. She stops, strains to listen. She hears the sound of kitchen cupboard doors closing. Shit.

There's somebody out there. She glances at the knob and sees that it's locked. Flimsy but better than nothing.

Shit shit shit.

Hell, she doesn't even have her cell, it's charging on the nightstand. She towels off quickly, then wraps the towel around her hair. She looks around for a weapon. Who keeps weapons in the bathroom? Draino maybe? Yeah right. like she's got any hope of getting some sneak thief to imbibe. Shit.

Who is she kidding. No way it's a thief, she knows damned well it's the goddamn rapist. Psycho is still scary, lousy special effects and outdated medical theory and all, because it doesn't get much more vulnerable than this. They oughta sell mace-on-a-rope so you could at least feel safe in the fucking shower.

Shit shit shit.

What could she use? The curtain rod, no, too damned flimsy. Wait. how about that lavender air freshener Quentin hates. A squirt of that shit in the creep's face ought to be as good as mace. She pulls on her robe, stuffs the aerosol can in her pocket, takes a deep breath and carefully pulls the door open. It's not a very big apartment but still she can't see in the kitchen without going down the hall. Maybe the best thing would be to take off out the bedroom window. It isn't like she wants to tangle with that bastard.

Nope, getting beaten and raped is not on the 'to do' list.

Tamara quietly pads along the hall away from the kitchen and into the bedroom. She pulls the door closed ohhhh so gently. She can barely hear the snick of the latch, so no way the bad guys heard it. Pushing her clothes off the chair onto the floor she tries to prop the chair under the doorknob like they always do in the movies. Doesn't work, though, chair's too short. Tamara settles for standing the chair in the doorway.

Well, hell, get some clothes on.

Gingerly, carefully, quietly opening the closet.

Grabbing a pink sweat suit off the shelf and pulling it on. Now she doesn't feel so vulnerable. Good.

Next thing. Gotta get the heck out. Tamara crosses to the window. She leaves the heavy drape closed and just slips behind it.

Quiet as a mouse, she releases the catch and slides open the window. Damn. The screen. There's a trick to getting it out, but she doesn't know it. Q does but she doesn't.

Tamara tries pushing, pulling, shimmying. Every sound is too loud. Gotta be quiet.

Suddenly it's out, but she has no idea how she did it, it's just done.

She eases open the drape, drops the screen on the bed, then lifts her leg up and out the window. She needs her morning coffee. Once she's out of here she'll get the cops and... the smell of fresh coffee in the hall.

Which is when it hits her: how many rapists make coffee in their victim's apartments?

Shit. It must be Q come home. Bastard. Scaring

her out of her skin like this.

She pulls her leg back inside, glances at the screen. Not knowing what she did to get it out, she sure as shit has no idea how to get it back in so, what? Stuff it under the bed. Don't let him know he scared her.

Good. She's in a position of strength here. He's in the wrong, but he's come back. That's something. Barbie thinks she's nuts to care, but, hell, Q is her guy. Q has always been her guy. Sometimes he acts like a jerk, in a lot of ways he's like a little boy, but... she loves him. What else is there, right?

She pulls the sash of the robe tighter and moves the chair back to its usual position by the wall. Great.

Quentin is pouring coffee when she walks in.

"What are you doing here?" she asks.

He says, "I thought maybe we could talk."

"Why? You never wanted to talk before."

"Maybe that's 'cause talking wasn't necessary before."

"Maybe not for you. Look, I've got to get ready for class."

Q gestures to the dinette. "This won't take long." He carries the mugs over and sets them on the table before taking a seat on the bench. Tamara sighs and joins him.

His whole demeanour is wrong. What gives?

"Aren't you even going to apologize?" she asks.

"There was a time I would have, but this isn't it."

"Fine. Whatever, Q, just get to the point, okay?"

"Paperwork's in. I'm withdrawn from the program."

Blood drains from her face. "What? Why... you can't..."

"It's done Tam. It hasn't been working out for me."

"Maybe it would have if you actually went to classes, or did your assignments instead of just smoking up all the time. There's no degree program in being high, Q."

He shakes his head. "I guess I deserve that. But you don't see that toking was the effect, not the cause. Photography just isn't my thing. I thought it'd be an adjunct to film, but it's something completely different. I thought I could do it so we could be together but I just can't."

"So you're saying it's my fault?"

"No, Tam, if it's anybody's fault it's mine. You did the right thing for you; picked the program you needed. I'm the one screwed up. I should have gone to Ryerson. It's just, I wanted to be with you. I thought I could make Christie work for me, but it's never been right. And now I'm screwing you up too."

"What about us?" Tamara asks, tears welling in her eyes. "You wanted to get married. It was your idea. Now you're gonna blow it off?"

"You're in a heavy duty program, Tam. You don't have time for me. I can switch to a different school or pull out and go back later. Sticking out photography here is a waste of money. And they're still willing to take me at Ryerson."

"So you're just gonna up and leave me?"

"That's why I'm here now, Tam, I wanted to talk it over with you. But you haven't let me talk to you at all. It sure as hell feels as though you've left me."

"You're the one who doesn't show up. Who spends all the time smoking up. I've been wondering why you married me. You never want to spend time with me. But the worst kick in the head was walking in to find you fucking some other woman in our bed."

The look of horror on his face almost convinces her. Almost. But Tamara knows what she knows. She was there. "That was my tipping point, Q."

"I've never been unfaithful to you, Tam. I just wouldn't."

"In our bed!"

"Wait a minute, are you talking about Friday?" Tamara nods, unable to form words. Quentin shakes his head. "Jesus, Tam, that wasn't me. Mouse and Jose were here and we all got high watching Harold and Kumar. I passed out on the recliner and they got to messing around and ended up in our room. That's it. You don't believe me ask either of them. But then, hell, if you don't believe me there really isn't much point anymore, is there."

He looks so angry. Is he telling the truth? Tamara feels her eyes filling. She wants to believe him. Is he playing her? She says, "I don't know what to believe anymore."

"Look, Tamara, I've been miserable. I haven't felt good here at all. It's a waste of money for me to stay.

Say the word and I'll pass on Ryerson and grab a job here. After you're done it'll be my turn, and we'll be together. It might be better if I just go to Ryerson now. Hell, it's not like you have any free time. And from the sounds of it, that's only gonna get worse, not better."

Tamara is stunned. "Wait a minute. Why didn't you ever say anything about any of this before? This is the first I've heard."

"I didn't really understand why I was miserable at first. It seemed easier to smoke up than figure out what the problem was. Made me feel better for a while. Kinda forget there's even a problem. It makes you think it's licked, but it isn't really."

Tamara shakes her head. "What do you want to do?"

"I think Ryerson is the best choice for me now. But I don't want you to think I'm running out on you or anything."

"We wouldn't hardly see each other."

"We don't hardly see each other now, Tammy."

"Not what I thought married life would be like."

"Things are worse than I thought, but this isn't exactly unexpected. I mean not really. Neither of us have been having fun. Even if you never noticed how miserable I've been."

"That is crap. You haven't been acting miserable, you've been acting like an asshole who's having too much fun getting high to waste his time going to class."

"I deserve that but... I guess I thought you'd be able to tell."

"How? By magic? It doesn't work like that."

"I know that now. But that's what it felt like to me. I mean, you're the smart one. But when I started figuring it out how was I supposed to talk to you? You wouldn't let me near."

She looks at him. "When would you leave?"

"I thought tonight. Give me a day to pack up and say my good byes, then I get a good night with my lady before I head out. Please tell me you're not doing an allnighter tonight."

Tamara sees that he's serious. "We'll talk tonight?"

"Yeah. Hey, did you notice? I cleaned the place up for you. Think I can figure out how to make dinner for you by the time you get back?"

Tamara looks at him. Q is offering to make dinner. The world is spinning and she just doesn't know what to think. Maybe. Maybe they can start over. Make it work.

132 . . .

Barbie's blonde hair is back lit by the sunlight streaming through the library windows behind the reading table. Stacks of books fan out around her, some laid face down, others heaped in jumbles, paper bookmarks conspicuously protrude as she makes notes, drumming her fingers on her laptop until she feels the glare of the other patrons.

Digging in her purse, she extracts an HB pencil, now idly tapping the eraser end against her front teeth while she works. Her brow creases into a frown of concentration as she plows through a particularly weighty tome.

Suddenly her concentration slips. Blinking myopically she readjusts her focus to take in the wider world. Even the pencil stills as she looks around the room. It feels as if she's being watched, except everyone else seems caught up in their work. What gives?

Laying down the pencil, she looks again. She scans back and forth. Still nothing. But the feeling of being watched is even stronger. So she lifts her head and looks up at the second floor balcony that rings the reading room. And there he is. Jose, leaning up against the rail, is looking down at her.

"So gorgeous," she thinks, smiling up at him, giving a little wave. He returns her wave with a crisp salute but doesn't smile, just looks down at her expressionlessly. Barbie feels her body betray her.

She uses both hands to indicate her ostentatious research display, then gives him a palms up pantomime "what can I do ?   ' He shrugs and she tears away her gaze, lowering her eyes to her work. Concentrate.

She's got to get this paper done or she'll be in big trouble. But she is dying to look up to see if he's still watching her. Barbie pushes the impulse down. Hard. She picks up the pencil again, tightens her grip. No. Don't look, work.

Don't encourage him. Flip through pages. Pretend to work, real work will follow soon enough.

Someone drops into the chair beside her. Barbie's first thought is that it's Jose come down from above, so although her heart is pounding, she doesn't look.

But then she knows it's not Jose. Looking over she sees it's only Tamara. "Are you busy?" Tamara asks.

Barbie shakes her head in amazement, waving her hand at the reference materials.

"Of course I'm busy. I've got to get my term paper done or I'm toast. Is yours done?"

Tamara shakes her head. "Not exactly, about half."

"It's due the end of the week."

"I know." Barbie is telling *her* when things are due? The whole world is upside down. "I thought I'd let you know Q's leaving. He's gonna switch to Ryerson. Probably make my work easier."

Tamara gets up to leave but Barbie reaches out a hand to grab her arm. "Wait. Are you all right?"

"Could be worse." Tamara nods tersely, although she looks on the verge of tears. "At least it wasn't him screwing Mouse."

"What?" Barbie isn't following this conversation at all.

"On Friday night. It wasn't Q, it was Jose."

"I missed something somewhere, Tam, you're saying Jose slept with Mouse?" Barbie asks, not quite believing it. She thought-- no, don't go there.

"Yeah, that's what Q said."

"Don't tell me you can't tell Jose and Q apart."

"I was freaking out, and it was dark." Seeing Barbie's agitation, Tamara realizes Barbie is jealous that Jose got it on with Mouse.

"Hey, sorry. I didn't think it'd bother you. I kinda thought you'd be, you know, happy, if, I mean, Jose and Mouse..."

"Yeah, that's great. Takes the pressure off," Barbie lies. "Look, Tam, why don't you go grab your books and get your research done. It'll take your mind off things."

"Yeah, okay. I think I will." She smiles wanly at her friend. Who'd have thought. Barbie may be flight, but she has really been a good friend. "Can I leave my stuff here then?"

Barbie nods, "Sure. Here, spread out on the table so nobody else takes your spot. We can talk at lunch, okay?" Thinking, Jose and Mouse?

Tamara nods, and does as she's told. Barbie watches Tamara head into the stacks and takes advantage of the moment to glance casually up at the balcony. Wishing he was there. Here. But he isn't. He's gone.

Lucky Mouse.

Barbie sighs, then turns back to her book.

133 · · ·

No one is eating outside today because it's cold. Kate is trying to find them a table while Nick gets their lunch. She's thinking they'd be better off to go home to eat as she cruises through the caf. There is an occasional empty seat but no place to squeeze two. This is nuts.

A flash of movement and she looks over and sees

Adam waving at her. Oh look, he's at a corner table with his friend Dave and -- joy oh joy -- empty seats.

Great! Kate grins and gives him a thumbs up and looks back to see where Nick is at. Perfect.

Nick's heading her way with a couple of bowls of soup balanced on a tray. And coffee. Nick knows she needs her caffeine fix. He's even stopped lecturing her about it. She beckons him to follow and she pushes on to Adam's table.

"Thanks Adam, you're a lifesaver." Kate pulls out a chair.

Adam smiles shyly. "I am happy to help the computer club hostess."

"Well, you sure did, big time." She grins. "I was thinking we were gonna have to take our lunch home. I sure don't plan on having lunch in Nick's lab. Ever."

Adam laughs while Dave raises his eyebrows.

"My husband's a med student," Kate says while stacking abandoned dishes on her side of the table onto an empty tray.

Dave gets it. "I see your point."

Nick arrives with his full tray and Kate asks, "You guys met?" as she carries the tray of debris to a clearing station.

Adam nods. "Hi , Nick."

Nick sets the tray down, and tells them "Thanks. I wasn't looking forward to lunch in the lab."

"Yeah, Kate said."

Nick comes around the table beside Dave, extending a hand. "Nick Stone, med school."

Shaking hands, "Dave LeBlanc, engineering."

Nick grins, distributing the tray contents. "This your first year?" Nick asks as Kate returns.

"Yes. It's much more intense than high school was."

Nick laughs as Kate crumbles the sealed package of crackers into dust then sprinkles it into her tomato soup.

"You know, your accent sounds just like my friend Krys. Whereabouts are you from, Dave?" Kate asks.

Dave says, "I'm from Walkerton. But I don't have an accent."

Kate laughs. "Sure you do. I guess it's not the same, then, because she's from a place called Paisley."

"That would have put us in the same school. Paisley doesn't have a high school; they get bussed to Walkerton." Dave says. Then he frowns. "I have an accent?"

"Just a little one." Kate smiles back. "You mean I was right? Awesome."

"What do you know," grins Nick. "Henry Higgins."

"I had no idea Christine ended up at Christie."

"Not Christine, Krystal. In computer science."

Dave nods. "It was a small school, Kate, and everybody knows everybody. We didn't have a Krystal, but there was Computer Chris. It would have to be Christine. Must be she's reinvented herself." Dave shrugs. "I guess I would too if I were her."

134 . . .

Kate walks into the computer lab, settling into her usual spot between Oscar and Maggie. As she fires up her machine, Kate leans over to Maggie, "I just had the strangest lunch." Kate says, quietly.

"Wait a minute. Isn't this is lunch with Nick day? I don't wanna hear anything kinky."

Kate rolls her eyes. "The caf was a zoo so it was lunch with a whole herd."

Maggie grins. "That's why we went downtown. Much more civilized."

"You may be better at planning than I am, Maggie, but I'm still better at digging up dirt."

"Ooooh," grins Maggie, "Sounds like I missed something good. What's the scoop?"

Just then Jake and Krystal come in and Kate freezes. Maggie says, "What?" Following Kate's line of sight she realizes the subject of the gossip has just entered.

Jake? She can't mean he's the rapist? Hard to believe. No way. Impossible.

It's got to be something else. Something with Krystal. How did Kate find out about Krystal? If anybody in CSIS had any brains, they'd be recruiting Kate. Begging her to sign on 'cause that girl would make an awesome spy.

Better keep it under wraps, it isn't something Krystal needs spread around. Maggie taps her keyboard and Kate nods an acknowledgement.

They can discuss it in a private IM chat.

Jake sets down Krystal's laptop across the aisle in her usual spot beside Adam's place. Maggie wonders where Adam is. It isn't like him to miss class. This'd be his second time. What's going on with that guy?

Krystal smiles brightly, "Thanks Jake."

Jake says, "No problem," with nonchalance belied by the tell tale grin spreading from ear to ear as he leaves the room.

Maggie sets up the chatroom while Kate settles in, firing off invites to Oscar and Kate to participate just as the professor makes her appearance. Krystal has been plugging in her laptop but looks up as Gates announces the class can use the time to do project work or meet with her for individual consultations.

As Gates settles in at her desk, Krystal roots through her bag and pulls our a tattered paper notebook and heads over to join the line that's already forming She perches on an empty desk to reread some notes while she waits.

Maggie
whazzup k8?

Kate
You'll never believe it. I had lunch with Adam + his pal Dave.

Oscar
Right, Adam brought him along the other night.

Kate
Dave has a weird story to tell. He grew up in a small town, everybody knows everybody, and kids from the nearby towns are bused to Walkerton for high school.

Maggie
I hv work 2 do K8. This going somewhere?

Kate
Big time. Seems a redhead named Chris from small town Paisley told friends she was dying so they'd tell the guy she was hot for.

Maggie and Oscar exchange glances, then they all look over at Krystal talking to Professor Gates.

Oscar
So he'd pity her and give her a tumble?

Maggie
There's never been any question the blonde is out of a bottle. I thought it was a fashion statement, not a disguise.

Oscar
Jake argued with Jose whether it was real blonde.

Maggie
Poor Jake.

Oscar
What happened? She get the guy?

Kate
Sort of worked, somebody told the guy, but
instead of dating her he went to pray with her
mom, and the mom set him straight.

Maggie
Holy shit that's... just...

Kate
Sick?

Oscar
Stupid, really. Y try it on again? Didn't work the
first time.

Maggie
Different time, different place.

Kate
Nick says this is way beyond a prank. Only a
sociopath would try to pull a scam like this. Twice.

Maggie
So Oscar told you?

Oscar
Guilty

Maggie
Just can't keep a secret, can you Oz.

Kate
Just as well. Y do u think Adam decided to cut.

INCONSTANT MOON

Maggie
Maybe this Dave guy is just trying to do her dirt?

Kate
Can't see any reason he'd have to lie.

Maggie
Cold chills. Need 2 hear it from her tho.

Kate
I wanna confront her. This is my last class today

Oscar
Can't believe I fell for it.

Maggie
It's funny, we weren't really friends until she was dying.

Oscar
I rather doubt we were ever really friends at all.

Kate
You guys believe it's all been a lie? even without talking to her?

Maggie
Yeah, I do.

Oscar
How could you lie about something like this?
Inconceivable.

Maggie
I couldn't. You'd pretty much have to be a pathological liar to pull it off.

Kate
Word Nick used was sociopath.

Maggie
it's not something that a friend would do, that's for damn sure.

Kate
She mustn't think very highly of us.

Oscar
I've helped her with a bloody lot of school work.
Kate
Me too.

Maggie
I guess between us we're probably getting her pretty good marks.

Kate
And poor Jake... not just the mooning over her, he's been her servant,oh, she's coming back. What now?

Maggie
Shh then. Talk to her after class. I'm sure as shit am not leaving this room until I know for sure. And she isn't either.

INCONSTANT MOON

Oscar
Sounds like a plan. Back to work kiddies.

Krystal takes her seat, seeing her friends are pretty wrapped up in their work she opens her own laptop.

135 · · ·

Although quite close to the road, the traffic noise is almost nonexistent due to the thick stand of trees. The path meanders through the woods, interspersed every so often with concrete stanchions bearing street lights.

Even with cast off leaves providing a colourful carpet there's still more than enough evergreen stuff to muffle sound. Except for the occasional crunching as people hurry along the path.

At least the stump is still here.

Oh look, all the cigarette butts have been cleaned up. Very thoughtful of the police. Still, given a choice. he'd be anywhere but here. But there really isn't a choice.

Resting his elbows on his knees, deep in the forest shadow, he takes a drag on the joint he lit just a moment ago. He hears giggling and tenses but it's a false alarm. Just a bunch of girls. He doesn't want them. He only needs one. Just one.

The one that's got him by the balls and won't let go. He draws on the joint, sucking the smoke deep into his lungs and letting it out slow, watching expelled smoke drift upward through the trees. Not too much foot traffic. It's getting too cold. He rocks a little, rubs his arms. She should be along momentarily.

After all, it's skive Thursday.

Barbie always did cut the last class so she could get her salon hit. A girl needs to get her nails done.

He is breathing heavily now, the corners of his mouth twitching as he waits. The spliff is done. He carefully stubs it out on an empty matchbook, then places it in an envelope in his inside breast pocket.

Looking down, he sees they haven't just swept, they've scraped off a layer of dirt from around the tree stump. He scuffs the bits of ash into the dirt. No DNA from ash. He smiles, tucking his hands into his armpits.

Footsteps. Glancing at his watch he knows it could be her. No talking. It isn't like she has friends.

An entourage maybe. Fans. High heels clattering. Good. He stands up. He can see her beautiful golden hair, floating in a cloud. Never dressed warmly enough for the weather. She goes around the curve of the path and he steps forward to follow her.

He's ready. He knows it's now or never. Increasing his speed, he closes the gap between them. He can tell just when she hears him, she tenses up a walks faster. He smiles. How fast can you go in those stupid shoes?

As he continues to close the gap he watches the way the heels make her butt move. Sensual.

Maybe that's all it was. Shoes.

Suddenly she stops, and whirls around to face him, Her hand is extended toward him, arm straight. What has she got pointed at him... oh, mace. Time to play. He stops. Draws back, raises his hands in mock surrender.

"Hey, it's just me," he says. She lowers her hand, looking over at him.

Barbie shakes her head at her foolishness when she recognizes him. She smiles an automatic greeting. Good. She feels foolish. Guilty. Use it.

"Where are you going?" asks Barbie.

"I'm just starting a part time job. Um, could I... ? " He wiggles his hands above his head, reminding her she has the drop on him.

"Oh sorry, Jose." Barbie grins. "Sorry, you gave me a scare." She stuffs the mace tube in her pocket.

He shakes his head. "That's okay. I gotta hurry if I'm gonna make the bus." He fingers the scarf in his pocket as he starts to pass her, but she reaches up and touches him.

"I can give you a ride."

He stops and turns to face her. "Okay."

Jose can feel his heart pounding. He looks down at her. She's smiling up at him, lips parted. She's so beautiful he can hardly breathe. He places his hands on her shoulders and bends down and kisses her. She responds with a passion that overwhelms him and for one brief shining moment it is enough.

The kiss deepens and she closes her eyes and pushes in closer, rubbing her body against his, hard, like an animal in heat. He's tempted. Last week it would have been everything.

Not anymore. His hands slide across her shoulders and encircle her neck. Her eyes fly open when he starts to squeeze.

Laurel L Russwurm

He can see the fear in her eyes... she has learned enough anatomy to know that this pressure will at the least render her unconscious.

He feels the power as he continues the kiss, but now it's lost all pretence; it's an honest straightforward violation as his lips block her mouth from screaming and his tongue retracts from the attack launched by her teeth.

Still, he maintains the pressure, keeping her mouth sealed. He notices that her hands have been scrabbling at him. The impacts of her ineffectual fists are muffled by the thickness of his coat. She tries to kick him, twist, pull away but he can see that she knows she's losing it here... she is not getting enough air... her resistance is waning, her strength trickling away.

He feels triumphant as her ungloved hands flutter up toward him in supplication. He's starting to smile when the fluttering hands transform into talons and rake the sides of his face. The sting is sharp, he can feel wetness on his cheek. Grimly he tightens his grip ignoring the pain and she slumps. Finally. He opens his hands allowing her to slip through his fingers, and fall into a rag doll sprawl in the mud.

He looks down at her laying there, legs splayed, skirt hiked up, undone jacket only partially covering her. He runs his palms down his cheeks and comes away bloody. Bitch scratched him.

He kneels and slides his hands under her armpits, trying to get a grip, but at best it's an awkward embrace. This won't work. Instead, moves around to her side, sliding one arm under her neck, and the other under her butt. Bracing himself he takes a deep breath and lifts. Once standing it's not so bad. Still, they make this shit look so much easier in the movies. She smells just as good as ever, even if she looks a mess.

He stares at the woman cradled in his arms. She shudders and sucks in a breath. Not dead then. But still unconscious.

Good. Gotta get her off the path. For a brief moment he thinks he should have gone with her to her car. It's too far now. She's much heavier than he thought.

Back to plan A. He carries her dead weight off the path and back into the bushes. He lays her down on the clean patch by the stump, but he knows this is much too close to the path.

But first he has to clean up.

Jose hurries back to the walkway and gathers up her purse and her laptop. Some of the vegetation is looking a little too smashed so he gives it a bit of a fluff up with his toe before carrying her things back to be deposited on the stump.

136 . . .

The computer class is breaking up and students are streaming out. Krystal is almost packed when she sees Oscar and Maggie with their heads bent together, already packed up. Oscar glances over at her, looking at her funny. OMG, he better not be thinking about hitting on her. She is *so* not into these pasty white geeks.

Especially arrogant jerks like Oz. Guy thinks he's so charming when he's really only pretentious.

Kate slides into the seat usually occupied by Adam, Maggie perches on the desk. Kate glances around, pleased to see that the class has left them with the room to themselves.

"What's up?" Krystal asks Kate.

Maggie says, "Just wanted to ask you something."

"Sure. Just make it quick. Got a meeting with my faculty adviser."

Maggie nods her head. "It can be quick. I wanted to ask you..." Maggie studies Krystal's face and decides to hit her with it full on. "How could you lie about dying?"

Kate notes that Krystal hasn't even flinched.

Krystal says, "I didn't lie to you. Why would anybody lie about something like that? You dragged it out of me, Maggie. And honestly, this isn't in very good taste."

Kate says, "Come on, Christine, if it didn't work the first time why did you think it'd work this time?"

Krystal realizes the game is up. That fucking Dave. She knew he'd ruin everything. "It did work the first time. And it would have worked this time too if you boneheads would have told him. God, what a bunch of losers I confided in."

Maggie just stares at her in shock. "You... don't think you did anything wrong."

Krystal stares back. "Of course I didn't do anything wrong. I didn't take your money. I didn't punch you out. All I did was take you into my confidence."

"Yeah, it was a confidence trick alright," agrees Maggie.

"No it wasn't. I didn't con you out of any money, I just I told you stuff that any real friend would have passed along to the man I loved as a kindness. But you couldn't even get that right."

Maggie just stares. "We were respecting your wishes."

Krystal glares at her a minute before saying, "Bullshit. A real friend would have told Jose how awesome I was and how I needed him. A real friend would have helped me."

Maggie shakes her head. "I guess you don't understand respect. Any more than you understand about real friendship."

Krystal laughs harshly. "You bitches just better be careful about spreading any slander about me. My Dad's a lawyer and I'll make sure you pay for it if you do."

Maggie says, "The legal defence against slander is truth, and we have that on our side."

Krystal glowers. "You think? I haven't admitted a thing."

"You told me that you were dying." Maggie says.

"Isn't everybody?"

"You said you had an inoperable brain tumour..."

Krystal stares at her. "Says you."

"You did say that."

"So what?" Krystal laughs. "I think it would boil down to a classic case of she says she says in a court of law. It could go either way so you'd better not try it. My Dad would take you to the cleaners. Not that he'd get much out of you losers."

Kate shakes her head ruefully. "Somehow, I have a hard time believing that. Especially since your mother busted you the last time. Even if your father is a lawyer I doubt he'd risk his career helping you commit perjury."

"That shows how much you know." Krystal stands.

Maggie gets up too, staring at this woman she has lost sleep over, ached over, cared about. This woman she thought was a friend. "Do what you want, Krystal, Christine, whatever the hell your name is, but I won't stand by and let you hurt anyone else with your lies."

Krystal glares back defiantly. "You can't make me leave Christie. I have a right to be here."

"That's up to you. But if I hear about you spreading any more lies I will bust you to the whole school. Understand?"

Krystal draws herself up. "You think? I got nothing to lose if I speak my mind. I might have to tell people about how Nick put the moves on me."

Maggie is aghast at this threat but Kate laughs out loud. "You go right ahead, if you think you can find one person who'll believe it more power to you. I think you're just going to find yourself in a world of trouble."

"You're not such hot shit Kate. You're just jealous of me."

Kate snorts derisively, stepping closer to Krystal, getting in her face. "You just don't get it, do you?"

"The only thing to 'get' is away from you losers."

"You stepped over the line. You've been outed. Enough people know about your BS that any attempt at a smear campaign will backfire on you so big that you won't have any choice but to leave the school. It might already be too late. You're on probation. Step over the line and the sky will fall."

Krystal glares at Kate. "You are so enjoying this."

Kate grins, crossing her arms, "You know, I am, Christine. I am enjoying this."

"Bitch." Krystal grabs her things and stomps out.

Maggie simply slumps back down into her chair. Kate turns to her friend. "Are you all right?"

"Yes. No. I guess... I guess I didn't really believe she lied. Intellectually, yeah, sure, it made sense in a warped sort of way. But emotionally? How could someone do something like that? I mean she is supposed to be our friend but it was all bullshit to get her the guy she wants? How could she do that?"

"Classic definition of a sociopath." Kate says, "I think she made it pretty clear the only person she cares about is herself. We aren't real to her."

"You got that right. I saw it, but I still don't hardly believe it. Incredible, she didn't even try to deny it."

"She was expecting it, Maggie. I'll bet you anything she saw Dave with Adam. That would explain why she skipped the meeting the other night. Lets just cut class. Go to a movie or something."

"Or something. Hey, you know Stu said there's supposed to be some great pinball palace downtown."

"Pinball?"

"Yeah, they're like really cool mechanical arcade games. They're great 'cause you get to hit the machines."

"That sounds cool. Where is this place."

Oscar pops his head in. "Got it all."

Kate looks up, "What?"

Grinning, Oscar says, "I made a surveillance video."

"You recorded that?"

Oscar nods. "It may do no good in a court of law but it will provide excellent corroboration should Miss Krys try anything else."

"We were thinking of calling it a day and going to play pinball. Wanna come?"

Oscar nods. "Sure. But first I think we need to find Jake."

"Will he believe it?"

"He will when he sees the video."

137 · · ·

Jose looks down at Barbie's form sprawled loosely on the muddy ground. She doesn't look like much. He drops her stuff in the dirt and takes a seat on the stump. Feeling the stirrings of excitement. He lights a joint and watches her. He wants to take his time this time. Savour it.

He watches her breasts rise and fall, breathing regular. Bit of bruising on her neck, nothing too bad. Mud in her hair. She'd hate that the most. Hell, she got off a lot easier than that red headed girl. It was really Barbie he should have been pounding that day.

He watches the smoke twist and writhe as it drifts upward, thinking that he can still walk away. Maybe she'd go to the cops. Maybe not though.

He looks at her face pressed in the mud. Clothes dishevelled. Little bit of drool pooling in the corner of her mouth.

This is the girl that's tied him in knots for so long.

So messed up he hasn't been able to see straight for most of the semester.

He takes a deep drag and really looks at her. She was always happy to smoke his drugs but he always knew that she'd never really accept him. She'd never think he was good enough. Golden girl. Princess. Cock tease.

No account bitch is what she is. Doesn't look so hot now.

He's thinking he should maybe tie her up first. Immobilize her. He looks in her purse. All kinds of crap.

Not even dental floss. Gloves. Who knew the girl was such an idiot. Day as cold as this and her gloves are in her purse, not on her hands?

Chocolate. Gum wrappers. Pantyhose? She's wearing pantyhose why does she have more in her bag?

And the make up. Holy shit. The girl has a beauty parlour's worth of crap in here. Perfume, paints, who knows what all these tubes and bottles are. Maybe when all the crap comes off she's really a dog?

Thick wallet. Let the wallet go. Don't touch it. He's

no fucking thief, no way.

He upends the purse and watches with satisfaction as the wallet bounces and everything else spills out all over the ground. Tubes scattering, bottles bouncing, keys, a metal disk rolls away into a clump of dead wildflowers. Who gives a shit. He's wearing his gloves. He's no fool.

In fact, it's a good thing he found out what an airhead this one was. Just think, he might have married the bitch and been stuck with her his whole life.

She's probably not even a real blonde like that Krystal. No way Jose. He grins to himself as he picks up her laptop bag, rifling though it. He drops the notebook computer into the dirt and pulls out the cables.

These ought to work.

Kneeling by her head, he grabs her under her armpits and drags her over to a sturdy young sapling at the edge of the little clearing. He wraps the power cord around one of Barbie's wrists and then pulls her cold hand above her head. He looks at her face. Yeah, she's still breathing. Just cold.

Stupid girl not to wear her gloves. He wraps the middle of the cord around a sapling and then pulls up her other wrist so he can bind it to the end. He gets up and goes back to the pile of girl crap beside the stump.

He picks up the gloves, admiring the softness of the leather. Too small for him, for sure, but he thinks they might make a great gag. Keep her from making noise.

He looks over at her, with her arms stretched over her head like that, she's certainly appealing. The coat is open, and the fabric of her dress is some kind of slippery shit. Doesn't look warm. And look at those nipples poking up against the cloth.

He reaches for the pantyhose, and carries it back to his dream girl. He runs his gloved finger along her lower lip and she shudders a little.

Tucking his finger into her mouth he pulls her jaw down and starts to push a glove into her open mouth when she spasms and her teeth clamp shut like a trap. Jesus, she almost bit his finger. He tries to open her mouth again but her eyes open.

Barbie's icy blue eyes look at him, confused.

"Jose, what..." she tries to sit up and she realizes that her wrists are bound. "Come on Jose, this isn't a very good game. How about you untie me and we pretend none of this ever happened."

"This isn't a game Barbie."

"Look, I didn't mean to... give you the wrong idea, lead you on, whatever. I mean, Jose, I really like you, I've always really liked you, it's just, just, I'm just not ready to settle down. That's all. I don't want to end up married too young, that's all."

Jose crouches beside her. "You've played me all along. And then you just dump me like garbage. Is that what you think I am? Garbage?"

"No, of course not. I think you're a great guy. Don't you realize how much I like you? It's not you that's the problem, it's me. Come on Jose, just help me up and we can start again, okay. Go get a cup of coffee. Sit down together and really talk about stuff, you know?"

Laurel L Russwurm

"I think it's too late for that."

"Jose, come on, let's give it a rest. Just untie me and..."

"And what?" asks Jose. "You'll be my friend? No, Barbie, you were never my friend."

"I promise I..."

Jose cuts her short with a short sharp blow to her midriff. As she gasps for air he stuffs the gloves into her mouth.

Barbie squirms as her breath comes back, trying to spit the gloves out while he in turn struggles to get the pantyhose tied around her head to hold the gloves in.

Barbie is wriggling sideways and pulling her knees up. Jose realizes she's trying to get her feet under her so she can stand. No way he's letting her off that easy.

No way.

In a smooth motion he lets go the pantyhose ends and slams his palms squarely on her breasts. Shocked at the suddenness of the change in attack Barbie even stops trying to spit out the gloves for a moment, and Jose swings his leg over to straddle her.

Jose has been worried that he might not be able to get it up since his failure with Mouse, but his erection is enormous. Breathless again from his weight on her stomach, Barbie looks up at him in supplication. Now she knows his power.

With her pinned down he's finally free to tie the god damn pantyhose. He can feel her subside as she realizes how helpless she actually is. Good. Oh, he thinks, this is so much better than the red head. The blonde goddess yields to him. What a rush.

He's on fire, so he pulls his jacket off and casts it aside, then reaches down to unbutton her shiny blouse.

But the blouse is slippery, especially with gloves on, there is no way. Fuck it. Jose grabs the fabric and gives it a mighty yank.

Buttons pop off and roll away in the dirt. The blouse fabric slithers down her sides and out of his way, revealing a lacy little bra barely covering those amazing breasts that makes his heart race.

He bends down and rests his chest on hers in a parody of a hug as he forces his hands underneath her to unfasten the bra. He can feel her panting under him as her breast rises and falls, throbbing against his chest.

The snap gives and he's about to sit back up when he feels an enormous searing pain in his shoulder, as if it's on fire. He sits up and releases an agonized groan when the full load of pain hits. Glancing down he sees one of the gloves in the dirt, but the other one, now bloody, is still in her mouth.

She bit him.

Well, no more mister nice guy.

He rears back and punches her in the face.

He can feel the cheek bone give way and he smiles as her eyes flutter and roll back in her head. Jesus God he is dripping blood from his shoulder. First things first.

He needs to stop the blood. He looks at the pantyhose and decides they'll have to do.

Jose pulls the damned pantyhose out from under her head again. After all the work to get it there in the first place.

Jose presses the big part against the ragged bite she's ripped out of his shoulder then struggles to wind the legs around his arm.

Although awkward to do with one hand he manages a rough knot and pulls it together by pulling one panty hose leg taut with his hand, the other with his teeth. Difficult but possible. This is starting to be more trouble than it's worth.

He hits her in the face again.

That feels good.

Jose looks at the pathetic bra and grabs it but the damn thing doesn't rip open, It stretches, He lets it go and it makes a satisfying sling shot thwapping sound as it snaps back against her skin. Jose can feel her body heat warming him where he straddles her. His excitement is rising as he punches her in the breast.

Again.

And again.

Suddenly he is hitting, beating, pummelling, bashing, striking, punching, slapping, rapping, pounding...

Blood is mixing with mud in the golden hair and he begins to sob quietly in counterpoint to the punches he's delivering. Why did she make him do this, he wonders. She should have loved him and not been so selfish, he thinks, not for the first time.

Suddenly Jose feels strong hands grabbing his shoulders and pulling him backward off of Barbie. As Jose is yanked to his feet the fingers connect with the bitten shoulder and Jose howls in agony. He whirls on his attacker with raised fists until he sees it's Eric.

He relaxes and shakes his head. "Gee man, I almost took your head off. Don't sneak up on a guy like that."

Eric stares at Jose. "What are you doing?"

Jose shrugs, "Barbie has been giving me trouble, man. I just had enough. You can't just let women stomp all over you, I mean after Elsie I think you can relate. We've just been working it out. You know how it is."

Eric looks down at the twisted still form laying bound to the tree. The left side of her face is mush, and Eric can see that blood has been oozing out of her ear for some time, forming a large puddle around her head. Barbie's bright blonde hair appears scarlet at the tips. Eric kneels beside her, looking for a flicker in her eyes, or the rise and fall of her chest. He feels for a pulse, but there isn't any.

"Hey now," Jose tells him, "Get your own girl, Eric. This one's mine."

"Jose," Eric stands and meets his eye. "She's dead."

Jose shakes his head. "No, she's just a little pissed off at me. The bitch is just punishing me is all. That's one of the things we have to work out."

Jose looks up at the sound of twigs breaking and leaves crackling and smiles.

"Hey Eric, there's your girlfriend. Why don't the two of you just run along and leave Barbie and me to work things out."

Eric turns to see Amelia and Mouse pushing their way through the brush. Amelia and Eric make eye contact and Eric tries to signal her away but Mouse sees Jose and calls out, "Hey, Jose."

But Mouse stops in mid stride as she takes in the bloody scratches on Jose's face and Barbie's limp form bound to the tree at his feet. Mouse lets out a blood curdling scream that splits the afternoon and seems to snap Jose out of his daze.

Jose tries to go around Eric, and although stunned by what he's found, Eric holds up his hands, shoving his friend's chest.

"What have you done? Jesus, Jose, you can't just..."

But Jose pushes back, and Eric stumbles backward, tripping over a root then falling down into sitting in the mud. Jose ignores Eric, who stares stupidly up at him, Mouse weeping like a baby and Amelia dialling her cellphone. Jose realizes there is only one course of action, so he scoops Barbie's car keys off the ground.

Fuck it, she won't mind.

Since the other students are ranged between him and the walkway, Jose opts for the path of least resistance and plunges the other way, deeper into the woods. Gotta be easier than fighting his way through the assholes. Gotta get the car and take off.

Amelia watches him go, and she tells the police dispatcher where they are and that there's a dead student here in the woods. Eric pulls himself to his feet and stumbles toward the girls. Mouse isn't screaming any more but she's crying. He pulls her into a hug.

Eric asks Amelia, "You called the cops?"

Amelia nods, "Now I'm calling the campus cops."

Inconstant Moon

"Okay, I'll gonna call Boris." While still cradling Mouse with one arm, Eric pulls out his cell with the other and fumbles one handed with the buttons.

"No." Amelia says, "Don't do that Eric."

"I know you like Jose, but he's gotta be stopped."

"You think I give a shit about that rat bastard murderer Jose? He's gotta be stopped but not by Boris." Amelia starts toward him. "What do you think Bo would do if he caught the guy?"

"Oh. Shit. You're right." Eric disconnects, putting the phone away.

"We've been living with a monster." Amelia shudders.

Eric looks stricken. "I can't believe... that I could even know somebody who'd do this... "

"Maybe she's just hurt..." says Mouse, but Eric emphatically shakes his head. Mouse looks at Barbie's unnaturally still form in disbelief. "Are you sure?

Eric nods miserably. "Yeah, Mouse. I'm sure."

Mouse starts wailing again, and Eric puts his hands on Mouse's shoulders. "Hey Mouse, come on. Let's get back to the path and wait for help to come."

Amelia takes her hand. "Yeah. We have to go wait for them, so she doesn't have to... to stay here."

Mouse nods and pulls a handkerchief out of her pocket and scrubs her face with it, then follows Amelia. Mouse says, "Barbie is, Barbie was... she was so full of life always, you know?"

Eric looks at Barbie again, still trying to believe it himself. He tears his eyes away and follows his friends.

They are all careful not to look back. Mouse snuffles as they struggle over the uneven mushy ground. "How could Jose do that? He said he loved her."

"I don't know Mouse. I guess he's the rapist too." Mouse blanches, thinking about the time she spent with Jose and their one night stand.

But then Mouse hands Eric her handkerchief because he is weeping too.

138 . . .

Jake climbs out from under the rough lean-to of branches he's assembled to create a 'hide' which he set up so he could photograph wildlife. The problem is that all the wild things took off when that girl screamed. He's been dead still for probably ten minutes and there hasn't been any sign.

But it's just occurred to Jake that it might be another attack happening out there. After all they never did catch the real rapist.

Jake starts back along the deer trail he followed to get to this spot. He's pretty sure the scream came from this way. The more he thinks about it, the more sure he is that that prick is actually attacking someone out there. Right now.

The creep didn't just rape Natasha, he beat the shit out of her too. Jake knows very well that he himself is not a big powerful guy. If he goes over there and tries to confront the rapist he's just going to end up getting beaten to a pulp.

Wouldn't it be smarter, not to mention a better use of resources, simply to call the police? It would be smarter to get out of the woods and back to the Res where he can find help. Somebody tough like Boris.

Suddenly it occurs to Jake that maybe it's Krystal being attacked. All bets are off. Jake starts moving faster. Then he starts to run.

139 . . .

Boris slides the phone back in his pocket. "That's weird, he's not answering. Wonder what Eric wanted."

"It's probably just a phantom call." says Natasha.

"A what?"

"You know, one of those calls your cell makes on its own. It happens when you stuff your phone in your bag or pocket and all it takes is a little bitty bump and then it starts auto-dialling."

Boris nods, noting with satisfaction Natasha's face is almost back to normal size and hue. She's sitting cross legged on her bed, hunched over a fistful of UNO cards, while Boris balances on a purple exercise ball at the foot, and Ethan and Liz flank on either side. Boris wishes Sarah could be here too, but she had a shift at the hospital. He wants Natasha and Sarah to be friends.

Liz tosses down a plus four card and Boris groans dramatically before waving his extra thick handful of cards at her. "Gee Liz, how many of those can one person have. I can barely hold the damned cards I have already." He picks up the four cards and tosses down a green change direction card.

Liz laughs and throws down a blue change direction card. Boris wails "Argghhh" and counters with a yellow change direction card.

"No, no, not yellow!" squeals Liz.

"Mwah hahaha" chortles Boris. "Oh yeah... yelloooow rocks!"

Natasha asks Ethan, "Think we'll get a chance to play?"

"Eventually, when those two stop being evil." Ethan frowns and gets up and goes to the window, leaning on the sill.

"What is it?" asks Natasha, suddenly pale.

"Sirens." The others all crowd around, Ethan steps back to cede Natasha the best view of the police cars coming up the road.

"Wonder what's happening."

140 . . .

Adam pulls into the parking lot, shaking his head as the engine continues to run on even after he pulls the key out. He sighs, hoping that it'll hold together until he can afford to do something about it. He pats the dashboard and murmurs his ritual, "Hear me baby, hold together," with the tiniest glimmer of a smile.

Adam picks up his laptop case and gets out, locking the door, idly wondering why, since if someone stole this piece of junk maybe he'd get a better one out of the insurance.

But with his luck, he would end up with something worse. Adam is just starting across the lot when he catches movement out of the corner of his eye.

Glancing over, he sees some guy leaning over Barbie's car. He stops, and turns back. It is not Barbie, but it is her car. He heads over, getting closer to the guy as he moves between the parked cars. The guy looks a bit familiar but Adam can't place him. And the man is definitely trying to get into Barbie's car.

"Hey!" Adam calls out. "What do you think you are doing?"

"I'm just borrowing my friend's car. Do you mind?" Jose answers back, then he turns holding up a keyring dangling with keys.

Adam steps closer, and yes, he recognizes Barbie's key ring from the night they went to the concert.

"Alright." Adam nods with a sigh, but he keeps approaching. Must be another one of Barbie's hordes of admirers. But what is wrong with his face?

Adam narrows his eyes to try and make sense of the vertical lines on the guy's cheeks. Is it paint? No, it's too regular, it looks kind of like blood. No, that does not make sense. The guy goes back to the door and finally gets the correct key in the door lock as Adam comes within a few feet.

He swings the door open and Adam extends a hand, "I'm Barbie's friend Adam from the computer club."

Ignoring his outstretched hand, the guy frowns,

then says, "You're the one put Linux on her laptop?"

Adam feels a momentary burst of pleasure -- Barbie must have been talking about him. But then it dissolves as he realizes Barbie must like this man a lot to lend him her car. Adam says, "Yes."

But then he looks at the man. He is a real mess. Adam squints a little, trying to figure out what's wrong with his face without actually staring or anything.

"I gotta go pick some stuff up." Jose stops and realizes that Adam is scrutinizing his face. He's gotta get out of here before Dilbert gets the picture.

Jose resists the urge to self consciously reach up and touch his face. Shit. "Look, pal, I don't have a beef with you, so just back off, Okay?"

"What's wrong with your face?"

"I got a rash. Barbie's just lending me her car so I can, so I can go home and get cleaned up."

Recognizing he has just been lied to, Adam stops pretending nonchalance and just stares at the guy. "Is that blood?"

"Look, pal, just take off, and you won't get hurt."

"You stole Barbie's keys?"

"I'm not a fucking thief. She gave me her keys so I could use her car." Jose glowers. "Barbie's lending me her car. She gave me her keys. She's my girlfriend."

But Adam remembers the guy with the fancy red car. That would be Barbie's real boyfriend. Not this man. Another lie.

"I'll ask Barbie, then." Adam unclips the brand new

cellphone on his belt and starts to punch in Barbie's number.

"Just leave it alone. Go away."

Adam ignores him and punches in Barbie's number from memory. But before it can ring, Jose steps forward and knocks Adam's cellphone out of his hand.

The phone flies through the air and then bounces twice on the asphalt before shattering. Adam stares at his new phone in horror. He just got it programmed. And only used it once.

Jose turns back toward Barbie's car and Adam swings his computer bag at him. It hits Jose in the back, making him stagger into the car door. Only grabbing onto the handle keeps him from falling down but it makes the door slam shut again. Jose doesn't care, he is just too angry at this stupid nerd.

Turning back to Adam he says. "What the hell did you do that for?"

"First you broke my cellphone and now you are attempting to steal Barbie's car."

"Piss off, I'm just borrowing her car. Besides, why should you care, she was only ever nice to you so you'd fix her computer for free. She was just using you, you loser. So just bug the hell off."

"Why should I believe you? Why would I believe anything a car thief says, Mister Loser?"

Jose just flips him the bird and reaches for the door handle again. Adam steps in even closer, crowding him. "No. This is not your car."

Jose tries to elbow Adam, but somehow finds

himself sitting in the dirt. His bloody balance must be off after the ruckus with Barbie. He scrambles to his feet and takes a swing at the guy and misses again.

This is getting annoying. especially since he can hear sirens. Goddamn, are they coming for him already? He can't even get off the bloody campus because of this crazy geek. He looks over at the scrawny little guy in a tie. A fuckin' tie, for god's sake.

"What is your problem?"

"You can't just go around breaking people's phones and pushing them around. I am just so sick of bullies."

Jose launches himself at Adam who easily sidesteps. Jose ends up skidding and sliding onto his knees on the asphalt.

"Who the fuck do you think you are, Batman?"

"No, just a geek who thought martial arts training might help me deal with neanderthals like you. Have you had enough?"

Jose picks himself up. This is so ridiculous. This 98 pound weakling in a tie is stopping him getting away. That's it, no more mister nice guy.

With a mighty roar Jose lunges at Adam with all the force he can muster. This time Adam does not step away but rather steps in, grasping Jose's wrist and somehow transforming the attack into a kind of ballet, altering the direction of movement and somehow sending Jose face first into the side door of the hummer parked in the adjacent parking spot.

Blinding pain.

God that hurt. For a second it's like a hot needle in

his nose, then Jose realizes his nose is broken, as blood spurts out his left nostril and the swelling starts. Shit. It fucking hurts. Jose slides to the ground. His face is throbbing. This is not good. He rolls over and lays on his back, looking up at the clouds. He can taste blood in the back of his throat. His head is ringing. He's so tired. It's just not his day. Hearing the sirens getting closer he thinks, WTF.

Reaching inside his jacket, Jose pulls out a joint and puts it in his mouth. Fumbling in his other pocket for the lighter he fires it up, and the first drag is heaven.

As the sweet smoke slides in, he sucks it deep into his lungs, where he holds it a moment to let the calm envelop him. Letting it out in a rush, he watches stray wisps of smoke float away, up into the sky.

NOTES ON THE TYPE

I chose Jay Batchelor's REBELCAPS to set the titles, and the sharp art deco edge of his debut font set the tone for my debut novel's stunning book design.

Tangerine

The Chapter segment numbers and titles are rendered in Toshi Omagari's classically elegant script font.

I chose Dave Crossland's Cantarell to represent the on-screen displays that are such an important element in any story set among the digital generation.

Gentium Book Basic

According to designer Victor Gaultney, Gentium was created for SIL International as "a free multilingual font to bring better typography to thousands of languages around the globe." This compact font is highly readable and visually attractive, so I chose Gentium Book for the body of the text.

All of these gorgeous fonts have been emancipated through licensing.

Acknowledgements

Writing a novel isn't as solitary a pursuit as I once thought. I have been fortunate to benefit from the advice, assistance and inspiration of many who helped make my debut novel become a reality. I would like to offer my heartfelt thanks for invaluable contributions to:

NaNoWriMo provided focus, a deadline, and the impetus to get back in the water.

The Public Domain is a powerful cultural resource. Its existence allows creators to learn and share culture. I used excerpts from William Shakespeare's **Romeo and Juliet** found online at the **MIT Shakespeare Project. Classic texts like Don Quixote** are available from the fabulous **Project Gutenberg Free Digital Library** http://www.gutenberg.org/ebooks/996

Tech Advice

I was fortunate in finding online formatting advice from **Identi.ca**'s free software community:

Charles H. Schulz, Roman Gelbort, Viktor Lindberg, Kevin Smith, Luke Slater, Matěj Cepl, François Revol, Brewster Malevich, Paul Philippov, Mike Linksvayer, Jake Kromer, Jan Wildeboer, Fanen Ahua, @rpcutts, Fabian Rodriguez, David Butt, Marjolein Katsma, Morten Juhl-Johansen Zölde-Fejér, @agentsmith, @marcelwink, and @openuniverse

and from the **Mobileread Forums:**

jackie_w, JSWolf, Jellby, Toxaris, Adjust, Pablo, HarryT, pholy and dwig.

Special Thanks

to

Cory Doctorow, Nina Paley and **Allison Crowe**
for questioning copyright and leading by example,

Nicolle DeCoppel
for depressing movie suggestions,

Graham Linehan
for resolving a last minute Irish question,

Debbi Mack
for reading my novel and writing a lovely blurb,

Eric Swett
for writing the first review,

and **Charles Roth** for biblification:
http://encyclomundi.org/wiki/Inconstant_Moon

Extra Special Thanks

to

my wonderful crew of **Beta Readers**
for their generosity, and heroic efforts to provide
invaluable feedback in a ridiculously short span of time:

§ **Larry Russwurm** § **Nienke Hinton** §
§ **Bob Jonkman** § **Wayne Borean** §
§ **Nicole Russwurm** § **Sameena Topan** §
§ Enkanowen § Lawrence Yeh § @openuniverse §
I could not have done it without you.

Laurel Russwurm

Laurel L. Russwurm, July 1st, 2013

Laurel L. Russwurm, Author

http://laurel.russwurm.org/blogs/

writing & copyright

http://laurelrusswurm.wordpress.com/

visual laurel

http://laurelrusswurm.tumblr.com/

LibraryThing

www.librarything.com/author/russwurmlaurell

goodreads

www.goodreads.com/author/show/4986579.Laurel_L_Russwurm

Follow Laurel on Twitter @laurelrusswurm

https://twitter.com/#!/laurelrusswurm

Subscribe to Laurel's Federated StatusNet microblog:

http://s.russwurm.org/laurelrusswurm

@laurelrusswurm@s.russwurm.org

Drop Laurel a line at laurel.l@russwurm.org

About the Author

Laurel L. Russwurm first learned how *not* to write a novel at the age of thirteen. A few years later she embarked on her first adventure in self-publishing, the Star Trek & science fiction fanzine **CANEKTION**.

Studying Media Arts at **Sheridan College** helped to launch Laurel's television career. Her credits span projects as diverse as Rob Iscove's sublime Emmy winning television special, **Romeo and Juliet on Ice** and John Zaritsky's powerfully disturbing documentary, **Rapists: Can They Be Stopped**?

Laurel's television writing rages from the **CTV/CBS** police procedural series **Night Heat**, to animation scripts for Nelvana's **Tintin** and **NeverEnding Story**, series. Laurel's apprenticeship was served in the story editing trenches of **Hot Shots** and **T. and T.**

While on parental hiatus, Laurel enjoyed the opportunity to roam the Internet, learning about free culture and hand coding XHTML, dabbling in digital photography, photo restoration, image manipulation and blogging. But fiction is in her blood, and novelling in her heart.

INCONSTANT MOON is Laurel's debut novel. She is currently laying the groundwork for her third novel, **"Incoherent,"** while editing her fast paced mystery thriller, **"The Girl In The Blue Flame Cafe."**

INCONSTANT MOON

was written with OpenOffice Writer running on Ubuntu, a distribution of the GNU/Linux operating system. The final proof was done in LibreOffice Writer running on Trisquel, another distribution of GNU/Linux. This paperback edition was formatted and edited with LibreOffice Writer on Ubuntu.

The ebook and online serialization versions were crafted using Wordpress, gedit, and Libre Office, and the ePub was created using the Sigil ebook editor in Trisquel.

Look for the special features pages on the

INCONSTANT MOON serialization blog
http://inconstantmoon.russwurm.org/blogs/

libreleft.com